The Restaurant Inspector

The Restaurant Inspector

Alex Pickett

THE UNIVERSITY OF WISCONSIN PRESS

The University of Wisconsin Press
728 State Street, Suite 443
Madison, Wisconsin 53706
uwpress.wisc.edu

Gray's Inn House, 127 Clerkenwell Road
London EC1R 5DB, United Kingdom
eurospanbookstore.com

Printed in the United States of America
This book may be available in a digital edition.

Library of Congress Cataloging-in-Publication Data
Names: Pickett, Alex, author.
Title: The restaurant inspector / Alex Pickett.
Description: Madison, Wisconsin : The University of Wisconsin Press, [2021]
Identifiers: LCCN 2020035435 | ISBN 9780299331641 (paperback)
Subjects: LCGFT: Fiction. | Novels.
Classification: LCC PS3616.I284 R47 2021 | DDC 813/.6—dc23
LC record available at https://lccn.loc.gov/2020035435

For
Elena

These are the regulations concerning animals, birds, every living thing that moves about in the water and every creature that moves along the ground. You must distinguish between the unclean and the clean, between living creatures that may be eaten and those that may not be eaten.

—LEVITICUS 11:46–47, spoken by God, the original restaurant inspector

Remember: Inspectors want to see operators succeed, and your sanitarian will be proud for you when you do.

—*Wisconsin Food Processing Guide: A Handbook for Entrepreneurs and Managers*

The Restaurant Inspector

Millsville

Adam Bender took a break from fighting with his wife to look out his bedroom window. It was two in the morning and he had just heard a door slam outside. In a moment he saw his neighbor Arthur Reilly running down the block at full speed wearing only a bath towel, which he clutched to himself. It was much too cold outside to be running like that—earlier that evening he had heard the first frost warning of the season on the radio. Adam had been surprised to hear the door slam, to see a man running in only a bath towel. Until he realized it was Arthur. If anyone had a reason to be running like that right now, Adam reasoned, it would be Arthur.

Adam wore a vivid yellow pajama top and multicolored pajama pants that were decorated with flowers and parrots. The fight he was currently having with his wife—one where he was in the moral right, and wielding his justness in such a way that he could take a break to go to the window and not be outwardly crushed by the sight of her sobbing on the bed—was in large part because of Arthur. Even so, as he watched his friend rounding the bend of their street, high-legged and powerful, completely determined in his path, Adam couldn't help but be impressed at Arthur's newfound determination. Before turning back to his wife to resume their quarrel, Adam thought how even two days ago he had never seen such resolution in this man. It would have been a shame to miss it.

≈

County Commissioner Janet Vosberg was still in her office at two in the morning. After the events of the past two days, she needed to make some decisions that all appeared at this moment to be the lesser of evils. And though there was nothing in the office that helped her to make these decisions, there were also fewer distractions here than at home, and sitting at her desk in the stately old courthouse building put her in the right frame of mind. She stared blankly ahead, and resting across her upturned palms was a softball bat. She silently gauged its weight, as if it were a bar of gold. The chill from the open window helped keep her awake and sharp enough to think. For almost twenty years, ever since she'd quit working maintenance for the county and gone back to finish college, she had angled to put herself in position to run for higher office. Now she had to consider whether or not it had all been a waste of time. Two days ago had been the perfect moment. But things had changed.

From outside her office window she heard the slapping of bare feet against the pavement. At first she thought it sounded like rain lashing the ground, but it was too cold for that. She went to the window and opened it wider, letting in an icy burst of air. Below, she saw a man sprinting down Maple Street nearly naked. He was too far away to identify, and after all the excitement lately she wasn't all that fazed by the sight of a naked, running man. If she had seen it was Arthur, however, she would have called the police immediately out of spite. But, since she couldn't see the man clearly, she only said out loud to herself, "Wow, that guy is *fast*!"

≈

From his pickup truck, resting at a stop sign, Sasha Bykov saw a blurry figure running past his headlights. Over the past two days, Sasha had seen enough of Arthur Reilly to recognize his stiff posture and determined stride, and by instinct he gunned his engine, hoping to clip him with his bumper. The truck lurched sharply ahead, barely missing Arthur's hip and juggling loose the hot dog cart hitched to Sasha's truck. Free from the hitch, the cart tipped backward like a seesaw abruptly relieved of one rider. The jolt caused stainless-steel covers to come loose and clatter to the asphalt. Sasha closed his eyes—he didn't want to think about the work it would take to clean up the mess. He had spent all night preparing to leave town, and this was one more thing to do.

Right away he was glad he hadn't hit Arthur with his truck. The impact itself—the crunch, the groan—would have been satisfying, but he couldn't have handled the guilt. Plus, even if he had gotten away with it (he definitely would have tried to get away with it), for months and maybe years after he would have had to worry about being pegged for the crime. All that stress would not have been worth a few minutes of satisfaction. If Arthur had stayed out of his way, Sasha might have become, for the first time since his wife died, a happy man. Instead, Sasha's life was currently ruined. So, as he sat for a moment, catching a final glimpse of Arthur's form before the darkness swallowed it, Sasha Bykov felt more hatred toward another person than he had ever felt in his entire life.

≈

Calvin Luedtke—Cal to almost everyone—had the windows in his truck rolled down and the heat turned up full blast. The truck was idling in the parking lot of County Building C—where during the day he worked—and on the seat beside him was a three-quarters-empty bottle of Wild Turkey. He was crying and waiting for his lover, in order to end things. He tried not to think about how it had all gone so wrong so quickly. Every so often he wiped his nose on the sleeve of a camouflage hunting jacket he kept in the extended cab. He had told his wife that he was going out this late to shine deer. Cal had been parked here for over an hour and by now assumed his girlfriend was not going to show.

When he heard the approaching footfalls, he leaned forward and fumbled blindly for the bottle in order to take a drink in celebration and for courage, instead of the pity gulps he had been ingesting thus far. The sounds signaled the satisfaction of sex and love, until he remembered why he was there. So seeing Arthur's sprint into the parking lot was a crushing emotional blow as well as a relief to Cal. It was a sign that he was no longer waiting for anyone, that he should go home. He was drunk enough not to wonder why Arthur was there, and any animosity Cal had felt toward him over the past couple of days dropped away in a haze of alcoholic camaraderie. Arthur was his colleague, and they were both at work. The flood of normalcy was soothing. Cal melted into his seat and watched as Arthur—for some reason clad only in a bath towel—fumbled for two minutes with his keys, trying to unlock the front door of the building with cold, shaking hands.

≈

Arthur assumed that even if he had been observed, nobody cared enough to stop him. He even took the time to warm himself under the hot-air dryer in the bathroom. Once inside the darkened health department office, he rubbed his hands, checked if the trash bin had been emptied by the cleaners, and flipped the switch to warm up the paper shredder. He took the nail file from the pen holder on the reception desk and jiggered open the locked filing cabinet. There he found the folder marked in red Sharpie: Inspections September 2013. He extracted the report he had written almost exactly twenty-four hours ago.

He held the paper firmly with both hands, not reading so much as ingesting it. The panic that compelled him to dash from his shower—stopping only to grab towel and keys before running wet and nearly naked through the biting cold—returned with frightening force. But he hadn't killed anyone. He saw now that what he had written might actually help clear him of that, if not incriminate him in lesser ways. Of course, even the charge, the implication, would completely upend his life. As he read, it dawned on him that the most damning information was what the report revealed about himself. It showed what he was capable of when he was afraid. It proved that he was no better than anyone else; he was a selfish coward who valued only his own petty comforts. Perhaps he was in hypothermic shock, but he felt that to shred the paper now would be like destroying a piece of himself. His towel dropped away. He didn't move. The hum of the shredder was the only sound in the office. From down the hall he either heard or imagined footsteps. He tried to will himself to act, to get it over with, but he couldn't budge. A question cycled through his head: "Am I actually corrupt?"

Wednesday, September 18

He watched as the man whose kitchen he had just inspected finished wiping down a table. The table was covered with a plastic sheet. The man wiped it with a dirty rag. There was only one customer in the restaurant, an old man Arthur did not recognize sitting in a booth in the back corner—he had been staring directly at Arthur ever since Arthur arrived fifteen minutes earlier. Arthur did not hurry the wiping man along, though he had been wiping for over a minute and there wasn't anything left to clean. The man rubbed the same spot over and over. Like an anthropologist observing a human sacrifice, Arthur tried to watch with professional disinterest, but he couldn't prevent concern from clouding his judgment.

The man, Arthur assumed, was lost in his thoughts, and the repetition of wiping only helped him lose himself further. Or maybe the man knew something bad was about to happen and was trying to delay the inevitable. In truth, it didn't matter to Arthur why the man was wiping for so long. But the fact that he was doing it was interesting. In fifteen years as an inspector, Arthur had never seen anyone do this, and he knew it was strange that he, Arthur, was staring at the man and in turn the man in the corner was staring at him. But Arthur was in no hurry yet and—since Arthur was at work and so, by simply being there, was, in effect, in action—did not care about how he appeared to anyone else. For now he was content to stand an awkward distance away and watch this man wipe. He considered it a short, almost pleasant break before the unpleasantness of having to shut down the restaurant.

As the man slowly and laboriously circled the rag, his hand passed from the dark of the dimly lit restaurant into the nine o'clock sunlight coming in through the large front window. Arthur couldn't take his eyes off the scene. Something about the smooth movement of the wiping in the otherwise still space, the curve of the man's back as he hunched over the table, and the view out the window of the rest of the world carrying on as usual engrossed him. He found himself wishing he was still an artist so he could sketch the scene in charcoal. The most striking aspect of the image would be the man's face, which seemed to be straining to conceal his immense pain. When he viewed the man's expression with this critical eye, Arthur felt a stab of something—anxiety or regret—in his chest.

Arthur knew he would never have been able to recreate that expression. He had always been a fair hand at sketching (he had even minored in art at Hunter College and briefly considered having a go at using his skills to make a living), but he'd struggled to convey human emotion or instill life in objects. Any living being he had drawn—men, women, babies, dogs, once an iguana—immediately looked soulless, frightening. Arthur Reilly was better at depicting surfaces, which was what drew him to inspecting in the first place. In college his still lifes had been exact, if not captivating. When he first started inspecting, in New York City, he used to go home after work and draw the faces of the people he'd inspected—pushcart operators, ice cream truck drivers, restaurant managers, all with angry or frightened faces that turned blank at his hand. But he'd given up drawing them after less than a year, when the drag of routine exhausted his creative reserves.

Or perhaps it was only this early morning September light that made him think about drawing the man wiping the table. He had never performed an inspection this early. He had always gone into the office before setting out on his inspections. But today he had been woken by an anonymous complaint and figured he would stop by before work, since it was on his way. Nothing was not on the way here. That and the affordable housing were the only clear advantages to living in this place that Arthur could think of offhand.

For the seventh time since he began his inspection, he felt the buzz of a text message in his pocket. The vibration broke him out of the trance, but he didn't check his phone. The other men did not react—the one kept wiping and the other kept staring—though they surely heard the buzz in the deadly silent restaurant. Something must be happening—seven texts over the course of a whole day was an extraordinary amount, and now it was only ten after nine. No matter how disagreeable a task, he had to hurry Bogdani along. Until then, Arthur had tried to not consciously think of him by name, only as someone with a kitchen that did not come anywhere near to being up to code. It was easier that way, though never entirely possible. But having thought of him as a sketch forced Arthur to think of him as a person.

Arthur knew the basics of his story. First off, his name was Mërgim Bogdani, but Arthur, like everyone around there, called him Bogdani. He had emigrated from Albania in the late nineties and, along with many other Albanians who came to the state at that time, settled in a small town and started a restaurant. Arthur had never understood how or why someone would do that. Sure, getting away from a cruel and corrupt government was understandable, but why come here, to basically nowhere? Perhaps small Wisconsin towns somehow resemble Albanian towns. Arthur wondered if Albania were similarly full of unassuming people and beautiful scenery and so they feel right at home. Maybe they start small restaurants because old men in Millsville, Wisconsin, sitting at the counter gabbing about high school football over coffee and crullers remind them of similar old men in Tirana talking about high school soccer over coffee and baklava. Or perhaps they are thankful to be somewhere, anywhere, that is not Albania, and quaint Wisconsin towns are definitely not Albania—though sometimes Arthur felt he was as isolated and out of place in Millsville as he would be if he were living in the Balkans. Arthur did not know why Bogdani came here because he had never asked. He did not want to intimately know the people whose lives he might one day have to ruin.

As Arthur watched, Bogdani slumped down in a chair and put his head on the table but kept on wiping, his shoulder pumping his arm forward in the same circle. Arthur instinctively took a step toward him and stopped. He had learned long ago that showing concern would only make the situation worse. Something was obviously wrong—Bogdani was moving like a machine with a broken part—and Arthur could only watch. He shifted his gaze to the man in the corner, hoping to convey that Bogdani needed help and that he, Arthur, was not the man to provide it. But the man in the corner only caught and held Arthur's eye with a hint of a smile, as though he had beaten Arthur in a game they had long been playing. Arthur jerked his head back to Bogdani, annoyed.

If only the violations weren't so egregious. Then he could watch while Bogdani cleaned up, give him a warning or fine, and get the hell out of there. Arthur mentally went through his inspection again, hoping that he was making too much of it. He was not. Were he to make a case to the public, he would start by telling them about the dead raccoon. Nothing more than a ball of fur, like roadkill behind the stack of hamburger bun boxes in the pantry. Probably long dead and decayed, though Arthur didn't give it an autopsy. But to Arthur the raccoon could be removed, the area cleaned with bleach, the buns thrown away. Poor guy probably wandered in there to die somewhere cozy. If it was only the raccoon, Arthur would let it go.

The worst violations were the unsexy ones: the refrigeration system, the meat, the fire suppression system. The refrigerators and freezers had all been off overnight—from a short in the electrical system, Arthur assumed. Not only that, but when turned back on they refused to cool to the necessary temperature. More disturbing (but easier to fix) were the boxes of previously frozen chicken and pork that were, for some reason, out on the counter and the prep tables, leaking. Arthur was not comfortable allowing food that touched any surface in the kitchen to be served. Perhaps most damaging of all, the range hood above the stove wouldn't turn on, all of the fire extinguishers were completely empty, and the wires of the sprinkler system were sticking out from the ceiling. Even a small fire would set the whole block ablaze. On top of that, there were nearly enough other violations (evidence of live insects—i.e., flies in and around the thawed meat; evidence of mold—i.e., mold on refrigerator lining (which almost everyone has); evidence of personnel smoking—i.e., about a carton's worth of cigarette butts on the floor; improperly stored poisonous or toxic items—i.e., pesticide sitting out on a cutting board) to justify closure.

Considering all this, Arthur was worried. Bogdani's kitchen had, until then, always received near-perfect scores, and now it was as if it had endured a natural disaster. By his estimation he had performed over ten thousand inspections and had never seen a once-clean kitchen in such poor shape or somebody taking closure this badly. It was almost understandable, of course, in a way, that Bogdani would act like this. In a town this small, it would be impossible for a restaurant to live down the shame and distrust that closure on such extreme grounds would produce.

Arthur tried to will Bogdani to stand up and act normal. Not only did this erratic behavior not bode well for a quick and easy end to the inspection, but Arthur had always felt a kinship with Bogdani (even though he knew Bogdani felt none with him). They were both outsiders in a place where outsiders were looked upon with skepticism. Only now Arthur felt as if he was on the wrong side—the persecutor, the fascist, someone who discriminated out of resentment or fear. But it was also as though he was watching himself at his worst moments, barely able to function after an immense disappointment. Arthur had never mentioned this perceived connection to Bogdani, because it was ridiculous. Arthur had suffered no political oppression. He simply had no place else to go. He had been justifiably fired from the health department in New York, and soon after that his wife had divorced him for valid reasons, leaving him with nothing. While Bogdani's story of arriving in town and starting a restaurant was a tale of struggle and success, a testament to the human will worthy of a brief newspaper story, Arthur's was merely a record of a series of failures.

He had never before caused anyone—not even his ex-wife—this amount of agony. Watching it made his own pulse quicken with rising panic, though he forced himself to be outwardly calm. Bogdani's nose and forehead were pressed against the table, and his hand kept moving. The rag made a squeaking sound at the same point in every loop, which highlighted the silence. A pinched grimace was discernible on Bogdani's face even as he shoved it against the tabletop. He emitted an occasional slow groan. Arthur cleared his throat as he felt the buzz of another text. The time had come to move things along. Whether that meant to try to help Bogdani or to begin closing the restaurant, Arthur didn't know. But he had to get on with his day. Arthur glanced back at the old man in the corner. The old man was not concerned.

As Arthur was about to speak, he heard, from above him and to his left, a shuffling, bumping sound. He saw two skinny legs on the top step of the stairs that led to the apartment above the diner. Bogdani's son, no doubt.

Bogdani had sent his wife and son up there when Arthur first arrived, but the kid had crept back to watch. This was unnerving, to say the least. Arthur did not want to do this at all, and certainly did not want to do it in front of this boy.

"Mr. Bogdani," Arthur said gently.

Bogdani's hand did not break its pattern of wiping.

"Mr. Bogdani," Arthur said more firmly.

The wiping stopped but he did not raise his head.

"Mr. Bogdani," Arthur said, his voice whisper-like in tone though not volume. "Your son."

At this Bogdani raised his head from the table and made eye contact with Arthur. His eyes were tired and bloodshot, the eyeballs set above swollen purple bags and below bushy black eyebrows. Like a drowned man—puffy and waterlogged.

When Arthur shifted his eyes quickly toward the son, Ismail, all Bogdani did was squint, as though Arthur was doing something inexplicable. Then he scanned the table, as though wondering how he had got there, before tossing aside the rag and walking unsteadily toward Arthur. Arthur resisted the urge to take a step back and ready himself for a physical confrontation.

"What is it?" Bogdani asked when he was near.

Arthur gestured his chin toward the stairwell and said, "Your boy."

"Yes, so?"

"Maybe you'd like to send him back upstairs."

Bogdani stared at Arthur as he barked, "Ismail!"

"What?"

Arthur couldn't understand what Bogdani said next—possibly it was in Albanian or perhaps Arthur couldn't make out the words under the meaty, guttural voice Bogdani used when ordering his son. The boy responded by dragging his feet down the stairs and standing next to his father, who put his arm around his son's shoulder like a junior officer who had the trust of the general.

"You can speak in front of him," Bogdani said.

Arthur scratched his bald spot and wearily examined the boy, now standing embarrassed by his father's side. He had seen Ismail before, busing tables during past inspections, sneaking glances at the badge attached to

Arthur's belt. (Arthur liked to imagine that kids were impressed by his badge, though he figured this was not actually the case.) He was in seventh grade but small for his age, and because of his swarthiness, his eyebrows that seemed too big for a child, his adolescent puffiness, Arthur gave him the secret nickname Miniature Joe Pesci. That's what reluctantly came to his mind whenever he saw the kid—even now, when he was about to deliver such devastating news.

"Mr. Bogdani," Arthur said, trying to swallow his annoyance. "Your kitchen is dangerous."

"Look, it was not like that last night," Bogdani said. There was no contrition in his voice. Only defiance.

"It doesn't technically matter how it was last night."

"No," Bogdani said. "It wouldn't to you."

"Mr. Bogdani, we're going to have to shut you down." Arthur tried to avoid saying "I'm sorry" while delivering bad news.

Bogdani snorted. "We," he said.

"Yes 'we,'" Arthur said. "The health department."

"Do you even see anyone in here? We are not open to customers," Bogdani said, making a sweeping gesture with his hand.

Arthur pointed to the man in the back. While his finger was extended he recognized he was simply trying to win an argument.

"Him," was all Bogdani said.

"Yes, him," Arthur said. "Plus the Open sign. Mr. Bogdani, what happened?"

Before Bogdani could speak there was a crash from the back table, where the man sat. Arthur and Ismail both jerked their heads toward the sound but Bogdani did not flinch and kept staring directly at Arthur. The man's coffee cup had overturned and rolled to the floor. The handle of the thick porcelain cup had broken off and skittered across the tile, landing a few feet from where Arthur stood, and the cup itself rolled in a half circle before settling noisily upside down. Coffee dripped down from the table and pooled in Rorschach blots. The old man seemed pleased.

"Now this!" said Bogdani with humor and despair.

"It doesn't technically matter how your kitchen was last night," Arthur repeated, masking his irritation with calm official-speak, "and it doesn't technically matter if the only customer is having a cup of coffee. There *is* a customer. It doesn't matter why your kitchen is how it is. It only matters, to me, and to the health department, that you don't serve another customer and that you close down this restaurant."

Bogdani put a hand to his face, then his eyes narrowed until the bags below nearly met his impressive brows. "You are coming in here and telling me about *my* kitchen?"

"It's your kitchen only insofar as we *allow* it to be your kitchen," Arthur said, a thought he had had plenty of times before but had never spoken out loud.

"I would be better off in Albania," Bogdani said, not taking his eyes off of Arthur but speaking as though to himself. "At least there they don't pretend to give a shit about you. They'll ruin your kitchen while you watch and then close you down and then make you bribe them. You act like you care. You act like you don't see what's actually happening."

Arthur had no idea what he was talking about, but he did not like being compared to an Albanian official. He took a breath to calm himself.

"I didn't ruin your kitchen," Arthur said. "If you'll come back with me, I'll show you what I'm talking about."

"I *paid* for that kitchen. You are nobody to tell me what happened in my own house."

A hoot of laughter came from the old man in back as the coffee continued to drip from his table. Arthur clenched his teeth and focused on the boy at Bogdani's side, who was looking up at his father in confused solidarity.

"Is anyone going to clean up that mess?" Arthur said, his voice louder than he intended.

Ismail took an obedient step toward the spilled coffee, and his father grabbed his T-shirt and pulled him back into place.

"Fine," Arthur said. "Let's go back to the kitchen and I'll detail your violations for you."

"You are not going to tell me about my own kitchen."

"If you won't go back, I can show you right here," Arthur said, and sighed, knowing that he would have to go through the evidence on his old, bible-sized digital camera that was all the department would provide, despite Arthur's weekly written requests to the budget office for newer models. (The only answer the single employee of the "budget office" ever gave him was that he should be happy they weren't still using Polaroids.) He pulled it out of his pack and turned it on, then shifted it away from the light so Bogdani could see the matchbook-sized screen showing a box of thawed chicken bleeding through the cardboard, spreading a salmonella pool across the floor.

"I am not going to look at my kitchen on that camera," Bogdani said, then immediately added, to nobody or perhaps to the man in the back, "I am getting told what to do by a man with this camera!"

"My camera hardly matters," Arthur said through his teeth.

"Big as a brick!" Bogdani said, smiling now.

The boy and old man laughed at Arthur's camera.

Like a fuse that burns out rather than allowing a power surge to ruin the whole electrical system, when Arthur reached a certain level of frustration he became completely calm. One of the first lessons he'd learned about inspecting was that nothing anyone could say was important enough to rile you. So he smiled, and waited for reality to sink in.

"You can't!" Bogdani said.

"I can't *not*," Arthur said, immediately wishing he had been clearer. As it happened he sounded like an argumentative child.

Bogdani straightened, he gaped at Arthur, his hands clung so tightly to his apron straps his knuckles turned white. He realized he was too late to seek understanding. He said, "I'm telling you it was not like that when I left last night. I came in. I saw it. Then you were here."

"Mr. Bogdani," Arthur said, tearing off Bogdani's yellow carbon-copied version of the report and handing it to him, "I really am sorry."

Bogdani took the report and considered it blankly, as if it were sheet music or a doctor's prescription in incomprehensible chicken scratch. His face clouded as his eyes ran over the page, then, all at once, he relaxed and appeared somehow calm and paternal, like a Buddhist monk at the moment of enlightenment.

"Do you know," Bogdani said, balling up the report in his hands and tossing it unthinkingly to the floor, "what we all call you behind your back?"

The man in the back gasped like a delighted studio-audience member.

"All of us, every restaurant owner in the county? Do you know what we call you?"

Arthur did not answer. Instead, he watched Ismail, who seemed hurt and lost by the news that their restaurant was going to close. He allowed his eyes to travel the room, trying to focus on anything except Bogdani's face. There was nothing to see but scuffed tile, tables covered with plastic tablecloths, fake potted plants, a bulletin board posting lost cats and horses for sale, a gumball machine selling Lions Club mints, and thin, fake-wood-paneled walls with precious little decoration except some nondescript framed paintings of flowers and a cheap Green Bay Packers pennant meant to convince customers of the Bogdanis' local loyalty. On a table near the entrance, Arthur spotted copies of the local paper for customers to read while they ate. On the cover was a picture of an elderly white guy and preteen white girl holding up a large fish. Both looked confused, or at least unready for their picture to be taken. Above the picture was the headline "Bass Winners." Arthur studied the picture as he considered walking out of the restaurant. He knew he should leave before Bogdani could tell him something he didn't want to hear. But Arthur had given Bogdani bad news and thought it was only fair to hear him out.

"We all call you the Dickless Wonder," Bogdani said.

Arthur shifted his eyes to Bogdani, who was stifling a laugh.

"Seriously, all of us!" A burst of laughter came through but he got it under control. Then he added conversationally, "Someone else thought of it. I do not even know what it means exactly—well, I understand that it suggests *you* don't have a dick, but I have never heard this expression." He shook his head quickly and snorted. "Anyway, now whenever we see each other we will, you know, we will say something like, 'Did the Dickless Wonder give you another lecture about mold on refrigerator lining?' or 'Do you think the Dickless Wonder's wife left him because he made her wear a hairnet while they fucked?'"

Only the man in the back laughed, but not as hard as Arthur would have expected. This had gone too far. The nickname itself Arthur could shrug off as childish name calling. He didn't enjoy knowing that people made fun of him behind his back, but that came with the job. He was aware the people he inspected didn't like him. His standards were inflexible, his demeanor bordered on cold. But that was how he survived this long after all he'd been through. To be safe he had to be inscrutable. And sure, since he was from New York and didn't care for hunting or sports, Arthur assumed people around here thought of him as unmanly or gay. He could take Bogdani's slur, but it was the last part, about his wife, that he couldn't move past. In New York he had been insulted plenty during inspections. He'd been spit on many times, once had a gun pulled on him, and twice had been punched in the face. Nothing before now had felt so calculated and personal. Arthur noticed his foot was tapping quickly against the floor. When he consciously held it still, his body filled with heat.

"I'll bet if you ever did fuck her, she made faces behind your back afterward like we all do when you give us one of your bacteria sermons," Bogdani continued. "I'll bet she fucked everyone you ever inspected and told them all about how you don't have a dick."

Bogdani's voice seemed on the verge of cracking as he spoke. The old man in the back was strangely quiet. Something was wrong with Bogdani, there was no doubt now. If he hadn't mentioned Arthur's ex-wife, Arthur would have been clearheaded enough to recognize this and feel the necessary concern. Instead, Arthur was doing everything he could to restrain his rage. He knew he should walk away. No matter what was said, Arthur was leaving here better off than Bogdani. But Arthur did not move.

Instead of answering Bogdani directly, Arthur bit his lip and shifted his focus to Ismail, who was even more Joe Pesci–like because his face was scrunched up in confusion or perhaps on the verge of tears. Arthur should not have said anything else—he should have been quiet and gone away and seethed and later patted himself on the back for his restraint. Instead, he spoke directly to Bogdani's son.

"Ismail," Arthur said with the distaste of the action already in his mouth, "I didn't want to bring you into this. I thought your father was wrong to drag you down here and make you witness his . . ." Arthur hesitated and then plunged headlong into what he knew he would later despise having said, " . . . his failure. This is the type of memory that sticks with people their whole lives, and I want to apologize for my part in putting you through it. But I did nothing wrong. I was doing my job. This is all your father's fault. He failed. He failed you and your mother. Hopefully one day you can forgive him."

With that, Arthur turned on his heels and walked toward the exit. As his hand hit the door he heard Ismail mutter after him, "Get the shit out of here, you Dickless Wonder." All Arthur thought as he walked toward his car was that now the boy didn't just look like Joe Pesci but sounded like him as well.

≈

That morning Arthur had received two phone calls before he was fully awake. The first, from an unknown number, woke him at six thirty. He didn't pick up but immediately listened to the voice mail. It was a complaint about the Bogdanis' restaurant from what sounded like an old woman on a crackling landline. "Hello," the woman said on the message, "is this the inspector? I thought you should know that the restaurant has a bad kitchen." There was a pause. "The Millsville Family Restaurant—the kitchen is bad, it made me sick. We are all sick from it." Then she hung up.

While Arthur contemplated the message, he fell back to sleep and had a dream about kitchens. (They frequently haunted his rest.) When he was woken up by the second call he assumed the first call had been a dream as well. The kitchen he had dreamt about was spotless, and as he walked along inspecting the gleaming surfaces, the room kept extending, so he had to keep walking and walking without checking off any violations on his clipboard. He couldn't tell if the dream made him happy or disturbed him.

"Inspector," the familiar jovial voice on the other end of the second call said.

"Editor," Arthur said, shifting his voice a few octaves up from gravelly so he didn't sound nervous or roused from sleep.

On the other line was Adam, Arthur's friend and neighbor, the editor of the local weekly paper. Arthur immediately reached out a hand to the other side of the bed, to make sure Adam's wife, Katie, was not there. From time to time she stopped by in the middle of the night. But not last night. Arthur was relieved, and a little sad that he was alone. Every time they spoke, Arthur assumed for the first few minutes of their conversation that Adam was finally going to expose the affair. When he didn't, Arthur was strangely disappointed.

"Inspector," Adam said again, as though he had called to say that one word.

Ever since he had learned about Arthur's occupation, Adam had called him nothing but "Inspector." Adam said he liked to pretend Arthur was a character in a detective novel. Arthur continued the lame joke by calling Adam "Editor" but was never quite sure if they were gently mocking each other's low positions in the greater scheme of things. In his more paranoid moments, Arthur wondered if Adam knew about the affair and could not bring himself to say Arthur's name out of some kind of repressed disgust. More likely, though, the nicknames simply turned their newfound familiarity into a comforting joke.

"Adam," Arthur said, hoping to speed the exchange along. It was already eight thirty and he had to figure out if the call he'd gotten earlier had been real or a dream.

"I have a friend," Adam said. "He's moving here and starting a restaurant."

"Think that's a good idea?" Arthur asked.

"It isn't my idea," Adam said sternly. "It's his. He can do what he wants."

Katie had made the first move. Though Arthur was the one who fell in love. He never cared that her eyes would glaze over every few minutes when they were together. It was understandable that she so often thought about Adam, who had abruptly taken off on an extended motorcycle trip only weeks before she invited herself over. When Katie was around, Arthur felt at home in his own house for the first time. He was willing to be used as a rebound as long as he had someone to hold, someone to talk to about the trivial distractions of his day. Katie must have gotten comfort from him as well—their final hug before she departed each night gave away her desperation for closeness, if not specifically for him.

As the weeks passed, they began to form two relationships. One, face to face, was based on polite talk and sex. The other, over email and texts, expressed their inner desires. They created whole narrative worlds on their screens. She wrote how she wanted Arthur to be a part of her life, to "give Caitlyn and Jenny the father they deserve," though she barely mentioned them in Arthur's presence. Arthur endorsed these plans completely. In his correspondences he mostly wrote about his longing for her, about what he would do to her when he saw her, and how much he hurt when she left.

But when she was around he mostly asked about her day, let her initiate intimacy, and never badgered her to stay longer than she suggested.

Then Adam suddenly returned, and Arthur began to suspect he was the only one who had meant what he wrote. She stopped replying to his emails. His calls went unanswered. To cover his pain and embarrassment, Arthur began seeking out Adam's friendship. He'd invite his neighbor over for back-deck beers and even once broke his own bicycle so he had an excuse to wheel it over and borrow Adam's tools and technical expertise. Despite the pretext, they became pals. The friendship managed to fill part of the emotional void Katie left, as well as get back at her for dropping him without so much as a text. It also somehow assuaged his own guilt for how he'd deceived Adam. As soon as Arthur settled into this new routine and managed to smooth over some of his inner turmoil, however, Katie began returning for brief, unannounced, wordless, late-night visits.

As he and Adam became close, Arthur recognized that, though they were very different, the two men had a true affinity for each other. He came to look forward to Adam's visits almost as much as Katie's. Adam rekindled Arthur's desire for friendship, as Katie had given him companionship after he thought he'd lost his ability to open himself up to anyone new. The idea that both relationships were so necessary for Arthur's emotional well-being and yet so tenuous frightened Arthur, and so, for now, he was doing his best to extract what enjoyment he could and not examine it too much. If he considered it too deeply, it could make him realize just how untenable the situation was.

"Anyway," Adam said, daring Arthur to interrupt, "my friend. He's a Russian. I met him on my trip. I was wondering if you could help him out."

"Of course."

"Good!" Adam said. "You know the permits and codes. It's all so much hassle."

Arthur assumed this was a slight dig at their political differences, a comfortable banter between friends. He said, "I know what he needs."

"Thank you," Adam said. "I understand what it is to ask for a favor in a professional capacity. I don't take it lightly."

His sincerity embarrassed Arthur and made him freshly ashamed that he slept with Katie so often, and even more ashamed for knowing that he would continue sleeping with her whenever she wanted. So he demurred and only said, "Yeah, yeah. I'm going to be late for my professional capacity, so I should go."

"One more thing," Adam said. "I heard there's an illness going around. People getting sick."

"Illness?" Arthur said, glancing at the clock.

"Kates told me right before I called. People going to the hospital? Might be something with the food?"

"Oh, that," Arthur said with a wave of his hand. He had no idea what Adam was talking about, and was now anxious to get up and go to work. But at the mention of an illness, a kind of instinct kicked in, an air of knowing stoicism that Arthur thought was unique to inspectors during potentially serious situations in which they are ignorant of facts. This mask concealed how little he knew, yet also radiated a vital calm that could mitigate if the danger was, on the off chance, real. This allowed him to confidently state, "We're on top of that. Sounds worse than it is. We're professionals. So you rest easy and have a good day, Editor."

"Inspector," Adam said, apparently placated.

~

Arthur felt Bogdani and his son watching him as he walked out of the restaurant. He was completely conscious of his gait as he crossed the street. For some reason he nodded at each passing car and pedestrian, as though he was assuring them that despite the ugly scene inside the restaurant he still had things under control. His keys became stuck in his pocket, and he fought the urge to forcefully wrangle them out. Once inside his dented, forest green, high-mileage, oil-leaking, county-issued Jeep Cherokee, he finally extricated his key and inserted it into the ignition. He then said a short prayer aloud. His prayer went, "Please please please for the love of god start." It didn't always start.

It started.

If it had been dead, he didn't think he had the energy to get out and walk to the courthouse to ask someone for a jump, though it was only a couple hundred yards behind where he was parked. Knowing that his every movement was tracked, he couldn't give the men in the restaurant the satisfaction of witnessing that walk of shame. Beyond that, though, the interaction had drained him. His legs felt heavy, as though he had walked a great distance. A tremor of anxiety was running through his body. His hands trembled. In a minute he would calm down. He always did eventually, when his body was overcome with regret and adrenaline like this. It was best to let his car warm up anyway. That way it wouldn't stall out when it shifted into gear.

Moving deliberately, trying to avoid detection, he took his phone from his pants pocket. He assumed the three missed calls and eight new texts were all from his office, probably Sandy checking why he wasn't in yet, since he had never before arrived late without calling first. And though he was supervising inspector and so he did not technically have to call in, the people in his office loved having a mystery to solve, no matter how minor. His being a half hour late to work without an explanation would be the most exciting event since that goose crashed through a window of the County Works office a couple of weeks ago.

It turned out the calls and texts were not merely fishing for information about his tardiness. They weren't even all from his office. One call and one text were from Katie. And though seeing her name provided welcome relief, the call was from her work phone, so she was probably reaching out in her official capacity as assistant county commissioner. He still decided to wait and open her text, saving it as a reward. The texts from Sandy, the receptionist in his office, read: *Where ru?* and *Janet wants u in her office rn* and *Whats up with these people getting sick?* and *Srsly where ARE YOU? We're getting calls what should we tell them?* and *JANET. OFFICE.* and *We can't handle all these calls!!!*

Katie's text read: *CALL ME its about Janet and IMPORTANT*.

He was already beginning to obsess about his behavior at the restaurant, and now an apparently serious event was about to unfold. He had really hoped Katie's message would provide a glimmer of hope or joy during this already shitty day, which was sure to only get worse. Instead, he felt leaden as he put his Jeep into gear. He decided to drive around the block to get to the courthouse to meet with Katie and Janet, though it was faster to walk. The least he could do for Bogdani was to not burden his lot any longer.

He reread the texts as he drove. Though disturbing, the messages also provided a welcome distraction and a stimulating air of mystery. They read like clues. He wanted to both delay the trip to the courthouse and be in the loop. He flipped the dial on the radio to see if anything out of the ordinary was being reported by the local station, but the radio had shorted out last week. At first he had actually liked the change and found the silence soothing. Now it was like a breach of basic human communication. He felt acutely alone.

As he began typing his reply to Sandy, he caught sight of people gathered near the bridge over the Grouse River. Though it was out of the way, he turned to drive past them. Whereas in New York he automatically avoided such scenes so he didn't become embroiled in some sidewalk drama, now he needed to see what was happening, though he still did not desire to become involved. It was like that goose through the window of the County Works. Everyone else rushed out at the first sound of the crash, while Arthur remained at his desk for a few minutes, telling himself it was none of his business and that he was not a rubbernecker. But sure enough, he soon followed. The mangled goose was dead on the floor, surrounded by shattered glass. Arthur wasn't exactly sure what he was looking at, but he had to admit he was glad he saw it. He couldn't explain why.

So now he turned because people were gathered, and gatherings were unusual. There were no street magicians or buskers here. When he passed by, he saw five people standing in a half circle and one person kneeling, all of them staring at a lump of a man supine on the sidewalk. Arthur initially increased his speed, but by the time he reached the end of the bridge he knew he had to turn around. He was a public servant in a town where a person in his position could actually help. Plus, after what he had done to the Bogdanis, he wanted the opportunity to provide someone with comfort and aid, as though making one person feel better would make up for ruining other people's lives.

≈

As soon as Arthur had left the restaurant—the moment the front door banged shut—the old man in the corner got up, stepped over the spilled coffee on the floor, and approached Bogdani. Bogdani was breathing heavily, and Ismail was furious and walked toward the front of their restaurant to eyeball the man who had ruined their lives. Bogdani wasn't sure it had been right to bring his son down. He had wanted the boy there to prove to the inspector that he wasn't afraid of him and to show his son how cold and disturbed the real world actually was. But after his outburst to the inspector and the inspector's cruelty toward Ismail, Bogdani considered that though his son probably learned something it might have been the wrong lesson.

"Look at his shitty goddamn car," Ismail said.

"Mouth!" Bogdani said sternly.

Ismail's stomach clenched as he absorbed the familiar tension that accompanied his father's disapproval. That he had been allowed to participate in the scene with the inspector and then hadn't been reprimanded for his previous swear made him think of them as equals in sorrow, but now he saw that he was still just his stern father's son. This was as much of a loss to him as their restaurant.

"They never give a break," the old man said, keeping a respectful distance from Bogdani. He had a thick Russian accent and wagged his head as he spoke. "But what was he to do? Your kitchen is in shambles."

Bogdani recovered his breathing and bit his tongue between his front teeth for a few seconds before answering. He wanted this man to shut up and leave, but the man had made him an offer to buy the restaurant. Bogdani knew he might have to take it, even though he assumed the man had sabotaged his kitchen. Bogdani did not have any illusions that the world worked fairly.

"You did that to my kitchen," Bogdani said.

"Please," the Russian man said, "give me more credit than that. If that was true, why not tell inspector? Why not report it?"

"Because I will die before I give that man the satisfaction." The satisfaction of what he was not sure. He only knew that he did not want to speculate to the inspector. The inspector was nothing but a slave to the system, a bean counter, a bureaucrat. Guesses would not be enough for him. People like government inspectors—whether here or in Albania—did not care about what actually happened, they only saw what they wanted to see in order to profit off misfortune. The inspector probably had a friend waiting to take over the restaurant after it was shuttered. He had never trusted the inspector. Ever since the first time that man came into his restaurant, when he used to smile and pretend to be Bogdani's friend, Bogdani knew that one day something like this would happen.

But even if the inspector had been a decent, honest man, Bogdani would still need evidence before openly alleging a crime had been committed. Baseless accusations had tormented Bogdani's youth. When he was a boy, his friend's father spent months in jail as a political prisoner, charged with complaining about a shop having no bread. (There was, officially, always enough bread in Communist Albania.) Bogdani needed proof. Not only would it have not helped anything but also, after seeing the damage of false allegations, he was nearly constitutionally unable to accuse.

"You don't want to give that. Far better to have restaurant closed down," the Russian man said with no apparent irony. "But now I suppose you will be more inclined to sell? The price now could be reasonable? Nobody will want to eat here ever again. It is good that somebody will give you anything."

Bogdani didn't answer. He instead focused on Ismail, who was obviously listening while he peered outside at that inspector in his horrible truck. He knew he should put an arm around his son's shoulder and let him know that everything, in one way or another, would be OK. But Bogdani didn't move. If the Russian man was not there, perhaps he would have, but instead he shifted his focus past his son and out the window. The inspector seemed to be studying his hands or perhaps fiddling with his phone. Bogdani wished he would go away.

The Russian man did not push the issue. He had all the time in the world. He didn't think about his own daughter as he watched this man stare at his son. He did not doubt that the restaurant would soon be his. He was accustomed to waiting, so he only counted the number of times Bogdani's face twitched as he waited impatiently for the inspector to drive off.

"What do you want with this restaurant anyway?" Bogdani asked, his eyes still on the idling vehicle that was emitting a thin line of black smoke from its exhaust.

"I like it here. It is relaxing," the old man said. "I want to fish. I can buy house here. It is like upstate New York but less taxes."

"But why here? Why come all this way just to ruin me?" Bogdani asked.

"Ruin. Who ruins?" the Russian man said with a shrug. "I come because I have friend here. He tells me what a nice town this is. Wholesome. He says an Albanian has a restaurant and I hope it was for sale. I like it here and want to stay."

Bogdani didn't know what he was talking about. All Bogdani knew was that it didn't matter if he and his wife and son liked it here or not. They had no place else to go.

≈

The people standing around the man on the sidewalk parted for Arthur, possibly because they saw the emblem on his truck or the badge on his belt and thought he was more equipped to help. He wasn't. But from years of inspecting he did know how to stay calm and take control of a situation, so he walked through the parted circle. He saw the man on the ground was Eldred Holmwood. Arthur knew him only as the man who wandered the town—summer or winter—wearing a snowmobile suit covered in buttons and who had always, since before Arthur had arrived, had a cast on his left arm. Arthur regarded him for a moment, saw a button on his left shoulder that read Dollar Days, saw a line of spittle bubbling out of his mouth that attached itself to his large and tangled beard, saw the man's eyes flutter and then open wide and then close hard, heard a low moaning seemingly coming from the inside of the man's body. The phrase "the least of us" went through Arthur's head, and he felt ashamed for thinking it. This was not the face he wanted to connect with his first encounter with a potentially serious illness, and he felt the fear that accompanied the recognition of a disease's ugliness. He turned and addressed the man kneeling beside Eldred.

"Are you a doctor?" Arthur asked.

"Me?" the man said, perhaps a little impressed that the mistake could even be made. "Heck no. Just saw him here."

"Anyone call an ambulance?"

The man shrugged and the others didn't move at all.

"Someone should probably call one," Arthur said.

"Just figured it was Eldred and all," a woman said, as though she specifically had been accused of not aiding her fellow man.

"Could be sleeping," a man chimed in. "Sleeps in the gazebo sometimes, figured he was just here now."

As the man spoke, Eldred's limbs convulsed and his cast banged hollowly against the sidewalk, causing the group to jump and Arthur to recoil as though a shot had gone off.

Arthur wanted to say, "What could it possibly hurt to call an ambulance?" but instead he gently said, "Let's call one as a precaution." Addressing the kneeling man he said, "Do you mind handling that?"

The man nodded, and as he fished the phone from his pocket an until-then-quiet man—the oldest of the bystanders—said to Arthur, "Say, you from the health department, right?"

Arthur glared at his truck's emblem for a moment as if it had betrayed him, and nodded.

"What's doing with this illness? Heard about it on the radio. That not your department?"

All the eyes went off the man on the ground and on Arthur. The kneeling man, who was now holding his phone to his ear, shifted a couple feet away from Eldred.

"We're on top of it," Arthur said, hoping it would be enough.

"How?" the kneeling man asked, the cell phone pressed to his ear.

"Are they coming?" Arthur asked.

"No, how you guys on top of it?"

"Are they coming?"

"On hold," the man said. "They're all booked up. Might have to send one from Danville."

"Think the ambulances are busy because of the illness?" the old man persisted. "Think that's what Eldred's got?"

"I have no idea what's wrong with him," Arthur said. "For now let's focus on getting Mr. Holmwood some help. That's what's important. That's all we can do."

The two who hadn't spoken yet—people Arthur had taken to be husband and wife but who could have also been siblings—whispered to each other for a moment. Arthur heard one of them say, "He's the inspector." That two of these people recognized him made Arthur refocus to examine each individual.

They were all familiar though he had never spoken to any of them. The husband and wife owned and operated a butcher shop/catering business down the road. And though the other inspector in his office had so far inspected them, Arthur now wondered if they also referred to him as the Dickless Wonder behind his back. The old man was one of the group of ball-capped retirees who most mornings sat at the counter of the Millsville Family Restaurant and drank coffee while discussing high school football. The other woman was the crossing guard he saw every morning on his way to work. She always seemed angry at both children and motorists. Another man lived in Arthur's subdivision and was always out with his dog but never picked up after it. Arthur couldn't place the kneeling man but knew he had interacted with him before.

Identifying these people did not help the situation. All it did was bring to mind that he was speaking to actual people, not to "the public," so diverting them with imprecise statements was a losing game. If he had it his way, Arthur's sole focus would be on this helpless and troubled man on the sidewalk. But he knew what was expected of him, so he shifted his attention to the healthy people. He found it was easy to put Eldred out of his mind, probably since, even when awake, Eldred was a cause for concern.

"Heard on the radio that twenty-two people are in the hospital," the man from Arthur's subdivision said.

"I heard it was something in the food," the kneeling man said. When Arthur held up his hands in disbelief that the guy wasn't taking his ambulance-calling duties seriously enough, the guy said, "Still on hold. Maybe all the ambulances *are* busy picking up sick people."

All eyes went back to Arthur, as though a truth had been spoken.

"Statements like these are what cause overreactions," Arthur said evenly. "The truth is that we are still investigating and that we will definitely find out what this is and we'll put a stop to it. That's fact."

"You hope," the crossing guard muttered.

"But right now," Arthur continued, ignoring her but acknowledging to himself that she was right, "we don't know what's causing this. They think food because the symptoms are similar to other foodborne problems" (he was making all this up—until he called his office he had as little, or probably less, knowledge than any of these people), "but this could be from the water or even the air for all we know. Most likely it's a bug that's going around and will go away soon on its own, or it's nothing and people are going to the hospital because they heard about an illness when all they have is heartburn."

His speech relieved no one, and they all stared at him with wide eyes, much more frightened than before.

"The water?" one of the butchers said.

"The air?" the other butcher said.

"So you don't know?" the old man said.

≈

At the courthouse, County Commissioner Janet Vosberg threw a softball at the wall to summon Katie Bender, the assistant county commissioner, whose office was next door. Janet had no idea (and probably never would) how much this annoyed Katie, how Katie dreaded the heavy thump that reverberated around her office when the softball hit. It forced her to leave the shelves on that wall empty ever since a particularly hard toss knocked down a picture of Katie's two daughters and broke the frame. Janet barely even thought about it anymore. It simply reminded her of her softball days, of having teammates, of screwing around and calling it work.

Janet had been an excellent softball player, had even been an unselected alternate for the US Women's team at the Atlanta Olympics. Her office was filled with softball memorabilia: a bat that had hit a pinch-hit, two-out, walk-off home run in the Pan American Games in 1990 (everyone who came into her office heard the story of the bat); a picture of Janet shaking hands with then First Lady Barbara Bush, who was smiling rather wearily while Janet stared seriously into the camera; team pictures; a picture with the governor of Wisconsin at the time; and a few with smiling white men nobody really cared about anymore. She still coached the girls' high school team and was given much of the credit for their recent success. Besides coaching and memorabilia, her softball proficiency now mostly showed up in the form of metaphors shoehorned in emails. (*We have to tuck in our chin and take one for the team if that's what this comes to!*) It was as though Janet didn't really want to use them, but felt the need to remind people that she once had a distinctiveness that separated her from everyone else in the town.

As she sat at her desk waiting for Katie, she was the same woman as in the pictures, only more bulked up. She still wore a ponytail, and her jaw retained its youthful squareness though perhaps was now less angular, and her shoulders were more rounded. Janet was so much a physical object that she preferred to think of herself first and foremost as a body. She earned it. She took pride in it and was right to. She still worked out with weights four days a week.

Nothing ever came easy for her. A bad knee forced her to quit softball and work full time for the county road crew. She had commuted an hour and a half each way to get her college degree, only to then suffer through tedious government administrative jobs. Her first campaign for office, for county clerk, had been unsuccessful. She had modeled herself as a Laura Bush Republican and tried softening her edges without sacrificing her professional veneer. She went to the Sears in Danville and bought four tasteful, if too floral, dresses and a few conservative skirts. By the end of each day, her face ached from the gentle smile she constantly wore in public. People who had known her since preschool asked why she was dressed like that, and Janet would smile, shrug, and say, "Don't you like it?" Once, when she wasn't able to change after work before going to visit her girlfriend Whitney in La Motte, she found herself standing in her doorway in a dress and that Stepford-wife smile plastered on her face. Whitney told her she looked demented.

Losing that first election refueled her competitive spirit. The next time, taking the advice of people who told her to "just be yourself," she changed her tack. When she ran for the much higher office of county commissioner, she kept, or even enhanced, her outer image as a hard-ass competitor who could keep up with the boys at the bar. In order to pull this off, though, she broke up with Whitney, even though Janet didn't think anyone in town was wise to their relationship. But she couldn't take any chances. The serenity and sense of completeness she felt when she was with Whitney couldn't compete with the rush of victory, even if she had never felt so broken and alone as she did during the last long drive back from La Motte. Voters could relate to her being "a jock," and if she chugged a beer, it meant she was "down to earth," but if she had a girlfriend, it meant she was a liberal, and that was political death this far north in the state.

She managed her image just as carefully as she had during her unsuccessful run for county clerk. When picking out clothes she would think, "What would 'Janet' wear?" But the biggest difference was that now there was no Whitney keeping her grounded, nobody to call for reassurance or advice. To be safe she even stopped making the occasional weekend trip to Minneapolis to hang out with her old softball pals in Powderhorn Park. Janet knew she wasn't exactly being brave. She reasoned that there was plenty of time for relationships, but her professional life could never recover if she didn't get into office soon. Anyway, it worked. People accepted her as the same old Janet, though she had a difficult time recognizing herself when she was alone.

Luckily, between working full time and running a campaign she had little time for a personal life. She found that the harder she pushed her athletic persona the more support she gained, as though physical ability somehow made her a more capable leader. Later she would trace back the source of that first victory to the day she gave a short speech prior to the steer-roping competition at the county fair. When she finished speaking she chased a calf, tackled it, and tied its legs together. She has since repeated the feat at every county fair since. This was still how most of the town knew her: as a softball player and tackler of calves.

"Yes?" Katie said, peeking her head in the door and speaking with an urgency that she hoped conveyed that she had other work to do.

"Should I just do it?" Janet said, picking up a thin folder that held the candidate forms that Katie had filled out for Janet to run for Congress. "Should I file them?" She spoke like someone about to jump out of an airplane.

"I don't know," Katie said, though it would have sounded pretty obvious to anyone but Janet that she was tactfully holding back. "If this sickness turns out to be something big, it might be bad timing. Like when Bush was reading to those kids on nine-eleven."

She knew Janet would like being compared to George W. Bush in any way possible, even if it had the faint whiff of ridicule. Indeed, she saw Janet's eyes shift over to her picture with Barbara.

Katie came in and closed the door. "Maybe wait a couple days? The election isn't going anywhere."

Janet nodded. Then she groaned and said, "It's been so long. I want to start campaigning already. Did I ever tell you I used to dream about being in Congress, even back when I was picking up roadkill and filling potholes for the county?"

Katie nodded quickly, hoping she wouldn't have to hear this again.

"Those assholes used to say that my coveralls shrunk in the wash when they'd put a size smaller in my locker so my tits would pop out. God, I wish some of them were still working so I could fire them." She added thoughtfully, "Though Jim Uloff did die last summer."

"I was just on the phone with the hospital," Katie said. "I finally got through to a doctor. They still aren't sure what's causing it."

"Is it the food?"

"They don't know. It's possible."

"That inspector get in here yet? Alton?"

"Arthur. Reilly," Katie said, aware Janet was pretending not to know who Arthur was. "I called his office but nobody knows where he is."

"I guess it doesn't matter, but keep calling them. Make it seem like a big deal."

Katie went over and placed a hand gently on the handle of the Pan Am bat. "Do you think this is the best way to handle it? Why have we already designated a scapegoat when we don't even really know what's happening yet?"

Janet's eyes were on the spot where Katie's hand made contact with the bat. "Because," she said distractedly, "if this turns out to be a big deal, we'll be on top of it. We'll be able to buy time by pointing out who was responsible—this Reilly guy—deal with him, then when we figure out what's wrong it'll look like I did it myself, despite the stupidity of the people around me."

Katie took her hand off the bat. Janet didn't know Katie was sleeping with Arthur (or at least Katie hoped she didn't but you never knew in this town) so Katie didn't jump up to defend him now, though she wanted to. Arthur had been there when her husband left to ride around on a midlife motorcycle and Katie had needed someone to be nice to her, to want to be with her. Of course, she cringed now when she recalled how they made plans to be together—of introducing him to her daughters as her *boyfriend*—but that wasn't his fault. He was just a lonely, attractive-enough guy and he *was* nice. Mostly she was annoyed with herself for getting attached when Arthur should have been a meaningless fling. She had gotten married young and hadn't made nearly enough mistakes—she wished she had simply let Arthur be a fun misstep and left it at that. Still, she assumed they were done once Adam came back. But Adam became even more aloof after his trip—by now he barely spoke to her and treated her like a stranger in their own house—so she started sneaking away to Arthur's whenever she needed to feel wanted.

Without the specter of commitment, Katie felt unfettered and wildly free during her time with Arthur. It turned out that when she stopped speaking to him, Arthur fulfilled a need that she had never known existed. For the first time in her life, she used somebody with no thought to what the other person wanted. Everything was on her terms—as far as she was concerned, Arthur existed only to satisfy her. She had never known what it felt like to be desired to the point of need, and nobody had ever really sacrificed anything on her behalf. Now, for her, Arthur—a paranoid New Yorker—kept his back door unlocked every night so she could come in whenever she felt like it. He even told her once, after they were finished and she was getting dressed to leave, that he had stopped masturbating because he didn't know when she would show up and he wanted to always be ready. She hadn't replied. She only turned her face away from him so he couldn't see her smile. That a man left himself open to danger and deprived himself of pleasure for her was thrilling, and she was proud that she never thanked him or apologized or felt the need to point out how she had much more to lose. How she handled herself in this one secret way was perhaps the most convincing evidence of personal growth in her entire adult life.

And yet she did her best not to examine these encounters much. She had grown up Catholic, so the guilt of cheating was always present—though luckily she was also midwestern, so she was skilled at blocking out emotions. It was only in the blissful moments after arriving home from Arthur's, when she was safe in bed and could finally allow herself to relax, that she became aware of how necessary the affair was to her overall well-being. Without the release Arthur provided, she didn't know how she would cope with what her life had become.

To throw Arthur under the bus was unfair. But she didn't say anything to Janet. She ultimately wasn't willing to risk much for a guy she slept with maybe once a week, even if he did stop jerking off for her. Most likely this was all going to blow over quickly, and it wasn't worth losing her job over Arthur, especially when her career might be taking off after the next election.

"I'll keep calling his office," Katie said. "What should we tell the radio station? They've been calling for updates. I'm telling them the same numbers the hospital gave us earlier, even though there are a bunch more now."

"Anything from TV yet?"

"No, only WCSN."

Janet nodded. "That works, for now. Put the radio off. Don't tell them anything new until we have good news or until we have someone to blame. Oh, and see if there are any Danishes left downstairs. Grab me one if there are."

Katie and Janet had gone to school together. Back then they had not been close, though Janet would have liked to have been. Unbeknownst to them, Katie and her friends had plagued Janet's thoughts since the eighth grade, after she overheard one of them calling her Janet the Hulk behind her back. Even now, whenever Janet applied even a modest amount of makeup, she recalled the first time she wore makeup to school and one of those girls drew a picture of a pig's face wearing bright red lipstick, and a boy had stuck it on Janet's locker. Katie's group had not specifically targeted her, but every time Janet had seen those girls together in the hallway a hard ball of dread formed in her stomach.

Perhaps Janet hired Katie as a way to mitigate this past persecution. Winning an election made it clear that she had to believe herself worthy of people's attention and support, so building up her confidence became as essential now as exercising had been for her softball career. After some fitful introspection, she concluded that the main obstacle to her progress was that she hadn't moved past this childish bullying as much as she told herself she had. She eventually struck on the idea of hiring Katie, whom she saw in the courthouse sometimes filing paperwork while clerking part time for a local lawyer. Hiring Katie could serve as a reminder (largely to herself) of how far above her tormentors she had risen. It gave Janet someone to push around as well. Based on how stressed Katie seemed during their interactions, and how little money her husband made at the paper, Katie's finances must have been tight and she would jump at the chance at steadier work. Janet had to fire her entire part-time staff to free up enough money to create Katie's full-time position, but it was worth it. With only two people in the office they had to band together, and Janet didn't have to worry about overworking Katie since she provided so much for Katie and her family. Besides her official duties, Katie took dictation, answered phones, and fetched coffee and the occasional Danish. Yet despite these tasks, Janet made sure that she never needed Katie as much as Katie needed her.

Katie, for her part, was relieved to find a secure, well-paying position. Before Janet called out of the blue, Katie had struggled to raise her daughters while working two part-time jobs. Long ago she'd read about Janet's sports exploits, and then Katie saw her name on a ballot before voting against her. Otherwise Janet had been a name and a set of features on the periphery of Katie's life. Janet's call had been such a lifeline, though, that Katie hadn't considered why Janet was offering it. She could only accept.

The new position allowed Katie and her family to move into a better house and buy a second car, though they came with a hidden cost. Whenever Janet asked Katie to take on an ever-expanding range of tasks, she would not-so-subtly remind Katie who was responsible for these luxuries and how easily they could be taken away. And so, while her life outside of work improved dramatically, during office hours Katie found herself as a kind of servant—responsible for running the office as well as attending to Janet's emotional well-being. She quickly discovered that Janet had no personal life and, since Katie was her entire staff, relied solely on Katie for duties as friend and assistant. Katie desperately hated her job and wanted out but had no reference outside of Janet. Plus there was no chance of her finding anything else around there that paid nearly as well.

When Janet told her about running for Congress, Katie thought first about herself and her daughters. If Janet won, she would surely take Katie along, which would mean even more time away from home and with Janet. And if she lost, Katie would be out of a job, and she would most likely lose her house. Katie could not imagine Janet winning anything but a local election. Janet's unique personality played well in Chase County, where people had some strange appreciation for her calf-wrestling ways, but Congress meant she would have to win the entire northwest section of the state. Lately Wisconsin seemed like a kind of political Wild West, though, so maybe Janet could have some appeal. Until she figured out what she wanted, Katie was going to keep tentatively supporting all Janet's decisions and hope she would not file her candidate papers anytime soon.

Katie went back to her office to carry out Janet's orders. She would contact Arthur and then the radio station. As annoying as Janet could be, Katie trusted her judgment during a crisis. In all the years Katie had worked for her, Janet rarely made a wrong call when her own well-being was at stake.

Back at her desk, Katie, while glaring at the wall of empty shelves, dialed the health department and after two rings got the voice mail. She hung up without leaving a message.

≈

No ambulance could make it for another half an hour, so the dispatcher recommended that they take Mr. Holmwood to the hospital themselves. Kent—the kneeling man who made the call—had not been as insistent as Arthur would have liked. He had actually said, "Oh yeah, Eldred's probably just sleeping one off. We can get him there, no problem."

While Kent and the butchers and the crossing guard loaded Eldred into the back seat of the Jeep, Arthur called his office. There was no answer and he left a voice mail. Setting out on the twenty-mile drive to the hospital, he called back and was directed to voice mail again, only this time the mailbox was full. Being unable to contact his normally sleepy office was disconcerting, and he stared down at his phone as the recording repeated itself. He hung up, immediately checked around to see if the town was going up in flames, and briefly wondered if people were looting the Piggly Wiggly. Hoping for some sign of civilization, he flipped the radio dial before remembering the radio was broken. His mind was not put at ease.

As he drove, Arthur tried to put the situation into perspective. He did not know what was wrong with Eldred. The people in his office—since they were as confused and worried about the rumors as the general public—were probably all making personal calls, which would tie up the phone lines and direct all incoming calls to voice mail. All Arthur was in control of was his own actions, and he had already made the choice to drive Eldred to Danville because it made the most sense to take him in a government vehicle.

And yet he was nagged by doubt. Mostly, he wondered why he had speculated about the water and air being possible causes of this illness.

Even as the words were coming out of his mouth he knew it was a dumb thing to say. It was technically true, of course, that those could be the sources—but for all he knew it could also be caused by monkeys or vampires or Anthrax, or there could be no illness at all. He shouldn't have worried people more than they already were. His job was to help, to put people's minds at ease, not to raise more fear. Or was his only job to keep his job? And, if so, wasn't the best way to stay employed to use his modest authority to keep the situation as confusing as possible, since the less people blamed the food the less they could blame him? As they neared the hospital he had the baffling urge to confess to Kent. But Kent was in the back with Eldred, and Arthur wasn't sure he could convey the nuances of this speech above the rush of air from the open windows.

The waiting room was full of coughing, groaning people. For the first time, Arthur thought something serious was going on. Still, after Kent said, "Man, this is scary!" Arthur only replied, "It's the emergency room. Do you think people should be doing jumping jacks?"

They were in line to sign in Eldred after depositing him in a wheelchair with a preoccupied orderly. Arthur tried to skip ahead, but the nurse at the desk rolled her eyes at his badge. When he pushed the issue she said, "Chase County? No jurisdiction here." Her tone implied that she was right, but Arthur knew that tone counted about 90 percent toward convincing people. Nonetheless, humbled, he went to the back of the line.

He managed to send a few texts but received no replies. Fear kept him from calling the courthouse to explain his absence—if he called, something bad could happen.

The chatter in the waiting area was not optimistic. People recounted rumors and paraphrased radio reports. A gaunt woman in a loose-fitting dress stood on a bench and cried out, "Why won't anyone give us *answers*? That's my son in there!" but lost her confidence to continue after everyone else got quiet and kept their eyes on the floor. She sheepishly and shakily got down off the bench. Nobody offered her a steadying hand.

The man at the front of the line was vociferously arguing with the nurse and didn't seem likely to stop anytime soon. When a doctor walked by, Arthur hooked her with his arm. Halfheartedly producing his badge, he identified himself as Inspector Reilly and asked what was going on.

"We don't know what exactly is causing it, to tell you the truth," Dr. Reddy, by her nametag, said cautiously. She was, Arthur assumed, of Indian descent and spoke with a British accent that sounded out of place alongside the long midwestern vowels sailing around the room. She was short, with hair a bit below her ears, and young, but she seemed to know what she was talking about—or perhaps she knew how to convey confidence to people who knew nothing about treating the sick and infirm.

"When do you expect to know more about their condition?" Arthur asked.

"We wish we already knew more."

"Of course. But are there tests you're waiting to hear back on? Or will it start to show itself after a certain amount of time?"

"Who are you again?" she asked, with a slight shake of her head.

"I work for the county," Arthur said, as though that meant that he deserved more information than anyone else.

"Even if we had information to give, we couldn't give it to just anyone."

"I'm the supervising health inspector," Arthur said. "I need to know about the illness so I can find its source and prevent more people from becoming sick. I need to tell people what to stay away from."

The doctor hesitated and said, "I have very little to tell you other than that many people are very sick, and since it is gastrointestinal in nature there is a chance it is from food. What kind of food, I couldn't guess. But we really don't know yet. People are exposed to a lot of the same things, Mr. Really."

"Reilly."

"Come again?"

"My name. It doesn't matter. Wait, it does kind of. If you could please keep me updated"—he handed the doctor his business card—"and if you call the office number, make sure to ask for me, and pronounce it correctly or else the receptionist might get confused."

The doctor glanced warily at the card. Arthur saw she was very tired.

"She's not a very good receptionist," Arthur said.

"They never are around here," Dr. Reddy said and sighed, tucking the card into her front pocket.

The doctor took a step away and turned sharply back. "Why are you here?" she asked. "In the registration line?"

≈

Back at the office of the Chase County Department of Health and Human Services, staff members were at a breaking point and it wasn't yet eleven o'clock. The office was quiet, but red lights on the phones twinkled like stars with incoming calls. They had long before turned off the ringers, unable to bear the sound any longer and knowing they had nothing to say to the people demanding answers. Just before they stopped picking up, they started answering honestly, admitting that they knew as little as the callers did and that they too were scared. This only induced confusion, and sometimes weeping or angry shouting.

Instinctively they turned their chairs to the entryways of their cubicles, the same as they did five years ago after learning of the death of Arthur's predecessor. A popular old-timer who had been with the department since the eighties, he died on the job, having slid off the road and into a tree during a snowstorm and not dying upon impact but freezing to death over the weekend. Nobody realized until Monday that he was missing. That time, as now, they all turned their chairs toward the small aisle between the partitions, as though around a campfire, to share their feelings.

There were five of them: Sandra, the office manager/receptionist; three accountants; and Cal, the other inspector. They had all worked together for twelve years (people with city jobs held on to them like grim death) and knew how to operate as a unit. Arthur had temporarily disrupted their harmony, but since they weren't going to quit they accepted him like a dog accepts going blind. At least, they all agreed, he was willing to shoulder more work than anyone else.

Now they were all thinking the same thing: how to leave the office. Individually they had nothing to offer to improve the situation, so collectively they had to decide how to extricate themselves. Finally, Cal spoke.

"I mean, we got families and he don't." In their group discussions, "he" always meant Arthur.

"They could get sick," Jenny, an accountant, added.

"If Jeremy gets sick and I'm sitting in this office not doing anything, I'm going to kill him," Sandra said.

The oldest and longest tenured of the group, an accountant named Jill—who in the mid-1990s had presented to the governor's office a formal petition with over a hundred signatures (many of them suspiciously like her own) protesting new laws that prohibited smoking in government buildings—settled the question when she said, "He can't fire us all."

They all knew Arthur couldn't fire any of them, let alone all of them, but they still nodded as though she had made a good point. Arthur had authority in the office only because he had negotiated for a higher civil service rank and taken on the role of supervisor when nobody else wanted the responsibility for the relatively modest pay raise. They were going to leave early. Fighting an absent Arthur was just the simplest way to lessen their own fear of censure—much more satisfying than approaching the byzantine system for legitimate permission.

While he waited for someone else to make the first move, Cal covered his right hand with his left and crossed the fingers on his right hand for luck, as he did while watching close football games. Sure, he was worried about his wife and son, but leaving work in the middle of the day without his wife's knowledge was just too enticing. It's not like there was anything he could actually do to prevent his family from getting sick. But if he could manage it, a whole day alone with Kristi—the high school girl he had recently begun sleeping with—would rank amongst the best days of his life.

If nobody was going to make a move, he at least wanted to grab his phone and send a text. Something like *U ready for your big cal bear?* or *Yr cal bear is getting out of hibernation early lets explore a cave!* (He recently explained to her about the University of California, Berkeley Golden Bears—or Cal Bears—and how the current quarterback of the Green Bay Packers had played football there. Now, if only to her, he referred to himself this way in the third person and hoped she would one day refer to him this way as well, as her Cal Bear.) His plan was to convince her to skip the rest of the day. The chance of spending a whole afternoon together made him cross his pinky and ring finger as well, a gesture usually reserved only for last-second field goals.

He was not the type who had affairs. At least he hadn't thought himself to be before last spring. Sure, he'd always ogled other women, but to him, keeping the image of the woman fresh in his mind and masturbating it away as soon as possible was the most salubrious course of action. Then he met Kristi while he was teaching a gun safety certification course to make some extra money. She was getting her license to go deer hunting with her father in the fall. Through a scheduling error, and the typically low enrollment in spring classes, she was his only pupil. They spent the day leaning shoulder-to-shoulder as he taught her to sight a gun. She was bright and eager and, if not very pretty, well, she was young and seemed to admire him, and it wasn't as though women were beating down Cal's door. In fact, she was only the third woman—his wife included—who had gotten Cal off since he came back to Millsville after graduating from Redhawk Technical College nearly twenty years ago. (A masseuse, whose name tag read Jade, at an interstate massage parlor off I-75 in Georgia, took care of the other one. A product of his very brief stint as a long-haul truck driver, on his way back from delivering a load of mattresses in Jacksonville, Florida.)

And though Kristi was two years below his son in school (but, as she pointed out, actually two years ahead of him in math placement) he justified going through with the affair by telling himself that these kinds of relationships weren't unusual (just look at all those boys getting seduced by high school teachers he'd read about) and that, hell, he needed something else in life. He spent the night after they had first done it (in her father's tree stand) staring at his bedroom ceiling wondering if he had undergone a spiritual experience. Nothing other than a miracle, he concluded, could bring him such joy. Therefore, he didn't care what the law and society deemed appropriate. His eyes were wide open. This feeling of love and defiance of authority was as profound a feeling as he'd ever experienced. Of course, he didn't dare dwell on another possibility: that he was a middle-aged lech who was taking advantage of a young girl. He also never considered what she thought and felt as he hurried to pull off his boxers and his body contorted to mount her. Not once did he entertain the idea that she might soon grow repulsed by him as the thrill receded, while he would surely grow more attached to her youth and vitality. He did, right before he drifted to sleep, convince himself that maybe he had it wrong and that sixteen was the age of consent in Wisconsin.

In the office, as precious seconds ticked away and the phones' lights kept blinking with calls and the fantasy of hours alone with Kristi—indoors, with no metal bar of a tree stand pressing into his back—became a real possibility, Cal uncrossed his fingers, pushed back his chair, and stood up. He decided to make his own luck.

"I don't know about you guys, but this here is B.S., if you ask me. He can C.S.I. his way to solve the mystery, but I'm making sure my family is safe."

As he gathered his things and grabbed his cell phone, he heard the hesitant scraping of chairs moving toward their desks. His day suddenly seemed very promising.

≈

On the drive back to town, Eldred sat in back, awake and alert as a kitten. After the doctor had explained to Arthur and Kent that Eldred had woken up confused and verbally abused the attending orderlies and nurses, she asked them to take him back, since space at the hospital was at a premium and Eldred had emphatically refused treatment. The doctor added that they all wondered why Eldred had been brought in at all. Before Arthur could explain, Kent piped up, "That's kind of what I said." He said it proudly, getting an answer right, and not to rub Arthur's face in it.

Now Arthur and Kent sat side by side with their windows down while Eldred mumbled to himself in the back seat and bent forward now and then to gaze at something far off in the distance.

To get fired from a job where you make $32,000 per year and have to trudge around to lousy restaurants all day (often in several feet of snow) would seem to have its upsides. But to Arthur—to whom getting fired appeared possible after the way he had treated Bogdani and now this time-wasting gaffe during an apparently serious food-related event—it was unthinkable.

He was scarred by those unemployed months in New York when he could almost feel his bank account draining away as he listlessly read ads for jobs he did not want or could not get. All he could do was email résumés showing one item of Work Experience that ended with his being fired for suspected corruption. He had no references. He had only one skill. He had never before been neither in school nor without a job, and the loss of security had held no thrill for him. Plus, his wife had recently filed for divorce and that only promised to get more expensive. Others had it worse, he told himself, but that hadn't helped him get out of bed in the morning. Once, to see what would happen, he applied for a position to hold up a sign on the side of the Belt Parkway for a tax preparation service. He was pretty sure he would not have taken the job, but they hadn't called back—he hoped because he was overqualified.

When faced with the looming possibility of moving in with his father, now retired in Pennsylvania, Arthur began widening his job search, first to places he could commute to from New York, then to all of New England and, wider still, west and south, his scope spreading quickly like those C.D.C. disease maps in pandemic movies. He sent dozens of résumés to increasingly less desirable areas with no luck. (He had what he considered his first panic attack after a phone interview with the Marion County, Indiana, health department, when he searched for images of the county on Google Maps and tried to picture himself actually living there—yet even they did not call him back after checking his references.)

Finally, he understood that he would have to lie about being fired. To do so, he bought a burner phone, listed himself as his own fake reference (a made-up supervisor, Harvey Stanthorpe), and gave misleading contact information for the New York City health department. Only then did he get the interview here, in Millsville, which, from its Google Map, did not appear quite as bleak as Indiana and, though perhaps equally off the grid, was at least surrounded by lush rolling hills and had a pretty, old-timey downtown with not a single Confederate flag in sight (three were visible in Indiana).

After a promising interview and a single missed call on his burner phone, he began to imagine, for the first time in months, the relief of having a job again. His fantasies were fascinatingly dull: name-brand cereal, cable TV, new shoes. During the week between his interview and the offer, he found himself drifting off for twenty or thirty minutes at a time, thinking about what his new life would be like if he were hired. He pictured himself winning over the most attractive woman in town—a veterinarian, possibly inspired by the movie *Doc Hollywood*, though he wasn't sure—and single-handedly revamping the entire local government.

As the week progressed, he projected his better future self, starting fresh like a man who faked his own death. He would properly appreciate nature, use his knowledge of the world to somehow help the less fortunate, become friends with the locals, and enjoy small-town comforts, like getting his back slapped while walking into a bar. He could become an entirely different person, someone who liked these kinds of things. Now he cringed when he remembered these fantasies—he was so, so wrong about so much, most of all about himself. Yet he was still grateful to be able to buy groceries and pay his mortgage and own his own car and afford new shoes. Anytime he felt homesick for New York and thought life was unbearable here, he only had to think about those jobless months to scare himself straight.

Joblessness was his only thought as he drove back to Millsville with Kent and Eldred. He was always finding reasons why he might be fired—the fear was close to an obsession—and now his worry was justified. Being out of work made Arthur act like a cowardly drowning man who would use a living companion as his flotation device. He'd repeat his shameful performance at the diner this morning a hundred times before he would face the prospect of being out of work again.

"Is that a hot dog cart up there?" Kent said, pointing an incredulous finger, indicating a yellow speck about a half mile ahead on the side of the road.

As they neared the speck, Arthur saw that it was indeed. Not just any hot dog cart, but, if Arthur saw it right, a New York City hot dog cart, Sabrett umbrella and all. Out here, at the side of a highway, it was as out of place as a cow standing at the median of the BQE. He wondered how they missed it on the drive up and concluded it must have just arrived. The cart had no legal right to operate—it needed to be licensed by his department—and it was the most logical source of the illness. If he could prove this, he could return to town a hero.

"Looks like it," Arthur said.

"You ever see anything like that?" Kent asked.

"Not out here," Arthur said.

"Eldred," Kent said, "you ever see anything like that? Cart way out here off Highway 9?"

"No," Eldred said definitively, as though his answer mattered greatly.

"You ever eaten a New York City hot dog, Eldred?" Kent asked with a wink toward Arthur.

Arthur didn't like the way Kent talked to Eldred. Ostensibly it was friendly—he used the same words he would use to a more lucid man—but he delivered them as though he was fishing for funny answers that he could tell people about later, to point out how crazy Eldred was, and by extension how normal Kent and his friends were. Eldred would never know he was doing this, but that didn't matter to Arthur. Arthur was frequently surprised by how unfeeling these seemingly overly polite midwesterners could be.

"In nineteen seventy-two," Eldred said.

"No shit," Kent said with delight.

Arthur pulled over across the road from the cart and told the other two men to stay in the car. The sight of the pushcart up close brought up a wave of nostalgia. He had inspected hundreds of carts thousands of times. That he missed doing it never occurred to him. There was nothing, after all, inherently good about inspecting pushcarts. It was merely an experience that recalled a unique blend of fond memories and pain. Nothing else could have brought the past back so powerfully.

His heart gave the odd thump or two, whether from seeing that familiar yellow-and-blue umbrella above a steaming hot dog tray or its potential as a link to the illness. He wasn't sure. All he knew, after taking a few steps toward the cart, was that he was so excited that he had forgotten his wallet, which contained his badge, in the center console of the car. And since he didn't want the operator to see him hesitate or retreat, he left it in there.

She smiled when Arthur first pulled over, but she must have noticed the decal on the side of the Jeep because her smile faded and she slumped onto the milk crate behind her. She wore too much makeup, and it was now coated in dust. She also wore bulky combat boots, which Arthur respected for their practicality. She was perhaps his age, but probably a little older. By the time he reached her, Arthur decided this all added up to an appeal that went beyond mere bone structure or body shape, and he went through his mental Rolodex to see if he had ever inspected her in New York. He would have remembered if he had, since most of his inspections were done in Queens where she would have been, by perhaps a large margin, the best-looking hot dog cart operator in the borough. This wasn't saying much, of course. It's rather like saying someone is the youngest resident in the nursing home, but it was still enough for Arthur to clear his throat before speaking. Sex with an attractive pushcart operator was a common yet still-unfulfilled fantasy.

"License and cart registration."

She huffed and handed him her New York City vending license, which gave her name as Anna Bykov. Then she pointed to the cart permit issued by the New York City Health Department affixed to the side of the cart.

Arthur calmly examined both the license and permit for longer than necessary, hoping she would get impatient and make a mistake. An old inspector's trick. After reading her vending license a second time, he heard her foot tapping quickly against the gravel.

"Don't need an individual license to vend here," he said, handing it back. "And your Chase County permit?"

"This is not expired," she said with a hint of a Russian accent while slapping the permit. The accent took Arthur by surprise. He stared at her a few seconds longer than he should have.

"No," he said. "You need a permit from us. From Chase County. This is New York's permit."

"My father has worked that out. He knows the inspector."

"I am the inspector. Wait, is he Adam's friend?" Arthur said, remembering Adam's call.

"Yes," she said, standing up and smiling wide, making her caked makeup crack in the places the dust had dried it up.

"Is this all he had in mind?" Arthur said, glancing around them, into the fields and green hills surrounding them. "A hot dog cart in the middle of nowhere?"

"Not just a cart," she said, her smile fading. "He will also open a restaurant in town. Gyros, pizza, everything. This is temporary. He says it is OK."

"It's not up to him. There are rules. Fees. I have to inspect the cart and make sure it's up to our standards. You need to file for a business permit. There are steps."

"Did all of those places that got people sick follow your steps?"

"We don't even know that those people got sick from food."

"We did not get anyone sick. This is the first day I am here. People started getting sick last night."

Arthur paused. He knew these conversations went nowhere, that New York restaurateurs were adept at talking in circles. But since they hated silence, Arthur let the pause linger. A cow lowed in the distance and Arthur kicked a rock.

"How's business?" he asked, a sudden curiosity coming over him.

She frowned and shrugged. "Not bad. Soda, some chips, but already a couple hot dogs. People stop because they are curious."

"Profit?"

"Yes, by the end of the day for sure."

"Anyway," Arthur said, shaking his head, "you can't keep selling here."

"Inspector, you seem like a nice man," she smiled again.

"Where did you sell in New York?" he asked, to get his mind off how she smiled at him.

"Brighton Beach."

"Boardwalk?"

"Yes, my father owned part of a restaurant there, but it failed."

The mention of the boardwalk gave him pause. He swallowed hard. He remembered how he, like so many desperate New Yorkers, gravitated toward the beach during the worst times in his life. After breakups and when his mother died, he found himself getting on the N train, riding it to the end, and hearing the sound of gulls as he stepped off. He went there two or three times a week when he was out of a job. It was fitting that now, when his life may once again be on the brink of collapse, a representative of that place showed up seemingly out of thin air. The cart provided a strange solace on such a lousy day. He did not want the interaction to end.

"So you came here with only your father?" Arthur said.

"Inspector?" she said, running her fingers through her hair and holding in a laugh.

Arthur blushed and looked down the road. A car crested a far-off rise and drove steadily toward them. The passengers in his Jeep shifted in their seats as they watched him through the open windows. He tried to think of a lie to cover why he asked, but nothing came to mind.

"I am divorced," she said finally, saving him.

"Me too," he said, and kicked himself, wondering why he had spoken up. He tried to avoid coming off as a real person during inspections; it took away the leverage of being purely a representative of the state.

She smiled. Blood was in the water. "We will file everything soon, but can't we stay for today? Tomorrow everything will be taken care of."

The car was getting closer. Arthur could hear the engine cut through the country silence. He put his hand over his eyes to shade the sun. A windowless white conversion van. The kind of van a creep would drive.

"I'll look the other way for now," he said quickly as the van slowed down and made for the shoulder. "Just don't serve anything else, and please don't come out again until you get the permits. For your own sake. If more people get sick and they see you out here, they'll think you're the cause. People around here aren't always," he searched for the word, "open minded."

"Thank you," she said, Arthur thought, sincerely. She added, "Would you like anything, inspector? It is the least I can do."

The grinding of gravel under tires sounded close behind him. He hadn't thought of getting anything from the cart, but she was right—if they were not serving food when the illness started, it should be safe. Plus, he was starving. In his rush to inspect the diner he hadn't eaten breakfast that morning. While he contemplated, the wind shifted, or perhaps he became more acutely aware of his senses, and a sour waft came to him: the unmistakable smell of hot dog water. The smell made his stomach churn and his mouth water, and it always brought to mind the color of gasoline. In New York he had stopped eating hot dogs after becoming an inspector, but now the smell and the revulsion mixed with his desire for this woman made his old life wash over him like a wave. Craving overcame him.

"Maybe I will take something," he said, almost breathless, "but of course I will pay." Arthur had never taken anything for free from anyone he inspected. He tried not to buy anything from them at all.

"I will not accept," she said.

"No. You have to."

He reached for his wallet and remembered it was still in the center console of the Jeep. His hand was on his empty back pocket when the van cut its engine. Plenty of inspectors took food, and more, from carts and restaurants, and Arthur never thought less of them. He didn't think he'd get caught, and if he did, there wouldn't be any major consequences for taking a two-dollar hot dog. He wanted to pay though—he did not want to give her the leverage of witnessing this minor infraction. Free food was not important enough to him to undermine his job.

But this wasn't about food. This was about memory. He wanted to experience a time in his life that he could never get back for as long as it took for the nitrates to pass through his system and into his brain. He couldn't allow this opportunity to pass, so when she took the white-bread bun out of the clear plastic bag and opened the steaming bin where the mass of hot dogs floated, Arthur didn't stop her. The driver of the van would soon be near enough to identify him, but he didn't move as Anna took out the bun, placed the hot dog, tossed on a sludge of slimy orange onions and a mound of sauerkraut, mustard, and ketchup, and handed him the stinking mass, the bun already heavy with juices. He took it, looked her in the eye, and, without wanting to, without thinking at all really, winked at her. He had never winked at anyone, ever, in his entire life, but, for some reason, he decided to start now. He winked at her, she put her hand to her mouth playfully, yet in genuine surprise. Arthur walked back to his Jeep and, sitting behind the wheel, devoured the hot dog while Kent and Eldred sat wordlessly and the old woman in the van approached the cart and ordered a Pepsi. Arthur drove away without reprimanding Anna for continuing to operate the cart.

A few miles down the road, Arthur wondered if dust had perhaps gotten in his eye, and that was why he winked. But it had not.

≈

"I do not blame you," the old Russian man who had been in the restaurant that morning, Sasha, told Adam Bender as they sat at Adam's kitchen table.

"For what?" Adam asked.

"For anything," Sasha said. "You lose my money on scheme and you do nothing. Man sleeps with your wife and you let him continue. Both ways you keep what you have, you don't lose anything. I do not blame you. I blame myself."

Adam began wishing he hadn't told Sasha anything about Arthur and Katie, though it had been a relief to finally say it out loud. Sasha had been more understanding the night before.

"It wasn't a scheme," Adam said. He was unused to explaining himself and spoke through gritted teeth. "It was a miscalculation. You knew the risks."

"I knew the risks you told me!" Sasha said, sounding equally jovial and threatening. "I should have known not to trust a man who did not invest his own money."

Adam was about to say that he had no money to invest, that their meager savings account existed only because his wife made far more than he did. This, he was aware, would have provoked no sympathy from Sasha.

"The ancient Greeks!" Sasha blurted. "They have known this for thousands of years! And you, Adam Bender from Wisconsin, think that you know better. Better than cosmonauts who have seen!"

"It isn't that simple . . ."

"Yuri Gagarin saw that the earth was round over fifty years ago! You think he lied about it? *Laika* probably even knew! And I let you dupe me!" Sasha said.

"It's not like I profited," Adam said.

"No. Because then I could get my money back," Sasha said. "Now it is down the drain. Or, rather, buried in the—what is it—salt flats?"

"Well, it was pretty radioactive, we couldn't just leave it there," Adam said.

"Of course," Sasha said, "with that in mind it was sound investment."

Adam would never confess that he felt some relief after his failure out in Utah. Or he had until Sasha called, needing a place to stay after he lost his house in Brooklyn. Before Sasha reappeared, that chapter of Adam's life had finally been over. Years of secret planning, studying, gathering the people and resources, all for a glorious eight seconds of flight until his "Stabilizer" machine went up in electric flame. Nearly every night since his return, Adam had dreamt about those precious seconds. Only in his dream, his unmanned, golf-cart-sized craft—a machine he had designed with the help of an ex–UC Davis physics professor (whom Adam had reason to believe had recently become homeless) and was perfectly calibrated to fly, irrespective of curvature or gravity, along a flat path—was still chugging along, two inches above the earth's flat surface, verifying to everyone that Adam was right and exceptional. And though the results proved him spectacularly wrong, and he accepted that the project was dead, he did still *feel* he was right. That if, given one more chance . . . Luckily, it was true that he hadn't lost anything tangible. Except maybe Katie.

"Your wife sleeps with inspector even though she does not know what you did?" Sasha asked. "She thinks you were away riding motorcycle and she does that to you?"

Adam didn't answer. Sasha was simply digging his finger into Adam's wound. In fact, not telling his family about his project to prove the earth was flat had been the best decision Adam made over the past year. He'd told Katie he was taking off on his motorcycle for a while to "find himself." This corny explanation was to allow him to return home as a surprise conquering hero. Or, as turned out to be the case, to cover his tracks in case of failure.

He had been a shockingly faithful husband during his trip, despite bunking in close quarters with the long-haired swingers—the most devoted members of a particularly radical sector of the Flat Earth Society—who assisted him on his project. He had told himself that his abstention was driven by a need to focus, not by something as banal as fidelity. Though his contempt for the open-mindedness and poor hygiene of the potential mates was also a contributing factor. When he got home and read Katie's emails from the inspector, he was stung but also pleased that they proved the strength of his own resolve. Her affair fit somehow with his new, diminished version of himself—it was one more miscalculation that still didn't feel like his fault.

His impulse had been to divorce her, but the reality of this was much less satisfying. It would bring to light that she made far more money (imagine Adam asking for alimony!), that he had been cheated on, and surely it wouldn't be difficult to discover the true nature of his trip, which would expose what happened in Utah. Instead, he bided his time. While he waited he was consciously cold toward her, though this was no great change from the past couple of years. He then readily accepted Arthur's overtures of friendship, telling himself that it was his best chance to discover an inroad for revenge on them both. Oddly, Adam wanted to experiment with where it went. To his surprise, it had so far led to a deeper friendship between the two men.

What all this amounted to now, with Sasha, was that he didn't want to explain himself. He wanted Sasha to shut up or change the subject.

"It is admirable, the way you let man sleep with your wife," Sasha continued. "I would not have such restraint. Man does that to my wife I would . . ." Instead of finding the right word, he made a motion with his fist that could have indicated either stabbing the man in the gut or an unidentifiably lewd gesture. "But you," he continued, "much more under control." He shrugged and added, "Admirable."

Adam nodded.

Sasha went on, "And so what you are telling me is that I should *not* mention to her why I am here? She does not know that you lost all my money? She does not know where you were and what you were doing? She thinks I am just crazy man who came here out of the blue with my daughter?"

Adam nodded again.

"And you do not want her to know all this . . . why?" Sasha said. "Because you are ashamed, correct? You are embarrassed that you lost all my money and wasted everyone's time?"

Adam bit his lip and glared.

Sasha didn't actually lose all his money in Adam's venture. He lost a lot, not all. He was mostly done in by a bad real estate market, several other lousy investments, and his choice to sell drugs on the Brighton Beach Boardwalk. This last decision left him with loads of dirty money that he hoped Adam would unwittingly launder for him. Wasting it on Adam had been painful, but there had been a strong possibility he was going to lose most of it anyway. More damaging, selling drugs also caused him to lose his stake in a restaurant, and his business partners ordered him to leave Brooklyn. Adam was the only person who gave in when Sasha demanded help, and then only after Sasha threatened to call Adam's wife. Nobody else had even picked up his call. Sasha's only option now was to bull his way into making a life here in Wisconsin, as he had when he moved to New York from the Soviet Union over thirty years before.

His first priority was to make his daughter stay here with him. She had agreed to come along to help him get settled, but she adamantly refused to move permanently. He had tried everything to get her to stay—he ordered her to, he yelled, and he guilted—but she was as obstinate as he was when she made up her mind. Sasha suspected she had wanted to move away from him for some time now, and was using her disdain for small-town life as an excuse. Investing in Adam's risky project in the first place was a chance to induce Anna to stay with him by threatening to cut her off from his new fortune. Sasha had not, of course, considered being direct and explaining to his daughter that, since her mother died, he could not bear the idea of living alone.

His current plan was to get Adam to leave his wife and marry Anna. It was all he could think of to make her stay, though he was keenly seeking more plausible alternatives.

"And it is good it is just sex," Sasha continued. "Sex is sex. Though, my wife, god rest her, she does not tell me about sex with neighbor man after this long I would think there is more to things. For me, I think she would admit to sex, make you jealous, make you beat up man. My wife keeps secret and I begin to think there is more there. Just me."

Adam scratched the back of his head vigorously and asked, "And Bogdani wouldn't sell you the restaurant?"

Sasha nodded. He had already described the scene he had witnessed at the diner. There was little more to say on the matter.

In the ensuing silence, Sasha studied the bathrobe Adam wore, though it was almost noon. It was lime green with a magenta belt tied around his waist. Sasha had not been aware that Adam always wore bright colors—mismatching plaids and stripes and polka dots with electric blues and pinks and oranges—before he invested his money with him. Adam had explained his nonsense theories on the subject only last night, including the real, physical power of color. Adam had told him with a straight face that missiles should be painted like rainbows. Sasha did not entertain this for a second and could not believe he had invested his money with a man who did. Sure, Adam's claims about the flatness of the earth turned out to be bogus, but those had at least been backed up by science and were basically in line with what Sasha had always intuited. In the end, Sasha blamed these troubles on the internet, where he and Adam had met on a site that explored certain alternative views. But Adam was not stupid, and he was practical in so many other ways.

Sasha decided not to ask about the crystals hanging in the window and the copper wire strung with colored beads attached to the apricot-colored walls. He did not want Adam to explain these silly baubles because they were fictions for people with too much time on their hands. He didn't want to be reminded that he had put his trust in such a man. The only solace he found in any of this was that his wife had believed in certain magic as well. While packing his house to move he'd found evidence of her superstitions—crystals and the same dried bundles of yarrow, thistle, stinging nettles, and St.-John's-wort that his mother had used to ward off evil spirits when he was a boy—in the back of drawers and the nooks of closets. He hadn't the heart to throw them away. They currently resided in a shoebox labeled Business Items stored in the U-Haul trailer parked outside Adam's house.

"You have to go to work?" Sasha asked.

Adam shrugged and said, "It's a weekly." He didn't want to explain that his paper was mostly full of event calendars and marriage announcements and school lunch menus and Little League baseball scores and store openings and weather reports and columns where old women wrote about long-past quilting bees and legal notices and obituaries and, if they were lucky, a story about a new fire truck procured by the volunteer fire department or a four-page spread on the Heritage Days Festival. Explaining it would describe it dismissively, since he knew the paper was frivolous. But he cared for his paper like it was an orphan he adopted, a small child whose dirty face you could never get clean no matter how hard you wiped.

During his trip out West, he called his office every Wednesday, before the paper was printed, for a rundown of each page. He had called the office more than he had called his daughters. Despite having a newspaper he adored and a family who loved him, lately he needed more. He had always been aware that something special was inside him, a spark that could prove his worth to the world. If only he had properly actualized his potential in Utah, his outlook might be different.

"So Arthur failed the diner just like that, huh?" Adam said. "That's harsh. Perfect timing for you though, right?"

"Yes, it was fortunate."

That Sasha had surely destroyed the kitchen or paid someone to do it left Adam strangely conflicted. On the one hand, the Bogdanis didn't deserve that. On the other hand, lacking this killer instinct was probably what held Adam back.

"And this sickness that's going around?" Adam asked. "I heard on the radio that more than forty people are sick. Is that also fortunate?"

Sasha frowned deeply but not unhappily and rocked his head back and forth.

Though Sasha's complex schemes made him interesting to have around, Adam was already beginning to sense that this would soon become exhausting. He wanted to ask how much longer they were going to stay, but he was afraid of the answer. Katie and the girls obviously did not want these strangers around. If he were a different man, Adam would have warned his family in advance or would at least have pulled them aside and apologized for the intrusion. But he could no more imagine doing that than he could imagine initiating sex with his wife, which he had not done for almost three years now. Instead, last night when Katie and his daughters complained and rolled their eyes, Adam whispered a stern lecture about being gracious hosts and told his daughters they had plenty to learn from someone who had lived in a different country. Lately, for Adam, it felt like defeat to be forgiving.

"I called your friend after he left the restaurant but nobody in the office answered," Sasha said. "I will go to his office today. I want to open restaurant as soon as possible. People will know I had nothing to do with any sickness. They will trust me more than the others. Business advantage."

"Arthur's probably pretty busy, everything going on," Adam said.

Sasha squinted uncomprehendingly at him. "But he's your friend, of course he will see me. It will only take minute. I will sign the forms and pay in cash. That way they can process it right there."

"But you haven't even bought the restaurant yet."

"That," Sasha said, "is the least of my concerns."

≈

In town, people were wearing masks. Arthur, Kent, and Eldred drove by maybe eight people, and four or five of them wore surgical masks over nose and mouth. They reminded him of the tourists Arthur used to see in New York. Arthur swore under his breath.

"Maybe you were right," Kent said. "It is the air."

Arthur could not bring himself to nod. Not only was he sure that his remarks about the air or water causing the illness set off this new development, but his stomach was beginning to clench as his digestive system reacted to the hot dog he had eaten ten minutes before. He shifted his focus as much as possible to the masked pedestrians. So this, he thought, was what happened when people around here panicked. A slightly emptier street than usual and people wearing masks as a barrier between them and the world. Still, the fact that people partitioned themselves off from shared air, hid their faces, shut themselves in, distressed Arthur more than it perhaps should have. People panic when it comes to threats they can't see. He swore that if the hypothetical "Muslims" (whom many folks around here were fond of complaining about but had barely known or encountered) attacked, the gun owners, brandishing their AR-15s and deer rifles, would be thrilled to band together in order to act out their military fantasies.

The upshot to all this was that the more that people wrongly believed this illness was passed through the air, the better chance that Arthur was off the hook. Even if the food was indeed to blame, it made his job simpler if there was some confusion. That he might not have been totally wrong to obfuscate the situation gave him the courage to enter the town and confront its quietly panicking people.

After some discussion with Kent and a little input from Eldred, they dropped Eldred off at the town square—a small green area on the main street with a gazebo and a memorial bell (what its worn plaque memorialized was long forgotten and "bell" became an honorary term after the clapper was stolen at a homecoming pep rally). Kent helped Eldred out of the car, and Eldred walked away with no apparent cognition of what had just occurred—it was as though he was dropped off by his chauffeur at his place of business and was already concentrating on the work at hand.

"Funny thing," Kent said, as Arthur drove him back to work. "I kept thinking when we saw that cart out there how something like that happened up there in Oneida County. Not a hot dog cart or nothing, but someone at the side of the road like that, out there in the open, only they were selling heroin and meth to truck drivers."

"What?" said Arthur. "When?"

"Couple three years ago maybe. Big deal at the time—Buddy's got a cabin at the lake there so I take my sled every winter and heard about it. Story was even in the *New York Times* because some kids got hold of some too and a couple overdosed."

"Jesus," Arthur said.

Arthur had barely glanced at the cart. His stomach gave a squeeze.

They pulled up to the building where Kent worked: H & J Heating and Cooling.

"Oh!" Arthur said when he saw the sign. "You're my heating guy!"

"Been over to your place a couple times now," Kent said, a little hurt.

"Of course," Arthur said. "I knew I knew you, I just couldn't place you."

"Well," Kent said. "There you go."

Arthur parked but neither of them moved. What they had gone through seemed to call for more than a handshake, though they hadn't done anything at all.

"How's your system running?" Kent asked.

"Good, I think," Arthur said. "Haven't had to run the heat yet this year." Then he added, "And hey, I wouldn't mention anything about the heroin to anyone. You know how people around here talk."

"They do do that," Kent said. "All right, then, I'll be seeing you."

They shook hands with a bit of ceremony, and Kent got out of the car. Arthur wondered if Kent would get into trouble or even fired for being late. Maybe, but he could get another job. Kent could fix heating and air-conditioning units. That's a skill that people will always need. When the door closed and Kent was out of sight, Arthur realized that Kent was one of only five people who had ever stepped inside his house.

≈

"Come here," Janet said to Katie from the window. The softball was still rolling on the floor. "Are those people wearing masks?"

Katie nodded. They were indeed.

"Is there something we don't know about?" she said, glaring fiercely at Katie, who was her eyes and ears. It surprised Katie how intimidating Janet could still be, especially considering how vulnerable she often was when it was just the two of them. Katie thought how Janet's ability to demand accountability with a single scowl would serve her well in a debate.

"I don't think so," Katie said. "Maybe they were all painting a house?"

"We better get out in front of this," Janet said, ignoring her and putting her head farther out the window. She spoke in clipped, punctuated speech like a submarine lieutenant. "Call the radio station. Tell them we have definitive evidence that it is caused by food. Tell them this was reported by that inspector—Arnold, Amos, whoever—and that now he has gone rogue. Use that phrase. 'Gone rogue.' Say if anyone has any information about his whereabouts to call our number. Say he is wanted for suspicious activity. Make it vague enough and confusing enough where we can deny anything later."

"How about we give them the number for the health office?" Katie said, hoping to get out of taking dozens of useless messages that day. "I just called over there. Nobody picked up, and the mailbox was full."

Janet considered this.

"No," she said. "That would cause more panic. I want to be the face of this. I want to look like we're in control. I want you taking the calls and assuring people I have this taken care of. If they're thinking about Anton instead of this bug, that benefits us. And tell them to take off those stupid masks. Makes it look like we sprayed these people with Agent Orange."

"Have we really thought this through?" Katie asked, wondering if Janet thought Katie had the ability to force people to stop wearing masks. "Couldn't it blow up in our face? Plus Arthur probably hasn't done anything wrong. It isn't really right to do this to him."

Janet smiled and spoke as if to a squirrel. "We are talking about running for Congress here," she said. "He doesn't matter."

Katie didn't go back to her office after being dismissed. Instead, she left the courthouse through the back door and went out to the street to try to get an explanation for the masks. A woman a block away was walking toward her. The white of the mask was visible from where Katie stood.

"Excuse me," Katie said when she was near. "Can I ask why you're wearing that mask?"

The woman's eyes crinkled and Katie assumed she had frowned.

"Katie?" she asked with a muffled voice. "It's me, Barb Paepke."

"Oh my gosh, Barb!" Barb's girl played on the volleyball team with Katie's daughter. She and Katie once co-chaperoned an overnight trip to Waukesha for a preseason tournament, and on the bus there and back Barb talked about little other than antiquing. "I'm so sorry." Katie didn't know why she apologized. Barb was the one wearing the mask.

"It's fine," Barb said. "And you didn't hear? I guess you catch this thing through the air. You know, like sneezes and stuff, I guess? Heard it from Barry Colberger over at the Piggly Wiggly. They're selling these masks over there—big display right out front. All the employees have them on. Gloves too. I went ahead and bought up the rest of the soup and spaghetti and toilet paper left on the shelves. You know, just in case."

"In case of what?"

Barb shrugged. "Shouldn't you know all this? Doesn't Janet know what's going on?"

"Of course," Katie said, trying to smile. "But you have it wrong. It's not passed through the air." Katie held back from admitting that they didn't know what was going on. She also didn't immediately tell the lie that Janet wanted her to spread. Katie wouldn't, after all, want Barb to lie about something like this.

"Then what is it?" Barb asked, the frown coming back to her eyes.

"The food," Katie said, staring at Barb's mask as she spoke. She found it was much easier to lie to someone wearing a mask. "It's from the food. We know now for sure."

"Oh my!" Barb said. Then she thought a moment. "I suppose it's better than the air though, huh? Do you know what food exactly?"

Katie shook her head. "We'll make an announcement soon," she said. "I shouldn't have said even that much, to tell the truth."

"My lips are sealed," Barb said, making a zipping motion over her mask, which she apparently had no intention of taking off. "Thanks so much, Katie."

She felt empty as she watched Barb walk quickly away. The feeling reminded Katie of when she used to lie to her parents back in high school for no real reason. Her lies were largely harmless, like saying that she was taking algebra when she was really in geometry. Her most elaborate story unfurled over her junior year, when she told her parents that she was friends with a foreign-exchange student named Greta. She often spent her walk home from school concocting elaborately boring stories about Greta's life in Germany or Greta's efforts to assimilate to American culture. That her parents couldn't tell she was lying as she told these stories over dinner fascinated Katie. It was then she realized that her parents didn't know much more about the world than she did, that they were only legally in charge of her, thanks to nearly arbitrary circumstances. After the last day of school that year, she told them about her emotional farewell with Greta, that her friend vowed never to come back here. Her father perked up at this and asked what Greta meant by that. Katie shrugged and answered, "You know, like that there's no public transportation and stuff. I don't really know. I didn't ask." Her heart was pounding when she said this, thinking she was caught. But her father only muttered something about World War II, and they never spoke of Greta again. Rather than giving her a sense of superiority, these bouts of lying frightened Katie by exposing how chaotic and scary the world actually was. Remembering this, she almost called out to Barb that she should wear the mask if it made her feel better, just in case, since she didn't really know any more than Barb did about the illness.

Before she headed back inside, Katie saw Arthur's shitty green Cherokee rattling down the street. Now at least she wouldn't have to report to the radio about him, sigh, "going rogue." His presence was comforting—he might have the situation under control, but even if he didn't, she could bitch to him about Janet. Arthur was at his best when he was working, his most attractive. Seeing him now reminded her why she once had feelings for him and had briefly envisioned them together long term. After so long with Adam, she had found Arthur's dependability appealing.

He drove straight past without a glance.

Back in her office, Katie hesitated before calling the radio station and called Adam first. He might still be at home since his friends—who showed up yesterday with no warning—were visiting. The memory of those two strangers walking into her house still made her wince, but she didn't have time to worry about them. Last night, after a whispered lecture from Adam about their duties as hosts, she had thrown up her hands and said they were his responsibility. (Though she, of course, still made up their beds and set out clean towels and made them a meal.) She decided to try her best to view their visit in as positive a light as possible. At least

Adam was exposing them to his motorcycle episode, which he had barely mentioned in any detail since he came home.

She had texted Adam and both girls earlier to make sure they were safe. Now his phone rang and rang, just as it did when he drove that stupid motorcycle all over the country last year. If he had picked up, she would not have told him the truth about what she and Janet were doing. Adam had a strict and fickle moral compass, and she didn't want to be judged. She only wanted to be reassured that everything would work out. Adam's pragmatism in the face of real danger was a steadying force that made her put up with so much else from him. And though it seemed that over the past few years Adam's always-present quirks were slowly turning from aspects of his personality to its dominant features, for now she trusted him when it counted. That was enough, barely, at least until the girls were older. When she hung up she told herself that she wasn't going to tell her daughters to buy masks like Barb Paepke, though she would feel better if they were similarly protected. But the optics, as Janet liked to say, would be terrible if the assistant county commissioner's family wore masks.

≈

Arthur did not want to go to the courthouse until he was able to properly assess the situation. He was already so late that it wouldn't matter if he stopped at his office first to gather information and possibly use the bathroom.

He had no choice but to drive past both Bogdani's restaurant and the courthouse. The main street, Maple Street, was the only way across that section of town. It had no stoplights and took twenty-two seconds, going the speed limit. During this time Arthur did not take his eyes off the road. He was not curious to see if anyone he did not want to see saw him.

To get to his office he drove past the courthouse until Maple Street turned into Highway 9. Then he took a left through a perpetually half-finished industrial park (built, he was told, during the boom after the muffler plant expansion and containing one newish-looking building for Generac, a company whose nature Arthur had never bothered to figure out since, if he knew how depressing that building actually was, he might not have the will to drive to work each morning), turned right out of the industrial park, drove past the county garage where the school buses, snowplows, broken-down police cruisers, orange county highway pickup trucks, impounded vehicles, and green Jeep Cherokees were stored, and, just over a ridge, where the road began to gravel, arrived at his building, County Building C (though there were no County Buildings A or B, as far as Arthur knew). It was brown and squat, and when it rained mud ran over the sidewalk leading to the front doors. In his interview he had been given the impression that he would work in the recently updated, but still stately, Chase County Courthouse, where he could eat his lunch on a bench in the garden next to a fountain being perpetually filled by a peeing cherub. But he had been mistaken. At County Building C the only place to eat outdoors was a crooked picnic table in a clearing just inside the natural-growth woods that surrounded the parking lot. The one time he ate there he later had to pick four wood ticks off his leg and two out of his pubic hair and burn them with a match until they popped.

There were fewer cars in the lot than usual. Perhaps another department had off-site training. Anyway, today he wasn't even up to the Sisyphean endeavor of keeping his own office on task, so he certainly wasn't going to think beyond his department. His coworkers would be of little actual help in solving this problem. All he needed from them today was the minimum.

Nobody was in the lobby of the building, which was normal. And though he was in a hurry, he still scanned the building's directory with its white, tilting letters on black backing behind clear plastic. His office, the Chase County Department of Health and Human Services, was listed as CCDHS—Rm 206. Arthur had long ago given up reminding the custodian about this lack of a second *H* in their title. And yet he looked up at the board every workday and hoped it was changed, the same formless hope he sometimes got when gazing up at an airplane and thinking how, if it was going to crash anyway, it might as well fall from the sky while he was watching it.

The CCDHHS office was, of course, empty and strangely silent. Arthur checked his watch to make sure it wasn't later in the day than he knew it was. For maybe thirty seconds he stood there studying Sandra's desk, sans Sandra. On the desk were pictures of her kids, little framed signs of hope ("Sometimes Good Enough Is Good Enough"), knickknacks involving white bobbleheaded children in Green Bay Packer uniforms catching heart-shaped footballs, a day planner, and a green plastic hat that read Happy 40th!, though by now Sandra was at least forty-two.

He walked past the accountants' empty desks to his cubicle, across from where Cal should have been. Perhaps, Arthur tried to think generously, Cal wasn't at his desk because he was out performing inspections.

He called Cal's work cell, but there was no answer. He tried his personal cell, and the call went straight to voice mail. He sighed and tried his home phone, hoping to get no answer. Someone picked up.

"Cal?" a woman's voice answered.

"Mrs. Luedtke, this is Arthur Reilly, the other inspector in Cal's office."

"Cal's not here," she said drily in the tone people used when someone at work tried to interfere with a person's personal life, or as though the police were calling to inquire about a stashed fugitive. Then she quickly added, "Wait, is he OK?"

"I have no idea," Arthur said. "I was hoping you knew where he was. Nobody's in the office and he isn't picking up his cell."

"Probably left to check on their families," she said, matter-of-factly. "But he ain't here. I thought he was still at work, not picking up his phone like always. You think he's sick somewhere?"

"I doubt it," Arthur said. "He'd call someone."

"I got to get in touch with him," she said with renewed urgency. "Jake's sick. I got a call from the school. What is this thing, anyway? Shouldn't you know something? Why don't you know what's going on?"

"Mrs. Luedtke"—Arthur was in full professional inspector mode now—"go pick up Jake. Leave a note for Cal. I'll find him and let him know what's going on. You go take care of your boy."

"I know that! Was on my way out when you interrupted me."

Arthur assumed Cal's wife had an aversion to him. He apologized and hung up.

He stared uncomprehendingly at the blinking lights of the phones and felt his stomach roil with renewed vigor and surprising amplitude. The simultaneous realization that those lights were calls from ignored and frightened citizens being transferred to a full voice mail and that his digestive tract needed to evacuate this hot dog in the very near future came just as the door opened and a large, squat man called into the void of the office: "Hello? I am here to see Arthur Reilly, the inspector."

Instinctively, Arthur crouched lower behind his cubicle partition but was aware that the sounds from his stomach would soon give him away. He closed his eyes and made a solemn wish that this man would disappear. If he had even twenty seconds to settle himself, though, maybe he could talk to this man without shitting his pants or jumping out the window.

≈

"If it is the inspector who is in trouble, perhaps they will not make us close."

Bogdani eyed the untouched food on his plate. His wife, Drita, had a valid point, but he decided not to give her the satisfaction of a response. His kitchen was as it was. No matter what the inspector had done, nobody could change that. Not that he didn't enjoy the radio report about the inspector, but it only pleased him to know that the inspector might soon be miserable as well. He hoped the inspector lost his job and went to prison.

"Do you remember what they did to Shehu?" Bogdani asked. He didn't expect Drita to answer. He only wanted to share the mental image of the former Albanian deputy prime minister who had been taken hostage by protesters and was, as the legend went, beaten and raped by leeks. He knew the story not to be true—he was told that Shehu had been beaten and held hostage but not sodomized—but Shehu still had to live forever with that shame, since Albanians believed the story they wanted to believe. Bogdani liked tossing off the reference and knowing that his wife now had to think of a man with a leek up his ass. Her discomfort made Bogdani feel less alone.

"And even if they do, we will clean up and be ready to open in a day or two," Drita continued as though her husband hadn't spoken. "The other inspector—the dumb one who steals—will come and let us open. Customers will understand. They know us. They are good people. This is like their second home, Mërgim. Some of them eat here every day. We are a part of their lives and they are a part of ours."

"People will never eat here again."

All he could think was that he should have seen this coming. When the Russian came to him he should have been suspicious. In every word that man said to him the previous day—how he will never receive a better offer for his restaurant and how it is better for everyone if Bogdani sell to him—Bogdani now saw the implicit threat.

A gloominess pervaded his thoughts as they ate their lunch. This feeling wasn't new. Indeed it seemed as though it had existed within him his whole life, but he never before had had time to dwell on it. There had been happiness since moving to America, but in retrospect he saw even joyous moments as fraught. The birth of his son, for instance, came at a particularly inopportune time, forcing him to pass up what would have been a lucrative business deal with his brother-in-law because they needed their savings to pay the hospital bills. Then, after reading about an expansion to the muffler plant here in Millsville that could perhaps double the population of the town, he bought this restaurant. Soon after he signed the papers, though, he learned that the expansion had fallen through and they might actually close the plant altogether.

Now, eating with his family, he recalled the feeling he had while reading that news in the local newspaper. He hadn't felt an injustice occurred, and he wasn't sad, he was simply embarrassed that he had ever allowed himself to feel a sense of accomplishment. He blamed himself. He had read the news as he was walking into his new restaurant. It was also then, after he dropped the newspaper on the sidewalk, that he noticed a crack in the foundation of the building that both he and the building inspector had apparently missed. He assumed then that the inspector was a friend of the previous owner. As he walked into his restaurant for the first time as the owner, he imagined they were, right then, laughing at him.

If he had to pinpoint the last moment he had been truly happy, or at least hopeful, Mërgim would have said it was the hours between paying a gangster in Albania for two spots on a rusty, overfilled motorboat and arriving in Italy with Drita. Until they were onboard he assumed he would be bilked out of his money, and once in Italy they faced scorn from the locals during the months of uncertainty before a cousin was able to get them further passage to Chicago. The trip on the rickety vessel was the leg Mërgim had dreaded most. This was before the Otranto tragedy, when an Italian warship rammed and sank a gangster-run naval boat killing more than eighty Albanian refugees, or the Bogdanis might not have risked the passage at all, and almost certainly would have been turned away before they reached Italy. Even at the time of their departure, the crossing was obviously dangerous, but once they were underway, the calm seas and the unexpected smoothness of the ride bestowed Mërgim with a strange feeling of security, more than he had felt on land since the pyramid-scheme-based economy spectacularly crashed and the country devolved into civil war. When he finally saw the Italian shore and realized that they were going to physically make it and he no longer had to worry about drowning, everything suddenly seemed possible.

But now, instead of dealing with the prospect of selling his restaurant or keeping it and risking going bankrupt, he was paralyzed by the familiar gloom that came to the forefront with no corresponding hope. Or maybe he was just not willing to ask for their help, out of guilt as much as pride. If he did not have these two people in his life, he considered, he would have very little. If they did not have him, they might well be better off.

"Ismail," he said sharply, forcing himself to drive away such useless wallowing through its usual outlet, "why aren't you in school today?" The busboy had unexpectedly quit so they kept Ismail home that morning to help with the restaurant, though he should have gone to school after it was closed down.

"I told him not to go," Drita said. "Not with the illness. He will stay home today."

Bogdani caught the furtive, grateful eye contact between his wife and son. Another example of her saving him from his father. Bogdani wished he could lighten up and be friends with the boy, but though he could envision how this would go and even planned out the words he would say, when it came time to speak he was never able to begin. It was as though a great tiredness fell upon him and he would instead tell the boy to clean something or do his homework. Changing a relationship is a lot of work, and Bogdani was exhausted from a lifetime of working so hard with so little reward.

He thought again of Shehu getting violated by the leeks. It was a turning point in the revolt against the corrupt democratic-capitalist government, which only a few short years before had taken over for the corrupt dictator-led communist government. Bogdani's village was near Lushnjë, where the attack on Shehu took place, but he had had no interest in going there to take part. Sure, he would have liked to have gotten in a shot on a high-ranking official like Shehu. It wouldn't have done any good but would have been satisfying. Back then he had seen it only as the beginning of the end of his life in Albania and kept alert for his opportunity for escape.

His sentiments toward the inspector were no less acrimonious than that crowd's had been toward Shehu. He would gladly give the inspector the same treatment, if he could get away with it. The idea of hurting the inspector raised his spirits slightly (he even considered he could include Ismail, that it might be something they would bond over—like some fathers took their sons hunting). But if he beat the inspector with a leek, people around here would just ask each other what a leek was, and though most of them despised the government they would fear Bogdani more for being an outsider trying to upset the status quo.

"It is not worth sending him out there," Drita added in an effort to fortify her defenses before the start of the battle. "Even if it turns out not to be anything, I don't think it would do any good. It is only one day of school."

Drita worried about her husband. He had always been moody and defensive but lately had gotten worse. Now, after this offer on the restaurant and the inspector's visit, she wanted to make him feel comforted and loved. But his attitude made it difficult to reach out to him. She decided instead to try her best to protect her son, though it only created the impression that they were ganging up on her husband, who was much more vulnerable to the pain of isolation than he would ever let on.

"You are right," Bogdani said at last. "Not worth it." He put a bite of rice in his mouth and chewed for a long time before saying, "You should go to your sister's."

Drita carefully chewed her lamb to buy time. Her sister lived in East Troy, in the southern part of the state, a similarly small town where she and her husband had a restaurant of their own. Drita would love the opportunity to visit. If the restaurant was indeed going to be closed down for a couple of days, it would be an opportune time to go. It would also be nice to get a break from her husband, especially when he was in this mood. As she chewed she considered how this could possibly be a trap.

"We cannot go. There is too much to do around here."

Bogdani fluttered his hands theatrically around the silent, empty diner. "What the fuck is going on around here?"

In happier times Drita would have started a fight about his language and temper, but now things were too bad to quarrel.

"We will leave in the morning," she said.

"Leave now," Bogdani said. "What is the use of staying another day?"

For the rest of lunch there was no other sound than the scraping of forks and knives on plates. Bogdani had never bothered to turn around the Open sign but had not had to turn anyone away. Nobody had come in, whether because of the illness or because word of his being closed down had spread. He hoped it was the illness, but truly he was beginning not to care.

≈

"I know Adam," the man with the Russian accent said, sitting down in the seat Arthur eventually offered him. "Your friend."

"He called me today and said to expect you. But it's really not a good time. Come back next week," Arthur said, doing his impression of a calm man with regulated bowels.

"Next week is too late. By next week I cannot take advantage."

"You have a cart operating," Arthur said, suddenly making the connection.

"You saw my cart!" the man said brightly. "My daughter says it does good business."

"And you were in Bogdani's restaurant this morning."

"Unfortunate. But there was nothing you could do."

"Mr. Byk . . ." Arthur fumbled as he tried to remember the last name on the man's daughter's food-handling license.

"Close enough."

"No," Arthur said, "I'd like to know."

"Not important."

Arthur wanted to press but held back. He respected the withholding of information. Mr. B—as Arthur now thought of him—was probably unaccustomed to asking favors without utilizing leverage or offering anything in return. He was, however, probably the type of man who thrived on bypassing red tape. Arthur bet he hated filling out forms. He allowed the man to keep his name.

"I'm very busy," Arthur said. "I wish you had let me call you and set up an appointment."

"You are busy, I am busy," he smiled when he said this, his head hanging as he studied Arthur from the very top of his eyes so his dark pupils were partly covered by his bushy brows.

"No. You see, Mr. . . ." *shit,* Arthur thought, before continuing, "we have a situation here that is extremely important. And I have a personal matter that I must attend to."

"The sickness. That is why I am here."

"You know something about it?"

"Just what I hear on radio."

"I don't understand."

"The people, they are not going to want to eat at restaurants," the man smiled warmly, but also rather like a rascal, as though to say, *What can we do?* "So I want to get started while this is still problem."

His candor shocked and impressed Arthur, whose bowels calmed briefly as though they also wanted to hear what this man had to say. People here would also want to take advantage of a bad situation, would even take steps to do so, but they would go to great lengths to not admit it, even to themselves.

"You have to know that I . . ." Arthur paused and shook off a laugh, the gravity of what this man said—that he wants to use other people's suffering for his own gain—having just reached him. Arthur had an impulse to explain how Mr. B could best take advantage of the misery, not because Arthur thought it was right, but because it was interesting. Arthur had—if not a passion per se—a sincere respect for how laws and rules run people's lives, whether people knew it or not. By helping this man, Arthur could test the efficacy of his own regulations, like a man playing chess against himself.

Arthur was known not only for his strictness during restaurant inspections, but also for his love of rule-making. Since taking up his current post, he had created 147 new county ordinances. Now, for instance, ice cream trucks could play their music for only forty-five seconds per city block or risk a twenty-five-dollar fine. It was a funny hobby, a kind of sport, like fantasy football or a child's wiping out ants just by stepping on them. Once he got the hang of it, he came to delight in the process of carefully writing up the ordinance and presenting it to the county board. Arthur felt more in charge of his own life. If anything annoyed him, he held the keys to make it stop since nobody else cared as much.

But with Mr. B, Arthur could test his true reach by stretching his own rules. He wanted to say, approximately, *I can't give you special treatment, but if I were you . . .* but he didn't because an image came to him: Bogdani's son with his brave, crushed face while the father stood by in resignation. This memory seemed to cause an upheaval to Arthur's system, and Sasha didn't budge as a wet gurgle pealed from Arthur's midsection. Arthur wondered if that was how all those people in the hospital felt—*upheaved*. In the face of unpleasantness he couldn't risk contributing to, or abetting, further distress, so Arthur said, "I can't help you take advantage of this situation."

Mr. B's face clouded with confusion for a moment, then he shook his head quickly, met Arthur's eyes, and said, as though explaining a simple truth to a monkey, "People need to eat. People will not want to eat at places that made them sick. They will eat food from grocery store, or at restaurant far away. So why not eat at my restaurant? It is good food, only place that has not gotten anyone sick."

Arthur imagined banners advertising the fact that eating there will not kill you.

"You couldn't get ready in time to take advantage anyway. This isn't going to last long."

"I could be ready by tomorrow."

"No, you couldn't."

Mr. B raised his hands.

"I can't," Arthur said.

Mr. B got up and, as Arthur began to stand too, put a hand on his shoulder and pushed him back down gently.

"Mr. Reilly, I came to this country more than thirty years ago at great inconvenience. Wife, daughter. You know why I came? To get away from lines. Everywhere in Russia there were lines. Home, work, vacation—so many lines. Your friend Adam says you can help me with line here, but instead you say to wait." He paused and said, "I don't know."

"Any other time."

"Always any other time," Mr. B said. "But I am going to buy restaurant and I will open tomorrow, next day at latest. Maybe I will ask Adam's wife to help me to the front of your line. She is very nice, very helpful." He placed a hand on Arthur's desk and leaned so close Arthur could smell the pickled sweetness of the man's breath. "Do you find that she is helpful, Mr. Reilly? Do you think she is good person to help me? Perhaps I should tell your friend Adam how . . . helpful she is to you?"

Arthur met Mr. B's eye and hoped his outward appearance was less panicked than the red-alert pandemonium he was undergoing internally. "Katie is very nice and works for the government so she would be a good choice to ask for help," he said, shocked that he not only spoke coherently but also said the right thing.

Mr. B sighed, nodded weakly, and began to walk away.

"Where are you going to operate?" Arthur called after him, his curiosity overriding his better sense to allow this man further opportunity to detain him.

"The restaurant you shut down this morning," Mr. B called over his shoulder without slowing down.

Arthur watched him go until the door clicked shut. Then he waited exactly thirty seconds and ran off to the seldom-occupied third-floor bathroom.

≈

"Is this Inspector Reilly?" asked a familiar voice from an unfamiliar number.

"Yes?" Arthur said.

"This is Dr. Reddy from the Danville Clinic. We spoke in the ER."

"Of course!"

"Can you hear me? There's an echo on my end."

"Sounds fine here," Arthur said, and cleared his throat. "Have you found a cause?"

"Not exactly," she said, and paused. "Though we are quite sure it's food-borne. But that's not why I called. A woman passed away, we believe from infection."

"Jesus."

"To be honest, I'm still not convinced you're the one I should be speaking to, but I need to spread the word. There seems to be dreadful communication among official channels here."

"That's reasonable," Arthur said. "So was she old? Did she have underlying conditions?"

"I can't give you any personal information. She was older, though, yes."

"Like, could she have been a nurse in World War Two?"

"I'm hanging up now. Get in contact with the county health department here. You should have already had a coordination plan in place. I'm busy. Don't put me in this position again."

Arthur knew he couldn't delay any longer. He had to suck it up and meet with Janet.

On his way to the courthouse he saw Cal's truck parked on a tree-lined residential street. This legitimate reason to briefly delay his trip lifted Arthur's spirits, and he immediately pulled beside the truck to investigate.

Inside the cab of Cal's truck were candy wrappers, shotgun shells, empty Kwik Trip "Mega Buddy" cups so large they had to be forced into the cup holder, tins of Skoal chewing tobacco, a surprising number of feathers, a Green Bay Packers air freshener, and various items of camouflage clothing—but no Cal. Then he glanced down the block and saw his fellow inspector walking with his head on a swivel and finally darting behind a house. Sensing that nothing good could come from this kind of furtive movement, Arthur wanted nothing more than to drive on and pretend he hadn't seen anything, especially because his bowels, though calmed, could use more time to rest before he had to talk to the commissioner. But Cal's son was sick with a disease that had contributed to a person's death, so Arthur parked across from the house that Cal had disappeared behind and waited a moment to see if Cal emerged.

Who knew what would happen if he went after his fellow inspector now? Cal was obviously not working, and Arthur had valid reasons to chase him down, but Cal still had a right to do what he wanted without Arthur meddling. Not that Cal had any problems interfering with Arthur's life or loping into Arthur's space. Every morning when Arthur came into the office, Cal commenced an assault on Arthur's time in the form of boring stories from the night or weekend before: what Cal had watched on TV, what animals Cal hunted or fished to death, particularly good or bad dinners, how many tackles or "pancake blocks" his son had registered in his latest football game, how far his son had thrown the shot put or discus in the previous night's track meet. He would even go into detail about how well or poorly he had slept the night before ("perfect sleeping weather" was a phrase Arthur had heard Cal utter on five different occasions). The acceptance of Cal was a feat of forbearance that Arthur was especially proud of—some of the only proof of his growing and becoming a better person since moving to Millsville. Rage no longer filled him each morning when he saw Cal's open, eager face—bald and pink and round as a whoopie cushion—gawping down from over Arthur's cubicle wall, ready to dispense his tedium.

Cal was also a shockingly inept inspector. He resisted all innovations. He obviously skipped inspections altogether and just gave the restaurants perfect scores. When Cal did inspect, Arthur was pretty certain it was only to get free or discounted meals. Still, over time Arthur was able to force himself to look past all this. Before he accepted this man's large and jovial uselessness, he often spent whole evenings at home composing speeches that might penetrate Cal's skull and make him understand how stupid he actually was and why that stupidity could potentially injure innocent people. It took about a year before Arthur finally convinced himself that the most deleterious aspect of Cal's incompetence was the amount of time Arthur wasted dwelling on it.

And now it was he, Arthur, who was about to invade Cal's personal space.

The house Arthur presumed Cal went into belonged to a lawyer named Nils Vanderberg. Arthur had no idea how he knew this, but if he had reason to ruminate on any house in that town, he felt he could figure out whom exactly it belonged to. Perhaps Cal was writing his will or was in the early stages of a divorce—those were legitimate reasons to go to a lawyer's house. Neither of these seemed likely though, since Cal didn't plan any further ahead than his next meal and wasn't likely to be initiating a divorce proceeding because Cal, as far as Arthur knew, lacked all initiative.

Just as Arthur decided he couldn't wait any longer and started to open his car door, a purple Pontiac Sunfire pulled in the lawyer's driveway and parked in the empty three-car garage. A girl got out of the car and walked into the house.

This made Arthur tired. Everything that had happened so far that day seemed to heap upon him. He wanted to nap in his Jeep until Cal came out or the town was sucked into a vortex of sickness and stupidity and despair. To counteract this impulse he got out and walked up and down in front of the house, hoping Cal would see him and get the hint and come out. When he didn't, Arthur traced Cal's route to the back of the house, thinking that if Cal wanted to avoid detection, it might be best if Arthur did as well.

Not long after Arthur started work as an inspector, his mother got sick with cancer. Arthur did not handle this well and rarely visited her, though his parents lived not far away in the same town outside of Philadelphia where he had grown up. Soon her cancer went into remission, but when it came back two years later Arthur tried to redeem his past callousness by going to his parents' house at every opportunity. It was during one of these visits that he happened to walk into his parents' bedroom one morning to borrow a pair of his father's socks and witnessed his father and mother having sex in a noteworthy position: his father standing near the bed and his wigless mother with her head mashed into a pillow and her butt high in the air. Arthur stood there unnoticed, watching his spindly father pound ("pound" being the only verb that came to mind whenever he thought of this scene) his sick mother until Arthur's faculties returned and he swiftly and silently closed the door. A half hour later his father gave Arthur a hearty slap on the back as Arthur ate his breakfast, and all continued outwardly the same as it always had. Inwardly, however, Arthur was waging all-out war with himself to block out this image—not only because it disgusted him but also because he was worried it *wouldn't* disgust him enough. His thoughts ran wild all day. He recalled every instance of watching pornography involving mothers and sons (which wasn't considered that weird in Europe), and he also considered how he had never had sex with a woman in that particular position, and how wrong it seemed to be lagging behind his parents in terms of sexual adventurousness. He didn't return to his parents' house for almost a month and managed to move past the awkward incident. A year later, at his mother's funeral, the image returned, and he was able to contextualize it for what it was: a moment worth living. For them, not him. He would still rather not have seen it. But, as she lay in her coffin, he was at least able to recognize and appreciate an unexpected dimension of his mother's vitality for life.

What he had witnessed immediately came to mind when Arthur saw, through the back window, a huffing, shirtless, and mostly pantsless Cal and this young girl (surely the lawyer Vanderberg's daughter) groping each other in the lawyer's dining room. He stood transfixed as Cal held out his penis like an offering to this girl who was as overmatched as if she were trying to fend off a water buffalo. Cal's medium-length, mushroomy member filled Arthur's vision. He knew that, like seeing his parents that morning, this scene would fill him with many similar misgivings about his own sexual appetites and experience, but unlike witnessing his parents there would be no silver lining.

These conflicting images and thoughts made Arthur's mind pointlessly race like a dog on a treadmill and leashed to an owner watching television. He wanted to run away or, better yet, knock on the window to put a stop to this, but his body would not move no matter how hard he willed it to. Arthur's eyes remained locked on Cal until he heard a piercing scream and shifted his eyes from Cal's veiny phallus to his shocked and sweaty face staring back at Arthur.

≈

Adam Bender heard the radio report while driving to his office: the disease was caused by food, and Arthur was needed for some vague reason. He clicked off the radio and was glad he had ignored Katie's call earlier. Surely she was seeking reassurance that lying to the public was acceptable in this situation. Adam was her sympathetic ear when she had to carry out Janet's more unscrupulous orders. This was perhaps their strongest bond lately, other than their daughters. But since his conversation with Sasha, he was not in the mood to justify Katie's actions, even if carrying them out was necessary to keep them financially afloat.

According to the radio report, Arthur had "gone rogue." Janet's phrasing, no doubt. Adam didn't mind Janet lying—ruthless conviction was why he was a conservative in the first place—but he couldn't stand how dumb she sounded. She loved words like "rogue" and "maverick" and "paradigm." These buzzwords peppered Janet's quotes in his paper. Katie, he figured, was aware of Janet's inanity but was compelled to go along. He secretly wished his wife had confidence to match her good sense. If she did, though, she probably would not still be with him.

On Wednesdays, Adam went to the office in the afternoon and worked into the evening, setting the final layout before the paper was printed overnight. Tomorrow morning he would open at six, accept the wrapped bundles, and at six thirty open the doors to the delivery people: elementary school boys on bikes who delivered locally and couples with bad teeth in pickup trucks who delivered to the outskirts of the county and whose paychecks, Adam assumed, went straightaway toward the purchase of methamphetamines.

Then the paper would be in the hands of readers, to idly pass an hour or two. Adam always imagined an old woman clipping a picture of herself as a bake-off winner or a father cutting out the rundown of a volleyball game in which his daughter excelled for inclusion in the scrapbook that he would present at her high school graduation party. Though Adam had no interest whatsoever in doing this for his own family—he had never clipped anything from his own paper—he was proud that these activities still existed and that he was responsible for them, a personal and tangible thing. The *Register* had no online format. Actually, it barely broke even—it was the *Shopper* (composed entirely of classifieds and local business advertisements) that made enough money to keep the business afloat—but Adam felt it was important to maintain both papers to keep area traditions alive.

Adam arrived at the office wearing baby-blue-and-gold plaid pants, a lime button-down shirt with a pink fleur-de-lis crest on the breast pocket, and mauve socks. Before he reached his desk, Mitch, the only staff writer, handed him three sheets of paper. Adam could sense Mitch's pride in his work by the way he flicked the pages toward Adam, as though they were in a movie about a busy newsroom. Apparently, Mitch had spent his morning writing a lengthy and informative possible-front-pager about the illness. Adam bet that Mitch had been glancing at the door for the past hour, waiting for Adam's praise and approval.

Mitch, for his part, considered the article to be the best work he had ever done. He had called a contact at the Danville Clinic (a nurse friend of his) and gotten the latest facts and figures: which tests had been run, what he'd heard doctors say, his best guess when they would pin down the cause, the indicative symptoms, and how many false alarms had been reported. Mitch researched similar outbreaks and discovered a recent one in Minnesota. He included a couple of personal stories from people who had called the paper and tried to convey the general feeling around town. At the end he tossed in a perhaps-slightly-too-editorial plea for calm and rationality in the face of potential disaster. Trust in the government, he wrote, though he himself did not trust the local elected officials at all. He ended with a quote from *The Plague* by Albert Camus, despite never having read the whole book. He just turned to the last page because he figured that was where to find the strongest passages. He finished his piece: "And if this comes to the worst, we can take heart that we are in this together, as Albert Camus wrote in his book *The Plague*, that we are 'in the never ending fight against terror and its relentless onslaughts, despite their personal afflictions, by all who, while unable to be saints but refusing to bow down to pestilences, strive their utmost to be healers.'"

He reread it several times while waiting for Adam to arrive. He fixed this or that but mostly basked in his own words. He considered emailing it to his mother but couldn't think of any reason other than the itch to boast.

Adam read the article as he took off his marigold-colored fall jacket, flipped to the second page very quickly, looked away to turn on his computer, glanced back to the page for a moment but obviously was not reading, placed the pages in the trash, and said, "No."

Mitch was crestfallen, but quickly became angry. He and Adam had developed a kind of odd-couple relationship over the past couple years, but this was just mean.

"I worked on it all morning, I did all that investigating, and you're not even going to read it?" Mitch asked, doing his best to keep his irritation in check.

"I read it. We're not going to print anything about the illness."

"We're a *newspaper*," Mitch said. "That's obviously *news*."

Adam thought a moment, tipped his head sideways to concede the point, and then said, "Yeah, but we're not going to print it. Maybe next week when it's blown over we'll include a story about a dog who helped raise sick people's spirits or something."

"But I have sources," Mitch said lamely.

Adam took the pages out of the garbage, scanned them, and said, "Just because you're screwing some nurse at the hospital and they give you some gossip about what they heard a doctor say in passing doesn't mean we can print it."

Mitch bit his lip. He had always almost respected Adam, despite his political leanings, for generally being considerate of Mitch's lifestyle. Being gay around here meant that Mitch was, at best, tolerated. It was as though he had a tacit agreement with everyone in town that they would not put signs in his yard or openly call him faggot as long as he never lived with a partner or walked down the street holding hands with a man.

He used to challenge this. In the nineties, when he moved back to Millsville after college, he told himself he would not act differently than he felt. If that meant people were open about their hatred, then they could openly hate. He began a relationship with a man from Eau Claire named James and, the Wednesday after James had stayed for the weekend (when they took only one trip to town, to the hardware store), Mitch found a crudely lettered sign proclaiming God Hates Fags stuck in his front yard. Seeing the sign chilled him but, though he was hurt, he managed to roll his eyes and superficially laugh it off as he pulled it out and stuck it in his kindling pile. James also laughed as they speculated over the phone which overweight wife beater took the time to buy the sign-making materials and then Magic Marker the cardboard. Though he laughed, James never visited again. They continued to see each other for a while—at James's house in the more progressive Eau Claire—until the relationship ran its course.

That October, Mitch read about Matthew Shepard and began having trouble falling asleep. He became like a lion tamer who lost his nerve, realizing how often he had tempted fate. No matter how scared he became, though, he would not move to another town. He told himself they could not force him to leave. He was born here. This was his home as much as it was anyone's. Soon he resigned himself to the fact that he could no longer live as visibly as he'd like. People here were expert at wearing you down, outlasting you, of bringing you back to the herd. Mitch never wanted to stand out, but he didn't want to hide either. It turned out he had to do one or the other. The constant smirks and clucks, head shaking, open laughter, the red-faced drunks in bars jostling him and asking what cock tastes like. So he retreated and, so far, they allowed him to stay unmolested.

Now he referred to himself as a "bachelor" to most everyone except a few women and the most progressive men (the high school art and literature teachers, the community theater director, and a handful of other "bachelors" spread out around the edges of the town and in the surrounding communities). And while Adam never addressed Mitch's sexuality directly, he also occasionally joked about it the way he would to a straight man who had a lot of sex. But this last comment about the nurse—whom Mitch had never actually slept with—felt sharp and nasty. It implied Mitch wasn't a conscientious worker and that Adam did not respect him as a writer, and that somehow his sexuality called this into question.

"Whatever," Mitch said.

"If you say so," said Adam, with his eyes locked firmly on his computer screen.

Adam liked Mitch. He was glad to work so closely with one of the few intelligent, curious, genuinely interesting people around here. He respected Mitch for living openly, though he would never confess this admiration. Sure, Adam supported politicians who wanted to punish Mitch for who he was, but these fickle matters were necessary to win elections. Practically, that Mitch was gay only meant that Adam could pay him less, since nobody else around here would hire him. Not that Adam could afford to give him more. If Mitch quit, Adam would have no choice but to write every article himself. Nobody else with half of Mitch's skill would take that meager salary.

This didn't mean he was going to print the story. At most he would maybe concede a fifty-word item below the legal notices about an uptick in ER visits. Even then he'd try to skew it somehow to blame the Democrats. Something like this would suit: "According to sources, hospital overcrowding has been a rising problem since the implementation of the Affordable Care Act, otherwise known as Obamacare."

He opened a new document to write a short piece about the Bogdanis' restaurant being closed down. Normally he wouldn't include such a disheartening story unless he could tie in a dig on liberals, but Sasha made him promise. Adam couldn't stand being under someone's thumb, though it would be worse to face his family. That would confirm Adam's suspicions that he truly was a failure. If he thought Katie would simply get angry about his Utah trip, he would tell Sasha to leave tomorrow. But he knew that she would be outwardly understanding while inside she would rage. If only she would explode. At least that would be *honest*. He could scream back, restrain his anger, throw a lamp. Such a display of passion might lead to the spark of sex. They hadn't done it in almost three years. Now, though, if Sasha told Katie about Adam's failed attempt to prove that the earth was flat by utilizing hypercharged magnets and copper coils, Katie would just be disappointed by Adam's stupidity or mental illness or midlife crisis or whatever she would blame it on. Or, more likely, she would blame herself. She'd probably be chipper and praise him for trying and immediately start cleaning the bathtub. Their house was never so clean as after Adam or one of their daughters or even Katie herself made a mistake. He imagined that when she'd started up with Arthur, the house sparkled.

His plan was to stick the restaurant story in the local section on page three, not page one as Sasha wanted. Whatever was on the front page of a weekly paper stayed in the public's view for seven days. The grandfather and granddaughter team who won that fishing tournament were currently staring out from the previous *Chase County Register* in the waiting room of every dentist office and mechanic in the county—hell, a couple well-thumbed copies were probably on a table near the front door of the closed restaurant. Though it would placate Sasha, it wasn't Adam's place to sabotage a business. Sure, the Bogdanis had probably done nothing to deserve it, but mostly it was too depressing. This was also why he wouldn't print Mitch's illness story. Whether or not it ended up being a big deal, he didn't want it confronting people every time they saw a copy of the paper.

He dashed off his piece about the restaurant and, since Mitch was sulking and there wasn't time to write a new front-page article, moved up from page three Mitch's story about the recent success of the Millsville FFA team titled, "Local Future Farmers Have Success at State Fair." He considered putting a story about the upcoming county board election on page one but didn't want Mitch to think he had ousted his illness story for one of his own. The FFA one was probably better anyhow since the picture included both children and a baby goat.

As he was figuring out how to fit the articles, there was a sharp increase in volume from Mitch's radio as he turned up a report on the illnesses. Adam initially rolled his eyes, but got an idea when he heard the part about Arthur. He called Katie and asked to speak to Janet.

"Why?" Katie asked, obviously distressed that he didn't even ask why she had called earlier.

"Something for the paper."

"Trust me, if you want information, you're better off asking me."

"I need a quote from her though," Adam said.

"But I'm authorized. Remember how I told you I gave all those quotes to the student paper about softball last week? How I actually said, 'We're trying to knock our preparation out of the park this offseason.'"

"Seriously, Kates, the paper has to go to press in an hour and a half. Can I talk to her, or do I have go over there myself?"

Without a word Katie patched him through and for a minute sat at her desk pressing her hand on the bridge of her nose and letting an incoming call ring to voice mail. For one minute she couldn't handle another call from someone who saw Arthur driving around town and asked what foods they should avoid. She was tired of lying to people.

When Janet picked up, Adam asked, "Would it help if we ran a story about that inspector?"

~

"But you don't *understand*," Cal, now fully dressed, said to Arthur in the Vanderbergs' kitchen.

Arthur nodded quickly and continued to stare at the kitchen tiles. He couldn't look Cal in the face. He'd never felt such genuine revulsion for another person and was desperate to get the hell out of there. But Cal refused to budge, and Arthur couldn't leave him there alone with this young girl.

"Let's go back to the office and discuss this," Arthur said.

"But nobody's there," Cal said, surprised.

Arthur glared at him until the girl came shyly into the kitchen.

"You won't tell my dad will you?" she asked.

"Please, just go back to school," Arthur said, putting his eyes back down. "We're leaving. Please go back. Let's all leave."

"Didn't you hear?" she asked both of them.

"What?" Arthur asked.

"They let us out early today because of whatever's going around," she said, and crossed her forearms, entwined her finger, and twisted it all together over her head in a nervous stretch. To Cal, she added, "I tried to tell you that but, you know, you didn't give me the chance?"

This brought to Arthur's mind scenes of animals pouncing, specifically a bear snatching a salmon midair over the waters of a raging river. He shuddered. Then he weighed this information about the school closing with everything else. It mattered.

"Oh, Kriss, you OK? Not sick are you?" Cal asked, his concern overriding his shame.

"Cal," Arthur said, "please do me this favor—no, I'm demanding you come outside with me. As your boss and," Arthur hesitated, "friend, I know that your best course of action is to leave now with me and for the two of you"—Arthur shifted his focus to Kristi. "You're not eighteen are you?" She shook her head—"to never see each other again."

Cal set his jaw, turned toward Kristi, and said, "She's the best thing that ever happened to me."

"Uh-huh," Kristi added.

"I can't leave you two alone here," Arthur said. "If nothing else, I don't think it would be legal. If I leave here alone, I have to call the police."

"You wouldn't!" Cal said. He took a breath, straightened with self-possession, and added, "Fine, call them. That's how real this is."

Arthur watched Kristi's reaction—how her features sharpened in rising panic—and was encouraged that she would help coax Cal out the door. Then Arthur remembered Cal's son.

"Jake," Arthur said, and Cal's head jerked up. "He's sick. I talked to your wife and she went to get him from school."

"Jake?" Cal's eyes began floating around in their sockets. "What's wrong?"

Arthur waved his hands around the room to indicate it was probably the illness.

"Forgot to tell you," Kristi said, nudging a chair leg with her bare foot. "Jake threw up in study hall. Didn't see it but heard about it."

"Threw up?" Cal said, with no apparent understanding of the words.

Sympathy was beginning to cloud Arthur's judgment. The disturbing thought of the woman's death came to him and he decided not to mention it. An overload of upsetting news might send Cal into catatonia, just when he was anticipating this forbidden and substantial joy. It could be like dropping someone with hypothermia into a hot tub and watching them go into shock.

"Go home," Arthur said. "Tell your wife that you were inspecting and your phone died. Say that I went out searching for you and found you while you were—I don't know—inspecting a restaurant. Get a specific restaurant in mind."

"For sure. OK," Cal said.

Arthur didn't want to stop speaking. Cal listened as though hypnotized. "And never see this young woman," he glanced at her.

"Kristi," she said quietly.

"Don't ever see Kristi ever again. Not even just one more time. Not even just once where you don't touch or do anything wrong. You have no reason to ever talk to Kristi again." Cal seemed to be stirring awake, so Arthur cut him off before he could begin speaking, "No matter how real your feelings are, they aren't worth ruining your lives. You'll get over it in time."

Nobody agreed or disagreed, and this was good enough for Arthur, the best he could hope for. He decided not to contact the police, whether to save himself the hassle or to spare Kristi from shame or because he had, in some baffling, unconscious way, grown attached to Cal and was squeamish to make him suffer. Though who was he kidding, they weren't friends. He should call the police or at least let Kristi's father know. He hoped he wasn't refraining because he didn't want to explain why he was here instead of doing something about this disease that he knew nothing about, except that it was deadly.

All he knew was that they finally got to leave the house, and after sitting in his Jeep long enough to watch Cal drive past the Vanderbergs' house, Arthur put his key in the ignition and turned. Nothing happened.

≈

The sight of Katie Bender at her desk made Arthur think about his ex-wife. They bore no physical resemblance, but seeing the person he was sleeping with in the course of everyday life made him almost feel normal. This had happened a few times in the past, when he saw Katie out gardening or lugging in groceries and had to restrain himself from strolling over and giving her a hand. Now he had the urge to walk around the desk and give her a quick kiss and ask how her day has been. He never entertained these fantasies for long, knowing that indulging even in the idea might expose a cave of desperation and desire that he would rather not probe. Seeing her now, though, he couldn't help but imagine what he could have done differently and how close they had come to being together.

Nothing about her made him feel welcome. Her expression actually reminded him of the last time he had seen his ex-wife, when he slunk by their old apartment to pick up a chair he had requested but did not necessarily need. Back then, he had arrived after their appointed time and she was on her way out, having waited for him not so much to come but to be gone. They had been separated for almost two months, and Arthur had been fired. He had almost hoped she would deny his request, since animosity was at least a strong emotion. Instead, when he called, she sighed and said he could take whatever he needed.

Walking through the apartment to retrieve the chair felt like being at a morgue, about to identify the body of a friend who long ago had disappeared and recently washed ashore. His footsteps echoed on the wood floors, and she responded to his small talk with single syllables. The chair itself was padded and bulky. He scratched a wall with one of its legs on his way out and had to turn it to crazy angles to fit it through the door. When he thanked her, she only said, "Goodbye, Arthur." She had never said his name as a greeting or farewell before. It sounded strange and forced. In the subway back to his new apartment, he put the chair down and sat in it to keep it from sliding around. People sighed at his blocking the aisle but he ignored them while he continued to ruminate on his wife's phrasing. Hurtling along, sitting in that familiar and unremarkable IKEA chair, he held on to a sad, slim hope that his wife had exaggerated her disinterest in seeing him again. "Goodbye, Arthur"—that was how people spoke in movies. He knew that when she was uncomfortable she resorted to trying to act like everyone else. He didn't even want to get back with her—what they had seemed irrevocably gone—but it would have helped him sleep to know that somebody still cared for him and might be available to him. That was Arthur's last hope for his former life. All optimism vanished as soon as he picked up his chair and lugged it home.

Katie's expression when he arrived—a mix of frustration at his tardiness and relief that he finally showed up—reminded him of that depressing chore. He feared that these recent reminders of his old life (first the pushcart and now Katie) portended a repetition. He became almost desperate for Katie to give him any optimistic sign. But as he approached, the phone on her desk rang, and she unthinkingly lifted the receiver an inch off the cradle and let it drop down with a clang, never taking her eyes off Arthur. He didn't know why she was angry with him—as far as he knew, he hadn't done anything so wrong. She of all people should understand why he put off meeting with Janet.

"*There* you are," she said.

"I know."

"You know you are here?"

Arthur lifted his hands. He didn't want to argue. It would mean so much if they could have a few seconds of familiarity, proof that she still cared about him one way or another. On his way to the courthouse he had walked by five people wearing masks and saw two others driving with them on. He had never felt more incompetent.

All he could think to say was, "Sorry."

She opened her mouth as though to speak but instead stood and led him into Janet's office after giving a sharp knock.

"Here's Arthur Reilly," Katie said, pronouncing his name very clearly.

Arthur had heard that Janet had kicked off her first campaign for commissioner at the county fair by tackling a calf and tying its legs together. He supposed he felt now pretty much like that calf did when it saw young, softball-toned Janet bearing down on it with rope in hand—not frightened of death but knowing you are going to be uncomfortable for a while and that it will still take a good deal of strength and agility to take you down.

"I suppose you know why you are here," Janet said from behind her desk.

"The illness."

"You didn't hear the radio?" Janet asked, eyebrows raised and nearly openly gleeful at his ignorance.

"The one in my Jeep is broken. I heard about the school being closed down though," he said, and quickly added, "and that a woman died."

"And the people wearing masks?" she asked, unfazed by the mention of the dead woman.

"Yes," Arthur said, as though it was an actual answer.

"Why did it take you so long to come? We called your office at nine a.m."

He told her a version of the truth, about taking Eldred to the hospital and investigating a pushcart on the highway. Janet fiddled impatiently with a softball until he mentioned the cart.

"So the cart's the cause?" she asked, ready to accept it as truth.

"No," Arthur said quickly, aware he was accountable for it since he hadn't shut it down.

"Then what is it?" Janet asked. "What have you been doing all day?"

So far, Arthur had purposefully left out that he had shut down the Bogdanis' restaurant. If he said anything, they would automatically be held responsible. It would also, he knew, be the best way to clear himself.

"This sickness is one of those things that happen from time to time," Arthur said. "Until we know what it is, we can't make a judgment on what caused it."

Janet smiled and tossed the softball about a foot into the air and caught it. Arthur recognized it as probably the same softball she used to summon Katie. When he and Katie had been together she used to complain about this softball-against-wall tactic, and Arthur, for reasons still unknown to him, had defended Janet. At the time he had argued that it didn't appear much different from an intercom buzzer. Now, seeing the softball, he couldn't think why in the world he took Janet's side. He wondered briefly if moments like that were why he was now alone.

"I'm going to let you in on a secret," Janet said.

Arthur nodded.

"I'm running for Congress."

"Congratulations," Arthur said.

"But that means that I can't tell people I'm not in control of this simple situation."

"This is hardly a simple situation," Arthur said, adding, "someone died."

"But people see it as simple: some people they know are sick, and they could get sick as well. They want someone in control. They don't want people coming in from out of town in hazmat suits and gas masks."

Arthur wasn't sure about this, but he didn't know these people nearly as well as Janet did.

"What about closing the school?" he asked. "Won't that make people panic?"

"It will calm people down. After a couple kids got sick, I called the superintendent and told him that our department of health ordered the school shut down. People don't want their children in harm's way. And now with this woman dead, I might also impose a curfew if this isn't under control by nightfall."

"Curfew?" Arthur asked, and realized something. "Wait, I'm the head of the health department. Wouldn't I be the one to give that order?" He was pretty sure this was right, though he was also almost certain that he didn't have the power to close the school.

"Officially you had been reported as having gone rogue, and since nobody else was available in your office I took control."

"Rogue?" Arthur asked. "Who reported me as 'going rogue'? What the hell does that even mean?"

"I did. You were given and had dismissed several direct orders, and our only conclusion was that you had gone off the grid."

"You're just making things up as you go along."

"Hardly," she said, "but now that you are here, let's get to the bottom of this. As of now, you're the one everyone is blaming since it was on the radio that you're wanted for questioning in relation to the illness."

"Because you told them that! I was helping someone. I was the only one at least trying to do my job."

"But it's on the radio. People are calling in and reporting all your movements to our office." She set the softball on her desk and looked at him. "Now we need to figure something out to shift the blame away from you—unless you're willing to take it on?" She cocked her head with eyebrows raised, and when he didn't react she continued. "Or, if we can show people that you were useful in solving this, you could be valuable in my campaign.

I certainly wouldn't forget that when I get elected. So," she said, refocusing her eyes so they seemed to be staring an inch or two inside his skull, "can you think of anything or anyone that could be causing this illness?"

Arthur watched the softball roll against its seams and finally rock gently into place on the desk. He didn't want to answer. He didn't know the answer. She knew he didn't know the answer. Nobody knew the answer yet. He didn't believe anything she had said so far would actually hold up. The "rogue" thing was ridiculous. But she knew how to work this system, and he knew how to work only within it. If she had put him in harm's way, he very well might be in danger.

He glanced back at the closed office door. Without witnesses it nearly felt as though he wasn't doing anything wrong. Besides, it *was* reasonable that the Bogdanis' kitchen got people sick. It was a conclusion other people could reach as well. Bogdani didn't deserve blame, but neither did Arthur.

From Janet's expression Arthur assumed he didn't have much more time to ponder. He had to tell her that he didn't know—which meant he would continue to be on the hook—or that it was Bogdani. He reached over some picture frames and around a trophy and picked up the softball so he could watch annoyance flash over Janet's features. A minor victory before a larger defeat. He rubbed the ball as though he were about to throw a pitch. Then he spoke.

≈

Sasha Bykov had wanted to live in a place like this for a long time. Taxes were low. The roads were in perfect condition. There was no traffic whatsoever. The one homeless person seemed more a charming quirk of the place than blight. The farmland smelled more crisp, less earthy than he imagined it would, and he never dreamed there would actually be this many cows.

Back in the Soviet Union he had lived in Belgorod, on what is now the Russian/Ukrainian border halfway between Kiev and Moscow. His whole adult life he worked in shipping, mostly loading timber and minerals to send to places he never had the opportunity to visit. He had been able to travel on vacation only once: to the Black Sea for his honeymoon with his wife, who was now dead. They had to share a room with a strange family, and he spent the last two days of his trip standing in line trying to procure train tickets home. And though he proclaimed a love of fishing, he had never caught a fish. Never, not even during his vacation (or subsequent vacations since moving to America), had he actually put a line in the water. He just assumed he would like it and, though not a patient man when it came to entertainment, figured he could be patient if at any moment a fish might strike his line. If he was able to start over here, drive on these roads, and smell this land and fish whenever he pleased, he would have no reason not to call himself a happy man.

Behind him he heard his daughter grunt as she pulled the pushcart closer to the hitch. Hooking up the cart was easier with two people but by no means a two-person job. His daughter was strong. If she had agreed to move here with him, he would probably be over there helping her and the hitch would be connected. Instead, his daughter was staying only until he was settled and then moving back to New York. Though she had little to go back to, she did not entertain the idea of joining him. She said she would go crazy here. On the drive over he tried explaining the joys of simplicity, but she replied that he would get bored within a month.

"Cows," he said, breathing deeply as he gazed out over the farmland.

"So how is your scheme coming along?" Anna asked between grunts.

"Scheme?" he said. "Who schemes? It is business proposition. Fair. If the Albanian wants to come work for us . . ."

"You, not us."

"If Albanian wants job, I will give him. After troubles pass, of course."

"How generous," Anna said.

"Who is greedy?" Sasha asked, glancing at her as she inched the trailer along. "I am semiretired. If restaurant makes profit, I am happy. I will fix, make into nice place. Plants. Marble countertop. Someday it will be yours."

Anna laughed loudly. She'd heard all this a hundred times already. Her father repeated the words "semiretired" and "profit" and "happy" like mantras.

"And if he won't sell?" Anna asked.

Sasha only shook his head. Life was an unending series of conflicts; if Sasha did not create difficulties for others, his own life would be difficult. So what was the difference?

"He is still young man," Sasha said. "Hardships are good for the soul at that age."

Anna laughed while she grunted. "He's from Albania, right? I'm pretty sure he's known more hardship than everyone in this town combined."

"And you? You had no troubles today?"

"Only from the truckers grabbing me when I bent over to take it out of my boot."

"Those shoes," Sasha grumbled. He didn't like his daughter talking about her ugly boots any more than he liked hearing about someone touching her while she sold them drugs. "Not too much longer with any of that, yes? Only to secure profit until restaurant is open. Then no more."

Sasha had his fill of pushing legal boundaries simply to stay afloat. It seemed he had been doing so ever since he came to America. It was never his plan. For twenty years he hustled work as a mechanic and an off-the-books security guard before he had enough to buy a stake in a small restaurant on the Brighton Beach Boardwalk. There they sold pastries and tea to the old Russians from a dilapidated retirement home located on the same block and to passersby as well in summer. But the Russians in the neighborhood who sunned themselves on the beach brought coolers full of food, and the few tourists came in only for snacks and bottles of water and never returned.

For years the space in the back of the restaurant had been reserved for late-night meetings that conducted the real business of Brighton Beach. Sasha and his partners did not actively take part, but they were allowed certain perks in the neighborhood in return for hosting. Sasha, for instance, was given permission to sell small amounts of drugs out of the pushcart he operated in front of the restaurant. This extra income allowed him to buy a home and take his family to the Poconos every summer. He and his partners thrived until the parks police conducted a silly, overblown raid and confiscated the pushcart along with the outdoor tables and chairs. They knew nothing of the drugs, but Sasha had never obtained a permit to operate on the boardwalk and then disregarded many registered letters warning of the seizure.

And though the fines had been minimal and the pushcart easy to reacquire, the presence of police—parks or otherwise—had been enough to shift the location of these backroom meetings to a restaurant farther down the beach. After that, all their privileges were revoked and people in the neighborhood began to consider the restaurant off limits. This dried up the income, the restaurant closed, and—since his pushcart had caused the trouble—Sasha's partners threatened him with specific violence if he ever worked in the borough again. Had he not, while he was still flush with money that needed to be laundered, invested so much in Adam's scheme, perhaps he could have reinvested it and soon retired in a manner befitting someone who had worked as hard as Sasha had his whole life. Instead, Sasha had no choice but to move and keep hustling.

Now he longed to be free from the inevitable hassles of illicit activity. He would further bend the law, if necessary, only to force Bogdani to sell. After he obtained the restaurant he would flush Anna's drugs and live a simple life here in the middle of the country where everything was clean and cheap.

"There," his daughter said behind him. "Thank you for your help."

"My back," he said without looking at her.

Though there was an underlying chill in the air, Anna felt sunburned, and her pores were clogged by the flying dust and dirt of passing cars. But her feet did not hurt because she wore clunky combat boots all the time, from the moment she woke up until the moment she went to bed. Ever since she was a teenager and had visited an army surplus store with her first boyfriend—a funny Brooklyn boy who had already enlisted in the Marines and a year later would die in Iraq—she had held on to this trademark of her style. She bought her first pair of bulky boots in that store after he dared her to when she took a liking to them. From the time she walked into the house with them on, her parents barked at her like yapping dogs, decrying the assumed cost (though they were the cheapest footwear she had ever purchased) and informing her that she would never net a husband in them (she did not dare tell them about the Brooklyn boy or they would have surely ruined it for her somehow), she loved her boots and everything they stood for. She attended her boyfriend's military funeral in the same boots, in tribute to the first person in her life who encouraged her to depart from her parents' strange and often befuddling rules. She wore slightly more appropriate boots with a small heel for her own weddings.

The only time she put on high heels was for her mother's funeral. When her father saw them below the hem of her black dress, he nodded and walked back to his bedroom so she could not see him cry.

In almost everything other than footwear, she had always obeyed her parents. After the death of her secret boyfriend, she no longer had the energy to fight them. She married the first boot-agnostic Russian that her parents introduced her to, a small-time contractor who bought the largest house he could afford, in Millburn, New Jersey, soon after the betrothal. She had her first miscarriage right before he filed for bankruptcy, her second the week before their house was foreclosed on, her third just before he divorced her for not being able to bear him a child, her fourth soon after getting married again, and her fifth after finding out her new husband was cheating on her.

During all this, she had managed to build up a small but profitable business selling hair extensions out of her home. She advertised to be the only supplier of Slavyanka hair in Millburn, and Russian women came from miles away to sit in Anna's bathroom and have her tape in long blonde locks. Of course, Anna had no idea where the hair actually came from, only that she bought it from the same man who provided her father's restaurant with caviar. If she had to guess, she'd assume it was taken off Russian prisoners or corpses and supplemented with synthetic fibers. But her customers couldn't tell the difference, they cared only about making the claim of Slavyanka. Anna's dream was to expand, to get her own shop, to go on a buying trip to Ukraine and Russia to find her own suppliers, perhaps even legitimate ones. But her business made money, so her parents and husbands discouraged expansion as risky. Then, soon after her second divorce, the business quickly dried up. She assumed her ex-husband poisoned people against her somehow, but an influx of legitimate salons was more likely the reason. For weeks after the separation she was alone, surrounded by a dozen mannequin heads modeling her imported hair.

Her parents blamed her for every one of these tragedies, more than once insinuating that perhaps the boots were to blame. If you witnessed the fights—the way she yelled at her mother for telling her about the psychic who said that Anna would never get pregnant, or how she stormed away from her father who always sided with Andrei and then Oleg—you might think she did not care what her parents thought. But in fact all she wished to do was please them, or at least pacify them, obtaining brief respite from this constant meddling.

As it stood, listening to her parents caused her two failed marriages, five miscarriages, and three wasted years since her last divorce, living in her father's house and tending a pushcart on the Brighton Beach Boardwalk. She drew the line at moving to the middle of nowhere. If her father had moved to Florida, maybe. But he was the only old Russian who didn't like the heat. By now she recognized he was no more capable of navigating the world than she was, and though she was still tethered to him by the near gravitational pull of his will, this was the first major decision in her life in which she would openly disobey him. She didn't want to leave New York. After a couple weeks, a month at most, she would head back and figure out what to do. Until then she would do what her father asked and then be free of him. It felt as though she was about to abandon a bulky yet useful pack so she could more freely explore the wild.

She had, from time to time, sold the small amounts of pot and meth and cocaine from her father's cart on the boardwalk, so it wasn't all that strange to sell meth and heroin on the side of the road here. Her father had come up with the idea after reading about kids in Wisconsin who overdosed on heroin and seeing a movie about truckers who took methamphetamines to stay awake. This, to Anna, sounded like an easy way to make money from their cart, so she immediately acquired the drugs from old high school friends who still hung around the boardwalk. When she approved the idea, her father initially hedged. Though he would obviously welcome the revenue, he wanted his new life to begin legally—it wasn't right for him to put her in danger. She snapped back that he wasn't putting her in anything, and if he didn't want a share of the profits, he could refuse them. The matter was closed.

The plan worked relatively well since almost all the truckers stopped out of curiosity, and she could tell easily enough who was interested in drugs by their readiness to proposition her for sex. Today, their first day, they had made only sixty dollars from the meth that Anna kept stored in a zippered pocket, a false platform heel, and the toes of her large combat boots, but she knew they would make more once the word got around.

"It is nice out here. So much better than the city," Sasha said. "Crisp."

"The cow shit is overwhelming," Anna said. "Just wait until the wind shifts."

"How are you feeling?" Sasha asked.

Anna didn't know what to say. She wondered if it was some kind of trick. Her father did not often ask about her. He preferred to tell her how she was feeling.

"People are getting sick," Sasha said, turning to walk to the truck.

Anna shrugged. It was no wonder people got sick around here. What else was there to do?

≈

Janet accepted Bogdani's guilt without question. After Arthur told her, she simply raised her eyebrows and said, "The immigrant? What is he, Greek?" and dismissed Arthur with a wave. He scrambled away, thankful to be in the clear and disgusted with himself for what he had done.

Outside the office Katie was scowling at him.

"Please don't scowl at me. Be nice," he said.

Katie didn't mean to scowl at him specifically. She supposed she was punishing him for creating so many problems for her that day.

"How'd it go?" she asked.

Arthur waved his hand back and forth at the wrist, indicating nothing.

"I don't know how to interpret that," she said. "Just tell me."

He had rarely seen her this tired and removed. Lately when she snuck into his house at night she seemed full of desire and on the verge of tears, and when they had first started up together she had been eager to please and ready for fun in an effort, Arthur assumed, to get her mind off Adam. But when she started to ignore him after Adam returned, Arthur assumed she had never cared much about him either way—that his role could have been filled by any willing and convenient person. And yet Arthur was still in love with her. All this surely would have hurt much more if he hadn't become friends with Adam. Here in the office, in an effort to strengthen their bond, he was desperate to talk to her since she finally seemed to be willing. He just wished he had better news to share.

"I passed the blame," Arthur said.

"I'm sure that made Janet happy."

The phone rang. Katie picked it up and said, "We found him. Turns out he was out of radio range while he was figuring all this out," she shrugged at Arthur. "For sure. We'll be making an announcement real soon then about what you should and shouldn't eat. Thanks so much for calling, Mr. Kolinski."

"All day?" Arthur said.

"Nonstop. Thanks for that. And thanks for driving right by me earlier so I had to call in a bogus news report to the radio. You could have at least called."

Arthur leaned against her desk, and Katie worried that Janet would come out and piece things together. He used to do this back when they were dating. Whenever she was about to leave he'd somehow linger in his own home, never saying directly that he wanted her to stay longer but obviously not wanting her to go. He had no idea, she thought, that sometimes people need to hear the words.

"Who'd you blame?" she asked.

"Bogdani. The guy who owns MFR."

"Poor guy," she said. "You know he emigrated from Albania?"

Arthur nodded.

"Did he do anything wrong?" she asked.

"I don't know. Maybe."

"What did he do? Why blame him?" she asked, anger creeping into her voice.

"How about you? How's your family?"

She knew he just didn't want to respond, but it was refreshing to be asked about herself. Still, she wasn't going to answer. Ever since she had considered introducing him to her daughters, talking to him about them was a violation. The idea that she had nearly put them through that made her almost physically ill. And though it was obvious that he would still eagerly accept that role in her life, that was the last thing she wanted from him, at least for now.

But she couldn't simply ignore him here, outside of his bedroom. Arthur was important to her. He satisfied a basic, vital need and she didn't know what she would do without him. Besides making her feel desired, the act of going to him in the night, sneaking out of the house, ducking behind trees, and entering through his back door still held a salacious thrill. She could think about it (the trip to Arthur's house, not the sex itself) during the day and be transported away from herself. She had to keep Arthur away from her real life or she would lose the only aspect of herself that she could call exhilarating and truly hers. It was unfortunate for him that the need he fulfilled in her meant that she could not give him what he needed—she couldn't allow him to be part of her real life or else she would lose what he provided.

When she took too long to answer, Arthur decided to spare her. He said, "I hate walking through the lobby of this place. It's all lawyers and people with rotten teeth."

"Meth," she said. "This place runs on it. That and drunk driving. The fines probably pay both our salaries."

This cynical insight showed a side of her that Arthur hadn't witnessed since they were dating. Back then she would get tipsy drinking wine on his back deck and complain about Janet and anyone else who annoyed her during the day. He liked when she did this. It was when she appeared most at ease and seemed to forget for a minute that she didn't always need to put on the mask of affable midwestern niceness. He liked to imagine that she didn't show this side of herself to many other people.

The phone rang again and Katie answered it. Their brief camaraderie alleviated some unknown pressure in him, and Arthur wanted to extend the meeting, to wait until she finished speaking so he could ask her to come over that night. He would tell her that he recognized the risk she took but that, for once, it would mean a lot to him if she came. But then she laughed at something the person on the phone said—maybe it was a friend or maybe some stranger made a joke—and Arthur felt deflated. He knew he should leave before someone saw them together, before he got her into trouble. It had, on the whole, been a good interaction, and as a rule it was best to leave while he was ahead. The people who stayed and asked for things were probably the people who more often got what they wanted, but they were also the ones other people did not like. So, without saying anything, he knocked softly on Katie's desk, and when she jerked her head up as though surprised he was still there, he gave a short wave and walked out the door, toward the lawyers and the people with bad teeth.

≈

Adam had time to give it only a quick line edit. He put the Future Farmers piece back on page three. The Pulitzer committee would have to search a bit to find their prizewinner, he thought with a laugh. If he had more time, he might reconsider, but the paper had to go to press. As it stood, the article implying that Arthur was responsible for the illness was under the banner headline, "Rogue Inspector Sought for Questioning in Illness Terror," and below that was a story about the Bogdanis' restaurant titled, "Is Closed Restaurant to Blame?"

It was true that he'd become friends with Arthur only to one day screw him over, but now it didn't feel as satisfying as he had hoped. Though Adam had every right to be vengeful, the nagging, rational part of his brain pointed out that he was the one who'd left, that Katie and Arthur both surely acted out of loneliness, and that he had stopped paying attention to Katie long ago. She may well have wanted Adam to catch her out. How many times had they sat there in icy silence, surely sharing the same thought, him repeating his first line over and over in his head—"I know about you and Arthur I know about you and Arthur I know about you and Arthur"—hoping it would overflow and tumble out of his mouth. Honestly, he couldn't tell how he felt about the affair anymore. It was like he had eaten a distasteful fruit for so long that he had gotten used to it, perhaps even craved its bitterness in some perverse way. At some point in the last few months he began wondering if they were technically polyamorous, since Adam allowed it to continue and was now genuinely friends with Arthur. And if so, what really separated him from the Utah swingers except his intolerance of people like them?

He'd written the bulk of this article months ago to show Katie what an asshole she had gotten herself mixed up with, and in the process also ideally get Arthur fired. A virtuoso act of passive aggression, he had thought at the time. Then Arthur made the effort to become friends, and Adam decided to hold off publishing it to see what happened. Today he had to modify it only slightly to suggest Arthur had a hand in this illness and add Janet's stupid quotes about him going rogue and her "proactive" search for causes of the outbreak. It was the perfect time to strike, yet Adam hesitated. He realized with some horror that he actually cared about Arthur and didn't want to lose him as a friend.

Adam glanced at the clock and back down at his article. He respected Arthur's corrupt and callous past, which the article clearly detailed. It certainly didn't fit his straight-and-narrow neighbor. An interesting specimen, this Arthur Reilly. What kind of a person makes an effort to become friends out of guilt? If Adam were in his shoes, he wouldn't be able to face the man out of remorse and pity, like Katie, who could barely meet Adam's eyes now. Reilly was a contradiction, which was probably why their friendship worked. Trained as an artist but now only involved in facts and surfaces. So defined by his job, but Adam didn't think for a second that Arthur believed in the benefits of his work, only in the act of work itself. A New Yorker, yet he now made no attempt to seek out excitement or culture. He was younger than Adam but acted like a pensioner. So lonely, but he went after someone who was not available for long-term companionship. He obviously disagreed with Adam's political stances but refused to state his own beliefs and rarely took the bait when Adam tried to start arguments. Adam figured he was some kind of left-leaning libertarian, if that was even possible anymore. Arthur's comically overzealous enforcement seemed to drive home the pointlessness of rules when carried out to the letter. He doubtless had little regard for regulations in his own life. Could these dichotomies be why Katie went to him? That he could be anything she needed him to be instead of Adam being so intractably himself? Could this also be why Adam was drawn to him? That Arthur's malleability was exactly what Adam needed too? Was Reilly inspecting them while he remained the inscrutable inspector . . .

"I thought we weren't printing anything about this," Mitch said coldly, reading over Adam's shoulder.

"I got it from Janet Vosberg. She asked we do it as a favor," Adam said.

"What'd this guy do, anyway?" Mitch asked cautiously. He, like many people, knew about Katie's affair and that Adam and the inspector were friends. Mitch liked to believe it was some kind of arrangement. Maybe underneath the gruff, barely veiled, judgmental exterior Adam had a progressive side.

Adam stifled the urge to answer, "Don't worry about it," and instead said, "They can't get in touch with him. They think he knows something about this illness."

"So your source said she doesn't know where he is and based on that thinks he might know something?"

"Stop saying 'source.' It's just Janet."

Mitch gave up and walked away muttering, "Source source source source . . ."

Adam turned back toward his article. Most of the information about Arthur was taken from a *New York Post* article from 2009, a story on page 36 titled "Health Inspector Fired after City Probe." Thanks to the *Post*'s sensationalized version, Adam had been able to write an arguably accurate account of Arthur's past misdeeds that would surely shock the locals, who were already skeptical of what they saw as lazy, greedy, tax-leeching civil servants. Even if he wanted to, Adam didn't have time to soften the language to cut Arthur a bit of a break while still appeasing Janet and exposing Arthur's true character to Katie.

He carefully finished the layout with the Arthur story (along with his picture) on the cover. He was dragging his feet. He considered calling Sasha for reassurance, but then he'd have to talk to Sasha. For lack of a better idea, he called Katie. At least he was sure she would pick up.

As it rang, he decided to be charming. He wanted to be on the same side for a few minutes.

"I have some information about the killer," he said in a James Cagney voice when she picked up the phone.

She laughed.

"Sorry about before, Kates," he said, now doing his imitation of a thoughtful husband.

"It's no problem," she said.

He hadn't heard Katie so relaxed since before he went to Utah. Perhaps, he considered, softness was more effective in manipulating people than his natural gravelly demeanor.

"I'm under deadline and it wouldn't have been ethical to get a quote from you since we're married," he said.

She laughed again and said, "It's not ethical even if we weren't. Don't worry about it. I'm sorry too. I've had a shitty day. Though everyone around here has, I suppose, so I shouldn't complain."

"You worry about your shitty day. Just because other people have it worse than you doesn't mean you need to be happy. Shittiness can't be created or destroyed, it is or isn't," he said, not able to tell if he was being funny or wise but hoping he was both. He was still adjusting to his new supportive role, and like anyone in unfamiliar territory he had to learn to speak the language and conform to the customs.

"I'm sorry, what was that?" she asked.

"You just—" he began, and then stopped. Repeating it would be tedious and pompous, and he realized what he said hadn't made much sense. He was slightly embarrassed for some reason, though Katie apparently hadn't heard him. He became annoyed that his effort to connect had been wasted.

"Are you busy with something else? Should I go?" he asked petulantly.

"No, not at all, I'm sorry, I'm listening," she said with some urgency, wanting to keep him attentive and kind with the same effort it would take to hold onto an eel. "I was talking to Arthur. He was leaving his meeting with Janet and stopped by my desk."

"Arthur's there?"

"He was. He just left."

Adam momentarily forgot why he called. He wished he had not.

"If he's there, why are we printing this article?"

"What article? Do you need to talk to Janet?"

"Forget it," Adam said.

"Adam, I want to help."

Picturing the two of them in the same room flooded Adam with images he hadn't summoned since he first learned of the affair, a masochistic exercise of imagining which sex acts Katie and Arthur indulged in.

"It's too late, it has to go in," he said.

"I'm sorry. I want to help," she said again. She wished she knew what he was talking about.

He didn't answer, knowing she would become desperate to keep him on the line.

"I'm supposed to call the radio station and tell them we're not searching for Arthur anymore," she said, hesitating, guessing what he wanted to hear. "I guess he pinned it on Bogdani—the guy who runs the MFR—for all these people getting sick. I'll probably have to tell that to the radio too, that the MFR is to blame."

"I heard he closed that place down," Adam said with renewed interest, keeping an ear open for quotes to add to the articles.

"He did!" Katie said, though that was the first she had heard of it. "Who knows if it even made anyone sick though. Janet's grasping for anything to get people to believe that we're on top of this."

"So Reilly passed it off to save himself? What an asshole," Adam said, easily converting his irritation into righteous indignation.

Katie was going to defend Arthur, say that it was difficult to not give Janet what she wanted when she dug in, but didn't want to give away that she cared about Arthur in any way. Instead, she said, "It's a tough situation."

In the ensuing silence Katie felt the weight of her husband's displeasure. She always blamed herself for other people's discomfort.

"Oh, and someone died!" she said, glad to figure out something to say to change the subject but accidentally sounding pleased about the event.

"Died? How?"

"Just an old woman. I mean, not 'just,' I just mean that an old woman died." She scrambled up the muddy banks of her thoughts for a moment before adding, "From the illness, I mean."

"Who is it? How'd you hear?"

"You know Mary Dorshorst's mother? Theresa? Her. The hospital called the office about an hour ago. Janet's keeping it quiet for now so don't tell anyone or write about it yet."

They hung up and Adam checked the clock. No more time to dither. He would put the entire strength of his puny paper against Arthur and, by extension, against the Millsville Family Restaurant, which "an unnamed source at the County Commissioner's office" confirmed as being the cause. He would ignore the fact that Arthur had indeed been found, since Janet never confirmed that she wasn't pursuing him anymore.

By switching the location of the articles and swapping a few words, his front page ended up with the banner headline "Closed Restaurant Confirmed as Origin of Illness Terror" and the lower front-page article, "Is Rogue Inspector Also to Blame?" Arthur's picture remained.

He didn't have time for a final round of copy edits. That step was only for him anyway. Nobody who read this paper would notice or care about grammatical errors or typos as long as he correctly identified the local boys who caught touchdown passes or who got what ribbon at which agricultural competition. Instead, he quickly scanned the layout, decided against adding the information about the woman who died, and sent another edition of the *Chase County Register* to the printer.

≈

During his mother's illness, Arthur had spent so much time at home that, after she died, he felt a break was necessary. When he finally visited his father again, about two years later, he did so to share his own good news: he had been promoted to investigator at the health department, and, because of that promotion, he and his wife had decided to try to adopt a baby. Coming up with enough news to carry the conversation over two days was standard visiting-home procedure, and he especially didn't want any lags because he felt guilty about not checking in more. But his father had never required emotional tending, and Arthur hadn't heard any troubling news, so he assumed his father was carrying on more or less as usual.

He was wrong.

Since the last time he visited, Arthur discovered, his father seemed to have turned the house upside down. The floor was littered with clothes. Food bits were cemented onto the dirty dishes that sat on every available surface. Flies buzzed in the kitchen. The air was rank with rot and sweat. For some reason, the lamps had been removed and all the overhead lights were on. Arthur wondered if he had accidentally stumbled into a crack house until his father came out and greeted him. His dad's appearance was only slightly better. Arthur guessed he had tried to spruce himself up by showering, but he was a few days unshaven and his clothes smelled moldy. Most disturbing of all, his father didn't mention the disarray.

At the Olive Garden, after guzzling a martini the size of a hand grenade, Arthur gained perspective and realized how all this wasn't completely surprising, and was in no small part his fault for not visiting more. His father had retired when his mother relapsed, vowing to spend as much time as possible taking care of her, and then simply being with her. Now he was too young to be without work, and the person who had taken care of him for over forty years was suddenly gone. Surely that was a petri dish for allowing depression to fester. For a brief moment at the restaurant, Arthur wondered if he would be any different if he were in his father's situation. He quickly ordered another martini.

Arthur didn't feel right asking his father about his life. He didn't have the security clearance to access his father's feelings. Instead, he remained in the comfortable conversational terrain of his own accomplishments, recounting his promotion. He explained how his new position entailed investigating each case thoroughly, a welcome change to the slash-and-burn style of street inspecting. In an effort to thwart silence he went into far too much detail about his most pressing case involving a new sub shop chain.

His father's eyes skipped across the room, unable to concentrate. This hurt Arthur, who had, since deciding to make the trip, often imagined his father's pride and encouragement at this moment. Though, he supposed, he had never been very interested in his father's work stories, and would only feign interest now if forced to listen to one. He decided to not tell his father that he and his wife had begun the process of adoption, though he had mentally rehearsed how he would tell it. The story was to be the emotional highpoint of the trip. He had looked forward to explaining how the decision had been influenced by his mother's expressed regret, in the final months of her life, that she had never become a grandmother. But now that he saw he might not get the tender reaction he desired, he kept it to himself.

When, after a painful lull, Arthur finally asked his father, in vague terms, about himself, his father replied, "Oh, I'm fine. I need to find ways to keep busy, I think." So, instead of trying to get to the core of his father's obvious problems, Arthur suggested various hobbies, rather forcefully promoting gardening. His dad nodded and said he would think about it.

Back at his own home, Arthur didn't go into detail about his father's troubling state. He told his wife only that his dad was "a bit depressed." Lately, he treated her comfort as though it was made of easily shatterable glass. He imagined she would see his father's issues as a reason to delay the adoption process. She could worry that they would be responsible for his care sooner than they ever imagined.

During a drunken moment on their first date, they had both laughed when his future wife, Susan, blurted out, "There's no way a baby is ever coming out of me." She never contradicted this statement. Six years later, when Arthur brought up the idea of having a child, she received him calmly. He had told her what his dying mother had said and imagined ever since that she anticipated him bringing it up. She told him that she was open to having a child if it was what he wanted, but she did not see herself as a receptacle. Those were her words: "I am not a receptacle." She also said, "I'm not going to cause trauma to my body just to bring another version of you into the world." She said both "receptacle" and "trauma to my body" several times during the conversation.

It all sounded fair to Arthur. He didn't have a keen desire to carry forth his genes. Mountains of paperwork and negotiating the labyrinthine corridors of an adoption agency were actually preferable to months or years of trying to conceive followed by nine months of worrying.

Luckily, after he returned from his father's house, his work soon became a lively distraction. The case of the sub shop proved even more interesting than he originally imagined. Shops had begun popping up all over the city, and almost each new franchisee tried to pass similarly bad checks or otherwise fudged the paperwork to some degree, which held up their licenses to operate. It seemed a coordinated effort of ineptitude, but this made no sense, considering that only a couple shops had opened. Arthur was fascinated. He called a meeting.

The man representing the franchises was a small, bearded, apologetic fellow named Jeff Geller. This Geller appeared overmatched even by the rather straightforward layout of the New York City Department of Health and Human Services. Indeed, he was twenty minutes late to the meeting and arrived with his papers falling from the folder under his arm. By the time he finished his lengthy explanation for his tardiness, the time allotted for the meeting was nearly over. Arthur barely had time to ask him about the bounced checks.

"It's my fault," Geller moaned. "I didn't think these shops would take off so fast. If I can find it, I can show you that we have the capital—money is not the issue, it's just these accounts. We've been working with a Mr. Coglan here at your department."

Arthur sighed. Coglan was a particularly troublesome accountant.

"And, to be honest," the man said, "I've been dealing with personal issues."

Arthur did not want to hear the rest but Jeff continued.

"My father died a couple months back," Jeff said. "It was sudden. Now there's all this stuff with the will, my mother expects me to handle it, it's all in New Jersey. I'm sorry, this has nothing to do with anything. I'm not making an excuse."

"No, I get it," Arthur said, to his surprise, truthfully.

"You do, don't you?" the man said, catching and holding Arthur's eye.

"I'm going through a similar situation myself," Arthur said, realizing how little he had ever talked about his mother's death.

Arthur was about to continue when his phone rang. He couldn't tell if he felt saved or vexed by the interruption. The meeting had gone long and he was now expecting a call from the adoption agency.

"Go ahead and answer," Geller said, sitting back in his chair.

"Actually I need to take this in private," Arthur said, not wanting the call to go to voice mail, knowing how difficult it was to get through when he called back.

"Is it about your mother?" the man asked.

"No," Arthur said, his eyes on the phone, whose rings now sounded desperate, like the cries of a swimmer about to tumble over a waterfall, "I'm actually trying to adopt. I really need to take this."

Jeff nodded quickly. "We should reschedule? I'll have all the paperwork and I'll know how to find your desk. Next month?"

Arthur did not want to push the meeting an entire month but had to pick up the phone. He nodded.

Between the two meetings Arthur's life seemed to improve. First, the adoption agency informed him that his application had been fast-tracked. This meant everything could be processed in weeks instead of months, that it could be over in months instead of years. Perhaps the best part was that Susan was thrilled with this news. Until then, Arthur had felt that the adoption was his thing, and that she was simply signing the paperwork for his sake. The expedition of their application, however, seemed to unlock some gratification in the process for her. Maybe, he considered, she had been steeling herself against the disappointment of having their application rejected. Or perhaps the sudden ease of procedure made her see the adoption as a puzzle to be solved instead of a hassle to fight against. After that, he regularly saw websites for cribs and children's clothes on her screen. They began to have funny conversations about names. This new ease made Arthur aware that for some time a tension had existed between them.

Also around this time, Arthur's father began to call late at night, three or four times per week, just before or after Arthur went to bed. These calls did not have a point. His father would often start the conversation the same way. For a week it was "I'm beginning to take an interest in the Eagles. You know, the football team. Do you know anything about them? Are you an Eagles fan?" Arthur had never had the slightest interest in sports and was surprised his dad could have thought otherwise. The next week, his father began each call, "What did we used to eat for dinner? What did your mother make? I can only remember about three things. Did we only eat three things? What do you guys eat? Does Susan cook? Or do you?" The lateness and irregularity of the calls combined with the repetition of subjects and phrases ("So what exactly is a superfood?") became exasperating. He kept as much as he could from Susan.

He considered himself too young to have a dead mother and a father with dementia (if indeed that was where his father was heading). These were supposed to be the problems of his fifties and sixties. He emailed his brother, who hadn't been any help. Jay, in San Jose, replied, "You know the old guy can be kind of wacky." Arthur did not know this at all. "Wacky" was far from how he would describe his father, either now or when he was younger. Arthur was ten years younger than Jay, though, so they had basically been raised by a different version of the same man. He was jealous that Jay knew this side of their father when all Arthur knew was a rather uptight, distant person. But he didn't relay any of this to Jay, choosing instead to keep the interaction as superficial as possible. They had not spoken since their mother's funeral, which was not unusual for them. At this point they had seemed to accept that they were simply two men who happened to have the same parents. Their relationship was almost one of joint ownership, as though they were the majority shareholders of a small company that basically ran itself.

Jeff Geller was on time to his next meeting. He was organized and alert. The change in his demeanor confused Arthur. For some reason, he preferred the old, disheveled version.

Arthur expressed his delight that four of the franchises had given good checks and were now fully licensed to operate. Jeff nodded. Arthur asked for more specifics, and Geller only either nodded or shrugged.

Getting nowhere, Arthur asked if something was wrong.

"How is your adoption going?" Jeff asked, and smiled wide.

Arthur stared at him for maybe a full minute before it came to him. He wondered if he had, on some level, known what was going on, if he was aware that this man had somehow orchestrated his fast-tracked adoption application. No, he couldn't have. And if he had known, would he have wanted it to turn out any different? That didn't matter now.

"Is your father even dead?" was all Arthur could think to ask.

"Why? Do you care?" Jeff answered.

Arthur couldn't answer.

"What do we do now?" Arthur asked.

"Nothing," Jeff said, standing. "Don't. Do. Anything."

Arthur remained seated for a long time after Geller left, trying to grasp what had just happened. His options going forward were limited. Telling the truth was appealing, but he couldn't imagine actually going into his supervisor's office and explaining. He couldn't even imagine telling his wife. Where would he begin? With his father? And why would they believe that he wasn't in on the plan? Even if they did believe him, the adoption agency surely would frown upon it. Leaving yourself open to unsuspected collusion wasn't exactly the best trait in a potential father.

He considered going to Coglan, the accountant assigned to the case. But the idea exhausted him. Coglan was one of those guys—not an uncommon type in their office, really—who thought he had a system to cut every corner in life, though these systems took up most of his time. Every two hours, for instance, Coglan painstakingly cleaned his teeth in the department bathroom using complicated tools kept in a black leather kit, and always explained to anyone who came in that this method would save him tens of thousands in dental costs in the long run. Arthur hated Coglan because he saw in Coglan his own worst traits taken to the most extreme degree. He couldn't figure out if he was jealous of Coglan's dedication or annoyed at his uselessness. No, he wouldn't go to him. If nothing else, he couldn't stand Coglan explaining exactly what Arthur had done wrong and what he should have done instead.

Instead, Arthur did nothing. He left his wife in the dark. He did nothing about the sub franchises. He tried not to speculate how big of an undertaking it must have been if they could afford this level of organization. Were they a front for drugs? Did they store mob-hit bodies in the buildings? Did they force teenage prostitutes to work in the back rooms? The binder he kept on the sub shops stayed on the same corner of his desk, untouched, for weeks after the meeting. If it had been up to Arthur, it would have stayed there forever.

A sense of unreality came over him. Until now he had always felt he could predict his future to some degree of certainty. At least the big things. The signposts of his life had been placed, and he was content to follow them, with little unpredictable side trips along the way. Now he felt himself veering from the path, though everything was still in place, if out of his control. This drifting changed him. He found himself acting less scrupulously. Maybe it was the recognition of his own vulnerability, or maybe he was trying to karmically make up for whatever crimes he was possibly now abetting, but he began to find himself siding more and more with the vendors in his cases. He took time with them, listened sympathetically while they explained their situations, even when they spoke of unrelated matters. Many spoke of children they hadn't seen in years, or sick parents they were sending all their money to halfway around the world. He began unofficially factoring these stories into cases. Soon his leniency became known, and operators requested that he handle their cases.

His problems caused him an overall hesitancy that blurred the lines between his work and home lives. He thought of his own father while vendors spoke of family troubles. He wondered if he would ever be forced away from his own child one day and, if so, if he would bear it as stoically. Hearing their stories about what they were doing for their families made him want to expand his own even more. Without consulting his wife or father, he started considering what it would take to move his father in with them.

Arthur eventually met Coglan in the bathroom. His tool kit was open, and he was using an intricate metal hook to clean the gums behind his bottom teeth. The scraping sound made Arthur slightly sick. While Arthur was at the urinal, Coglan told him not to be stupid. Arthur asked him to clarify, and Coglan spat into the sink. He went back to his cleaning before he spoke again. "About Gavildeli's. Don't be an idiot. Don't ruin it for everyone." Arthur couldn't tell if he was relieved or frightened that someone else knew what was going on. He wasn't sure if he should keep quiet to avoid further conspiracy or confront Coglan for guidance on how to proceed. He went to wash his hands and saw thick streaky blood in the sink where Coglan had been spitting.

"Jesus. Are you okay?" Arthur asked.

Coglan turned on the faucet and said, "It's nothing." He softened his tone and added, "Just cool it with that place. It'll be fine. Close the file and I'll take care of the rest."

For the first time, Coglan appeared vulnerable, his systems a front for hiding weakness. Arthur wondered what Geller had on Coglan. Did the blood mean he was sick? Did he need some serious dental work? Or did he just happen to bleed and was in it for money?

"Did you know I used to want to be an artist?" Arthur asked. Coglan paused in his cleaning. They made eye contact in the mirror. Arthur continued, "The sink reminded me of it. The way the red swirled like that. It was disgusting and scary but . . . I don't know. It reminded me of my dad for some reason."

Arthur didn't know what made him say that. Especially to Coglan, and especially now. Maybe he felt connected to him in a way he hadn't been to anyone before, and that he could be completely honest. Or maybe he wanted to show Coglan that he was, or at least once was, concerned with ideas rather than efficiency. Coglan continued with his cleaning before he replied.

"Whatever you say, Van Gogh. Just keep your fucking mouth shut."

This interaction only made Arthur worry more. He couldn't bring himself to close the case and actively contribute to the scheme, whatever it was. But he wouldn't pursue it either. He wanted his old life back but didn't even know when it had ended.

His father called him at work. Arthur felt a pang of remorse upon hearing his voice. But he sounded strong, and angry. Apparently Jay had suggested their father move in with him.

"Can you believe the nerve?" Arthur's father asked. "I'm sixty-five years old. I'm not eighty."

Arthur was elated that he had dragged his feet and was the one to receive this call.

"But you're doing better?" Arthur asked.

"Of course. That's actually why I called. I went to my office yesterday. Sorry I didn't call." His father had worked in Midtown and for twenty-five years had made the commute. This meant he had recently been two stops from Arthur's office and had not called. Arthur was hurt but kept quiet. "I might go back part-time, maybe do some consulting. Apparently the guys who took my clients are bungling it."

"No surprise there," Arthur said, buttering the old guy up.

His father laughed. "No, no," he said. "Anyway, I talked to Tariq—you know, the guy I bought coffee from outside my building?"

Arthur knew of Tariq. His father bought coffee and a bagel from him every morning for more than twenty years, more than once joking that he had paid for Tariq's kids to go to college. He explained that a cart was trying to push Tariq out of his spot and asked if Arthur could intervene.

Arthur wanted to explain that he wasn't inspecting anymore, that he had moved beyond petty pushcart squabbles. But this was his opportunity to make up for his recent neglect and further entrench himself as the better son. Arthur said he would go down that afternoon.

Being on the street again, mediating cart locations, throwing his weight around in person, took Arthur back to an easier time. And though he had no authority to do so—since the infringing cart was not actually breaking any rules—he made them move down the block to a less desirable location. The operator was furious, but obeyed. Arthur gave Tariq his card and told him to call if he needed anything else.

The spurned cart almost immediately lodged a complaint about Arthur. This prompted a cursory exploration into Arthur's cases that uncovered a recent pattern of questionable decisions in certain vendors' favor. That triggered a deeper dive into Arthur's history, and the sub shop file was flagged. One day the binder was gone from the corner of his desk.

Susan was unaware of any of this. She was impressed with how he was negotiating the adoption process and pleased at the ease and speed at which it was progressing. He didn't want to jeopardize that with uncertainty. He also didn't tell her about his father's apparent rebound, in case it was short lived. Even when it was clear everything was about to cave in, he still kept quiet, hoping for a miracle.

It did not come. On the Friday after the binder was taken, he and Coglan were called into the health commissioner's office—an impressive place, by city office standards, with a view facing south onto Ground Zero, which at that time was still basically a hole in the ground. Coglan had a story ready that insinuated Arthur alone was in on the scheme. Arthur was so tired and stressed from the past few months that it did not take him long to break.

His union rep was angry he hadn't called her before he went into the meeting. She managed only to postpone the final decision until Monday. The adoption agency was contacted and immediately dropped the application and began an investigation of its own. Nobody would tell him what else they had discovered about Jeff Geller and the sub shops.

His plan on the ride home from work was to let it all play out, to not tell Susan what had happened, to have a veneer of normalcy for two more days before everything fell apart. But the adoption agency had contacted her already, and she was waiting for him on the couch, eyeing him as if he was a stranger.

"You made me want it," she said.

"I know."

"It's too much."

"I'm sorry."

"It's all just too much," she said.

Arthur knew her well enough not to say anything else.

A couple weeks later, after he was fired but luckily not arrested, he read about the sub shops in the paper. (The article about his own firing came out right after he was let go, and garnered little attention.) It turned out that the franchise was an arm of a $23 million Ponzi-and-money-laundering scheme that would have been front-page news had Bernie Madoff not gotten caught stealing $65 billion not long before. The article made no mention of Jeff Geller, who, if that was even his real name, was probably, Arthur assumed, a fixer of some kind. Arthur was mentioned only as "a low-level city employee" who was fired for implication in the scheme. The scam mostly involved middle-income investors. Apparently many people in Arthur's tax bracket lost everything they had. Arthur tried to tell himself that he, too, lost everything because of this scheme, but that wasn't exactly true. He chose to stay silent. He chose not to do what was right. He wanted his inaction to allow him to escape complicity. If he had more actively contributed one way or another, he might have either gotten away with it or stopped it. Instead, he had done nothing.

Not long after this, he agreed to meet his father at his office to go to lunch. Somehow Arthur had managed to keep everything from his old man, electing not to invite a lecture about responsibility from the person Arthur considered partly accountable for his own downfall. That his father was back on his feet so quickly and easily had almost been enough to make Arthur turn down the lunch offer, but he figured this was as good a time as any to come clean. If nothing else, there was always the possibility of a job at his dad's company, even if he had no desire to work there.

A couple blocks from his father's office, he heard someone angrily yell his name and saw, encased in his stainless-steel coffee cart, Tariq. Now in a much less desirable location, he beckoned Arthur over with two fingers.

For the first time in a long time Arthur felt a rush of retaliatory anger. Through the controlled conflict of inspection, he had managed to quell his visceral reaction to aggression, but now he was simply a person being screamed at by a man he had once tried to help. He saw Tariq as though in slow motion, heard him repeating the word "motherfucker."

Luckily the screen in those carts is made of plastic, or else Arthur would have broken his hand when he punched it. Tariq immediately quieted down, and Arthur took a breath, telling himself not to get petty, not to throw the napkin dispenser or the tray of swizzle sticks or the packets of Sweet'N Low. Not to punch Tariq, whose anger was, in a way, valid. Instead, Arthur decided to conduct an experiment he had often calculated in his mind during inspections but never expected to have the opportunity to play out. The design of these coffee carts—with their two big back wheels opposite a long hitch—appeared imbalanced in an easily exploitable way. And so, with adrenaline coursing through him, Arthur kicked away the weighted blocks from the hitch. Tariq was somewhere close, yelling, but Arthur paid him no mind as he stooped and took the hitch in hand. As he lifted, the big back wheels served as a fulcrum, and he easily tipped the cart until he heard the crash of dishes and machinery from inside. In his mind he saw himself flipping the cart upside down, like a person doing a half a cartwheel, but when it reached a certain point he realized this was impossible. After shoving Tariq away with one arm, Arthur heaved until the cart tipped over, awkwardly, sideways, so the service window was flat against the sidewalk. Milk and coffee bled out from under the structure, reminding Arthur that he hadn't checked if anyone was in the way before he toppled it.

The cart was unalterably there, smashed, and a crowd of people—a couple of them recording everything with smartphones—stood gawking. Heaving with exertion, suddenly spent of energy, Arthur didn't know what to do next. Tariq had gone to get help. He could sense the crowd's desire for him to do something else crazy, to further act out for their amusement. But all he could do was stare at the cart, thinking how the act had been so much more satisfying than the result. After a few seconds he ran away.

≈

By the time Bogdani heard the radio report that blamed him for an illness that had apparently killed someone, his wife and son had already left to visit her sister and presumably were out of range of the radio station, since they had not called or come back. He had been halfheartedly cleaning his kitchen, but now he grabbed the only bottle of liquor in the house (a dusty bottle of scotch—a gift upon their arrival), turned up the radio (which had switched from the news back to classic rock, so Foghat was playing), and sat down at the table farthest from the front window. He poured a large belt of scotch into a coffee cup—the same kind of cup that was still overturned and broken next to the corner booth where earlier Sasha had sat watching him fight with the inspector.

Bogdani drank the cup empty and lobbed it across the restaurant. It hit with a clunk and bounced as it skipped across the floor. Good, solid cup—it didn't shatter. He had bought the cups years ago at a restaurant supply wholesaler in Grouse River Falls. The hollow, echoing cup sounded strange in this place that was normally bustling with chatter and cooking at this time. He grabbed another cup from the prep counter, filled it with scotch, and when he finished tossed it in the same direction.

He poured the third and hesitated. This was what was meant by feeling sorry for oneself. He had felt this way almost all his life but had never stopped and taken note. It almost felt good to allow himself to do this. Even in Albania he had not indulged his self-pity. There, at the end, after he and everyone he knew had lost everything to the pyramid schemes, and rebels with stolen government guns overran the country, his only thought had been to get out. Back then he was able to focus his efforts on escaping. There was something definite to flee and places willing to take them in. Even if escape often involved riding in leaky boats, at least they had somewhere to go. There had been enough aggrieved people to make other countries feel sorry for them and accept them with begrudging tolerance.

His lot had been easier to accept back then because nobody had done him any specific wrong—the Albanian government was mistreating everyone equally out of outright greed and incompetence. He could understand a government harming its own people for those reasons. At least he hadn't been in it alone. Here, now, people seemed to be explicitly against him. He was an outlier, targeted by those who wanted to skirt blame. A scapegoat. From now on he would simply be considered a failure at business and a recklessly ignorant man who put lives in danger. That they had been so calculating in bringing about his demise made him feel personally aggrieved and yet more powerless than ever. It drained his energy.

He took a kind of pleasure, then, in openly feeling sorry for himself. He had worked no less hard than any of the hundreds of thriving Albanians around the state. Indeed, years ago he had gotten his now-prosperous brother-in-law—whose large house his wife and son were currently visiting—his first job. They'd worked for the same wage in the same warehouse while all sharing a small apartment. But just as they had been ready to quit and buy a restaurant together, Drita announced she was pregnant. Without health insurance he did not have the money to invest, so he stayed on at the warehouse and his brother-in-law invested wisely. When it was finally time to make his own move, he had chosen Millsville based on news that the muffler plant would soon be expanding. His brother-in-law told him not to go that far north—that part of the state had only farms and dying businesses, the people were drunk and small minded and wouldn't tolerate a foreigner. But Bogdani persisted and signed the deed weeks before the expansion fell through and the plant closed. There had been other problems too—his mother's illness required him to send money and take two trips to Albania for the treatment and then funeral, the structural damage and subsequent flooding problems in the building that the inspector had so conveniently not foreseen. Still, he never felt sorry for himself until now. Every decision he made had been sound, considering the information he had at the time.

He didn't spend much time pondering whether he was actually responsible for this sickness. He assumed he was not. It didn't matter now though, except that someone had died. If he had been so reckless that someone died, he could understand why his life was ruined, grieve for what he had lost, and not argue the circumstances. But to be unjustly deemed responsible for a person's death would be too much to bear.

He kept the overhead lights off during the day to save on utilities and now was glad the restaurant was dim. The tablecloths gleamed blue against the whiteness of the floor and brown of the walls. Everything in that room appeared solid and immovable. He could sit on any table and it would not topple over. He could punch a wall and his fist would not go through. He could try to tear apart the stems of the fake plants his wife had placed in each corner but they would hold firm against his grasp. That he had built up something so strong and so real—that this space was, for now, his—comforted him. He hadn't made many wrong decisions in his life, and if he could do it all over again, he would do everything the same and hope for a different outcome. He preferred circumstances being against him to having made the wrong choices.

A flickering of the light made him glance up. Two people stood outside. They shaded their eyes and peered into his restaurant, blocking the familiar view of the street. Both wore masks, and he could not tell if they were men or women, young or old. Maybe, he thought, they were there to rob him. He laughed when he realized this would only bring him relief, since he had so little to take and could file an insurance claim for more than what was stolen. When he laughed the people jerked their heads up and abruptly walked away, perhaps frightened of being so close to this now contaminated place.

If he were to leave, he would miss almost nothing about this town. It would not be like leaving Albania, where he had left everything he had ever known. He had never believed in the outward friendliness of the people in Millsville. Nobody was his friend. They smiled at him, they spoke louder when addressing him because they thought that helped him understand, they allowed his wife to be a part of the PTA, they bought food from his restaurant. If they were all to go, though, he wouldn't think about any of them individually. Maybe the inspector, but only because the inspector infuriated him, reminded him that he was always under governmental control. The inspector would have done well under communism—his ability to treat humans as subordinate to ideas would have been an asset. Even before today that man got to him. The way he took his job too seriously, had at first pretended to be Bogdani's friend, and soon came to address Bogdani like he mattered less than his oven, since the inspector cared if the oven was up to code. No, the inspector he would be glad to get rid of, but the rest of the people could just fade away. Bogdani didn't know why he was thinking about leaving. The scotch may have been affecting him. He did not drink often.

He raised his glass in salute to the objects in the room that he had, until then, taken care of more attentively than his own son. A last conciliatory thought came to him: those masks might mean that they had discovered the illness was from a different source. Then he smiled, knowing that even if that were true, one radio report was enough. That and being closed down meant there was no chance his restaurant would ever reopen. He tossed back too much scotch, and as it went down his throat the inspector came to mind. The liquid held there for a moment and burned, making him cough and gasp. When he recovered his breath he felt exhausted, and instead of tossing the cup across the room he merely batted it toward the edge of the table with the back of his left hand and then nudged it off with his right, as a cat would, and stared down at the broken pieces.

≈

"Wasn't my fault. Arthur told us not to answer our phones for anyone but him," Cal told his wife outside their son's hospital room. "Wasn't supposed to pick up for anybody, not even you."

"Sickness going around and he doesn't let you leave, doesn't even let you talk to your family," Cal's wife, Tara, said distractedly. "But yeah, I went and called the nurse soon as I heard he threw up, and she said his symptoms matched, told me to run him on over here. Now doctors say he's got it. Won't let us in his room even, not until they know what they're dealing with."

Cal shifted his head to get a better view of his son through the narrow window. He was asleep or unconscious. Tape was stuck around the door in makeshift quarantine measures. Cal wanted to tear the whole thing off its hinges and go inside. Only the boy's face was visible, and even that was half obscured by his heft. Seeing his son's sheet-covered bulk reminded him that it was football season, so Jake was in jeopardy of missing the last few games of his high school career.

"Guess there's a lot of fakers," Tara told him. "Been coming in wasting everyone's time and not even sick. Just a bunch of liars or wanting attention."

"What?" Cal said, furious. "Coming in here like they're sick? Swear to god, if he don't get enough attention, I'll sue the goddamn phonies and the hospital. Goddamn doctors. Whoever started this illness in the first place. I'll even sue work for not letting me come down sooner. Would have grabbed a doctor by the coat and made him help Jake right away, instead of helping some faker first."

Tara nodded in agreement.

Cal sat next to his wife and folded his hands in prayer. When he saw she was on her phone, he pulled out his own, tilting it away from her in case Kristi had texted. He wanted to post a picture of Jake on Facebook and ask people to pray for him, but he didn't want to search his photos this close to Tara in case there were any Kristi pics still in there. He hoped Tara posted something. And though he was aware the illness might be foodborne, and that he was a member of the health department, he still felt helpless and unfairly persecuted.

Not one to sit patiently, Cal eventually roamed the halls looking, ostensibly, for answers, but was willing to settle for a cafeteria or a vending machine since he skipped lunch to make it to Kristi's as quickly as possible. (Though he then had to wait in his truck for forty-five minutes, hunched down like a stalker, until moments before she arrived.) He was surprised by his detachment from the frantic energy around him. People in scrubs rushed around, holding clipboards, guiding a patient either by the elbow or on a wheeled stretcher. Visitors seemed to contain their fright and anxiety in eyes that searched anywhere—even Cal's face—for information. Cal never knew it but he was one of these people, seeking with more urgency and even less ability than he had ever searched for a violation in a restaurant.

The muffled sound of a hidden radio got his attention. A Foghat song. He followed the music to one of the only rooms with an open door.

"There any news?" he asked from outside the doorway.

The four people sitting around the woman in bed all turned to him. Cal assumed the patient was a faker.

"Guess it's from that restaurant on Maple in Millsville," said the fraud.

"The MFR?" Cal asked.

"Yeah. So maybe I don't got it. Haven't eaten there," she said, and coughed.

Cal didn't know if Jake had gone to the MFR lately. Jake and his friends often left school to eat lunch, and he usually ate a meal after football practice before coming home to dinner—perhaps one of these had been at the Bogdanis' restaurant.

"And someone died," the patient said. "Old woman, I guess."

He was going to ask a follow-up question—what he didn't know, he just wanted to speak—when another desperate man shouldered past him and, while they both filled the doorway, asked if anyone had heard any news. The woman again answered, "Guess it's from the restaurant on Maple in Millsville." Cal walked away, disgusted.

Cal stopped searching for answers as he walked the hall. These people could do nothing for him. Considering the possibility of Jake dying was beyond his emotional capacity. He needed his son to be OK. He wanted him to have never gotten sick. If anyone had jostled him or gotten in his way, Cal might very well have beaten them to a pulp.

This was not his fault. He technically could have inspected that restaurant but there had been no reason to. If anything, as he now shifted his search completely, from answers to a vending machine, Cal felt tricked. He had inspected the MFR and there had never been any problems. And though he was pretty sure Bogdani was from one of those Muslim countries, he was also a family man, a hard worker. He never allowed Cal to pay for meals, not even if he stopped in for a quick snack, though most places only comped on inspection days. That this immigrant caused Jake to go to the hospital, potentially miss the remaining football games of his high school career, and, god forbid, maybe even die was an even graver betrayal, since Cal had until then given him the benefit of the doubt.

He spotted a group of vending machines at the end of the hall and lumbered toward them. Now that he knew the cause of his son's ailment he wanted to eat and get back to his room as soon as possible. He was preoccupied while standing in line, so when it was his turn he quickly assessed the situation: Normally he would have gotten the Cool Ranch Doritos, since it was the largest bag and he ate those at home, but the Chili Cheese Fritos—which he would normally not consider since it was a corn chip—was partially dangling so there was a chance he would get two for the price of one. Since he would eat either bag as quickly as possible, the nuances of the chip were not as important as quantity. He took a chance on the dangling Fritos.

When he put in his last two dollars and pushed the buttons, the metal coil that freed the Fritos jerked and caught hold of the bag as it rotated, spun the bag until it couldn't turn any farther, and proceeded to slice a perfect arc through the front of the bag. The chips spilled out into the bottom of the machine, like a deer's guts when sliced open while hanging from a hook in the garage.

Cal was confused. He could understand the bag not being released—that's a risk you take when you try to get two bags for the price of one—but he had never heard of this. The mangled bag still had chips inside, and if he hadn't been so distressed, he would have reached into the receptacle and scooped out the mouthful or so of fallen Fritos, happy to salvage something. But the violent end to this endeavor appeared to Cal to be yet another sign. Of what he didn't know. Since he was being unfairly punished for other people's mistakes, his only option was to find something—or someone—he could hurt back. Bogdani. He could make Bogdani experience at least a portion of the pain he was currently feeling. As he stalked back to his son's room, chipless and hungry and frightened, he wondered what if anything he could do to make Bogdani feel his pain.

≈

"What's it mean that Dad is the center of an investigation?" Ismail asked his mother a few minutes after she snapped the radio off, before the report was even finished. They had been driving in the hills and the Millsville station came in clear enough, though they were nearly an hour outside of town. He had, of course, understood the report perfectly well.

"It doesn't mean anything," Drita said, angrier than she intended. "And do not mention it to your auntie or your cousin. Try to put it out of your mind."

Ismail could see that the news report scared his mother. When she was worried her tongue pushed against the inside of her cheeks like it was trying to escape. He wanted to keep talking, preferably about the radio report and the illness and about the inspection earlier that day. His mother's demeanor, however, indicated that those subjects would not be appropriate. He considered reassuring her that he wouldn't say a word to his aunt or uncle or cousin during their visit. He planned to say nothing at all—he couldn't stand his cousin, who always made fun of him for having less money and living in a "hick town" up north. But he couldn't manage to say the words to his mom. Lately, bringing his mother joy seemed like a breach of etiquette. On the rare occasions when he did make her smile or laugh or thank him and kiss the top of his head, he immediately cringed, imagining the other boys in his class witnessing his kindness and mocking of him for it. He saw them interpreting it as weakness and calling him a "mother lover," a recent school-wide joke based on a *Saturday Night Live* song from a few years ago that his classmates had taken to singing loudly in the halls whenever Mrs. Eckley, an attractive and now-pregnant teacher, passed out of earshot. So, even in the car, Ismail stayed quiet and worried about everything without giving outlet to his concern. He only fiddled with the radio to see if he could find a station that did not either play country music or read from the Bible.

The radio report had sent waves of panic through Drita, who was doing everything she could to maintain focus and keep the car on the road. She wished she could do something to assuage her son's obvious concern, but she could barely keep herself together. She longed to use this as an opportunity to get closer to Ismail, who lately had been pulling away in an irritating display of self-conscious adolescence, but now she had to consider the right course of action. She should turn around and go back home or pull over and call her husband. But the way he had been acting all day told her that either option would probably earn her a reprimand, and she did not want to subject herself to further emotional strain. When she allowed herself to consider it, she felt incredible relief at pretending that she had not heard the report and driving on. She decided to call him when she arrived, feign surprise when he told her the news, and ask Ismail to lie about having heard it on the radio when they got back home. She didn't like asking her son to lie, but lately, as her husband's ill moods had become more frequent, lying had become necessary.

Soon their path took them through the town of Wisconsin Dells. An odd outpost in an otherwise wooded and unremarkable drive, the Dells provided a needed relief. The billboards for attractions had begun cropping up miles before, offering amazing experiences that could not possibly be as fulfilling as advertised. Still, the idea of such useless entertainment appealed to Drita just then. Every billboard featured happy people with amazed expressions on their faces.

"Should we stop?" Drita asked, trying to smirk.

"Can we?" Ismail asked, confused.

Drita had meant it as a joke, or maybe a wish. The tourist town was out of season and surely nearly desolate, though the weather was still pleasantly cool. But, thinking about it, she saw no reason not to stop. It would be cruel of her to suggest it and then not follow through. She did consider how sharing this experience alone with her son was unfair to her husband, who was so miserable and had been left to deal with such a mess alone. Her enjoyment would be tempered with the knowledge of his unhappiness, but she decided to stop, for Ismail. This would be one more thing they would keep from Mërgim, one more secret to ask her son to keep.

"Where should we go?" Drita asked. "What would you like to do?"

This unexpected treat took Ismail by surprise, and he felt like a game show contestant who suddenly had to decide among prizes.

"Go-Karts?" he said. "Or Ripley's Believe It or Not? Or the Robot Museum?" he had been keenly watching the billboards as they drove and found he was naming all the advertisements he could remember.

"You have to choose one," Drita said. "We don't have much time. Your auntie is expecting us." Though honestly, the closer they got to her sister's the more Drita began to dread getting there and wondered how much of her decision to stop was to delay their arrival. Lately, her sister had become expert at making one or two remarks over the course of an otherwise pleasant visit that managed to cut Drita with surgical precision and implant annoyances just under her skin that lasted for weeks after. Though perhaps it wasn't her sister who had changed but Drita, who was becoming more sensitive to the merest slight.

She took the exit into town to survey the options. Once on the main drive, however, they both fell silent and simply stared. The nearly empty street was lined with souvenir stores, most of which were closed. Advertised in the windows of many of these stores were the headdresses, moccasins, and fake bows and arrows of the "American Indians." There was even a shop called Indian Pottery. Drita wondered what exactly those were souvenirs of, other than a people that the founders of this town had willfully cleared away. There were Native Americans in Millsville as well, though Drita was not acquainted with any of them, and, for the most part, they did not frequent the restaurant. Drita had, on a couple of occasions, overheard customers talk offhandedly about how "Indians" were poor and alcoholics and acted as though the white people in town were responsible for taking away their land. Her customers seemed to think that "Indians" lacked ambition or drive to better their situation, despite receiving more government assistance than the white people. When she'd heard this in the past, Drita felt proud that she had worked hard for everything they had achieved, which seemed an ineradicable bottom line. Now when she considered these overheard assessments, she understood that measuring toil was hardly protection against a stacked deck. What was working hard when your world had been stolen?

"So what do you want to do?" Drita said, forcing as much cheerfulness into her voice as she could muster. "There are so many options."

In addition to the souvenirs (and, for some reason, many shops that exclusively sold fudge), there were such attractions as Pirate's Cove Adventure Golf, Timber Falls Adventure Park, an elaborately decorated building called Wizard Quest, and the much-advertised Ripley's Believe It or Not museum. She wondered vaguely if, should their restaurant be closed down, they could come here and operate a shop along this street, selling unnecessary items to people who were willing to waste money to prove they had had a good time. Ismail would surely like the excitement of such a place, at least at first. She glanced at her son who, out of lack of desire or inability to make a choice, did not tell her to stop. When the attractions and shops became fewer and the street began to turn into a highway out of town, Drita kept driving.

"What's that?" Ismail asked.

Startled by the break in the silence, Drita turned into the empty parking lot of the attraction in question and stopped the car.

"What is that?" Ismail asked again.

They stayed in the car while they tried to figure out what the giant structure represented. There were no signs, no markers directing patrons to an entrance, no posted price of admission. The building was meant to resemble a crumbled ruin—two big white boxes lined with windows, one box made to seem as though it was sinking into the ground.

"Oh!" Ismail said. "It's the White House! Only upside-down."

Indeed it was a full-scale representation of the White House, or at least the bottom half of it. Neither of them could figure out what kind of disaster could turn a building this large on its head.

"Why is it here?" he asked.

"I have no idea," Drita said. "Would you like to go inside?"

"I don't see a door," Ismail said.

They continued staring at the confusing spectacle. Perhaps it was a statue, a political statement of some kind, though that sentiment did not fit into this ridiculous town. It reminded Drita of when she was a girl, of seeing the destroyed statues of Enver Hoxha, the communist dictator who brutally ruled Albania for over forty years. After the communist regime fell, people pulled down the statues and left them similarly upside-down and crumbled as a reminder of what the country no longer was. But this was in many ways the opposite of that moment. That America could come to such ruin was so laughable that tourists were meant to have their picture taken in front of this fake disaster scene to show that reveling in America's ridiculous strength was great fun. The scene disturbed Drita, making her slightly queasy.

They sat for another minute without speaking. Then Ismail said, "Maybe just the Go-Karts?"

Drita nodded, and turned the car around.

≈

"Yes, a curfew," Janet said quietly into the phone. She worried that Katie could hear her despite the closed door, though Katie had claimed she could not.

"I hear you, but what I'm wondering . . ." The police chief didn't want to finish his thought. He assumed—but did not know for sure—that Janet was his superior, even though she worked for the county and he was city police.

Janet didn't save him from his unfinished sentence.

"What I'm wondering," he continued, "and it's not that I think you're wrong here—it's not that at all—it's just protocol I'm worried about here. Protocol." He hoped this sufficed for a complete thought.

Janet did not say anything.

"Because here's the thing," the police chief, whose name was Burt Butzler, added desperately, "I don't have any experience in enforcing a curfew. Maybe them county boys or state fellas could come in on relief, you know, give us a hand here, since—it's experience I'm talking about here."

Janet smiled and let him flounder a little longer.

"I gotta tell you," Burt said, his voice resigned to honesty, "I just don't honestly know—and it's not you here that I'm doubting, Janet, it's me—I don't honestly know if this is an order I get from your office. You know more than me when it comes down to rules and regulations, that I won't argue, but my issue here, well, the issue I'm concerned with is, what I'm saying—"

"Burt," Janet interrupted much to the officer's relief, "I have full confidence that your department will handle this capably."

"Thanks for that, I mean it, Janet, I do, and I don't know if I gave the wrong impression, but it isn't exactly the enforcement side of things that I'm worried about. It's more that I don't know—"

"If you feel like you need to ignore this direct order, then that's up to you, Burt. Maybe you know how the chain of command works better than I do. How long have you been a police officer in this town?"

"Eighteen years, Janet, but that isn't the—"

"That's a long time! And this is a lot to put on your plate. So you feel free to contact whoever you need to contact, Burt, to see if you need to do this. If you don't think you need to do it or if you aren't up to the task, then don't do anything, Burt."

"Gosh, Janet, it isn't a 'what I think' thing that we're talking about. I don't think anything." Burt's defenses were pretty well worn so he decided to retreat. "But yeah, we'll do our best tonight. Well, I will. It's Wednesday so it's only me on duty on the overnight."

"That's fine. Just fine."

"And Janet," Burt said, a thought coming to him quickly, "you don't think this'll happen tomorrow too, do you? You know Packers got the Thursday game against the Lions and most folks around here don't got DirecTV to watch at home since it isn't on network. Gotta go to Pokeys to watch." Burt had requested this Thursday night off months ago.

"I'm sure we'll get it sorted out by then," Janet said.

"Packers and all," Burt said.

Janet hung up.

Imposing a curfew! She worried people might think she was making the wrong call, that she was too full of herself, overreacting, and throwing her weight around. But it was a thrill to exert this much power. Because of her, an entire town had to stay indoors tonight. It made the back of her neck prickle. She did also legitimately think it was a sensible idea for people not to congregate or eat in restaurants tonight. Not only would separating people help to stop the spread of disease, but these already anxious people might, with enough alcohol, become desperate, and so it would head off any disturbance that might be brewing. It was Wednesday—people could drink and eat in their homes.

She didn't know if what she was doing was strictly legal, but with the death today she had to show she was in charge. And she *was*, she had to admit, having fun discovering the extent of her powers. To close down the school, she just called the principal and told him to send everyone home, though it was probably the superintendent's call. She called Burt and told him it was now illegal for anyone to stay out past nine o'clock that night. She almost hoped someone would get out the county charter and challenge her authority. She could then point them out as impeding her from preventing the spread of the illness if it gets worse. And if her supporters raised a fuss about obstructing individual liberties, she could always deflect the accusations by claiming that the health department closed the school and Burt was responsible for the curfew.

Janet did care about these people, but she didn't need to go down to the hospital like Rosalynn Carter touring the Vietnamese refugee camps to prove it. She grew up here. These were the only people she knew—she didn't want them to be miserable. She certainly didn't want them to die. Theresa Dorshorst's daughter Mary had been in the grade below Janet in school, and Theresa used to substitute-teach from time to time. While she sincerely wanted to ease people's suffering, she also wanted credit for doing so, and those were not conflicting ideas.

She wondered if she should call anyone else to make sure word of the curfew spread. She had already paved the way by having the radio announce the news of the death. She should also have Katie call the radio station and maybe the nearest TV station about the curfew, though its range might give them more exposure than she wanted.

She picked up her softball and cocked back to throw, then held off. Katie was so often critical of these big decisions in her noncommittal way, where she only took basic ethics into account. Janet put the softball down. She didn't feel like fighting with Katie. She would call the radio herself.

It was nearly four thirty. If Janet was going to file her candidate papers, Katie would have to walk down to the clerk of courts now to get them notarized and sent to Madison. She could wait another day. Katie was right about that: it wouldn't hurt to wait.

She turned to the county's website on her computer. A day like today—when disseminating information would be expected and possibly useful but ultimately harmful in exposing her own ignorance—made her glad they had never set up an official social media page. Before she began to check the Facebook pages of the biggest loudmouths in town to get the real scoop, she briefly wondered why she hesitated to ask Katie to call the radio station. Normally, making Katie squirm was the highlight of her day. Janet took note of this feeling and filed it away to ponder later.

≈

Arthur decided not to walk the three miles back to his office to write up his reports. Instead, for the first time ever, he cut out of work early. It wasn't all that early—a half hour—but it was not yet five o'clock. All he knew was that his attempts to ameliorate the situation only made everything worse, so he might as well go home.

Plus his stomach was still not right. During the excitement either it had settled itself temporarily for his benefit or he didn't notice his physical discomfort in the midst of so much other, more pressing, mental distress. The relief brought about by the glorious twenty minutes in the secluded third-floor bathroom in County Building C seemed like a distant memory now and, though he no longer needed a bathroom, he still felt the hot dog piled in the bottom of his stomach like a heap of compost. As he began his walk home, his mind was stuck on the dreamy wish of an extra-long ice-cream scoop that could snake down his esophagus and snatch up the rottenness.

In an effort to quell his queasiness by walking, as well as to not be cowed by Janet's stupid plan to sic the public on him, Arthur took the long way home, walking down Maple Street to observe the town without his professional detachment. The street was strangely empty, though it was near the time that cities call rush hour. Maybe Janet's curfew made sense. An official order could put people's minds at ease. It could take the decision of whether to leave the house out of their hands. No, that was stupid. The illness was surely caused by food—if people want to go outside, they should go outside. Janet was getting to him.

At the memorial park where earlier he and Kent dropped off Eldred, Arthur had to sit and wait for his stomach to settle. He was no hypochondriac. He had a professional obligation to take the illness seriously in general, but it was far more likely that his stomach was cramping because all he had to eat that day was a single slop-covered hot dog from a cart on the highway. So, while he would have advised anyone else in the county with these symptoms to head to the nearest hospital, Arthur focused on the oddly soothing fantasy of that extra-long ice-cream scoop.

Across the street was Adam's newspaper office and, a little farther down, the Bogdanis' restaurant. If his digestive tract wasn't staging a revolt, Arthur would have visited Adam to apologize for not being more helpful to Mr. B. He would have inquired about Adam's daughters, told him that he saw Katie at the courthouse, and vented about Janet's ridiculous manhunt. Adam was the one person Arthur knew around here who definitely recognized stupidity when he saw it, though Adam had many questionable beliefs himself.

He would have caught Adam with twenty minutes before the paper had to go to the printer. Arthur's friendly visit would have made Adam feel guilty. He would have realized that though Arthur was an asshole he was still a genuine friend. Plus, Adam would prefer to keep his position of moral authority. If Arthur had stopped in, Adam would have put the Future Farmers article back on the front page. But instead, Arthur had eaten a dubious hot dog earlier that day so he sat across the street clenching himself.

He shifted focus to see the Open sign in the window of the Bogdanis' restaurant. If he felt better, he would have made sure Bogdani wasn't operating, since even if the kitchen had been cleaned, there was a mandatory forty-eight-hour suspension after being closed down (another rule implemented by Arthur that he now wished he could break). Arthur would not have imposed further penalty if Bogdani were still serving food. In fact, Arthur would have hoped the diner was operating so he could make up for his previous insensitivity. He wanted the opportunity to apologize, take any abuse with stoic professionalism, and discuss how they could work together to spare his business further harm.

If he had gone in, Arthur would have found Bogdani at the table, half drunk. Bogdani would not have paid Arthur much attention except to mutter abuses in his direction. There would be broken cups on the ground. Arthur's presence would have only made Bogdani feel worse, but Arthur would have recognized something was seriously wrong. Arthur wouldn't have left him alone. He would have tried to track down his family. When unable to find them, Arthur would have stayed with Bogdani late into the night. Who knows if any of that would have helped.

When Arthur's stomach relaxed, he got off his bench and walked home. Eldred was not in the park or Arthur would have asked him how he felt about being half-kidnapped earlier. Nobody was on the street or Arthur would have asked why they were wearing a mask.

Arthur was glad that Katie and Adam were at work so there was no chance of seeing them. He decided that when he got home he would make himself a peanut butter sandwich to settle his stomach and then check his ex-wife's Facebook page. Arthur was not on Facebook but had created a fake profile just to follow his ex-wife. (In his friend invite he said that they had met at a party once and she accepted quickly.) Though he recognized this was the action of a stalking ex-husband, he wasn't doing it to keep tabs on her. He did it because his dad, of all people, once said that he felt sorry for Arthur's ex-wife because she posted such dumb jokes on Facebook and nobody ever "liked" them. They were so painfully unfunny, his dad said, that though he pitied her he could not bring himself to like them himself or people would think *he* was stupid. Arthur then felt lame for ever being her husband, even though it was her awkwardness that had drawn him to her in the first place. So Arthur created a profile with a fake name and liked much of what his ex-wife posted. Eating a sandwich and liking his ex-wife's Facebook page would make him feel better. He would salvage his day by not doing anyone, himself included, more harm.

≈

The neighbors peeked out their windows as Sasha and Anna parked their truck and pushcart in front of the Benders' house. Sasha didn't care about being observed, but Anna was furious. That these small-town assholes had nothing better to do but judge her while she was sweaty and dirt-smudged made her carry her head higher and mash her boots into the ground as she walked. She shooed her father away while she unhooked the cart from the hitch and set it up on a cinder block. Away from the isolation of the highway her father was her only ally and she was glad he was near.

"Why are we staying here?" she asked, though she knew the answer.

"Hotels are expensive. We would eat up profit."

"But she doesn't want us here. Why would she?" This argument would get her nowhere—her father was immune to the persuasion of inconvenience and imposition—but she needed to say the words.

Her father didn't answer. Instead, he looked around at the plastic-sided houses with closely trimmed yards still green against the yellowing autumn foliage. The sounds of children playing echoed from the backyards, there were no sirens in the air, and a man tossed a stick for a dog that had just pooped in the street. It was a crisp sixty degrees. Past the main roads of the subdivision began the natural-growth woods that predated the town. Between these trees that rustled with wind and cut the sun into shadow, Sasha saw the newly painted water tower announcing the town's name in the high school's colors.

"I could not live in this neighborhood," Sasha proclaimed.

Anna lifted her head and squinted dismissively at the banality, as though seeing it for the first time. She said, "Who could except for these people? But I thought you *wanted* simplicity."

"A house near a river. With a cherry tree."

Anna sighed. The world in her father's head was a very strange place.

As she was deciding whether to point out her father's mistakes in planning (which would have been satisfying but also might have made him reconsider moving here, thus saddling her with him until he died), the inspector turned the corner and walked toward them.

"That's him," she said.

Sasha quickly calculated if it was better to leave the inspector alone or to talk to him here, on neutral, personal ground. Since he generally considered it good policy to do something rather than to not, he called out.

"Inspector, we are neighbors!"

Arthur's face, already visibly pale from where they stood, became, if possible, even whiter after he saw who spoke. He scratched his head, gave a single open-handed wave, dropped his hand back into place, and refocused on the road directly in front of him.

"What a coincidence!" Sasha yelled, though he had long known Arthur lived nearby.

Arthur barely nodded until Anna came around the pushcart and said hello. He turned his head sharply and stumbled on a rock.

"Go over to him and talk!" Sasha whispered fiercely.

Anna was conditioned to obey her father and immediately stepped closer to the inspector. That she actually wanted to speak to him didn't cross her mind until she was already walking. She found him attractive enough—if a bit bald and without enough distinctiveness to call him handsome—to keep possibilities open, and they hadn't lagged for conversation during his inspection. Though she was glad to approach him and might not have if her father hadn't told her to, she wished she had done it on her own volition since it now had the aspect of a chore.

"Inspector," she said when she was a few steps away. She lightly kicked a rock and felt the last two bags of meth jostle against her toes.

"It's Arthur. Anna, right?" he said. She smelled of sweat and motor oil, which might have just been hot dog. His stomach clenched while his penis reluctantly stiffened halfway.

"Of course," she said. "Are you following me, Inspector Arthur?"

"No," Arthur said with alarm. "I live right over there."

"Sure you do," she said. "You're following me."

"I'm not," Arthur said, then to his surprise added, "but if I had known you were here, I would have looked forward to the possibility of seeing you." This struck him immediately as a clumsy and oddly formal statement, as if he was the more awkward but hopefully more upright suitor in a nineteenth-century Russian novel.

She saved him by saying, "That's sweet." It was sweet but his self-consciousness also made her reconsider her desire—he wasn't very charming and didn't take control like he did while inspecting. On the other hand, her father had told her about his continuing affair with the skinny blonde woman so maybe there was more to him than there appeared. If nothing else, Anna supposed, sleeping with him would be a kind of revenge on the blonde woman for her perfect life. Her important government job. Successful husband. Big house. Her daughters. That fake smile. Anna couldn't stand her—she was so unremarkable and yet she had everything Anna wanted. Anna couldn't align herself with people she envied. She instead fought to bring them down to what she considered her own level, and so she'd been trying to gain the upper hand since they arrived. A power struggle might make staying here tolerable, or at least interesting. She'd considered sleeping with Adam the night before—now *he'd* definitely take control—but he didn't extend the offer and the logistics were too complicated for her to initiate since Anna was already displacing one of the girls. Anyway, stealing the inspector seemed like a greater violation than sleeping with her husband. The blonde woman chose to sleep with the inspector at a great personal risk, and was probably with her husband only out of habit and for the children. Anna would never admit it, even to herself, but behind those feelings of detesting and envying her lay a hidden admiration. Anna could not help but respect her willingness to risk everything for pleasure.

"Jesus, I'm sorry," Arthur said. "I'm not feeling well. I should get going." He didn't want to leave, but he did want to stop saying stupid things. Also the walk had stirred awake his bowels, and as he got closer to home the desire for his bathroom was quickly becoming a need.

"Perhaps I could come by sometime?" she said. Then she put her cupped hand conspiratorially to the side of her mouth and added with a smile, "I need to get away from this house. There's someone else's family inside!"

"Yeah, yeah," Arthur said, and tried to think of something clever but only managed to add, "yeah."

Sasha watched his daughter talk to the inspector. When the man walked away she turned toward the cart and stomped toward him in her stupid impractical boots. His daughter knew what to do. She was a good daughter except that she wore those boots and wouldn't stay here with him. Maybe she could get close to the inspector. Marrying him would be even better than marrying Adam. That way he'd have a son-in-law in the government. It was not too late for his daughter to have a son who could visit his grandfather's house. If that happened—if his daughter was married and a mother and Sasha's grandson came to his house and they sat under a cherry tree and fished—then Sasha would be completely fulfilled. There were other, lesser ways for him to be happy, but this was the fantasy that went through Sasha's head as his daughter walked across the street in her boots. For the time it took her, he was pleased that they were here.

≈

Back in New York, Arthur occasionally saw people he inspected when he was off the clock, usually on the subway. Mostly he saw pushcart operators, since he inspected them far more than anything else. When they saw him across the subway car, they would smile broadly or shyly at him, depending on their most recent inspection. Initially these interactions unnerved Arthur. With no badge to protect him, the pushcart operators were free to point out that Arthur was a fraud, basically just a kid playing inspector, and that they were grown men. They were aware that Arthur spent his entire adult life enforcing mostly ineffective and meaningless rules. But as he became more comfortable with his job and these interactions outside of work became more frequent, he perfected a gesture that involved eye contact, a half grin, and a brisk but friendly nod that ended with him returning to his book or newspaper. He was no less a fraud than ever, but he understood how to deal with what his life had become. The next time he inspected the cart after one of these subway interactions, the man could only say, "So you take the J train, Inspector!" and Arthur could frown and nod and continue to give the man's cart the regular fines since nothing had been shared between them.

In Millsville he interacted everywhere with the people he inspected: the grocery store, the mechanic, in line at the Danville Cinema, at the library, the doctor's office, while jogging in his neighborhood. He hadn't eaten inside a restaurant around there in two years—he didn't want to make people nervous simply by eating their food. He accepted these conditions as inevitable and kept intimacies to a minimum. Such distance was why he never asked Bogdani about his life in Albania, though he was interested in the answer.

So he didn't know why he was so shaken by seeing Anna and her father. That they were staying with Adam wasn't surprising—he knew they were friends. Only after he appreciated his second bout of relief that day did he realize what had been so off-putting, especially since he had definitely wanted to speak to Anna again. It all went back to Bogdani. He currently felt the same shame and regret that he had felt after calling Bogdani a failure in front of his son. With everything else that had happened—the illness, Janet, Katie, Cal's cock—momentarily stripped from his consciousness following the fulfillment of this physical need, the interaction with Bogdani came back in a wave of remorse, and if anything was left inside of him, he would have felt sick all over again. Along with that shame came the connection between Bogdani and Sasha: Bogdani had said that his kitchen wasn't in such poor condition the night before, and Sasha had told Arthur that he was buying Bogdani's restaurant.

Arthur wished he had at least tried to help, if only to show he was on Bogdani's side. He could have accused Sasha of sabotage, he could have understood why the kitchen was how it was, and he could have sympathized with Bogdani and helped him file a police report. But he still would have had to shut the restaurant down. A kitchen is how it is, and Arthur would never not shut down a kitchen that was not up to code. If he didn't believe in this, he didn't believe in anything. Not for the first time, Arthur thought how boring and uptight he was, and how anyone else in his position would make an exception once in a while. If he didn't feel so physically unwell and mentally depleted, he would have laughed at himself.

He sat on his toilet and stared into his shower. He would never be able to pass his own home if he were to inspect it. His shower was covered in a thick black mold that appeared scorched by a fire. (In his lectures to restaurant operators, he called mold "the Silent Killer.") The growth was not only a product of his never cleaning his tub, but also a structural deficiency that did not allow the bathroom to ventilate—and further aided by a broken bathroom fan that he did not bother to fix. (Not that he would care about these reasons if he were inspecting this bathroom, of course: mold is mold no matter why it is there.)

He had considered attempting to remove the domestic fungus after Katie had used the shower the one time she stayed over at his house, when both her daughters were away overnight. Without discussing it, they had played house—Arthur bought groceries and they cooked dinner, they watched TV (which they had never done before and was still the most intimate moment they had ever shared), she brushed her teeth in his sink. Their nights until then had been hurried, broken up. Katie would stop by and have a drink on his deck, go home, come back when her daughters were asleep, leave before they woke up. Their night together felt normal, which was heartbreaking for Arthur because it made him realize how much he longed for the contentment of a shared routine.

But when she took a shower that morning, she had said, "How do you live like this? I feel like I'm going to get cancer in here," and Arthur became concerned. Not only had she confirmed his fears that the mold was perhaps indeed carcinogenic, but now he worried that Katie wouldn't want to spend time at his house. At the time, he reasoned that he would not remove the blight until she used the shower again, in order to judge how she would react the second time. He secretly wanted her to be concerned for his health, and he wanted her to want him to fix it because he wanted her to want to use it more. But not long after that, Adam came back and she stopped using anything but his bedroom (and, well, him), and Arthur stopped thinking about the black growth in his shower.

It wasn't only his bathroom that would not pass inspection, though. Other areas of his house would fail as well: his electrical system regularly shorted out; his heat worked sporadically, and his air conditioning, as far as he knew, didn't work at all; his kitchen was a disaster of spoiled food, crusty utensils, mysterious containers haunting the back of his refrigerator, broken sink disposal and dishwasher, hand towels left unwashed for half a year, empty bottles of soap, furry bread and cheese that he'd eat after lopping off the offending section, a sink constantly overflowing with dirty dishes, large areas of the counter covered in a gelatin-like substance that stuck to and tore the paper towel on the rare instances when he half-heartedly tried to clean it up, a freezer shrunken to three-quarters of its size from frost, an oven bottom caked with scorched cheese from dripping Tombstone pizzas, a microwave plastered with years' worth of splatter from exploding soups and sauces.

Despite all this, he believed he would pass if Cal inspected him. Arthur would be able to convince him that the violations were not as severe as they seemed. The passing or failing of an inspection has much more to do with the inspector than the entity being inspected—this was why Arthur believed in his job, because he was better at it than other people. Arthur could legitimately fail anything if he put his mind to it. Any competent inspector could. The truth was that Arthur's house was probably not going to hurt him in either the long term or short. He hadn't gotten sick once in the past three years despite living in the midst of all this filth, and though it was within the realm of possibility that his moldy shower could, over time, give him cancer, couldn't drinking too much diet soda do so as well? (Arthur had very little idea how cancer worked.)

Inspection was about intention and possibility: a person serving food to other people should try to keep them safe according to accepted norms and not allow for the risk of causing harm if it is not known exactly what can harm a person. This, to Arthur, was sound thinking. He believed this was how service industries should act but individuals could do whatever they wanted as long as they didn't expect people to come into their house and eat.

When Arthur finished on the toilet he nodded at his spore-coated shower as though in agreement with himself for being filthy and irresponsible. He then abruptly stood, as if he had concluded a business meeting in which a compromise had been struck that made nobody happy and had therefore been a sound deal for all.

≈

Bogdani had not moved from his chair in some time. He was finding it difficult to close the door after letting in the darkness of his thoughts. Or maybe it was only the scotch. No, the scotch had deepened the darkness, like gasoline fueling a fire, but the source of the darkness had always been there, waiting to get inside him. His mood made it impossible to get up from his chair, and he watched as the shadows lengthened across the street. If his eyes hadn't adjusted along with the setting sun, he would not have been able to see much at all.

He was no longer thinking of anything concrete. Snatches of ideas about betrayal and neglect and oppression swept through his mind without ever taking root. One moment he was imagining his wife and son laughing at his incompetence as they drove to her sister's mansion. Another moment he imagined the inspector was still inside his restaurant, judging Bogdani instead of his kitchen, ticking off boxes in the "fail" column and then tearing off his maddening yellow sheet and handing it over. Then he saw his mother in her sick bed after he arrived back in Lushnjë, too late to say goodbye, unable to ask if she forgave him for leaving her behind, though she never expressed anything but pride at what she perceived as his successful life in America. These thoughts all went by like smoke out a chimney blown by the wind. He didn't try to catch them or pin them down, they only poured out as he sat in his dark, empty restaurant. Still, an idea stuck in the back of his mind, just out of reach. A hard nugget, a fact, something he told himself to make sure to remember or something he had forgotten to do.

Outside the window, down the street a bit, a movement caught his eye—a man walking away from the memorial park. He assumed, since all day the streets had been nearly empty due to the illness, that it was that homeless man—Holmwood was his name—who spent much of his day in that park. Bogdani knew the man only because he came to the restaurant every morning for old donuts and the dregs of coffee. Nearly each day for years now, the man had stood in the alley behind the kitchen like a patient dog, waiting for Bogdani to open the door halfway and shove a white wax paper bag and a steaming takeaway cup into his hands. Neither man ever said anything, at most maybe one of them would grunt or nod, but the small act of kindness had become a part of Bogdani's morning routine, the same as taking the chairs down from the tables or pouring oil into the fryer. Bogdani didn't even know when or how the ritual began. When the man occasionally did not show up—like for a week last winter for reasons Bogdani never discovered—Bogdani found himself unsettled and more irritable than usual. The homeless man was probably the only person in this county who had never betrayed Bogdani, who accepted what Bogdani offered in a way that Bogdani respected and indeed needed—without pretense or expectation. That homeless man in his winter snowsuit covered with buttons and his arm in a cast was probably the closest that Bogdani came to having a friend around here. No, that couldn't be true. But it was! This struck Bogdani as unbearable and funny. Bursts of laughter came out of him like sobs, and he slapped the table.

The laugh seemed to shake loose the idea that had been nagging him. He held up a hand and stopped laughing, felt tears on his cheeks, but did not wipe them. Of course, the bag. Two days ago, after his morning busboy quit, Bogdani had found his backpack in the closet, and inside it, along with a sweatshirt and chewing tobacco and a half-empty bottle of Mountain Dew Code Red, was a handgun. Bogdani didn't know what kind specifically. Not a revolver but one with the clip.

The man who'd quit, the one who needed Bogdani's money but did not feel the need to come to work on time and thought it above his station to clean bathrooms, was obviously the type who needed a gun to make up for his numerous shortcomings. Indeed, there was even a possibility this man had ruined his kitchen, both in revenge and in a search for the forgotten bag.

Without realizing it, and without willing himself to do it, Bogdani found he was walking to where he had stored the bag, on the top shelf of the locked cupboard under the stairs. He'd hid it there while he figured out how to properly dispose of it. He should have taken it to the police but had long ago learned not to trust authorities. Plus, he imagined himself getting caught with the gun in his possession on the way to the station. He could have given the bag back to the busboy when he returned to the restaurant and asked for it, but the man had acted so superior while quitting that Bogdani enjoyed pretending he didn't know what the man was talking about and forced him to leave under threat of calling the authorities. (The confrontation had occurred, Bogdani now remembered, in front of the Russian man, moments after Bogdani had turned down his insulting offer to buy the restaurant.) Anyway, he didn't want the gun in the busboy's hands. He didn't trust the man carrying a tray of dishes, let alone a pistol.

The gun, when he lifted it out of the bag, had a satisfying heft of something well made. He placed the bag back on the shelf and carried the gun back to the table and sat down. He turned it back and forth in his hands, inspected it, but did not aim it or even place his finger on the trigger. It had more meaning for him as a crafted object, not as an instrument. He was not in the mood to think of a thing's capabilities or worth. Like how he drank the scotch not to get drunk but because scotch was there and it did not seem to matter if he drank it or not. Now, with this gun, he felt a similar hollowness. Whether or not the gun was loaded did not change anything about his life.

He considered throwing it across the room as he had done with his coffee mugs. Instead, he placed it indifferently on the table in front of him in such a way that the barrel happened to point toward his chest. Following the path from the barrel to his own body, he made the connection and a chill went through him, starting in his feet and traveling up to his bowels. It was the first time since he heard the radio report some time ago (had it been hours already?) that he felt something, though even now he was detached from the feeling—as though he saw someone on television wailing and knew approximately how they felt but had no connection to the pain itself.

The street outside his window was empty. He was so alone. A voice came to him then, but like the chill he recently experienced without a connection to the feeling, the voice came without his being aware of thinking. The voice spoke from deep within. It said how they were not the problem. Other people were not his oppressors. It was him, Mërgim Bogdani, who was the burden. Everyone else was fine, happy, adjusted; it was he who was in their way. He saw that his wife and son bristled when he came into a room, that the government wanted him to suffer because he came to their country unwanted, that people would rather have someone born in this country run his business. He was the impediment. Him and his stupid desire to have something of his own, to make his own way—his biggest failure was wanting to make his family happy but having succeeded only in making them miserable. He even makes himself miserable! The voice then said, *You might have even killed someone. Would it have been worth it? Or would that only have been expected?* Yes, he definitely killed someone, it was his fault, all his fault. It was all his fault. The ultimate failure, the voice told him, was that you have done all this to yourself. Circumstance could not be blamed for what your life has become. He made each choice. He was a knowing agent in the world, and misery was the result of his action.

As the voice spoke, Bogdani settled his eyes down at the table, at the gun, and listened, nodding, the same way he had listened to the radio report earlier in the day informing him of something he had already done, that he could not undo. Yes, he understood everything now.

He was still looking at the gun when the phone rang.

≈

Late that night, at the hospital, where Jake was still confined to his bed, Tara convinced Cal to go home. The door to the room was open now, and they sat next to their sleeping son, who had been awake a half hour before—lucid but weak. Cal didn't want to leave but Tara reminded him that he didn't have any vacation time or sick days remaining and if he lost his job, they wouldn't be able to afford to keep Jake in the hospital. After one last chat with the doctor and a long look at his son, Cal got in his truck and left.

The highway was pitch dark. When his eyes adjusted, he scoured the fields for animals and a few times considered stopping to shine for deer with the spotlight in his back seat. Shining was the only activity Cal preferred to do alone. He was just as satisfied scanning the light back and forth in empty fields as when he found a group of ten deer. Something about exposing the space behind the darkness, momentarily turning night into day, made him feel that the world was easier to control, or at least understand. It's one of the few experiences in Cal's life that, if asked why he liked it, he wouldn't try to explain.

But tonight he was too worried to shine, even though it seemed that Jake was going to pull through. Without another means of distraction, he found his thoughts stuck on the text Kristi had sent him hours earlier. It had simply read *How's Jake?* She had obeyed their "no sexting" rule, and the text came in under the name "Arthur Work" so he wasn't worried about getting caught. And yet he couldn't shake his irritation, though normally even the most innocuous text from her brought him a joy that was, to his wife, suspiciously out of place from a coworker.

Perhaps her text reminded him that the affair threatened his relationship with his son. Or he didn't want to remember how close he'd been to ejaculating earlier, considering he was not in the frame of mind to finish himself off when he got home. Or maybe being forced to examine his infatuation with Kristi in light of the current crisis made him feel stupid and childish. Worrying for so long outside his son's room clarified what should really matter.

He slowed his truck at the sight of two glinting eyes. A young doe stared unblinking in the middle of the road. Under his breath, Cal let slip the phrase, "There you go along now, little dogie." He shook his head and realized how exhausted he was. Before he could tap the horn the deer snapped out of it and loped away. As he resumed his drive, Cal was moved by the memory of the deer's innocent expression and felt a sense of loss that it wasn't still in his vision.

If he were the one sick in bed, worried he could die, he assumed he would think a lot about little fleeting things like that deer. Small moments that don't seem important, like spotting animals and eating good meals, were what made life worth living. And if that were true, then he would surely think as much about Kristi as his own family. Since meeting her, he couldn't remember going a few minutes without thinking about her, while he completely forgot about Jake's birthday last month until Tara told him to pick up a cake on his way home.

On that hypothetical sick bed he would be consoled that he had reached for such heights, felt that he had "left nothing on the field," as football announcers were so quick to say. Instead of trying to reconcile his conflicting feelings, his thoughts involuntarily shifted back to his hatred for Bogdani. That *immigrant*. That *Muslim*. If Bogdani had not poisoned half the town, Cal would be at home, satiated both by hours alone with Kristi and his wife's cooking, probably watching the late local news or that fishing show and contemplating whether he had the necessary reserves to have sex with his wife that night in order to prolong the sexual high of his afternoon as well as throw her off the scent. This was not too much to ask. This was simple and attainable.

He spent most of his drive fantasizing about harming Bogdani. (These fantasies all ended with Cal throwing a bloodied Bogdani through the large plate-glass window at the front of the restaurant.) Cal had his badge on him so he could perhaps go to Bogdani's front door and demand to be let in, and then inflict an equal amount of pain on the man who hurt his son. It would be difficult to prove his guilt after the beating, since it would be his word against Bogdani's, and because Cal had lived there his whole life and didn't poison anyone, his word would hold more water. Cal comforted himself with these thoughts. They made him feel sufficiently angry and somehow in control. Then he picked up his phone.

≈

Everyone playing the game of Scrabble wanted to be somewhere else. Perhaps this happens with most games of Scrabble; at the Benders' house, with Adam and Katie and Sasha and Anna, nobody had wanted to play in the first place. Katie just couldn't take the silence of the man or the staring of his daughter any longer and had suggested they play the only game in the house even arguably appropriate for adults. But she quickly realized she had only further brewed discomfort and that they were duty bound to play the game out. To counteract this awfulness Katie kept an enthusiastic running commentary about the game play. This also allowed her to stop asking these people questions that they grunted one-word answers to.

Behind her chatter, Katie mostly thought about sleeping in the same room as her husband. The previous night had been a surprise—she had noticed him next to her only after waking the next morning and now wished she had made a move. Tonight she was able to prepare herself. Her current plan was to initiate quiet and intense sex brought on by proximity and hope it ended in renewed intimacy. However, in the event of the more likely scenario—that Adam pops a sleeping pill and immediately falls asleep—she intended to play with herself as she imagines sneaking away to screw Arthur. Both options depressed her but also turned her on. Either way, at least she would get some release after a long and frustrating day that ended with her potentially assisting in the ruin of an innocent family. Ever since she had called the radio to report the Bogdanis' restaurant as the cause of the sickness, she'd had a tightness in her diaphragm that she hoped wasn't the beginnings of the mystery illness. In an ideal world she'd relieve this tightness by venting to a sympathetic Adam before he made love to her. Katie had long ago stopped believing in an ideal world, though—at this point she'd happily settle for these Russians going to bed. She placed the letters to spell MANDATE and winced as the pressure in her chest doubled. In the brief excruciating silence, she took a long swallow of wine and imagined what it would be like later when she walked naked from the bathroom to the bed in front of her husband for the first time in years. Those seven steps will almost—but not quite—be worth his friends' unannounced intrusion. She forced a smile to her lips and loudly proclaimed her excitement about her word score, both wishing she had the capacity to endure quiet and resenting these people for making her do all the work.

Anna knew the woman had suggested this game only to humiliate her. So what if Anna wasn't a champion speller? And though she was doing moderately well with sheer will and her grasp of the importance of bonus squares, her letter rack held a *V* and a *J* and an *X*. Soon she would have to attempt misspelling a complex word, thus allowing this horrible woman the satisfaction of proving Anna's stupidity. Now she definitely wanted to have sex with that inspector. That was worth much more in her silent war against this woman than points from a board game. If she would at least *shut up*. Her compliments about everyone's words (even Anna's father's egregiously misspelled and made up words) grated on Anna's nerves, and she found herself staring hard while tapping her toes quickly on the carpet. Earlier in the night, watching this woman expertly play the role of insipid mother and wife, Anna was surprised to discover a kernel of grudging respect. Good for the blonde woman for fooling everyone while getting satisfied by the inspector on the side. If this dull person had such hidden depth, maybe there was more to this town than Anna thought. But then Katie, with her blank smile, stood over her, shaking a game box, and any goodwill immediately drained away. She was dying for her father to start operating that restaurant so they had somewhere else to stay. Any misgivings she had about displacing the family who currently occupied the restaurant were tossed aside at the thought of having to play another game of Scrabble against this woman. That this annoying person had so much while Anna had so little allowed Anna to forget how wrong it was to make another family have less so she could have more. She suddenly realized that everyone was staring at her, that it was her turn. She quickly placed *J U T* around an *S* to make JUST and was momentarily relieved to have her turn over and to have gotten rid of her *J*. She desperately wanted to stop playing Scrabble.

At least, Adam thought, playing Scrabble allowed him to focus his annoyance at Katie for suggesting the game and at her inane comments that didn't put anyone else at ease but only made her feel less uncomfortable. All he could do now was win as quickly as possible, be annoyed, and devise a plan to sleep with Anna later that night to get back at Katie. So far all he came up with was a fantasy where Anna gave him a blow job under the table while Katie sat across from him, obliviously blathering. Despite these amusing distractions, he couldn't get his mind off the articles he had written that afternoon. He attributed his decision to print them to temporary insanity brought about by a deadline combined with a rare flare-up of jealousy. If this had happened on a Monday, his desire for revenge would have passed and he'd have churned out a regular edition of his paper that could only have offended people with discerning taste. Instead, now, as he contemplated his next Scrabble word, most of his guilt centered on the restaurant owner, Bogdani. Arthur at least deserved what he got—he put himself into this position. And though it was his turn to play, Adam found his thoughts centering on non-Scrabble-related word choice. Specifically, how he had written that the restaurant was "closed due to gross violations of the health code." And though by "gross" he had meant "flagrant" he knew many of his readers would take it to mean "disgusting." Writing the article had been to appease Sasha, but Adam chose how he wrote it. He didn't need to include words like "terror" and "gross." He also hadn't had to mention that the Bogdanis were immigrants, knowing how this knowledge would land with his readers, wary of "foreignness" of all kinds.

Pushing these thoughts from his head long enough to play, he placed the letters to spell SCRUPLE with the C in triple letter. Katie clapped delightedly at all the points. Adam glared at her as he surreptitiously reached into his pocket and tapped a flat piece of coiled copper wire strung with colored beads. Most days he tapped the coil dozens of times for luck and to ward off karmic reprisals, but since sending the article to the printers he had tapped it 206 times. Lately this tapping also reminded him of his failure in Utah, since copper and colors had been integral to the foundational mechanics of his machine. Undeterred by this unpleasant memory, Adam kept tapping. Relief flowed through him like morphine through an addict. The nearly electric charge drawn from the coil not only rejuvenated him, it also served to confirm the perfection of his own instinct and intellect for having discovered this power source all on his own. This certainty allowed him to convince himself that he could not have done anything wrong. He realized Bogdani wasn't unfairly crushed by history, but rather justifiably cleared away so that history could move forward unimpeded. Freed from guilt, his thoughts returned to being irritated by his wife and devising a plan to sleep with Anna, who was surely making eye contact now and seemed to be touching his foot under the table.

Sasha could not care less about Scrabble. How it could possibly matter one way or another if he received imaginary "points" for spelling out words on a board he could not fathom and didn't bother to try to figure out. But this was the price of free lodging, so he mechanically put down letters that seemed to spell out words and allowed Adam's wife to count them while talking to him like a child. Adam's wife was unusually interested in points. While she was distracted with them, Sasha would toe Adam's foot as Adam stared at Anna. The only way Sasha could ever imagine forgiving Adam for squandering Sasha's money was if Adam married his daughter and made her live here. As soon as Sasha's points were counted and noted, though, he'd go back to figuring out how to purchase and open his restaurant. The Albanian's former busboy—whom Sasha had tracked down and paid to destroy the kitchen as well as to keep Sasha informed of any new developments—told him that the man's wife and son had left town without him. This would make it easier for Sasha to pressure him, for he would never abuse a man in view of his family. That the inspector had done that in front of the man's son was offensive even to Sasha. But with the family gone, Sasha's options were open. Sasha was an expert bully, usually able to obtain his desired result without actually causing physical harm. All over New York there were building supers and fellow motorists and loud neighbors and competing vendors and overcharging merchants who could attest to Sasha's prowess when it came to intimidation. Threatening injury seemed the most prudent course here as well. His only concern was that Albanians were renowned for their toughness and brutality, as Sasha had heard from people who had tangled with their gangsters. He was willing to gamble that Bogdani had been sufficiently worn down by this isolating place to not put up a fight. As he considered this, he noticed that the others were staring at him with pleading eyes. Perhaps, Sasha thought as he placed three tiles next to an *E* to spell PUNE, if he needed to, he could get the former busboy to actually inflict the damage. He nodded to himself at the practicality of this plan though everyone else at the table thought he was nodding at the five-point word that nobody—out of apathy or politeness—challenged.

≈

Alone at home with her dogs, Janet Vosberg decided to take a swim. She lived about a quarter mile from a small lake and occasionally during the summer walked over with her three dogs—two Labs and a retriever—and took off her clothes, and they all swam across the lake and back. Then she rested for a while on the shore before walking back down the secluded path still unclothed. She had never swum in the lake this late in the year, but after her difficult day she thought the cold water would refresh her. It did, but she did not consider that the shock would shorten her breath and sap her strength, so by the time she was halfway back she had to turn on her back and change to a modified backstroke—floating as much as possible so only her stomach, breasts, and face were above the water like a series of small islands—in order to save energy. She emerged a few minutes later onto the muddy bank, shivering and gasping up at the stars while her dogs ran excitedly yapping down the path.

The exhaustion and relief made her feel like crying but she didn't allow herself the satisfaction. She had done something stupid and gotten in over her head through nobody's fault but her own. Crying would not help. She was mostly glad nobody witnessed her failure. A breeze made her skin tighten. The mud under her was gritty and slimy. She shivered but still needed a minute to gather the fortitude to get up and walk home. An image of that diner owner came to her, the immigrant that the inspector told her about. She pictured him and his family bustling around in that restaurant.

The thought further enervated her, and she felt her body loosen and settle into the mud as her eyes half closed. Only when she heard her dogs running back down the path to investigate her absence did she force herself up so they would not see her in such a weak position. There was a slight sucking sound as she lifted herself out of the mud, and she sat up heavily and waited for the barking to get closer. As they came into view she shifted her thoughts away from the restaurant owner. Now, in the middle of a crisis, was not the time to question her decisions. Her moment of weakness was over. The dogs ran to her and jockeyed for position to lick her face, then ran around the shore sniffing and barking to each other. She looked away from them and down at herself, at a layer of fat that had accumulated over the muscle around her midsection and rolled over itself as she sat hunched over still catching her breath. She told herself to focus on that area the next time she worked out. Flabby abs was a problem she could fix by working harder. She stood up, still naked and covered in mud, and walked back to her house.

≈

Later that same night, Arthur Reilly was at the Millsville Family Restaurant with Mërgim Bogdani's dead body. Arthur had tried to stay home but guilt overtook his desire to not fail any more than he already had that day. As he walked downtown to apologize for how he had acted that morning—but not for shutting down the restaurant—he thought that being alone gave him too much time to agonize over his decisions. It was as good a reason as any to be married. Even at the worst times of his marriage, when he felt uncomfortable and lonely in his own apartment with his wife next to him, there had been enough else to worry about without convincing himself to do something stupid, just to have something to do.

He should have gone back home as soon as he saw all the lights were out. Entering the diner could do no one, especially the Bogdanis, any good. But he had a professional curiosity about whether or not the door was open. It was. Since the Open sign was displayed and the door was unlocked, the restaurant could technically be considered to be operating. Whether he had the right, or even obligation, to go inside was arguable.

The smell tipped him off. He knew all the different ways a restaurant could smell and this—something like yogurt and sulfur—was not one of them. Later he would not know if he imagined that smell. He would also wonder if he entered the restaurant because of some feeling or premonition rather than professional concern. But no matter what he smelled or why he went in, he never understood why he didn't call out to see if anyone was inside. Perhaps he didn't want to wake anyone up. But this didn't add up since he immediately searched for the light switch. The fact was that it was too quiet, too still, and yet he felt he wasn't alone, so he wanted light simply so he wasn't in the dark. After feeling his way across the wall near the door without finding a switch, he went to check the kitchen. After three or four careful steps around tables and chairs he slipped, braced himself on a chair, and froze for a full minute before lifting his foot stickily off the floor and holding it six inches off the ground.

His options, as he saw them, were to continue on to the kitchen to find the light or to run away. Which was the responsible one he didn't know. He felt both that something in the restaurant was wrong and that he was doing something illegal; which of these was more true would determine his direction. The time to decide had already begun since he could hold his foot up in that position for only so long, and by the time his foot was trembling with exhaustion his eyes adjusted to the light sufficiently to see a form sitting in a nearby chair. He took a long step forward, past the pool, continued toward the kitchen, and found the light switch.

Now he was looking at Bogdani. He felt weak and sick, and when he finally dropped his eyes to the ground he saw his footprints leading from the pool of blood to the kitchen and then back to where he currently stood. The path brought to mind a placemat he had seen once with a child's puzzle where you tried to follow a pirate's footprints, discerning the correct set from other misleading footprints to find a buried treasure.

Like a wheel caught in snow that spins wildly until it melts everything below and finally catches on concrete and is able to lurch out, Arthur's thoughts came back under his control. He had two options: run out and throw his shoe in the river or call the police. Calling the police would ensure Bogdani's family didn't stumble across his body, but also might put Arthur under suspicion and cost him his job. Considering the inept Millsville police department, he assumed that if he ran nobody would ever know he had been there.

A car drove slowly down the street past the window. Without thinking, Arthur dashed back to the kitchen and turned out the lights. The car—which he now saw was a police car—abruptly stopped in the middle of the road. Arthur became aware of a gasping sound coming from deep within him. When he tried to quiet down he couldn't gather enough air to keep conscious and became dizzy. His gasping resumed but twice as loud, and just as he resolved to hold his breath and pass out, the police cruiser began moving again.

Arthur leaned back against the wall and slowly slid to the floor. He stared at where he knew Bogdani sat in the dark. Now that he had no option but to go, he saw how wrong it was to leave Bogdani like this just to save himself. He was still going to do it, of course. It was a line that he would never be able to uncross, but he walked over it willingly.

Thursday, September 19

When the knocking wouldn't stop Arthur forced himself to wake up. His head ached, there was a person next to him, and it was nearly time for his alarm to go off. Profoundly tired and miserable, he performed a quick review, hoping that by the time he finished, the person knocking would be gone: last night he found Bogdani dead; he stopped at the only bar that refused to adhere to the curfew (in order to not give in to big government, the owner told Arthur over and over); this was not Katie next to him but the pushcart woman—Anna—who had been waiting for Arthur on his front steps last night; his Cherokee was broken down and his own car was still parked at the office; a deadly illness was running unchecked and unidentified through the town; and, shit, he had walked all the way to his office after leaving the bar and written a report about what he had seen at the restaurant.

The knocking continued, so Arthur flung away his sheets and belched before preemptively turning off his alarm. He lifted the sheet just enough to glimpse Anna's naked body and nodded, allowing himself to be pleased about one decision the previous night.

Through the front window he saw Katie at the door. The panic this induced gave Arthur temporary reprieve from his headache, and he combed his hair with his hand to cover his receding hairline as much as possible.

"Did you hear?" she asked, pushing her way inside as soon as he unlocked the door.

He made a hesitant guttural sound and moved his head somewhere between a shake and nod.

"Drugs! Out of that stupid cart that's parked in front of my house. That's what I get a call about today. All these people still sick and now this," Katie said and collapsed into the only chair in Arthur's living room.

That Katie, without makeup and in pajama pants and a UW–Platteville sweatshirt, was sitting in his living room made Arthur feel that a goal had been accomplished. He had wanted this for a long time, even if he hadn't allowed himself to hope for it, and struggled to figure out what he could do to make her stay.

"They're staying at your house. Wouldn't you know?" he said.

"You inspected them, wouldn't you?"

"How'd you hear this?"

"Janet called this morning."

"Jesus, what time does she get up?"

Katie shook her head and sighed.

"I'm sure it's a rumor," Arthur said.

"Maybe," Katie said, seeming to relax a bit, "but the woman isn't at my place this morning. He," she rolled her eyes, "is up and making *fish* for breakfast, but she's gone."

Arthur nodded quickly.

"I asked where she was and he said something like, 'She is or she is not here. Who am I to say where daughter is?' I swear, Arthur, I can't have these people in my house for another second. They're unbearable. Last night we played Scrabble and I wanted to slit my wrists."

"Well," Arthur said judiciously.

"No, I'm serious, they're insane. And she's worse than him! He sits there like a sack of grapefruit but she constantly stares at me tapping those awful ugly boots on my carpet. I can't even talk to Adam about it or he'll give me a *look* like I'm too goddamn provincial to understand these New Yorkers."

"Well," Arthur said, glancing down the hall that led to his bedroom. He knew he needed to usher Katie out immediately. But she came to him because she could not talk to her husband. Her tired voice—like the sound of a dungeon door being unbolted—gave him hope.

"I almost hope they're selling this stuff so they'll be locked up. I want to know where they are so there's no chance they ever step foot in my house again. I don't know, Arthur. He brings these people into our home? I don't think I know him anymore. Sometimes I think back to when he was gone and marvel at how simple everything was."

Arthur didn't care, just then, about the conflict of interest of having had sex with the person Katie was complaining about. He also didn't care that his best friend (an odd term for an adult, but nevertheless apt) was her husband. She had longingly spoken of the time when they had been together. The joy this provided meant he could no longer pretend it wasn't exactly what he'd wanted all along.

He stopped listening and focused on her as a physical being, saw how her feet tucked under her, how she was swimming in the sweatshirt. He wanted to grab her like he was an out-of-control skydiver grasping onto the upper limb of a tree. He wanted to feel the closeness of her body when she actually wanted and needed it—he imagined her limbs squeezing back. He stifled the urge to lift her out of her chair and clutch her. It was at this moment he saw Anna storming down the hallway wrapped in a sheet.

"We aren't selling any drugs, you stupid bitch," she said as she entered the living room. "If you want to know, ask us. Don't come over to him and talk behind our backs."

Katie was shocked into silence. She only gaped at Arthur.

"What, I can't fuck him?" Anna said with a nod toward Arthur. "You have everything else so you need every man in the world too?"

"How do you," Katie began, then turned again to Arthur who tried to appear as confused as she was.

"Everyone knows," Anna said. "You think it's such a secret." She attempted to smirk triumphantly, but her expression fell and she only looked hurt and tired.

"Did you?" Katie said to Arthur.

"God, no," Arthur said, hoping he hadn't confessed anything to Anna while drunk.

Katie stood up slowly, like an elderly person. The look she gave him—not so much sad as frightened—as she walked out the door somehow didn't make Arthur feel much of anything. She was so afraid of getting caught. Or, more likely, was afraid of people *knowing*. Knowing she had done something bad. Knowing she had sex. Knowing she had wanted something she wasn't supposed to want. Maybe it was seeing her next to Anna—who certainly didn't seem to care what people knew or thought of her—but for a moment Arthur saw Katie with some distance, as some woman from a small town. Someone willing to sacrifice the more complex pleasures of life for comfort and anonymity. He wasn't entirely sure what this meant, only that he felt a little sorry for her. He was also aware that he might not be so different.

Before the door even clicked closed, Anna turned sharply and marched back to the bedroom, shouting to Arthur over her shoulder, "Now come in and fuck me before we have to go to work."

Arthur hesitated. For what seemed like a long time he stood in his living room and swiveled his head between the front door and the hallway leading to his bedroom. He had betrayed Katie more severely than they had ever betrayed her husband. He wanted to run outside to explain himself and tell her what she meant to him . . . but he also wanted to have sex with Anna again. Though he wavered, he was pretty sure what he was going to do. Maybe he was too tired of feeling guilty to care anymore. Or maybe, he rationalized, all this wasn't important when compared to other problems. Or maybe it dawned on him that the time to fight for Katie had been months ago. Maybe having sex was the imperfect remedy for the pain of what he'd lost. Or maybe he really was an asshole.

Whatever the reason, he had made his decision. When Anna called again from the bedroom he ran in and did what felt good.

≈

Showering in his moldy bathroom, Arthur had to figure out how to get to work without a car. He was toweling off when he heard the front door open and called out to Anna to see if he could ride with them to his office.

He regretted this almost immediately. Not only did he have to stand in Katie's front yard while they hooked the cart to the hitch, but he somehow ended up sitting between the Bykovs during the ride. He had to keep moving his legs out of the way of Sasha's vigorous shifting, which pushed him against Anna, who furtively rubbed against him with feline pressure, which brought uncomfortably salacious memories to Arthur's mind while his thigh was still in contact with her father's hand. Sasha also barraged him with questions about how they could begin operating as soon as possible, and Arthur was forced to thank him multiple times for the ride ("Office is far away! Is nice to not walk all of this distance, huh?").

The worst part was that Sasha refused to drop him anywhere but the front door of County Building C, despite Arthur's nearly begging him to let him out down the road. They both knew Sasha wanted as many witnesses as possible, but Arthur was in no position to insist since he had asked for the ride. Arthur closed his eyes in silent prayer as Sasha negotiated both truck and pushcart around the perimeter of the parking lot, twice loudly grinding the gears as he backed up. By the time Arthur finally emerged, people were watching the show out their office windows. Sasha then called out, "See you later, Inspector!" and beeped the horn twice. As the truck pulled away, he remembered he hadn't told them they couldn't legally operate their cart.

The upshot to his eventful morning was that Arthur had been able to keep his mind off the previous night as much as possible. Bogdani was always on the periphery of his thoughts. During any lull in activity (in the shower, for instance) and even a couple times when there was no lull (like while he was having sex with Anna), he could only think about his role in the man's death. Without considering it in depth Arthur saw himself as the primary cause for Bogdani's taking his own life (if, of course, he took his own life). He didn't know how he would be able to pretend nothing had happened.

It would have been a relief if the office were empty today, so of course everyone was there. The thought of reprimanding them for leaving early yesterday exhausted him. Before he went to the restaurant last night he had worked out his speech (something akin to "I'm not mad, I'm disappointed") but now he couldn't bring himself to deliver it. It wouldn't help anything, and he couldn't bear the contempt in their voices while they gave their lame excuses.

Sandra was on the phone when he came in. Not, of course, speaking to a concerned citizen or government official but, presumably, to her son—who must have been home from school—about the location of batteries for the TV remote. She squeezed the phone between her shoulder and ear and waved her hands at Arthur to get his attention. He waited at her desk for nearly three minutes until her son retrieved the batteries from the basement.

"Boys!" she said with a fake exasperated sigh when she finally hung up.

"Everything OK?" Arthur asked, as calmly as possible. "Not sick are they?"

"No," Sandra said, wary that Arthur bothered to inquire about her family at all, perhaps even worried it was some kind of trick. "Just home. Canceled school again today, you know. Illness and all."

"I didn't know that," Arthur said.

"They did!" she said eagerly. Then, wanting to continue to be the disseminator of gossip but not having additional information, she added, "Canceled it right up."

They didn't move for a moment, and she shifted her eyes from Arthur to her computer screen. "So . . . everything all right with you?"

"Did you have something for me, Sandy?" he said, reaching into his pocket and grasping his keys hard enough to cause himself a sharp pinch of pain.

She scrunched up her face, confused, then apparently remembered she had stopped him and sucked her lips against her teeth as though to say *I'm such a dope.* "Got a message for you." She handed him a slip of paper that read, "Dr. Ready (sp?) sounds British. Call back."

≈

"Tomatoes?" Janet said after a particularly hard softball toss against the wall.

"So that's what it's all from," an increasingly distracted Katie said as she picked up the softball and placed it back on Janet's desk. She had never picked up the ball before—her only act of rebellion had been to make Janet stand up and retrieve it after Katie had left the office.

"Do you not want me to throw the ball against the wall?" Janet asked suddenly.

"What?" Katie asked, taken off guard. "It's fine. It doesn't matter. I don't care. Tomatoes?"

Janet eyed her for a moment, then shrugged and regained her vitriol. "Tomatoes! All of this from a bad batch of tomatoes that happened to have been delivered here. I might have to wait another two years to run for Congress because of fucking tomatoes. I probably got screwed by a bunch of idiots in Guatemala who didn't wash their hands or took a shit on the floor of a truck or something."

Katie barely paid attention. She was furious at herself for not taking advantage of the opportunity to get Janet to stop throwing the softball. She always missed chances like this because she didn't want to hurt people's feelings. Like how she'd slunk out of Arthur's house that morning after the woman yelled at her, even though she was the one inconveniencing Katie. Or how Katie then lingered on Arthur's porch so he could come out and apologize, even though he shouldn't have let her leave in the first place. Or last night when she walked naked to bed and Adam only picked a fight about Scrabble and then worked on a crossword puzzle until after she fell asleep. She always gave people too many opportunities to do right, and when they were still jerks she thought of the perfect retort the minute after the right time had passed. Now, whether or not the moment was still ripe, she decided to finally say what she thought.

"A woman died," she said, "and we blamed that restaurant even though they probably didn't do anything wrong. It's despicable. What we did was unforgivable. We never considered other people."

"You're right," Janet said, biting her lip. "It doesn't look good for me. People won't like it."

Katie debated the merits of explaining the nuances of her argument to Janet.

"Then again," Janet continued, "it was better we did something instead of sitting on our hands. People won't care about that restaurant—it's not like we closed down the Piggly Wiggly."

"But the restaurant will probably have to close. Nobody will want to eat there anymore. What will those people do?"

"Yeah, well," Janet said, preoccupied and unconcerned. "Hopefully they'll move back to Armenia."

Who was this woman? And why was Katie trying to help her? Right now, Katie Bender's job was to figure out how to convince people that Janet didn't willingly deceive them and acted in everyone else's best interest, all so Janet could advance her own career. And though this was technically also in Katie's best interest, for maybe the first time in her life she couldn't convince herself to put her own family's comfort above what was right.

Katie studied the softball on Janet's desk, noting the scuffs and bruises from countless tosses against the wall. An idea formed, spreading through Katie like heat until she found herself on the verge of speaking.

"I think I'm going to quit," Katie said slowly, surprising herself with the news.

≈

Arthur sat at his desk staring at the report he had written the previous night after fleeing from Bogdani's body. The report's content and style reflected his state of mind at the time. He stopped reading halfway through (at the line, "I called him a failure in front of his son and fifteen hours later he was dead") because it stirred up the feelings he had tried to keep at bay all morning. When he leaned back he noticed Cal standing over him with his elbows draped over the cubicle partition, his eyes on Arthur's screen. He had the expression of a bored farmhand leaning over a fence waiting for the pigs to finish eating so he could take away the empty slop bucket.

"Fucking Bogdani, huh?" Cal said when Arthur finally acknowledged him.

"What about him?" Arthur said quickly, clicking the document closed.

"Reason for all this shit. Got Jake and everyone else sick. Killed that lady. You know she used to substitute-teach when I was in high school. You've been going to his place, right? Inspecting over there? Didn't you see nothing?"

Arthur exhaled deeply and tapped his desk with the knuckle of his middle finger, trying not to get annoyed. He wondered if Cal even remembered that he'd been caught with an underage girl yesterday.

"Actually just heard it isn't only that restaurant," Arthur said, finding himself unable to say Bogdani's name. "The doctor called. She said it was most likely caused by a shipment of tainted tomatoes—some offshoot of salmonella or E. coli or trichinosis. Apparently there was a similar outbreak in Minnesota recently. People here are displaying the same symptoms."

"Jeez," Cal said, a frown forming on his face and his eyes darting around as though he just realized he was hopelessly lost. He quickly became animated and slapped the cubicle partition. "I told them!" he said. "Ask anyone here, yesterday I said I bet it was something random. Something we couldn't do anything about anyway. All those people calling here and it wasn't even our fault. Doctors didn't even know."

"All true," Arthur said. Wanting to take advantage of Cal's eagerness, he added, "Why don't you get the numbers to all the restaurants in the county from the list and start calling them. Tell them to throw out all their tomatoes and to not serve them until we tell them different."

"I'm on it," Cal said. He stared blankly at Arthur, perhaps waiting for further instruction. Arthur shrugged and Cal slapped the cubicle wall once more and ducked away to his own desk.

Arthur kept his body completely still for about thirty seconds. He felt as if he had performed a trick that accidentally turned out to be real magic. Arthur had never heard "I'm on it" come out of Cal's mouth before, unless Cal perhaps said the words while telling a story and the "it" referred to a snowmobile.

Cal's newfound work ethic was even more peculiar since it was Arthur who was now dragging his feet. He had done nothing in the twenty minutes since hearing about the tomatoes, and he still had to figure out what to do about the report he wrote last night.

In his shock and drunkenness he had thought it was necessary to confess in some way, at least to himself, but of course he felt no relief. Now this evidence he created was out there waiting to be discovered. It could be deleted from the server easily enough. But, like every report he wrote, he had also placed a printed copy in the locked filing cabinet by Sandra's desk, and there was no way Sandra wouldn't notice him taking out a file and not returning it.

He was also anxiously awaiting the moment when the news of Bogdani's death would break, and he had to consider his expression when someone informed him. He doubted he would have been very affected by it if he hadn't been involved. He barely knew the guy—people he barely knew probably died all the time. If he hadn't already seen Bogdani dead, he would probably think about the need to fill out paperwork and how to sufficiently clean the dining room in order to begin serving food again. His lips would tighten, his eyebrows would lower, and his face would turn away as he calculated what to do. A cold but honest reaction. He couldn't react like this now, though. Not because it would give him away, but because he wasn't capable of such a detached response. The blood was sure to drain from his face, his mouth would open, sounds would come from his throat.

Assuming the body hadn't yet been discovered, Arthur could still go to the restaurant pretending to remove Bogdani's tomatoes. This was what he would do if Bogdani were still alive, and would be ideal to pretend to do now except that Arthur couldn't bring himself to do it. The idea of going over there and seeing the body again made Arthur shudder.

No, the most he was capable of was visiting other restaurants to ensure they removed their tomatoes, and when he heard the news he'd act as though he had already been told. That way he could shake his head and say, "What a shame."

Before he left for his inspections he took advantage of this reckless mood and quickly deleted the report from the database. After that he felt better and wondered if something was seriously wrong with him, since the relief was without contradiction. Then he got up and, without explanation, left to perform his inspections.

≈

Sasha Bykov drove directly to the Millsville Family Restaurant after dropping off Anna and the pushcart on the highway. He had no doubt he'd be able to begin operating right after the purchase since his daughter had slept at the inspector's and they'd driven him to work. He burst into the restaurant, full of confidence, and immediately saw the body. He wasn't so much afraid or surprised as he was confused, and he stood a respectful distance away and nodded sadly. Then he sat in a chair by the window and cursed out loud.

He tried to keep calm by telling himself that Bogdani had been too weak to deal with the pressure, that all this was his own fault, but that brought Sasha no consolation. He had gone too far, and even if he were able to buy the restaurant—which he now assumed would be a relatively simple cash transaction—he would be constantly reminded that he did not deserve his new life.

It was all over anyway, if anyone had seen Sasha enter the restaurant. He didn't think anyone had been watching, but it was so quiet and empty out on the street that any movement was surely acutely observed. A part of him hoped there had been a witness so he'd be forced to come clean, explain his role, and have no choice but to move on. He'd chosen Millsville only because he had a free place to stay—his only connection was Adam. But the idea had already lodged in Sasha's brain that he was going to start a restaurant here so he was going to do it. Motives and reason didn't play a role once the idea solidified. He'd have similar difficulties anywhere he went, so he might as well bull ahead.

He turned his head more toward the window, to keep the unpleasantness at the center of the room out of sight. Outside, a large figure with a black mask covering its nose and mouth loomed above him. Sasha jumped out of his seat and took a few steps back. His first thought was that Death had come to punish him. Death must have heard the chair shift because he put a large hand over his eyes to cover the glare so he could see inside the infected restaurant.

Sasha checked his breath, annoyed that he was spooked by his own ghost story. Then the phone rang and Sasha stifled a gasp and put a hand to his chest to rein his pounding heart. The ringing startled the man outside as well and he fled.

In the calmest of times, Sasha could not stand a ringing phone that was not picked up. Now it threatened to drive him insane. He walked around the perimeter of the dining area toward the kitchen, careful not to disturb the scene. At the swinging doors he examined the footprints leading from the congealed pool of blood. This gave him hope that he wasn't alone in the knowledge of Bogdani's death. Perhaps this man even killed Bogdani. If there was a murderer, it could be proven Sasha had done nothing wrong—he might even be a valuable witness. By the time the phone stopped ringing Sasha was convinced that these were the killer's footprints. He also decided to leave by the back door.

≈

Arthur began his tomato disposal at Subway, which had started serving breakfast a few months earlier. An easy inspection. The part-time employee wasn't likely to make a fuss, and the Subway would quickly recover if closed down. People trusted the Subway to have structures in place to quickly fix any issue and punish any offender but would feel betrayed and mistrustful of similar infractions by a restaurant like the MFR. There they'd assume one man's incompetence or laziness led to the dangerous condition. But the good faceless folks behind the Subway franchise know exactly how not to make people sick. They are tried and true. They know sickness is bad for business. The people of Millsville had never heard of anyone getting sick at a Subway, which has probably done research and spent money to figure out how to be safe and trustworthy. A family running a place like the Millsville Family Restaurant can't do that. Subway, however, has already considered how to impress people with cleanness. "I mean, just look at all that stainless steel, those sneeze guards, and the gloves on those sandwich artists' hands!" the people will say, should the Subway be accused. Outside of Subway, Hardee's, and Pizza Hut, no restaurant in Millsville had those safeguards in place. A family like the Bogdanis doesn't want to run that kind of business. They don't want to work in that sterile environment every day—it's soul crushing. It ensures bland, safe food.

The Subway opened nearly fifteen years before, and people in town still used it as a measure of time: "Oh sure, the Opelts bought that house about the time the Subway opened." Other benchmarks recalled the times that the football team won state, Arndt's flooring store burned down under mysterious circumstances, and the Grouse River flooded. The years of these events were in themselves unimportant. They were gauges of the town's own time. You'd never hear someone say, "Oh sure, I remember when Bush was elected, right around when Arndt's burned down." The election and the fire didn't happen on the same plane of time and space. Someone would have to do the math in their head, cohere the national and local. Arthur was not yet tuned in to this local scale, but lately, the more he heard it referenced, he started to understand how the flood fit into a distance of his own life. He wasn't sure how he felt about being absorbed into this system, indeed he didn't notice it enough to dwell on it—when he did, he tried not to let the fact that he was losing himself in this small town frighten him.

But he was fully aware that these past couple days—with a serious illness and two deaths—would become a major event on this town's time scale. Throwing away the tomatoes from a Subway sandwich shop off Highway 9 in Millsville, Wisconsin, was perhaps insignificant in the larger scheme, but hundreds or even a few thousand people were not going to forget it for perhaps the next fifty years. Arthur, in his capacity as a civil servant, was mostly concerned about how individuals were being affected right now, but this tug of local history—filled as it was with floods and fires and store openings—was present in his mind, as though it was forcing him to take his place here, like a kindergarten teacher pushing a reluctant child onto the stage of a school play.

Inside the Subway there were, surprisingly, three people sitting at tables and two others in line. Either these people trusted the corporation or they were passersby unaware of the risk. Arthur assumed the people at the table—two large-sweatered women with permed hair and a man with a Packers sweatshirt and a duck call dangling down like a necklace—were locals. When his glance lingered to check if they were eating tomatoes, one woman nudged the other and they all glared up at him with suspicion that bordered on contempt. Arthur was reminded of New York, where this expression was the norm toward anyone wearing a badge.

When the girl behind the counter spotted him, she became flustered. The man who was ordering repeated, "No spinach. No spinach. No spinach!" but the girl's gloved hand automatically moved toward the bin of spinach to complete the Egg White Spinach Flatbread Wrap. When the spinach touched the bread the customer threw up his hands: "Come on!" The girl hastily threw out the spinach-tainted wrap and apologized profusely.

Staring in fright at Arthur as he explained the situation, she watched silently as he stepped past her to check their stock for tomatoes, wringing her plastic-covered hands, unsure if she should let him do this but not daring to disrespect his badge and demeanor. This was a no-win situation for the girl, whose green name tag read Jodie. Today was simply the first time she had to negotiate a world of superiors, a life lesson in deciding who had more power over her: her employers or her government. She apparently decided government, since it would presumably have power over her for her entire life, while the owner of this particular Subway would merely have power over her until she quit.

Together they identified three sealed containers of tomatoes as well as yesterday's leftovers covered and stored in the refrigerator. Jodie threw these into the garbage as Arthur watched, and then she tied up the bag and took it outside. For the first time in the past two days, Arthur had done something potentially helpful.

As he emerged from the back room, he began humming a cheery little tune and realized with embarrassment that everyone in the restaurant was blatantly staring at him. He quieted, put up his hands as though protecting himself, and said, "What?" Nobody answered. They all shook their heads and began muttering among themselves.

After a few parting words with Jodie, he started to leave the restaurant with renewed vigor. A woman tossed a copy of the *Chase County Register* on a table as Arthur was passing. Seeing his picture and the headline, he said, "What's this?" The woman didn't reply. Her face remained stone still.

Arthur picked up the paper and walked absently out of the restaurant. Just before the door closed behind him, Jodie called out quietly, "Sir, the paper's ours," but he didn't hear. Now the restaurant began buzzing about the rogue inspector, how he threw out the tomatoes and stole the newspaper.

≈

In East Troy, Ismail and Drita Bogdani bickered with their relatives as they packed their bags. Actually, Drita and her sister did most of the fighting, but Ismail and his cousin had been the cause. As they folded up their shirts and searched for a lost sock, Drita spoke harshly in a mix of Albanian and English to her sister, who was standing alongside her crying daughter in the doorway as though blocking them from leaving, though they had ordered them to go.

Lately Drita had become increasingly aware that she was the cause of her and her sister growing apart. This awareness did nothing to lessen the tension, however. As her own misfortunes compounded, Drita couldn't stop thinking that she and Mërgim had come to this country first, had suffered nearly alone against poverty and the inability to communicate, had to impose on family friends—basically strangers—until Mërgim found a job and figured out how they would survive. Her sister and brother-in-law had it easy by comparison. Upon their arrival they moved into the Bogdanis' one-bedroom apartment. Mërgim got his brother-in-law a job at his warehouse. Drita introduced her sister to the language center and showed her where to shop, how to drive, and how to apply for a license. It took her younger sister weeks to learn everything Drita had struggled to figure out in months, and then her always-smarter sister began giving the lessons. They had never been anything but generous after their successes, always offered to bring the Bogdanis in, but both she and Mërgim were too proud to accept—he especially was convinced that the brother-in-law smirked as he gave the proposal. Now the wound created by unfortunate luck and unwise choices was beginning to fester, and Drita couldn't check her anger toward her sister, though she knew it was unwarranted.

In the car Drita's frustration turned to her son, who had started the fight. "Why did you hit her? My son does not hit girls."

Ismail slunk down in his seat and felt miserable. He much preferred being in the house where his mom had been on his side, fighting against her own family for his sake. Now all he had to look forward to was a long ride back to his father.

"Answer me. This is serious." She had started the car but didn't move from the driveway, though her sister and niece were staring at them from the front porch. "You can't hit someone, especially in their own house."

Ismail stared at his aunt and cousin out the car window. He wanted to apologize to his mom but knew he would begin crying if he said anything contrite. Possibly he could keep his composure if he were to swear at them or if he called his cousin a bad name, but anything else would cause him to break down and he didn't want his younger cousin to witness this weakness. She would surely use his tears against him for the rest of his life. He wanted his mom to drive away from this place, but he didn't want to go home.

"I will go back there and get the whole story from them. I will make you apologize to her if you don't tell me why you did what you did right now."

That his mom seemed to be taking their side was too much, and he slid farther down in his seat as a tear fell down his face. His cousin had made fun of their restaurant for its troubles and said her parents' restaurant always got perfect scores from the health department. She called them "dirty Albanians" even though she and her family were as Albanian as the Bogdanis. She told him that they were going to lose their restaurant and will be kicked out of the country for being too poor, but if he was lucky, Ismail's father could come work for her father busing tables—and that was when Ismail hit her in the mouth, cutting her lip and causing her to spit blood into the sink between wails. Ismail knew that his father had been in this country longer than hers and got her father his first job, but that her father had invested wisely and his had not. Just last summer his cousin's family visited the beaches of Albania for an entire month while someone else ran their restaurant. As far as Ismail knew, his father hadn't taken a day off in years. And though explaining all this to his mom could at least partially absolve Ismail of wrongdoing, he could not bring himself to repeat his cousin's words to her on the off-chance they could be confirmed as true.

His mother saw the tear fall and shifted the car into drive. They would go back to Millsville and take their chances getting sick. At least they would all be together. She called her husband as they drove but got no answer. He must have been either cleaning or brooding. She would call again.

≈

Eldred Holmwood had seen plenty of dead bodies. In Vietnam mostly, but over the past twenty-five years, since he began living on the streets of Millsville and in the basement of the United Church of Christ in winter, he had come across six corpses: two—a woman and a man, six years apart—washed up on the banks of the Grouse River; a drunk driver who had crashed his car into a retaining wall near the high school (the same night of a football game, shattered glass mixed in with the wrappers and napkins and ticket stubs, illuminated by the car's blinking emergency lights); folks who had died naturally—one in the park, one on a porch, and one on their lawn. And now he found Bogdani dead in his restaurant.

Mornings he came to the back door of the Millsville Family Restaurant and was given a coffee and a day-old donut. Today nobody was in the kitchen so he left. When, by instinct, he returned later, he entered and found Bogdani at the table, a gun a few feet away from his dangling hand. He went to the phone, dialed 911, told the operator what had happened, and went outside to wait for the police to arrive.

≈

Only the secretary was in the front office of the *Chase County Register* when Arthur arrived. She was around seventy-five, had tightly curled gray hair, and wrote the "Good Ol' Days" column for the paper about events (quilting bees, hay rides, parades, Halloween costume contests, county fairs, Miss Millsville beauty pageants) from the town's distant and not-so-distant past. Now she was knitting and looking down at the *Milwaukee Journal Sentinel* spread out over her desk. When Arthur said her name, she looked up sheepishly. When he asked if Adam was in, a voice from deeper in the office snorted and called out "Good luck!" She went to the back to get Adam.

Adam emerged from the back office wearing a subdued—for him—plum-colored polo shirt with yellow-and-emerald plaid golf pants. His eyes were down and his lips were curled, either angrily or apologetically. Arthur had never seen Adam contrite before—he didn't think Adam capable of remorse or admission of guilt. Seeing him like this did not square with his previous conceptions of his friend. Arthur stumbled over his thoughts, recalculating how to begin.

"Why?" Arthur asked.

"Christ," Adam began, but then stopped and lifted his head slightly.

Arthur was thrown off by the hesitation—Adam was not one to hesitate—until he heard sirens in the distance. Sirens were rare around here, and when they occurred people automatically made for the nearest window to identify police, fire, or ambulance, and then determined the direction and proximity. If close, they walked the dog over and investigated themselves. If it drifted into the distance, they turned on their radios. It had taken years for Arthur to conform to this routine—indeed, when he first arrived, the lack of sirens was alarming.

Hearing it coming closer, Adam and Arthur both made their way to the big front window and stood silently until first one and then another police car sped past with full lights and sirens. Without a word the two men went to the sidewalk and watched as the cars stopped in front of the Bogdanis' restaurant.

"Look, I'm sorry about the article," Adam said while they stared.

Arthur didn't respond. More people emerged from the doorways along Maple Street. Arthur should have said something to hide his fear, but at that moment he felt as though he had killed Bogdani. Not caused the man to kill himself but actually pulled the trigger. It took everything Arthur had to stay calm.

"I'd take it back if I could. At the time I was just thinking . . ." Adam hesitated and seemed about to continue but never started back up.

"What?" Arthur said. "What were you thinking at the time?" He wanted Adam to bring up the affair with Katie, wanted him to say that he knew about Arthur's desire to take Adam's place in his home. It would have been a welcome diversion. Anything was better than watching these police cars and pretending he didn't know what was going on. Even a beating from Adam would have been preferable, but he would accept having a conversation about Katie. Penance. Arthur had never truly understood what the word meant or why someone would ever welcome pain. He had always seen his problems arising from outside forces and the punishments he endured undeserved. Now he wanted to feel bad to keep from feeling worse.

"Nothing. I'm sorry is all," Adam said.

"No, what was it?" Arthur said, turning toward Adam and nearly panting as he spoke. "Tell me! Why did you print it? For fuck's sake, I'm your friend, you have to tell me. Why did you print it? Why would you write that about me? Why not talk to me first? Why not tell me why now? What did I do to deserve it? Fucking tell me! I can take it, tell me!"

"I'm sorry," Adam whispered as they watched a policeman walk unsteadily out of the restaurant, lean against his car, and throw up.

≈

Katie heard the sirens long before the police cars screamed by. Her instinct was to follow them, but she had decided to disentangle herself from the concerns of the county. Instead, she texted her daughters to make sure they were safe, and ignored the excitement.

Quitting had been a rash decision. And though in the right, she still felt the strong, nagging voice of responsibility asking how she expected to pay the mortgage and eat and put gas in the car (let alone pay for their daughters' college in a couple years) on only Adam's salary. She tried to numb herself to these concerns but she was not the type to push good sense aside.

It had been years since she truly had nothing to do. That she had gained the time by taking the moral high ground made her feel buoyant, and she wanted to explore her newfound independence. But the exhilaration soon wore off. She wasn't walking toward anything. She chose this path because it was the opposite direction of home and work. She wondered what a person who had nothing to do did. Eldred Holmwood seemed happy enough roaming around town. High school kids drove around the block over and over or sat on the hoods of their cars in front of the hardware store. Sad people sat in bars and drank in the middle of the day. None of these seemed appealing. She decided to go to the Kwik Trip and get a tin of chewing tobacco.

She chewed tobacco off and on since her freshman year of high school. Her first time had been on a dare when some older girls wanted her to throw up. They were rugged girls who grew up on farms and told her that for her first time she needed to swallow her disgusting mint-tobacco saliva. Katie knew better though, and after the initial spinning high and fiberglass irritation she calmly spit the waste into a Sprite bottle and told the girls she didn't know what the big deal was.

Throughout high school she capitalized on her disarmingly sweet looks to steal tins of Skoal from the display on the counter of the Kwik Trip, and at night she would happily stick a pinch in her upper lip as she did her homework. She never told anyone she did this. Even at parties while the other girls, to keep up, took dips from boys and made faces as they indelicately spit into empty cans of beer, Katie would staunchly refuse. It was a fun game but a terrible habit—at least for a girl. Boys let the tins rub circle outlines in the back pockets of their jeans, but Katie hid her stolen tins under the Pringles in a can she kept half filled. She would have far preferred her father caught her having sex than discover a stolen tin of chewing tobacco in her room. Sex was expected, but she didn't want to see the look on his face if he discovered his little girl chewed.

In college she more or less gave it up. The lack of privacy of dorms and shared apartments didn't allow her even the secret indulgence of keeping a dip in while she studied. From time to time, during Christmas break or when exams were at their most stressful, she would buy a tin and allow herself a single glorious dip before throwing the rest away—but she stopped altogether after getting married, at least until her daughters were born.

On her first solo trip (to a friend's wedding in Tomah) after giving birth to Jenny, she stopped to get gas and saw a cardboard advertisement for Skoal bending in the wind. The snowy mountain range depicted behind the hockey puck–like tin on the sign was meant to evoke Skoal's crisp mint flavor. By the time the pump clunked full Katie realized that this stupid advertisement, meant to entice people to buy a product designed to relieve them of their lower jaws, was making her cry. Still, she was haunted by the fact that, for a few years at least, chewing tobacco was the closest she would get to the sensation of being on a mountain. It also reminded her of those quiet nights alone in her room, lying on the floor with a book open and sucking on her silent pleasure. Basically, it was a siren call of freedom—a secret freedom in which only three farm girls had ever witnessed her participation.

Now, any time she was alone and out of town she bought a tin and chewed her brains out until she was near home. These opportunities rarely presented themselves, and when they did the expectation and immediate gratification left her feeling guilty and satisfied, much like having sex with Arthur. A predictable yet ever-surprising activity, and that she could walk to the Kwik Trip and buy a tin of Skoal renewed her faith in herself. For at least the next half hour or so, she had a way to bring herself joy.

She had never bought a tin from this Kwik Trip, but she knew from surreptitious glances while buying milk or chips or paying for gas that they had her brand. On the walk over she had decided on Skoal Mint because that had been her favorite growing up. She stood in front of the counter pretending to examine an LED flashlight keychain while someone checked out. She planned to buy a tin and a Diet Coke (her favorite combo), sit at the picnic tables behind the Pizza Hut (which didn't open until noon), and spend the morning blissed out with a sizable wad tucked in her lip.

Katie knew the cashier by name (Carol) and occupation only, and they would usually exchange a few words about Katie's purchases or the weather, so Katie had already planned what she would say if questioned: "Oh, I got the father-in-law in town." But when she finally got to the counter with her Diet Coke and cake donut, a man Katie knew as Jerry Bochinski came in and stood behind her in line while Carol examined and then wordlessly scanned Katie's purchases. Katie cursed this gigantic man and decided to abandon her plan. Another witness was too risky—she imagined them talking about her after she left the store. But when the cashier asked if Katie needed anything else, Bochinski seemed to take it as his cue to speak and said, "Hey Carol, hear about what happened downtown yet?"

"Something going on?" Carol asked.

"Just driving down Maple there when all these cop cars are pulled up in front of the MFR with lights going, so I pull over in the park to see what's going on when an ambulance comes. So a few minutes later I go up to Burt Butzler, who's outside the restaurant and ask him point blank, 'Burt, what's going on?' Thought it was the illness or something, you know? Turns out the guy there that runs the restaurant there killed himself."

"No way!" Carol said.

"Sure did," Bochinski said, with feeling, "that's the way Burt tells it. Guess the guy couldn't take getting all those people sick, killing Theresa Dorshorst like he did."

Katie had been holding her debit card about two inches above her open purse since Bochinski had launched into his story. She kept it there when she said quietly, "But he didn't do anything wrong. It turns out he wasn't any more to blame than anyone else."

Carol and Bochinski looked at each other and scrunched up their faces in confusion.

"Heard on the radio it was from the MFR. They even shut it down," Carol said.

"Tomatoes," Katie said, dropping her card back in her purse and noticing her hand begin to shake.

"What's that?" Carol asked.

"It was all caused by tomatoes."

"Nah," Bochinski delicately corrected. "I heard it too on the radio. Turns out the MFR did it. Makes sense, you know. Something funny about that place. You know, I think he might have been," he lowered his voice, "Muslim."

Carol shook her head as though shaking off disbelief, ready to move past the initial surprise of the news and get on with her day. "Well, it's all just a bunch of bad news," she said. Then she looked up at Katie and added, "Anything else, dear?"

"What?" Katie asked.

"Anything else for you?"

"Yes," Katie said. "A tin of Skoal Mint."

Carol nodded and grabbed the tin out of the dispenser.

"Didn't know you chewed," Carol said.

Katie examined the tin as though she had never seen such a thing before, then shifted her eyes up to meet Carol's and said absently, "I like to chew tobacco from time to time."

"Well, all right then," Carol said.

~

"Eldred," Adam said. "You don't think he could have done it?"

Arthur shook his head and said, "Why would he call it in?" He added, "Besides, Burt said it was suicide." Arthur was still running over how he had acted in the restaurant around those two pale, wide-eyed policemen and two EMTs. He didn't think he had been any more suspicious than anyone else. Once he had tried to get close to the pool of blood so he could conceivably argue that was how his footprints got on the floor, but Adam had warned him away.

"Could have been an accident," Adam said. "Guns have a way of going off."

"Could be," Arthur said. He swallowed and added, "For some reason I hope so."

"If it was, there's no way that police force is going to figure it out. You know what we used to call Burt in high school?" Adam asked.

"What?"

"Donkey dick."

Despite his mood Arthur chuckled at the schoolboy joke.

"Not because he has a big penis or anything," Adam said, "just because his head looks like one. He was that kid in high school you let hang around so there's an outlet for the teenage need to be an asshole. We abused that guy and he took it so we'd be his friend. Now he dishes it all back out." Adam paused and added, "He is the stupidest person I've ever known."

"That crime scene didn't exactly seem shipshape," Arthur said. "You see when someone spilled hot apple cider?"

"Right! Plus they let you in without a word." Adam dropped his eyes. "I only mean that you have actual motive. You were one of the last people to see him alive. You shut down his restaurant and blamed him for causing this illness. You guys might have fought. They should have questioned you or at least made you stay outside."

Arthur's breath became shaky. He forgot Adam was actually a capable journalist despite his weird beliefs and the product he turned out each week. Arthur forced himself to speak to fill in the guilty silence, "He didn't cause this sickness, you know?"

"I assumed as much. At least from what Katie told me."

"No, they found out it was from a contaminated shipment of tomatoes. We don't know where specifically—not even if they are from restaurants or grocery stores. They could be from an isolated source or they might have been delivered all over the county."

"Probably imported from Mexico," Adam said. "I'll bet they weren't from around here."

"It doesn't matter where they came from," Arthur said. "Tomatoes are tough to clean properly and aren't often cooked. If something's on them, it'll probably get eaten."

They were on their way to the Piggly Wiggly so Arthur could watch them throw away their tomatoes. Adam had joined him, Arthur assumed, to process what they had seen, or to mine some more dirt on Arthur. Now they were both silent and Arthur was grateful to let the subject of blaming Bogdani drop.

"So how long are those people staying at your house?" Arthur asked. He spoke to break the silence, to get out of his own head, but as soon as he said it he wished he had said something else.

"I don't think Katie likes it," Adam said. "But she doesn't like much of anything."

"I spoke to him yesterday," Arthur said, remembering Adam's favor. "Saw him twice actually. Once at the restaurant and then in my office."

"He said you couldn't help. I was hoping you could, but I understand. He's demanding."

"You don't think," Arthur said, hesitating, "that he could have had anything to do with it?"

"With what?"

Arthur raised his eyebrows and cleared his throat.

"That? God, no. Of course not," Adam said confidently, though as they continued on he began his compulsive jiggling of the copper coil in his pocket.

"Do you ever regret moving back here?" Arthur asked. He knew Adam had grown up in Millsville, gone to college in Chicago, worked on a couple different newspapers around the Midwest, and then moved back on his own volition to take over the *Chase County Register* after the editor-in-chief died. It fascinated Arthur that an intelligent person could choose to move here knowing what it had to offer. Of course, trying to predict Adam's behavior wasn't always a logical task.

"No," Adam said resolutely. This was the expected answer. Since leaving the restaurant Adam had been more thoughtful and less rigid than usual. This question seemed to set him straight. "Why, do you?" he asked.

"All the time," Arthur said. "Pretty much every day on my drive to work. But I had no choice. *You* know that."

"There's always a choice."

"You know this was the only job I applied for that didn't check my previous employment? I gave them all the general number for the health department in New York, and every other job I was considered for called and asked for a more direct number since it's impossible to navigate through the switchboard and actually speak to someone. Here I'll bet they just passed my résumé along." The one benefit of Adam's article was that it allowed Arthur to speak freely about his past.

"That's not right," Adam said.

"For me or them?" Arthur said, then continued, "I don't care anyway. I was desperate. You know I was on food stamps? A step away from welfare?"

He had never said any of this out loud and hadn't expected to feel such a rush of relief. Lying to get the job made him constantly fear getting fired, and he still felt distant shame when he bought groceries, remembering how he had walked to a supermarket thirteen blocks away from his tiny, post-divorce apartment in Astoria to make sure he wasn't recognized.

"I know plenty of people who had been on food stamps and welfare. Smart people. Writers and artists," Adam said.

"You don't believe in public assistance," Arthur said. "You're always saying people should make it on their own."

"But you took it. At least own up to it. Don't lie to cover it up."

Arthur shook his head. The frustration of talking to Adam surprised him every time.

"Those people you knew were creating something," Arthur said. "They were trying to do something difficult and meaningful. All I did was fail for no reason. I tried to live a normal life and I couldn't do it. I had nothing to overcome and I still needed help to live. It's humiliating to fail at being average."

"You tried to be average?"

"Not at the time," Arthur said. "Back then I was, you know, living my life. It was afterward when I was miserable. That was when I realized how nice it had been to be average."

Arthur didn't know why he was defending himself, or if they were fighting, or why either of them cared who was right or wrong. All this was in the past. It felt now as if it had happened a long time ago and to someone else.

They were outside the Piggly Wiggly. Adam seemed ready to accompany Arthur inside, and Arthur almost looked forward to telling his friend that he couldn't. They paused before the automatic door like they were at the end of a first date and one was about to inform the other that he wasn't interested.

But when Arthur turned toward Adam, he saw Sasha's truck parked in the lot.

Adam saw him staring and said, "Didn't he give you a ride to work this morning?"

Before Arthur could answer, Sasha came out of the store carrying two plastic grocery bags full of packages of hot dog buns. He was staring distractedly at the ground until he noticed the two of them, smiled broadly, and said, "Hello! My friend and neighbor."

Arthur turned and walked inside. He resolved that no matter what other pressing work he had to do that day, he would get to the bottom of Sasha's involvement in Bogdani's death. Whether to do any practical good or to alleviate his own guilt he didn't know and certainly did not care.

≈

Shortly after Katie quit, Janet received a call that Arthur Reilly had gotten a ride to work with those suspected drug dealers who were operating that cart out on the highway. She thanked the caller (Sandra at the health department), hung up, grabbed the softball, and set it back down on her desk when she remembered she was alone.

After what she had read in the paper that morning she could fire him (though her first reaction to the story had been that they had messed up by hiring him in the first place), but her instinct was to keep him. No reason to give up leverage, especially at the start of a campaign.

She quickly forgot about Arthur when the call came in about Mërgim Bogdani. Two people were dead in less than twenty-four hours from basically unnatural causes. People would not feel safe. But was a dead immigrant necessarily bad for her? Theresa Dorshorst, sure, people knew her. If Theresa could die, it could happen to anyone. But an immigrant who poisoned them and then commits suicide doesn't have much to do with her constituents. Maybe that's just what these people do? It wasn't for the residents of Chase County to speculate. Maybe, Janet thought, she could even incorporate an anti-immigration platform into her campaign. In a couple weeks, when people stop thinking they need to feel sad for the man's family, they might support keeping immigrants out of the state entirely so a mess like this wouldn't happen again.

She was suddenly glad she hadn't yet called the radio station about the tomatoes. She'd get in touch with Reilly and tell him to get every tomato out of her county as quickly and quietly as possible or she'd can him and press charges for lying on his résumé. The word would soon get out about the source of the illness, sure, but it would all be too confusing to ever know for certain. Plus, who knows, since the tomatoes might have come from Mexico (she had done some research and found that the US had recently made a trade agreement with Mexico specifically for the import of tomatoes, though she had no idea where the offending tomatoes were actually from), she could find a way to integrate it into her new platform anyway.

There, she thought, as she went to the window. She handled everything without anyone's help. She decided not to consider what Katie would say in response to her current plan (something weakly contrary, no doubt) and wondered if she even wanted her back. Yes, she did—there was too much history and intimacy between them to cut her out. It wasn't as fun without Katie around. Perhaps Janet wouldn't bring her along if she won her congressional seat, but she wanted her near now.

Outside, she was pleased to see that only one of the three pedestrians in view still wore a mask. Could be a sign life was getting back to normal.

This could all be a blip on the town's radar in a week or, more likely, a month.

≈

Anna had already sold two bags of meth to a truck driver and some heroin to a high school girl by the time her father arrived with the reinforcements of hot dog buns. The girl had been so nervous and overpaid by so much that Anna was sure the girl wouldn't rat her out. After listening outside of Katie's bedroom that morning and hearing they were under suspicion, her father had forbidden her from selling anything other than food, but ever since Anna caught Katie talking behind her back she refused to give in. She simply lied to her father and hid the drugs far off the road under a large clump of dirt.

When her father pulled up she was in the field near the hiding place, poking around the overgrown weeds and wildflowers in her boots. She had invented a game of throwing leftover bread for small birds to pluck out of the air, and when they missed the piece Anna would try to catch the bread on its way down. She looked so innocent as he watched from the road, throwing the bread with an awkward underhand motion, stalking to catch it as though she was walking on stilts, angrily shaking her head when it dropped to the ground, and clapping when the birds plucked it. Tears came to his eyes. This wholesome scene made him want to live here even more, so perhaps the purity of this place could rub off on them both. That her innocence was so out of character also allowed him to glimpse how his harshness—which he had considered necessary in order to give them a better life—had hardened his daughter. Normally he would shrug this off, recognizing it as a product of the world rather than the choices he had made, but he was still shaken after seeing what had happened to the Albanian and couldn't let himself off the hook.

He remembered fondly how he and his wife used to watch young Anna like this, from afar, commenting on how beautiful a person they had made, contemplating what she would one day become. He wondered what his wife would think of him now. She had never approved of Sasha breaking the law—well, outside of tax evasion—but always allowed him his secrets. She would not have tolerated involving Anna though. This sudden recognition of her judgment from the beyond made his feet go cold with dread.

Now, as he watched Anna play her game, he knew he had to change his ways in honor of his beloved wife. He vowed that from here on he would never commit another illegal act, though it was the cornerstone of his current plan.

A car pulled up across the road and he turned away from his daughter. A brown Dodge Charger—a Chase County patrol cruiser—crunched against the gravel shoulder and parked for a long time with its lights flashing. Sasha looked back at Anna but could not locate her in the field. She seemed to have disappeared.

The hassle of more governmental interference weighed heavily on him. Sasha quickly sized up the man as he got out of the cruiser and decided that flattery was his best tool to sway this crew-cut, acne-scarred, middle-aged police officer.

"What you got going here?" the policeman asked as he walked up.

"Hello, Officer! I am selling hot dogs on this beautiful day. I can get you something," Sasha said, feeling tired from the obsequious banter before he even finished speaking.

"Got a license I can look at?"

Sasha gave the officer his driver's license and New York City permits. "It is OK," he said. "Ask Arthur Reilly at health department. I give him ride to work this morning in my truck!"

The officer said they had received complaints, and Sasha, confused, told him that he couldn't imagine what they could be about.

He wished Anna was here—this would be her cue to step in and flirt with the man to put him off guard. He wished he were legally operating a pushcart that had never sold methamphetamines to truckers. He wished he wasn't going to bribe this guy.

It all came back to him, why it was necessary to bend the law from time to time. Ever since coming to this country, all he had known was obstacles. He saw little choice but to skirt some rules in order to get the same things that came so easily to other people. His whole life his desire to go through the proper channels had been eroded by the drudgery of waiting in lines only to be confronted with incompetence. He had never been part of the system because the system was run by people who only wanted to retain their place within it, or move up in it, but cared very little for people outside of it. He had seen plenty of this in New York City while he paid his fines or filed for permits or fought off litigants, but here, in the middle of nowhere, they didn't even seem to pretend to want to help. They held on to what they had as though it was worth having, as though someone else was always trying to grab it away.

If his behavior had made his daughter a little less happy-go-lucky, perhaps it was a blessing. What was his job as a father if not to prepare his daughter for the world?

He allowed the policeman to search his cart. The man found nothing and asked to see permits from the county.

"I can pay fee for paperwork to you so you know we are telling the truth. Forty dollars. I was about to leave and go pay but it is easier to give to you."

"No, sir," the policeman said, "I wouldn't know where to take it. You know, it's probably best there if you maybe take and move on."

"I give to you but I still go to office and pay. It is OK. If you go and see that I have not paid, you come back. You have never had New York City hot dog, Officer. You can have hot dog on the house."

Concealed in the wildflowers, Anna watched her father and the police officer talking. By the time the officer left, munching a hot dog, she assumed that, whether he knew it or not, he had taken a bribe. Her father was an expert at bribery. The induced person never knew what they were taking until after they had accepted.

She was glad she was not up there. She didn't feel like playing her part, flirting with some yokel so her father could beat the system and make thirty more dollars. She wanted to be away from this place, away from her father. Oddly, her most innocent act since arriving had been to sleep with that inspector. He had been so drunk and sad and grateful. She might even try to stay at his place until her father got his restaurant. That way she wouldn't have to go back to that woman's house. Maybe, she thought, she and the inspector could keep in touch. He could be the pure and naive influence that she hadn't known she wanted.

The policeman drove away and her father turned toward the field. She decided not to show herself. Soon he yelled for her but she stayed crouching, though her thighs were beginning to ache. She wanted another minute to herself. She wanted him to worry. He kept calling, louder and louder.

He looked like a frightened and confused old man, standing in the road screaming at nothing. But Anna knew him better than that.

≈

"This Reilly?" Janet asked. Before Arthur could answer she continued, "You read the paper? Read it. You get a ride to work with those Russians? I thought so. What you will do now is remove every tomato from this county without explanation—on my order you are unofficially working rogue now. You got that? You know nothing official but you aren't going to rule anything out. Don't link it to me. Do this and maybe, *maybe* I'll let you keep your job. If not, I'll make sure you never work anywhere, ever again. I'm hanging up."

As soon as the line cut he understood that by not disagreeing he had accepted his role in dragging Bogdani's corpse through the streets.

He retrieved his car from the newspaper building and wondered if there was anything he could have done differently. Quit. Said that he was not going to comply with Janet's plan. Not lied on his résumé. Not blamed Bogdani for getting people sick when he hadn't been responsible. Not humiliated Bogdani in front of his son. Told the proper authorities when he saw Bogdani's body the night before. Not written a detailed report about seeing Bogdani's dead body. Not slept with Anna when he knew her father wanted something from him. Not gotten fired. Not screwed up his marriage. Not moved to Millsville, Wisconsin.

The recognition of his poor decision-making skills did nothing to alleviate his misery. All he could do was press on so it would all be over quicker. He wished he had his Cherokee, which was still broken down in front of the Vanderbergs' house. That he was driving his personal vehicle—a 1999 Toyota Camry with nearly 200,000 miles, which he had bought for $1,500 after discovering a car was necessary—made him feel like a crazy person popping around town, asking people to throw out their tomatoes for no specific reason. There was no doubt he was official in his Cherokee: not only was the decal on the door but there was no way he would choose to drive it if he didn't have business to attend to.

At least now he had a working radio, from which he learned that 105 people had gotten sick. He had to put an end to this. Janet wasn't wrong about that. Skeptics were still wearing masks. Two people were dead. One person was killed by the illness and another perhaps from the fallout. It was after eleven o'clock and people would soon be eating tomatoes on their sandwiches and in their iceberg-lettuce-and-cheese salads.

He called Cal as he drove toward the Pizza Hut to remove the tomatoes from their salad bar. The pizza sauce, he assumed, had been made long ago and far, far away and did not pose any threat. He could then move on to the trickier diners, restaurants, and grocery stores scattered around the county that were sure to put up a fight. When Cal picked up on the second ring, Arthur hurriedly explained that he should be vague about the tomatoes when he called the restaurants. As he began to patiently re-explain, Arthur saw Drita and Ismail Bogdani driving in the opposite direction, toward their restaurant.

His voice trailed off and he heard Cal asking him to speak up. Arthur couldn't for the life of him remember where he was going or why he was on the phone. The surviving Bogdanis' presence muddled his thinking until it dawned on him that they might not have been informed of Bogdani's death.

These realizations, combined with Cal's voice asking him to explain, made safe driving a distant priority. By the time he decided he had to turn around and stop Ismail and Drita from entering that restaurant, his car had already veered over the curb and crashed against a light pole.

The impact of the accident deployed Arthur's airbag, but other than wooziness from getting hit in the face by that airbag, he didn't feel he was injured. Stepping out he saw the hood bent around the pole and steam or smoke rising from the engine. He stared at this for a long time before comprehending that he could not drive his car anymore. This understanding was accompanied by a certain sadness—the car that had served him so faithfully didn't deserve such an unceremonious end. He looked across the street and saw a woman staring at him.

"Arthur?" she asked.

"Yes?"

She raised both hands and he understood it was Katie.

"Are you OK?" she asked.

"I think so," Arthur said.

"You drove into that pole."

"I didn't mean to," he said.

"You drove right into it."

"Bogdani," Arthur said.

A truck stopped in the middle of the road, and the driver asked if everything was OK. Arthur nodded, though it was not at all OK.

"Call the police yet?" the driver asked.

Arthur looked at his empty hands and at the ground around his feet and said, "I don't know where my phone is. I think it broke in the crash."

"Not on it were you?" the driver asked accusingly.

Arthur pressed his lips against his teeth and barely restrained himself from telling this guy to shut up.

"Terry," Katie spoke to the man in the truck from the other side of the street, "it just happened. You're the first one here. If you could call someone, it would be a big help."

The man reached to his belt for his phone like a gunslinger called to draw. Informing about notable events was like currency around here, and he was not going to miss this opportunity.

Arthur couldn't think straight. He wanted to scream at the guy in the truck, call him a vulture or a vampire, but knew he had something more important to do.

"I heard about Mr. Bogdani," Katie whispered to him. "I'm on my way over to the restaurant to see what's going on. Figure it's calmed down by now."

He hadn't seen her cross the street and was grateful she was here.

"His son," Arthur said. "His wife and son are driving there now. I just saw them."

Katie eyed him steadily. The man's voice chirped behind them, "I called. They said they're busy but'll get here when they can. Didn't know nothing about it."

"Will you shut up!" Katie yelled over her shoulder.

The man muttered something but was not offended enough to drive away. He pulled to the curb to let the two cars that were stopped behind him pass. Each of them, when they came to the scene, gawked at Arthur and Katie and the smashed car, then rolled down the passenger-side window and asked the man in the truck what happened before driving off.

"What do we do?" Arthur asked.

"We have to go over there," Katie said.

"Why?"

"To help."

"To help do what? What can we do that they can't?"

"Explain what happened before someone else does. That's all," Katie said.

She took off toward the restaurant. Arthur immediately followed.

They were a block away when they heard the scream.

≈

Cal sighed, relieved when Arthur's phone call cut off with a loud crackling thud. He hadn't yet called a single restaurant and figured the interruption saved him from getting in trouble.

He had his reasons for not calling yet. First, Jake was awake and feeling a bit better so Cal had been on FaceTime for an hour with his wife and son, who convinced him there was no need to visit yet. He immediately texted this news about Jake to Kristi, and this led to another hour of texting with her. According to Kristi, Arthur's broken-down truck was causing people to talk. A neighbor informed her father that the truck's driver had gone into the Vanderbergs' house and, when questioned, Kristi admitted that it was Arthur's truck and couldn't come up with a reasonable excuse for his being there. Her father, she wrote, was—to put it mildly—concerned and would not let the matter drop. Cal was troubled by Kristi's admission (though he was greatly relieved that only Arthur's name was involved) and was disconcerted by her flippancy (when writing about her father's red, screaming face, she added "LMAO" and six tomato emojis). Cal actually found himself siding with her father on most of her grievances. Their conversation was cut short when Jill informed him that Bogdani had killed himself.

"No way," Cal replied.

"Yeah, guess he shot himself in the head," she said, anticipating the next question.

He tried to gather the courage to say something else but only stared at her and rubbed his tongue around his lips over and over.

"You all right there, Cal? You know the guy?"

He turned to his computer as though getting back to work.

Cal had called the restaurant on his way home the previous night and threatened Bogdani. And though he assumed his reaction to the news made him look guilty, he was queasy and unable to respond. He reminded himself that he hadn't killed anyone. He didn't even do anything very illegal and, besides, cell phones weren't (he didn't think) traceable. Anyway, why would they trace the call if the guy killed himself? And even if they did, couldn't Cal lie? But what if Bogdani had left a note?

If the call were discovered, somehow, people would understand that Cal was just angry about Jake. It's the truth. This didn't make Cal feel any better. In fact, after convincing himself that he probably didn't have anything to worry about legally, he still had to confront what he had done: he had verbally abused a man whose business was ruined after being falsely accused of poisoning the town.

Cal shuddered when he recalled the phone call. He had, twice, called Bogdani a "timber nigger," though that was, to Cal's understanding, a derogatory phrase for a Native American. To cover his bases he had also called him a "raghead" and told him to "get the hell out of my country." Cal had also told Bogdani that he would "do the same to your boy to see how you like it." Until Bogdani picked up, Cal hadn't known what he was going to say—the words seemed to form themselves. He had never in his life said anything so vile or even thought anything like it. Sure, he would occasionally speak negatively about "illegals," and he and his friends were in general agreement that other racial groups carried with them more problems than did the white people they knew. But he had always felt a certain pride that he wouldn't join in when someone else used racist terms, and would even sometimes silently rebuke them for their callousness.

Now there was no taking it back.

At least Arthur's abbreviated call allowed for hope that the tomato thing was bogus and Cal had been right to not do any work today. He might even be kind of a hero for not spreading false information. Plus he saved restaurants from throwing away perfectly good food. For all Cal knew, the MFR really was the source and his call, if still not nice or anything, had at least been justified. Cal sighed, gratified that he might be off the hook. He wondered if it was too early to go to lunch.

≈

By the time Arthur and Katie arrived, huffing, at the restaurant, Ismail and Drita had driven away. Stupidly, the police had left the place unattended, though they had at least removed the body. Their only precaution had been to string a single line of police tape across the doorway. It was now dangling and blowing in the breeze.

"Where do you think they went?" Katie asked.

"Police, I hope. Or maybe the hospital."

Katie sat down in a chair near the door, far away from the pool of blood.

"What did we do?" she asked.

Arthur decided to misinterpret her question and said, "Guess we missed them."

She frowned at him until he closed his eyes and nodded that he understood.

Arthur had too much to do to stay here but couldn't figure out how to begin. He sat down, then immediately stood with the irrational thought that it was the same chair Bogdani was in the night before. Gingerly he lowered himself back down.

"I saw him here last night," he said when he saw how Katie was looking at him.

"You mean, before?"

He shook his head, then tried a couple times to speak before he said, "I didn't handle it well. Went a little crazy. I'm still not handling it well."

There was a long pause. He wanted her to ask him questions so she could understand and tell him that it was going to be OK, that he hadn't done anything very wrong. Though after how he had treated her that morning he didn't think it was likely she cared much for his well-being.

She said, "Why are there so many broken coffee cups in here?"

The question hung in the air like the sulfur-and-yogurt smell had last night. It didn't matter why coffee cups were on the ground or that Arthur saw the body. Not now, at least.

"You know I ate here the first morning after I moved to this town?" Arthur said. "I was staying in this horrible temporary apartment above the thrift store down the block. I stared at water stains all night. I hated it so much and didn't think I could possibly spend another night here. That first-day-of-summer-camp feeling. Figured I'd eat breakfast here because

I started work in a few days and after inspecting them I wouldn't want to eat here anymore."

"What happened?" Katie asked.

"Nothing. It was fine. It's a diner. Bunch of meat. Oily eggs. Thin coffee. I spotted a few violations but not anything worth mentioning. I left as miserable as I came in."

"Great story," Katie said.

"You don't know anything about my life, do you?" Arthur said evenly. "Whatever has happened between us has never been about me. You don't care."

"Maybe," she said, and held in the apology that came to her throat like a reflex. "I thought I did though, for a minute." To be nice she added, "Why did you tell that story?"

"I'm just saying I do have connections to things around here. People who were born here think they have exclusive rights to all the boring crap in this town, as though having seen it their whole lives makes it mean more than it actually does."

"You don't care about that. You're above it."

"At best I have perspective," Arthur said. "But it's like I'm constantly not understanding an inside joke, and even after it's been explained to me it's still not funny. But that doesn't make it any better to not be included."

"What does that mean?" Katie said, meaning to encourage him to open up but sounding as though she doubted it meant anything at all.

"Who knows?" Arthur said, picking up a coffee cup shard and tossing it across the room. He wondered why all of this bothered him and if this was at all an appropriate time to apologize for this morning.

A siren began to sound and they both raised their heads before recognizing the high sustained wail of the Thursday noon whistle.

"Why do they do that?" Arthur asked. He'd asked this before but never remembered the answer.

"I think it's to test the alarm. It's the same one that goes off during tornadoes. Suppose it would go off if there was an air raid or something."

"Let's hope the air raid doesn't come at noon on a Thursday," Arthur said.

Katie chuckled a little. She'd heard that joke before.

They sat for a minute and Arthur heard a quiet scraping from the kitchen—possibly a mouse—and remembered that it must still be a disaster back there. So much of the restaurant was the same as the first time he inspected it, when he gave it a perfect score: counters, walls, floors, chairs, tables, windows, plants, bulletin board, gumball machine. And yet now it was a completely different space. No longer even inhabitable and the absolute last place in the county from which he would allow food to be served. That it could go from one thing to another so quickly suddenly frightened Arthur. He didn't know why. Maybe it was simply the recognition of the impermanence of things.

"I'm sorry about this morning," he said.

"Who cares," Katie said without looking up.

"I should have come after you," he said.

"Yes," she said. "You should have."

A woman poked her head in the front door and quickly withdrew when she saw Katie and Arthur sitting there.

"You know I quit today?" Katie said.

"After you heard?"

"No. Before. Somehow it makes me feel better that I recognized how awful it all was before I knew anything happened. Not that it made a difference. I just couldn't stand it anymore."

They were sitting at separate tables and Arthur moved near her and reached out his hand. She took it and they sat like that, content with the touch. Arthur was reminded how he once bought her a bracelet that she thanked him warmly for but never wore around him. He'd later found it tucked deep into the cushion of his couch.

"We need to do something," Arthur said with the dreaminess of someone who just hit the snooze button.

"Yeah," Katie said, also not moving.

"No," Arthur said, unable to resist his better judgment, wanting to stay at that table for as long as possible but reluctantly letting go of her hand. "I need to get rid of these tomatoes. I need to call Cal. We need to make sure his"—he indicated the last place he'd seen Bogdani—"family is all right."

"People are still eating those tomatoes?" Katie said. "We've known about that for hours."

Arthur nodded guiltily.

"Look," he said, "both my cars don't work and my phone probably broke in the crash. Can you help me out? Call the garage and get Gary to start my truck?"

Katie didn't respond right away. The virtuous high she got from quitting was all but lost, replaced by the gnawing feeling that she could have helped if she was still in her old position.

More sounds—maybe the soft closing of a door, a pan being set down—came from the kitchen and Arthur got up to look. This time he stayed along the edge of the wall. His bloody footprints were still there, only much more faded than they had become in his memory.

He eased open the kitchen door until he stood face-to-face with a bearded man wearing a camouflage cap and beat-up Carhartt jacket. The man slowly formed the words, "Oh, fuck," before shoving Arthur and turning to run out the back door.

Arthur felt like he was falling back in exaggerated slow motion, always at the cusp of regaining his balance, and, when his hand slipped off what he thought was a secure grip on the back of a chair, fell heavily into the mostly congealed pool of blood.

≈

Drita Bogdani was able to spare her son the scene inside their diner. She saw the police tape across the door and told Ismail to stay in the car while she went inside, saw the blood, screamed, and went directly back outside. She then drove aimlessly away while trying to hold herself together.

This, more closely than anything since, reminded her of leaving Lushnjë after the outbreak of the Albanian Civil War. She and Mërgim had to throw everything they could into a bag and jump in a truck bound for the port city of Durrës, paying far too much to dangle half out of the truck bed for hours until being deposited into a similarly fraught situation of finding safe passage to Italy. That truck ride, too, had come after arguing with her family, who never quite approved of Mërgim and did not fully trust him to keep her safe.

Now, driving away with no destination in mind, she felt as powerless as she had during that hasty departure and ragged journey, back when she did not know if she had the strength to hold on long enough to get there. She had simply been too charged to think or feel anything. And though she'd had no control over where she was being taken, at least her husband was there with her and she knew she wanted to escape. Now she was driving with her son in the seat next to her. There was a similar sense of a lack of control, but she had nowhere to go.

Ismail, for his part, was only slightly less troubled, though he had not gone inside the restaurant. The police tape had frightened him as much as it had his mother, and her scream confirmed that something terrible had happened. His mother drove stiffly now, with both hands on the wheel. She seemed to be constantly exhaling in short bursts, and tears poured in a steady stream from her eyes. He had no idea where they were going and did not ask.

Eventually his mother began muttering something that he couldn't understand. He stayed quiet and concentrated and soon he heard her repeating, "We have nowhere to go."

Ismail had no reference point to comprehend what was going on. His mind went to movies he had seen and books he had read, but nothing quite explained this. Something had happened with his father but he didn't know what. Did the police tape mean that the restaurant was closed down forever? Did his father leave them (as Ismail always suspected was possible)? He wouldn't consider anything worse. It did no good. He did think, though, that this might well have been how his parents felt when they left Albania: scared and confused, not quite sure where they were going or why, and having no concept of the damage already done—moving not to reach anything else but only to get away.

He couldn't bring himself to speak, though as they drove on, past the park at the edge of town where he had played baseball this past summer, he knew he had to do something.

"Mom, I have to pee," he said.

She clapped her hand over her mouth, and her whole body shook with sobs. In a minute she pulled over alongside a cornfield outside of town. She swallowed hard, and by the time she turned toward Ismail her face had returned to a semblance of its normal stern-featured yet attentive and caring form. She said, "Go."

Ismail had not expected this transformation and opened his door only about six inches, shut it, and said, "I don't have to go anymore."

His mother, wild-eyed, nodded and inhaled deeply. A semi rumbled past them from behind, shaking the car and causing them both to jump in their seats.

"Why are there so many of those?" his mother said angrily while smoothing her hair with a trembling hand. "On every road. So much stuff. What is so important that all these people need?"

"Mom," Ismail said, "where are we going?"

Drita winced and put her thumb against her forehead, then gripped her hands into fists to calm herself down.

"We're going back," she said, putting the car into drive and making a Y-turn on the narrow country road.

"Are you OK?" Ismail asked. "Is everything going to be OK?"

"Of course," his mother said, not taking her eyes from the road. "Of course."

≈

Oh god, the last thing she wanted was to see Cal. Texting with him was fine, but now he seemed pretty determined to meet in person. Kristi was already in trouble with her dad, who wasn't letting her out of the house because of the illness and because one of the neighbors told him two men had come over the day before. She couldn't deal with Cal. She set down her phone and stretched.

Cal was fun at first, but lately he'd become kind of exhausting. She worried that if she ended it he might go crazy and tell her dad. If only that other guy hadn't seen them together yesterday. If it was Cal's word against hers, she could say he was making it up.

If this was her life for the next two years, she would go crazy. She was so bored. She already planned to graduate early and immediately enroll at the University of Chicago. Her father wouldn't pay for any school farther away. She couldn't believe it when he told her he wouldn't pay for her to go to college on a coast, even though her brother went to NYU. She asked if she could at least *apply* to the Ivies and Stanford and Berkeley. It only seemed fair after all the work she'd already put in during summers and with private tutors. That she'd actually managed to maneuver herself into position to go to a top-tier college, though she attended Millsville High School, where she speculated some of her teachers were barely literate, was nothing short of a miracle. But he held remarkably firm. She didn't talk to him for two weeks after that.

She went to the hunter's safety course last spring to get her gun license only because she thought she could convince her dad to change his mind if they went hunting together. The idea of killing an innocent deer disgusted her, but that was how men like her father made bold decisions. Out in the cold, a gun resting on his shoulder, the primal thrill of waiting to kill something. That might give her dad the courage to let go.

When she started up with Cal, the gun safety instructor, she told herself it was a kind of experiment. Though, honestly, she also wanted to be loved, to see what all the fuss was about. Nobody had ever shown any serious interest in her before—her experiences with boys were all drunken party flings—and all of a sudden this grown man desired her to the point of obsession. The opportunity might never present itself again. She'd long promised herself she wouldn't become ensnared in a small-town relationship that might trick her into staying in this dead-end backwater. So Cal was kind of perfect. Despite her best efforts, after they started up she was surprised by how affected she became by his depth of feeling for her and hoped this would be the kind of endearing formative relationship she would look back on fondly. But sometimes, when her head muddled at the idea of what she was doing to his wife or when she saw his oafish son in the hallway at school, she wondered if she was actually struggling to maintain control of the situation or if she wasn't perhaps being taken advantage of somehow. She'd read a million articles and chatroom posts about people who had been in similar relationships at her age and saw that there was a chance she would one day tearfully recount this experience to a psychologist, or maybe she would never be able to hold down a decent relationship of her own because of some damage already inflicted.

But at least she hadn't become attached yet. She wouldn't stay in this town for one day longer for Cal Luedtke's sake. And even if her father never changed his mind about paying for a coastal school, she had already filled out her application to Chicago, written four practice personal statements, and received feedback on them from her brother, who tutored super-rich kids and knew all the tricks to getting into the best schools. She was consistently scoring in the low thirties on her ACT practice exams and in the fourteen hundreds on the SAT. She was enrolled in four different academic programs at the universities in Madison and Minneapolis for next summer.

Ever since she spent a week with her brother in New York, she'd been determined to get into a school in a major city. Hanging out with him and his friends, smoking pot in their tiny shared apartment, had been the first time she felt she belonged somewhere. They'd taken her under their collective wing and actually seemed to like her knowing so little about anything. Even she could tell that they relished playing the part of the worldly New Yorkers, though most of them were escapees from small flyover towns as well.

All week they dragged her around the city. They ate Thai food in Williamsburg. Using someone's expired ID, she got into her first bar and made her brother get her rum and Cokes because she was too afraid to order. Everyone filled Kristi's bag with little bottles of whisky and still-hot knishes while they stood in line at the Sunshine Cinema. Then they poured the whisky into fountain Cokes and watched *Spring Breakers* in Kristi's honor, since she was visiting during her own spring break.

One evening they took her to an art exhibit where they stood in a mirrored room full of tiny pinpricks of light. It felt to Kristi—only partially because she was stoned—like all the lights of the city were condensed into this single room and she was floating among them without a body. It was the most aware she had ever been of her own physical and emotional *thereness,* as though every synapse in her brain was firing off at the same time. She was so stimulated and happy that she almost burst out crying but was afraid of looking like a hick who couldn't control herself in front of her brother's friends. She soon found herself agreeably lost in the lights, and her brother had to retrieve her after everyone else left. While she was still formulating words to explain to him what she was feeling, they rejoined the group just in time to hear one of her brother's roommates say dismissively, "I don't know, I was underwhelmed . . . like, it was pretty and all, but ultimately the lights are just cheap spectacle." And Kristi felt both plummeted back to earth and in total awe that this was simply another night in their lives, and that they got to experience this whenever they desired.

The five days she spent in New York were a stream of new foods and films and art and, perhaps best of all, lazing around her brother's apartment with his friends, smoking pot and eating big slices of pizza and goofing off while watching stupid stuff on YouTube. At the end, when her brother put her into a cab and instructed the driver to take her to JFK, all he said to her by way of farewell was, "Don't tell Mom and Dad *anything*." And she had nodded and smiled, feeling once again like the little sister instead of like a fellow NYU student. She cried the entire way to the airport and for most of the flight home, devastated that she would have to spend three more years in this town before she could join that more sophisticated world. She was furious with her father for choosing to live in such a nothing place.

Now she had to figure out a way to pass the time.

Her phone was facedown on her bed.

Maybe she could text Cal that it might be best if they "take a break" for a while. Picturing the look on his face, though, broke her heart a little. He was just a big dumb lunk. He had never said an unkind word to her. She couldn't help but feel sorry for him and his pathetic life that revolved around killing animals and talking about his son's football games. Not that her life was so great, but at least she had hopes. Still, wasn't it better to let him down now before he got even more attached? Stuck on her dresser mirror was a long turkey feather he had gifted her on their second meeting, a week before she let him have sex with her up in that tree stand. She kept it only on the off chance he ever made it to her bedroom. It would be so satisfying to chuck that feather, not have to see it every time she checked her reflection.

She sighed and gazed at her phone. Surely there were already like twenty new texts from him. She went to the window.

Outside, leaning against that green Cherokee parked across the street, was the man from the day before, only now he was all stained and ragged. Arthur. The one who interrupted her and Cal. She didn't mind that he had interfered. In a way, it was the most interesting possible outcome. But why he was back she didn't know—perhaps he was there for her? He seemed nervous, craning his head to see down the block. An attractive enough guy, she thought. Like an extra in a movie. Balding and a bit doughy but certainly better looking than Cal. Probably not as fun or easy though. She didn't imagine that he could fall so completely for her like Cal had.

A tow truck turned onto her street. Glancing between Arthur and the truck, something clicked. All at once she figured out how to solve all her problems. If she tearfully told her father, who was working from home today, that one of the men from yesterday was back, he'd go ballistic and chaos would ensue. From this disorder, she worked out a logical chain of events that could culminate in Cal being forced to end their relationship under threat of exposure. At the very least, she could claim that her father's violent display frightened her, and he would shamefacedly allow her to go to Amanda's to study. Once free, she would go to Erin's. There was a rumor that one of the Bender girls had a heroin hookup and people were meeting at Erin's basement later to try it, though Kristi was still on the fence about whether or not she actually would.

With the truck negotiating its way down the narrow street, she didn't have time to consider all angles, but really how catastrophic could this become for her? With a shrug she went to the head of the stairs and yelled down, "Daddy, I think one of those men are back! He's standing across the street!"

She ran back to her bedroom window to watch.

≈

Despite Katie's best efforts, Arthur's khaki pants were ruined. Before giving up she explained, with the grim apology of a battle-tested midwestern stain-fighting mom, that she was not used to spot-cleaning that much blood.

As he leaned against his Cherokee and waited for Gary, he assumed it was obvious to everyone what the stain was, where he acquired it, and whose blood it was. His fears seemed to be confirmed by the passersby who scrutinized him as though assessing his features so they could accurately describe him to a police sketch artist in the near future.

Finally, Arthur heard the disconcerting belching and grinding of Gary's diesel-engine tow truck. If Gary got the Cherokee started, Arthur would ask him to tow his crashed Camry back to the garage. On his walk over from the restaurant Arthur saw the Camry was still smashed against the pole, causing traffic to slow but otherwise garnering no official attention. To Arthur the steaming car looked post-apocalyptic. A sign of a new era where petty misfortunes were the norm, not worth the time of the police who were overworked with problems of life and death.

As the truck neared, Arthur heard a door open and slam shut across the street and saw a short, tubby, curiously determined man emerge and walk straight toward him. Arthur tracked the man out of the corner of his eye but kept his attention on Gary's truck driving slowly down the street.

"You Reilly?" the tubby man asked.

"Yes," Arthur said, and before he was able to fully face him he was punched awkwardly on the cheek, the fist landing between jaw and cheekbone.

Arthur recoiled against the hood of his truck and saw lights pop and flash in the upper portion of his vision. He recognized it as "seeing stars," and his inability to make them go away frightened him. The man who hit him was hopping up and down in the middle of the street, flapping his hand and cursing about his own pain.

"You stay the hell away from my daughter," the man said, grimacing and holding his hand.

"Your daughter?" Arthur said, confused until memories of the previous day washed over him. "You Vanderberg?"

The man looked at him incredulously. "Of course I am! Stay the hell away from her, Reilly. I've heard all about you. Just stay the hell away."

Arthur didn't know where to begin. He looked over at Gary, who was standing with one foot out of his truck, frozen and waiting for whatever was going to happen to happen.

"You still need a start?" Gary asked.

≈

"Yeah, so the Armenian guy who runs the MFR, you know the place down on Maple?"

Sasha changed his facial features in a way that did not confirm or deny knowledge of the restaurant.

"Guy killed himself," the customer said. "Probably because he got all those people sick."

Sasha raised his eyebrows in disbelief.

"Saw the cops down there when I was leaving town."

Sasha shook his head sadly.

"Anyway, too sad," the customer said. "Oh, and I'll have a pop—Diet Coke if you got it—and you got any chips?"

Sasha handed him the soda and a bag of Utz potato chips.

The customer looked upon the chips with suspicion.

"Don't got any Wavy Lay's, do you?"

Sasha left Anna alone at the cart and drove back to town. He hadn't told her what he had seen and did not enlighten her now. He only said he had to go take advantage of the situation.

Since his own interaction with the police, Sasha had been able to get himself under some kind of control. Now that people knew what happened, he needed to stay sharp in order to take advantage before anyone else swooped in. On his way into town he called Adam's lawyer to amend the papers to both lower the offer and reflect the widow Bogdani as the sole owner of the restaurant. He wanted to present them to her as soon as possible, while she was still in shock.

Sasha loved lawyers. He respected how they were outside the government but had a seemingly supernatural ability to shape the process to their purposes. He had wanted to be one growing up, but it became clear early on that he did not have the test scores or connections to follow his dream. He instead studied at a vocational school and went on to work for the railroad, where he loaded freight for shipments of mostly lumber and minerals bound for Kiev and Moscow. Here he learned how the goods worth having were transferred—that is, in luggage cars and hidden underneath what was listed in the bill of lading. His daring allowed him to overcome his lack of connections. He earned his promotions. But because he had no protectors he was ultimately held responsible when someone from his crew had to take the fall for burying blue jeans, stacks of Beatles albums, American cigarettes, appliances, electronics, the occasional person, and so much else underneath loads of wood and coal. If only he had known a shrewd lawyer back then, maybe he would not have had to flee. Instead, he used every underground connection he had to shuttle him and his family out of the country the way they had shuttled contraband into it for so many years.

He had witnessed lawyers' magic plenty of times in New York when he would invest in a new business or buy a little property or have to sign permits or contracts. The lawyers would explain everything in a steady monotone voice, and if he asked them to clarify, they would simply repeat what they had said with the words in a slightly different order until he gave up and signed or nodded or did whatever they needed him to do. Though Sasha had been hurt by these deals, he never blamed the lawyers. That was the beauty of lawyers: it's never their fault. It was always Sasha's fault for not understanding what the lawyers had done. Blaming the lawyer would be like eating a whole meal and then blaming the waiter for bringing you the wrong dish—it's already too late so you just pay.

After he hung up with the lawyer Sasha listened to the radio report: the number of sick people was holding steady at 105; a man in downtown Millsville was dead from apparent suicide and the police were looking for a man with size ten-and-a-half shoes; and a car crashed into a pole on Maple Street and the driver fled the scene. The urgency in the announcer's voice made Sasha smile. It was quaint how important all this was to these people. To them, these were serious problems.

His lawyer was, of course, Vanderberg, who was working from home that day. Sasha laughed as he drove by the car crashed against the light pole, sitting there like a callback to a previously referenced joke.

A tow truck blocked the street so he parked and walked ahead to investigate. Two men—one of them the inspector—were reeling and contorting in the middle of the road. Sasha knew a fight when he saw one and clasped his hands together at his luck. Then he heard the short man addressed as "Vanderberg" and felt as though he had been given a gift. He was in the perfect position: a witness who did not see what had actually happened.

"I saw the whole thing!" Sasha yelled.

The inspector froze and the lawyer stopped flapping his hand. They both stared at him. Sasha saw recognition bloom in his lawyer's eye before the inspector's.

"You saw him swing at me first!" the lawyer said.

Sasha looked at the inspector like an auctioneer open to a higher bid. When the moment passed, Sasha said, "Yes! He hit you."

The inspector narrowed his eyes and Sasha wondered if he had made a mistake. It was never good to be on the wrong side of a civil servant but, he thought, at least he now had a powerful friend in his debt. And yes, it would have been nice if his daughter could have married the inspector, but there was still Adam. Tonight he would sow some more seeds of discord between Adam and his wife. Though less useful, Adam would be the more interesting son-in-law, and he came already with children. Overall he was glad he had at least done something.

"Gary," the inspector said, wincing and with his hand to his face, "you saw what really happened, right?"

"Jeez, sorry, Arthur," the tow-truck driver said with genuine emotion. "This thing's hard to manage down a narrow street, you know. I wasn't looking."

The lawyer broke in. "You stay the hell away from my family, Reilly, or I'll get you on battery too. I have witnesses."

"I didn't do anything to your family," Arthur growled through his painfully clenched jaw. He took a breath and considered how to explain this so it made sense. "I was here yesterday but I didn't—" he broke off. Then he started again. "It wasn't me."

"What wasn't?" the lawyer asked.

Arthur ordered himself to expose Cal but said nothing.

"Who was it then?" the lawyer asked.

Sasha observed this with great pleasure, as though he came in late to a play and didn't know which character to root for. Out of sheer curiosity Sasha wanted the inspector to confess so he, Sasha, knew what was going on and could possibly have something to use against him. Then Sasha remembered that his daughter had stayed at the inspector's house last night, and the protective father in him wanted Arthur to speak so Sasha could judge his character.

The inspector closed his eyes in frustration. "Gary," he said, "can you start this or not?"

The tow-truck driver hesitantly got out of his truck but moved quickly once he touched the ground. As he took Arthur's keys and popped the hood, the lawyer spoke again.

"I know people, Reilly. Important people. I don't care where you're from. You're a piece of shit. You won't get away with this."

≈

Arthur compulsively rubbed his tongue against the teeth on his left side, checking for chips or looseness. At least Gary had been able to start his Cherokee and would tow his Camry to the county lot. And, somehow, like a miracle, the restart had restored his Cherokee's radio to working order. These minor victories did little to lessen the blow of his many defeats, however. Impotent anger made him want to punch his steering wheel, but he was afraid it would break off from the dashboard completely. He was driving much too fast and without destination so he turned into a church parking lot overlooking a small, deserted park.

Sitting there, the engine running but motionless, he recalled, with a sense like déjà vu, his last subway ride to work in New York. That had been a Monday. The previous week he had to go in to the office but had not been allowed to do any actual work. Nobody spoke to him. Occasionally he attended a meeting with someone from legal or with his union rep but nothing was decided. That weekend he and his wife had either fought or sat in glacial silence. During that Monday train ride he was filled with frustrated, fruitless fury at himself that was somehow preferable to how he felt at home and how he'd feel at work. To prolong this feeling he got out at a random station and stood there, as though waiting for the next train.

He hadn't fought. He had seen it all coming and had done nothing. He didn't try to explain to his wife why he chose to act as he did. He only tried to placate her by saying what he thought she wanted to hear. By the time he was on that platform, watching train after train go by, he quietly panicked as it hit him that he had handled everything wrong and that the opportunity had passed. From there on out he could only take what others gave him.

Now, in Millsville, sitting in a running car that wasn't going anywhere, he had the same feeling, except it was perhaps not too late.

He wiggled the gear shift into reverse, ready to get back to work, when he was interrupted by a loud bang on his passenger-side door. Stunned, he stupidly contemplated the man yanking on the ever-sticky door handle before he scrambled into action, lunging to plunge down the lock before being thwarted by his own locked seat belt.

The door swung open with a loud pop and the man jumped in. Arthur recoiled and put his fists up, though he was too entangled to swing.

"What do you want?" Arthur said, fists still raised.

"Jesus," the man said petulantly, "been fuckin' following you since the restaurant there. Gotta catch my breath."

He recognized the man from the Bogdanis' kitchen—he had shoved Arthur into the pool of blood. Gaunt face with a patchy beard, chewing tobacco in his lip, stiff baggy pants that looked like they were made of burlap, his coat open so Arthur could see a black sweatshirt with a lime green picture of a deer.

"Caught up with you just when fat ass punched you, you know, then waited till you took off but you didn't see me. Been fuckin' running at you till I saw you turned, then cut through the Eggebrechts' yard there figuring you was up here at the park. Nothing else up here, you know."

That's a fantastic account of how you found me, Arthur wanted to say. Instead he said, "Please get out of my car. We can talk when you are outside."

The man's face drooped in disappointment that his feat of tracking went uncelebrated.

"Just saying how I got here," he said, not getting out of the car. "Back there at the restaurant, you know, I wasn't doing nothing. You scared me is all."

"OK."

"I mean," a sheepish grin came over the young man, "I was gonna take some stuff back is all, but I didn't, like, kill the guy or nothing."

"What were you going to take?" Arthur asked as he tried and failed to inconspicuously snake his hand to unlock himself.

"Not like I was going to steal. I used to work for him. He owed *me* money. Can't ask for fucking back pay after a guy's dead, you'll look like an asshole."

Much better to steal from the dead man, Arthur thought. But he said, "Makes sense."

"Right!" the man became animated again. "Quit a couple days ago. Fucking asshole yelled at me for coming in late. Called me lazy. Fucking Albanian or whatever saying shit about me."

"Why are you here now?" Arthur said.

"Saw your badge so I wanted to make sure you weren't with the cops or nothing. Then figured I didn't want you thinking I killed him, you know, just talk to you. Then when I saw that Russian fucker over there with you, wanted to make sure he didn't say any lies about me."

"You know Sasha?"

The guy snorted.

"Did you do anything to the MFR's kitchen two nights ago?" Arthur said, an idea coming on suddenly.

The man's head turned slowly toward Arthur.

"I won't turn you in. It hardly matters now," Arthur said, adding, to himself: the damage is already done.

The man gaped at him like a cornered raccoon, and Arthur didn't know if he should be afraid of the man bolting from the car or coming after him.

"Thing is," the man said carefully, "I kind of need a favor."

"Shouldn't be a problem," Arthur said, assuming it would definitely be a problem.

"Thing is," the man said, swallowing, "you know the gun he used to do it? I mean, were you there? You see what he used?"

"Why?" Arthur said. He recalled the vague outline of a gun but the recollection brought to mind the image of Bogdani's freshly dead body, so he shut it away.

"Thing is, think it might have been mine," he said and shook his head vigorously. "Seriously, I didn't do nothing. I left a bag of my stuff there, in the kitchen cabinet, and guy must have gone through it 'cause I couldn't find it there today."

Arthur considered this and said, "Yes. I saw it. I know exactly what gun was used. But you're going to have to give me some information first."

The guy nodded and they both stared at the park. Two kids, maybe brothers, were on the baseball diamond, one pitching to the other. They were both wearing masks over their nose and mouth like it was the most normal thing in the world.

≈

Adam was sitting at his desk when Katie came in and closed the door behind her. She sat for a couple minutes without speaking. Katie had never come to his office without calling first, and she always announced her entrance by chatting so long with Mitch and Norma that Adam would usually have to come out and bark at everyone to get back to work.

He finally said, "Yes?"

She said, "I'm sleeping with Arthur Reilly."

He got up and started toward the door.

She said, "Wait."

He turned.

She said, "And I quit my job."

What bothered him as he left the building was that the news had wormed past his rational defenses. Long ago he had worked out a plan for this announcement. He'd guessed she would confess at home when the kids were out or in bed, but he'd planned for the office scenario as well—it was almost preferable because he'd look powerful and in control sitting behind his desk. After she told him, he was to lean back in his chair, pause a beat, and say, "Is that what those emails were about?" or, if he didn't want to hand her the ammunition of admitting to invading her privacy, he could drily ask, "Oh, really, is that where you go at night when you think I'm asleep?" In his fantasies she always whispered, "So you knew all along? Why didn't you say anything?" To which he would answer, "We have daughters, Katie. Someone had to consider what was best for them. God knows *you* were only thinking about yourself." She would break down then, crying so hard that she'd choke on and actually spit out her tears, which he had only seen her do once, a few years back when they had to put their cat down.

But he'd spoiled the moment. It was as though he had let a fine wine age for years only to open it and find it rancid. Not only that, but she quit her job? Katie was the steady one. They couldn't both be impulsive and irresponsible. Adam needed the freedom to be unconventional if he were to have a chance to make his mark. The whole *point* of Katie was her constancy.

If only Anna had been in her room last night when Adam had snuck into it. At least then he'd have the solace of being even. He considered again where Anna could have possibly gone, and kicked himself for not overtly propositioning her earlier that evening, or maybe the night before. He couldn't grasp his thoughts. For all the time he spent calculating, he rarely came up with a backup plan. Everything always worked perfectly in his head. The outside world was the problem.

To improve his situation, he turned to forces he could not fully understand but nonetheless made sense to him. This was preferable to going back and talking it out with Katie. He took out his copper coil and fingered the beads, sliding them from side to side like an abacus. Usually this brought him a certain calm and strength.

He slowed his walk and fixed a distracted scowl on his face. The anxious constriction of his chest restricted his breathing. If stupid Sasha wasn't around, Adam could go home and hide away in his basement to settle down and devise a plan to regain the advantage over Katie. He paused at the corner near his car, pretending to scratch a persistent itch so he could pull his shirt free in a desperate attempt to improve airflow to his lungs. He bent down to feign tying his shoe, and as he undid the lace, a sharp bleat sent a shock wave through his body, making him steady himself. A man slowed his SUV and rolled down his window.

"All right, Rainbow Brite!" the man called with a friendly wave.

One of Katie's relatives. This town was crawling with them, but they all seemed to be distant. Third cousins and aunts' ex-husbands and great step-uncles. So much divorce involved that her family multiplied exponentially though nobody seemed related by blood.

Before he began refusing to attend the never-ending string of weddings and anniversaries and funerals and holidays, her family used to tease him about his clothes and beliefs. They eventually settled on "Rainbow Brite" after rejecting such winners as "Gay Flag" and, for some reason, "Leprechaun Larry." Katie insisted they said that stuff only to make him feel like part of the family—most everyone at these get-togethers had a nickname based on a particularity in character—but Adam disliked being called out for any reason other than praise. He felt he was specifically targeted because he was better than those mouth breathers.

This routine anger and annoyance at Katie's eighth cousin counteracted the deep shame and fear he'd felt since her confession. It made him able to pick himself up. As he stood he palmed the copper coil, closed his eyes, and waited for the object's power to flow through him. Nothing happened. Perhaps, he considered for the first time, he was just a nut holding a child's arts-and-crafts project.

Across the street was the post office, a low, solid structure that could have been part of a 1950s *Twilight Zone* set, down to the sign at the entrance designating the building as the local fallout shelter. The emblem reminded him of Utah. He considered that if he was wrong about copper and wrong about Katie, he might also be wrong about the earth being flat. Was it silly to assume that a machine utilizing magnets, copper, colors, crystals, and a relatively small amount of basically legally obtained enriched uranium procured by one of the swingers who worked at Oak Ridge Labs was the key to unlocking and monetarily exploiting the widely held misunderstanding of the earth's shape? No. His research and experiments definitely proved these methods to be correct. Plus the arguments against the fact of flatness were easily refutable. As were the arguments about roundness. Yes, a ship disappears over the horizon of the ocean, but that's the limit of human sight and obfuscation of dense, low-lying sea air. Pictures of the earth from space are obviously doctored. The curvilinear edges of the horizon as seen from a plane were an optical illusion. Adam was a journalist. He believed what he could see and trusted his instincts. He didn't trust the science simply because it had been told to him. If he discovered it for himself, surely he could imagine earth as a big basketball too. But he wasn't looking to proselytize. He was aware how audiences reacted to unconventional views that contradicted what they had been told in grade school. He only wanted to prove himself right. So it had long been an obsessive basement hobby, at least until the internet created alternative conservative websites and crowdsourcing. All it took was one advertisement on the most conspiracy theory–based radio show in the country to find investors and raise enough for his beautiful machine that rose two inches above the salt flats of Utah for eight magnificent seconds. He only wished the trip away hadn't cost him so dearly when he arrived home.

Trusting in the power of objects had gone from habit to belief over many years. When he was a boy, his mom used to give him seemingly useless old perfume bottles and slivers of driftwood and tell him that these objects would make his nervous tummy aches go away if he held them tight and took good care of them. When his family moved, these charms were the first items Adam packed. The box he kept them in never strayed from his lap while driving to their strange new home—he was sure that if it was misplaced, his sore stomach would burst. Even if he wanted to, he could never explain all the systems he'd come up with since then. He knew how many times to tap wood, particularities of magnet grades, appropriate crystal type and placement, proper copper wire density and shape, the precise strengths of each color. At nearly every moment of each day he was doing something to stay alive or gain an edge.

His systems had successfully gotten his two children born and raised into decent people; he also had a house, an understanding wife, two living parents, siblings who did not bother him for his time or money, an interesting job. A comfortable life.

Standing there with it all unraveling around him, he worried for the first time that these objects were the cause of his undoing. Perhaps, he considered, his life was heading in the wrong direction because he had become beholden to his objects, rather than the other way around. The copper in his hand was slightly cold, that was all. It felt like nothing. Like a *trinket.* It suddenly struck him as ridiculous to think that his wife wouldn't have said what she said if he had only surrounded himself with more copper, worn yellow on Tuesdays, had another magnet in his left shoe, or hung six more crystals in his westernmost bedroom window. His impulse was to fling his copper coil away, over these main street buildings, so he could see it hang in the air and, for a moment, hope it boomeranged back to him, confirming its validity, or else fly away and release him from its grip forever. But the old men lingering outside the post office had taken notice of him and surely wouldn't stand for such behavior. He shoved the coil back in his pocket and walked toward the river.

He stopped just before the bridge leading to the other side of town, at the mouth of a trail that led to a secret childhood fishing spot, which he hadn't visited in over twenty years. Such a perfect place to both hide and rediscover his essential self that he wondered if this was what he had had in mind since leaving the office. As he neared the water he kept waiting for nostalgia to course through him. He imagined movies where soft-focused, sun-flared scenes of children being chased by their father allowed for the possibility of youth and adulthood merging. But, once at the shore, he couldn't muster enthusiasm and only felt childish, as if he had not changed at all since the last time he stood in this spot. Nothing was down there except rusted lures, tangled fishing lines, used condoms, smashed beer cans, and a new-looking shoe.

He took the copper coil from his pocket and tossed it limply into the water.

It had been so impulsive that he thought he might weep from the shock. Not only did he lose his coil—though he had dozens at home—but it was the first time in years that he'd allowed himself to waver. He retroactively wondered if throwing in his precious copper had been a desperate attempt to regain his sense of self by merging his power with the river's, but his toss had lacked the ceremony.

Confusingly, though, after it sank from sight, he felt only a pleasant emptiness and climbed back up the bank in a daze. He emerged into the sunlight feeling renewed. Not from anything to do with the river but from the recognition that he was not, in fact, beholden to his own beliefs. That he could throw that copper away so easily meant he was stronger than he knew.

With newfound purpose, he went directly to the courthouse, where he was only momentarily dismayed by Katie's empty desk. He skirted quickly by and entered Janet's office without knocking.

She was at her desk holding up two mirrors, apparently to get a view of the back of her head. When Adam saw her like this he was filled with sudden, unexpected shame. He once again felt defeated and forgot why he had come.

Janet appeared similarly thrown off and set down the mirrors.

"I was just checking . . ." she began, paused, and said, "You don't knock? What are you doing?"

"Katie wasn't there," Adam said, as though this was a valid explanation.

"I know. She quit."

Adam nodded. He really wanted to know what she had been doing with those mirrors.

"Why are you here?" Janet asked, annoyed.

"Fire Reilly," Adam said, staring at Janet's hair.

"Who?"

He met her eyes.

"Oh, the inspector," she said.

≈

In exchange for Arthur confirming that the gun Bogdani had used matched the description of the man's gun, and that Arthur would, if needed, testify on the man's behalf (with what information, Arthur was not sure, though he was sincere in his promise), the man got out of his car.

The man was angry with Sasha for getting him involved, so he happily divulged everything he knew. Arthur was able to confirm his suspicions that Sasha was responsible for destroying the Bogdanis' kitchen (as well as, to Arthur's surprise, verify the rumor that the Bykovs were actually selling drugs) but, since the man refused to give Arthur even his first name and Arthur promised not to implicate him, Arthur had no tangible evidence to back all this up. And even if he did, what would happen? Bogdani was dead. It was already too late.

He removed the tomatoes at the Pizza Hut and Hardee's, though he assumed the food was too processed there to harm anybody. When they told him that Cal hadn't called, he gritted his teeth, which caused a sharp pain in his punched mouth. He used the phone at Hardee's to call Cal but there was no answer. He called the office and Sandra told him that Cal was away from his desk. From her hesitant tone Arthur figured she was covering for him. He pictured Cal waving both hands at her to indicate he didn't want to talk. Them against him.

On the way to the next inspection this report came on the radio: "OK, that was AC/DC ending your twelve-o'clock-rock-block brought to you by Dave's Ace Hardware. Little update on this big illness hitting our viewing area: no new cases to report so the number holds at one-hundred-and-five but we have reports that folks are being sent home from the hospital with the A-OK, so kids, start studying for those tests because it looks like you might be back to school tomorrow. One new item to report: police are on the lookout for a 'person of interest' involved in the apparent suicide at the Millsville Family Restaurant earlier today. They are on the hunt for a man with size ten-and-a-half Rockports. So keep your eyes on the pavement today and give Chief Butzler a call if you notice that particular leather. I only see my size seven Converse so no luck here in the booth. When we come back—a double dose of Van Halen . . ."

Arthur's eyes shifted involuntarily down to his feet, where his shoe perched on the pedal like a star witness at trial. He had thrown his shoes into the river last night but he didn't consider that his replacement pair was the exact same brand and model. (He had bought four pairs at once because they had been "Buy one, get one half off.") This time Arthur controlled himself and didn't allow his dizziness to cause him to crash.

At Marty's, the other supermarket in town (Arthur always forgot about Marty's because everyone he knew shopped at the much nicer and newer Piggly Wiggly—he assumed only the poorest people roamed the aisles of the underlit and dusty-canned Marty's), Arthur ran into resistance. He explained his position to a stock boy, the produce manager, the general manager, then, over the phone, to Marty himself. Marty was not having his tomatoes thrown away.

"I read all about you!" Marty squealed on the phone when Arthur identified himself. "You're a troublemaker."

"Mr. . . ." Arthur hesitated, then said, "Marty. Between you and me, these tomatoes could get people sick."

"Don't fool me with that bullshit. Colberger put you up to this?"

Barry Colberger owned the Piggly Wiggly.

"Of course not," Arthur said.

"Not enough that he gets all the customers, he needs my tomatoes too?"

"Marty, I'm telling you, I have an order from the courthouse to remove every tomato in Chase County. It's not up to me and it's certainly not up to Barry Colberger."

"You don't fool me! You don't fool me! I heard on the radio that that Armenian got those people sick. This is big government putting the strong arm on the small businessman."

"Albanian."

"You can take your tomatoes and go to hell!" Marty said, and hung up.

Arthur hung up the phone and gave a thumbs-up to the manager. "Good to go," he said.

They began loading the tomatoes from the display bin onto a cart when a loudspeaker called for the general manager. Arthur loaded as fast as he could.

When the last tomato had been packed the general manager yelled across the store for them to stop. Arthur wrenched the cart away from the produce manager and pushed it like a bobsledder beginning his run, determined to get it to the trash compactor in the back room. The produce manager gave chase and called to a stock boy at the end of the aisle.

The stock boy—or stock man in this case, a burly guy in his midtwenties—did not hesitate to obey orders and tackled Arthur like a running back. The wind went completely out of Arthur as soon as they hit the ground, and he heard a crunch that could very well have been ribs breaking. Around them tomatoes rolled, spilled from the tipped-over cart.

"Not two-time all-conference linebacker for nothing, huh?" Arthur heard the produce manager say to the stock boy, who stood up chuckling and dusting himself off.

At the order of the general manager they lifted Arthur off the ground, dragged him gasping out the automatic doors, and deposited him on the sidewalk against the generic cola machine where cans were still twenty-five cents apiece.

He regained his breath and checked his ribs for damage. He had to stop Janet and Sasha and restore Bogdani's name. If he was going to be publicly implicated in Bogdani's death and could no longer do his job anyway, he at least had to let the truth be known—no matter what it cost him.

≈

Janet never understood Adam. Ostensibly he was an ally—the rare conservative who controlled the media, no matter how insignificant his newspaper was—and in the past he had aided her campaigns and causes. But she always suspected Adam didn't think much of her. He seemed to suppress a smirk whenever they discussed politics, like it was cute that she was trying to keep up with him.

Now he was desperate for her help. That he had caught her trying to determine her "good side" for her campaign photos only strengthened her resolve to show him that no matter how smart he thought he was he didn't have nearly as much power as she did.

"Why do you have it in for this guy?" Janet said. "I thought you were friends."

"Personal matter," Adam said.

"Because of him and Katie?" Janet enjoyed seeing him pale and helplessly lick his lips.

"You knew?" he said.

"Did you not?"

Adam nodded and didn't say anything.

"What will firing Arthur Reilly do?" Janet asked slowly.

"He'll leave town," Adam said. "He'll hopefully be miserable."

"For me," Janet said. "What will it do for me?"

Adam bit down hard on his lip and sat down in the chair in front of Janet's desk.

"I didn't say you could sit down," Janet said.

Adam instantly stood back up, fists balled in frustration.

"Kidding," Janet said. "Have a seat, of course."

He sat down heavily.

"Right now," Janet said, "Reilly can help me. After your article today he's at my mercy. He'll do anything I say. Why would I give that up? I don't want him to leave. Plus we'll look incompetent if we admit we hired him without looking into his past."

"Do it as a favor?" Adam said hopelessly. "Fine—I'll back your campaign. You're running for Congress, right? I'll be as favorable as legally possible in the paper."

Janet scrunched up her face. "You will be anyway. Besides, I have everyone's vote who reads your paper."

"If you don't fire him, at least investigate him for that suicide. They're looking for someone. He might actually be involved." She didn't look convinced so he added, "That way you won't look bad. In fact, you'll look smart because you were the one who figured it out." She appeared to be on the fence so he reluctantly used a phrase he despised but she would relish: "You'd be a maverick—both lawmaker and sheriff."

"That's true," she said. "But still not worth it."

A solution came to him and he perked up, opened his mouth, closed it, then, before he could consider too much, he said, "I'll get Katie to come back to work for you."

Janet didn't see this coming. She picked up the softball from her desk and rolled it between one hand and the other. Since Katie left Janet felt not only the loss of her professional presence—Janet hadn't answered her own phone in years—but also some cosmic imbalance in her life from the shock of Katie asserting herself. Katie was a kind of living trophy to prove that Janet had conquered her past. Ever since she quit, Janet felt exposed.

"Can you do that?" Janet asked.

"Of course," Adam said.

"Do it. Then maybe we can work something out."

Janet set the softball back on her desk and Adam didn't move.

"Anything else?" Janet said.

Adam shook his head.

"Then go."

≈

The radio station broadcast out of a building off County Highway K-S heading north out of town. Just over a rolling hill two items become visible: the spire of the radio building/gift shop pointing up like a long, thin summer sausage with the word Wisconsin running down its side, and a pair of oversized horns set between two giant perky goat ears. The sausage-spired, octagonal building had been the main visitors center at the inaugural World Dairy Expo in 1967, a ten-day event meant to rival the spectacle of the World's Fair that, despite the attendance of Ladybird Johnson, flopped. The expo turned out to be too high concept for dairy farmers and too dairy-based for everyone else. The founder of the radio station, a recently deceased local legend named Sidney Graaf, seeing opportunity in failure, bought the building on the cheap and had it hauled back piece by piece to attract tourists. He also bought a motorized block of cheddar on wheels from the expo, officially named the Cheesemobile. Over the years its hue faded from orange to dusty red and was affectionately referred to as the Brick. Sidney drove it in the Fourth of July parade until the brakes went out and the insuranceless vehicle T-boned a school bus, causing minor injuries to a dozen members of the marching band. A few years later, undaunted, Sidney commissioned the enormous talking goat. The 21-foot-tall fiberglass goat, named Nattering Nanny Andersson, was billed as "the World's Largest Talking Goat" (a claim as unverifiable as it is useless). Sidney ordered it in a brief, ill-advised venture to stand out as the only cheese shop in the state to exclusively sell goat cheese. As Arthur had found out during his initial tour through the town, for ten cents you could still hear Nanny speak. Yet her once-chipper voice now sounds as though it is melting as it garbles off facts about Wisconsin cheese and the 1967 World Dairy Expo.

Such an odd outpost along this seldom-used road originally softened Arthur's affection. This kind of kitsch was part of the charm of a town like this, and he greeted the building and big goat and dented cheese car with the enthusiasm of an art dealer finding a useful painting at a thrift store. But, as he pulled into the parking lot after leaving Marty's, he realized he had not been back to this building since his initial visit, except once to investigate a complaint that the gift shop inside the octagon was simply cutting the mold off old blocks of cheese instead of throwing the whole block away. (The gift shop employee, who had no idea this wasn't an acceptable practice, verified this complaint.)

Now he came again to deliver his message to the townspeople.

Brittany Graaf, who had inherited the station/gift shop/goat from her late grandfather, was the only employee present, running both the store and the station. Arthur already had heard her give news updates twice and noticed a big difference in her radio voice (which sounded like a classic rock DJ) and her speaking voice (which sounded like a midwestern aunt). When he shook her hand he forced himself to maintain strict eye contact, realizing with alarm that he was still wearing the sought-after shoes, though his overall dishevelment might have been distraction enough. He explained to her about the tomatoes causing the sickness and that Bogdani was not to blame.

"So, I've been getting my updates straight from the horse's mouth up there at the courthouse with Katie Bender or even Janet, you know," Brittany told him. "Not that I don't trust you or something. You know more than I do for sure. I'm only the big mouth that says this stuff. Just that maybe I should give them a call over there to make sure."

"Of course," Arthur said, gulping. "Please do."

"You know," Brittany said, "I got another update here in three minutes. Guess, I mean, badge and all you probably know what's going on. I'll have to give your name as my source though."

His instinct was to give the name Calvin Luedtke. But she probably went to prom with him or something.

"Where have I heard that?" she asked after he gave his real name.

Arthur shrugged.

"You the guy in the paper this morning?"

"No," Arthur said. "I don't think so. You must be thinking of someone else."

Before he left she asked him, out of bland politeness or probing, where he was going next. He told her there was a shady hot dog cart at the edge of town and, between the two of them, he'd heard it was selling drugs. She raised her eyebrows and said, "Interesting!"

This was the second part of his plan: to spread rumors. He had inadvertently spread so many already that he was well versed in how it worked. Threatening, bribing, lying, or harming people were all in play until he cleared Bogdani, got people out of harm's way, and, if possible, kept his job.

≈

Anna was done with this pushcart. She could not take the confused looks of people driving by or the leers of the truck drivers. She was sick of being a curiosity. She had just called her father for the fifth time to come get her when Drita and Ismail Bogdani parked across the road.

Anna stiffened, knowing who they were. Her father was probably, at least in part, responsible for this woman's husband's death so she didn't know if they were coming to exact some kind of revenge. They were, after all, Albanians—as far as Anna knew they still adhered to the rules of the blood feud like their fellow countrymen. Anna gripped her hot dog tongs tightly.

"We are looking for your father," Drita said before she reached the cart. "We were told that we could find him here."

"I don't know where he is," Anna said automatically, though she assumed he was still at the lawyer's.

"How can someone be so difficult to find in this town?" Drita asked, looking at the ground. "Normally everyone is right outside the door. Your father especially."

Anna could see she was tired and desperate. So was the boy.

"I was just trying to call him," Anna said. "I want him to take me back to town but he's not picking up. I can't take these people looking at me." She didn't know why she added the last part. She hadn't spoken to anyone about her discomfort and thought this woman might understand.

"Can I have his phone number then?" Drita asked.

Anna hesitated and Drita spoke again.

"I want to take his offer. I want to sell the restaurant."

"Why?" Anna said, immediately wishing she hadn't spoken.

"To get away from this town. I do not want my son," she indicated Ismail, who was half hidden behind her and looking at Anna shyly, "growing up around here."

"It's not so bad," Anna said.

Drita screwed up her face. "You have been here two days and you already do not like how people look at you."

"I am not staying here. I'll go back to New York when my father gets settled."

"Do you really think that?" Drita said wearily. "We used to say the same thing when we first came here. We said we would save money and go somewhere better. Now I hope to be able to move in with my sister."

"I will leave in a couple weeks," Anna said defiantly. "You and I are not the same. You are a refugee."

She said the word much harsher than she intended. It seemed to hurt Drita.

"Please. Your father's phone number?" Drita asked.

"I didn't mean anything," Anna said.

"Can you give me the number?"

Anna gave her the number and Drita turned toward her car.

"I'm sorry about your husband," Anna said.

Drita stopped and said something in reply, but her words were obscured by a passing pickup truck. Anna watched as they got back into their car and drove away.

≈

Before entering County Building C, Arthur gathered himself like an actor about to go onstage. He was not angry with his coworkers—he expected nothing more from them than the inaction and incompetence they had so far displayed. But he would yell at them anyway while he still had some authority. Funny how he'd wanted to let loose on these people for so long, and now that he was finally going to he had to fake his enthusiasm.

He'd yell at Sandra for hiding Cal. He'd yell at Cal for being Cal. He'd be vague with the accountants and assume they'd fill in the blanks themselves. He'd guilt them, say that they were all to blame for anyone who got sick from now on and that he wouldn't take the fall for all this—even though he had already decided to. Somehow, planning to yell at them made him realize he will miss these people. That this could be the last time he entered this office was much more of a loss to him than he ever thought possible.

After he yelled he was going to write a detailed email to the statewide newspapers about the sickness, about Janet's attempts to manipulate the flow of information to aid her upcoming campaign, about Bogdani's death being the result of their efforts, and, for good measure, he'd include Sasha's role in all this and hint about the drugs.

He felt like whistling as he walked down the empty hallway. Maybe he had a concussion from the punch or the tackle or was still in shock from seeing Bogdani's body. If so, he was glad for the trauma—this elation was much better than the fear and frustration that he had felt all day. Hopefully, though, it was simply the result of taking control of a shitty situation. Now, when he was fired and back on food stamps and welfare and trying to lie his way into another lousy job, he could at least look back on this with some kind of pride. He had forgotten how satisfying moral victories were.

At the door to the office he checked his watch. It was later than he imagined and he frowned, worried that people had left early again. How disappointing if he couldn't yell at them! Reprimanding them had taken on an almost nostalgic feeling, like a speech at a going-away party.

He shook his head and laughed at himself for acting as though making them miserable one more time was a sweet gesture of farewell. At the exact moment he laughed, the building's security guard—an older woman Arthur knew existed but rarely saw—stepped out of the bathroom. They made eye contact. She blushed bright red and scuttled away.

Arthur wanted to shout that he wasn't laughing at her, but that would only have made it worse. Instead, he cursed his rotten luck and reminded himself that these people were to blame for their sensitivity about being seen doing anything even arguably unpleasant. Still, he had been here long enough to feel guilty at making someone uncomfortable. Why guilt was such an essential part of the social fabric of these people he could not begin to understand. All he knew was that to truly be one of them meant having to be perpetually disappointed in himself or another person. He accepted that he felt bad about the incident with the security guard but had done nothing wrong. Then he nodded to himself, grimly and bravely, and opened the door.

≈

With nothing else to do, Katie went home. It was the last place Adam would go, at least until he licked his wounds and strategized his counterattack. With her daughters out at friends' houses, maybe Katie could quietly eat a late lunch before another horrific evening unfolded. She was proud of how she had handled herself so far but dreaded the repercussions of her actions. She didn't want to have to silently endure Adam's scornful looks and comments; she didn't want to let those Russians invade her house again; most of all, she didn't want to put on a brave face in front of her daughters and act as though everything was normal. But of course she would. It was the only way she knew to make other people more comfortable.

While the bacon was in the microwave she spread mayonnaise on cracked wheat bread and got out the lettuce and tomato. The head of lettuce had already been washed but she ran it under water anyway, pulled off a couple leaves, cut off the white part closest to the base, and stuck the leaves into the mayo. Without grabbing a cutting board she sliced the tomato on the counter—first down the middle, then twice outward from each side of the first cut, giving her four big slices. She placed these on top of the lettuce and took the paper plate of greasy bacon out of the microwave, dabbed the bacon with a napkin, and put it on top of the tomato. Then she covered the bacon with the other slice of bread, grabbed a crumpled bag of Wavy Lay's, and stood at the counter flipping through an *Us Weekly* with her sandwich and chips within reach. She munched a chip.

This was her routine five days a week for the past ten years. She always went home for lunch. Sometimes she ate turkey or grabbed some Subway or ate leftovers. Sometimes she read *People* or turned on the TV and watched CNN or Dr. Oz. She always stood at this spot at the counter, never really paid attention to what she ate, but always appreciated the food and the break and the quiet without consciously acknowledging it. Now, as she glanced at pictures of celebrities she recognized instantly, mostly because she had seen them before in these magazines, she grabbed her sandwich. Just before taking a bite she hesitated.

Tomatoes.

She set the sandwich down and felt genuine horror. She turned to the sink and washed her hands. She grabbed a sponge, wet it, wiped down the spot where she had cut the tomato, and then threw the sponge away. All she was doing was eating a sandwich. This was what all those people who got sick did. This was what Theresa Dorshorst did. Everyone did this all the time until it turned the town upside down and caused a woman to die and a man to kill himself. Her eyes were locked on the sandwich. Tomatoes were pretty gross if she thought about them. They oozed.

She didn't know how long she stared at the sandwich. Minutes probably. She tried to remember where she bought the tomatoes. Soon the door slammed and she expected to see one of her daughters so she gathered herself and tried to pretend nothing was wrong. It was the Russian man.

"Lunchtime!" he exclaimed when he saw her.

She nodded and sighed.

"I have only come home for minute." She hated that he called her house his home. "The woman, she says she will sell me restaurant. It is good. It is right thing to do."

"Does that mean you'll be leaving tonight?"

"No," he said. "We have to clean up. There is lot of—" He broke off the description out of respect and instead gestured outward from his head, showing how an exit wound will spread brain and skull and blood.

Katie winced.

"Yes," he said sympathetically. "And who knows, maybe now I can get better price."

Katie shifted her eyes away from him and found herself looking at the sandwich. The bacon was getting cold, and the bread was soaking in the tomato's juices. She couldn't bear the sight and faced him squarely.

"How can you do that? Her husband just died," she asked.

He nodded sadly. "Tragic circumstances. Still. The business is not worth as much. Anyone would tell her so. This way she gets money now. It is what she needs. If I paid more, she would be taking advantage of me for being sympathetic. If I pay less, you say I will be exploiting her. I would rather pay less. It is fair."

It all sounded so reasonable but she knew it was unfair. She always found herself in this situation: with Adam, with Janet, and now with this guy. She didn't, at the moment, care if the world happened to operate this way. She would prefer everything to be a series of random events rather than a constant flow of people taking advantage of the less fortunate. She didn't want this guy to win, but she also knew that if Drita Bogdani needed money, this was her only option. Katie briefly ran through her own finances to see if she could buy the restaurant, but obviously this did not make sense.

"I want you out of my house," she said.

"Soon," he said calmly.

"No, I want you out tonight. Right now."

"I will ask Adam."

"I don't care what he says! It's my house too."

"All of our things are here. Your husband said we can stay. It is not right to make us leave. We would have nowhere to go."

Katie clenched her jaw and said nothing. It was no use to keep arguing.

When Sasha saw she had given in, he walked to the refrigerator and opened the door. Then he glanced back at Katie.

"Aren't you going to eat your sandwich?"

"No," she said.

"If it will go to waste . . ."

She hesitated for a couple of seconds and nudged the plate over to him.

"It's all yours," she said.

≈

Cal had never seen Arthur act that way before. He barged into the office with a swollen jaw and stained pants and winced and grabbed his ribs as he yelled at Cal for not calling restaurants to remove the tomatoes. Until then Cal had always thought of Arthur as uptight and kind of standoffish—and, probably because Arthur didn't hunt or regularly watch football, Cal thought of him as unmanly, even though Arthur was the most aggressive person in the office—but overall he considered Arthur an OK guy since he did so much of the work. Now he had to reassess his impression. Cal had a reasonable excuse for not calling those restaurants, two excuses really: he thought Arthur told him not to call and his son was sick so he had been distracted. Arthur had refused to listen.

As soon as Arthur left, everyone but Cal lifted their heads over their partitions, made quick eye contact, and shifted their gaze to Cal, who had received the brunt of Arthur's wrath.

"Fuck got into him? What'd I do?" Cal said from the safety of his cubicle.

"No call for that language," Jenny the accountant said.

"Just mean that it's not like I'm the one that got people sick. I didn't kill no one."

The mention of such unpleasantness took any fun out of gossiping about Arthur. Everyone slowly sat down to ponder—but not actively do anything about—the seriousness of their situation.

Cal didn't mind the silence. He wanted to be alone. He was angry with Arthur not only for reprimanding him unjustly in front of everyone but also for crushing Cal's hopes of continuing his tryst. After the initial screaming, Arthur calmed down enough to talk quietly to Cal about Kristi, telling him in no uncertain terms that Cal had to break it off with her immediately and that she had to tell her father—and anyone else who would listen—that Arthur had nothing to do with her. Otherwise Arthur would tell Cal's wife, Kristi's dad, and the police what Cal had done. Normally Cal might gamble that Arthur wouldn't go through with it, but after how he had just acted Cal couldn't hold it to chance.

He hated Arthur's stupid, calm face, he thought, as he desultorily searched his computer for contact info for food-service establishments in their county. Sure, Arthur had a right to get on him about not calling the restaurants. That was his job. But he had no power over what Cal did outside of work—he was not authorized to take away Cal's happiness. Ever since he heard that Bogdani had killed himself, thinking about Kristi had been the only way to get his mind off that phone call last night. In contrast to that call, his affair with Kristi seemed pure, and he needed her more than ever if he was going to move past his guilt and shame. Seized by poetic desperation, Cal pictured his life without Kristi. He saw an endless walk through deerless woods with an empty rifle. Perhaps he would describe this to Arthur if he got the chance to argue in favor of continuing the affair.

The first restaurant he called was a diner in Granger called Ruth's Comfy Kitchen. He regularly inspected Ruth's and, when he was there during lunchtime, got the open-faced turkey sandwich with extra gravy—hold the peas, no side salad.

"What do you mean tomatoes?" Ruth asked after Cal explained.

"Sorry, Ruth. You know, just one of those things."

"One of what things?"

"It's a—what do you call it?" he paused as he thought of the word. "A thing just in case." He thought more and Ruth waited. "A precaution! Just a precaution. Nothing to be worried about."

"Sounds a bit fishy, if you ask me. Throwing out my tomatoes. What if people want some? What am I supposed to tell them?"

"Oh, you know, just tell them you got a bad batch."

"I'm not telling them that! Got bad tomatoes, who knows what else bad you got. This got anything to do with that bug what's going around down there? Because nobody I know up here in Granger's got what's going on down there."

"No, Ruth, just a precaution," Cal said. Then he lowered his voice confidentially and said, "OK, well, between you and me, they think these tomatoes might have some kind of connection to these people getting sick. You know my boy's got it? Gonna be fine but gave us a scare there. But seriously, that goes no further than this call."

They continued to discuss the particulars, and with some reluctance Ruth agreed to throw out the tomatoes. Upon hanging up the phone Cal reflected that he hadn't even made it past one call without divulging the truth about the tomatoes, despite Arthur very specifically ordering him not to. He did not consider that Arthur told him this knowing Cal would still tell everyone anyway, and since Cal was letting them in on a secret the news would spread even quicker. Instead, Cal just reminded himself that it wasn't in his job description to lie to anybody. If Arthur got mad at him again, that's what he'd say. Everybody in the office would back him up.

He made another call and, forgetting himself, within a minute mentioned the real reason it was necessary to remove the tomatoes.

≈

In the quiet moments after signing away their restaurant, Drita Bogdani surveyed their apartment. They had lived here for the past twelve years. She felt no more connection to it now than she had at the beginning, when her husband had first bought the restaurant against the advice of several people, including her now-prosperous brother-in-law. But nobody could change her husband's mind after he had decided on something, not even her. She had told him she would not live here, above the restaurant, for long. He assured her they would buy a house soon.

She had always thought of the apartment as both a safe haven and a transitory place. She never even replaced the furniture that had been included in the sale. At the time, Drita had been thankful for the furniture since they had no money left after the purchase. The day they signed the papers had been one of the saddest since they had arrived—for her at least. Mërgim had been thrilled. After hoarding every penny for years they had finally saved a nice amount, enough to rent a better apartment. Maybe if Mërgim was promoted at the warehouse, they could eventually buy a house. They even had enough to invest with her brother-in-law, though it had been a long time since the offer to join them had been extended and Drita knew her husband would not beg. But why else did they come to this country if not to have something of their own, make a better life for their son? Once they paid off the restaurant they would own a part of this country for themselves, a part nobody could take away. The profits would send their son to college. The money from selling it could provide for them into their old age. Now all those dreams were gone.

The kitchen in the apartment still contained the same folding table and rickety metal chairs as when they first moved in. Sitting there for perhaps the last time, she admitted to herself that she could have replaced the lousy furniture at minimal cost and effort. The squeaky bedframes, the ugly sagging couch, the oversized oak coffee table, the TV stand with its flaking yellow paint—all could have been upgraded at the thrift store down the street or, like some of her neighbors, at the big box stores in Danville. Perhaps she kept it all as a reminder of where they had begun, but now she was not sure why. What was once supposed to be motivation had at some point turned to rebuke. Maybe, she thought, her husband would still be downstairs, cleaning, if she had only been more understanding. She never wanted to see any of it ever again. Not even their TV. Leaving this place with nothing was simply the fulfillment of her original expectations. She wanted no reminders.

Standing across the kitchen table was this horrible man who tried to offer her so much less than he had offered her husband the day before. He was reading the signed contract over very closely with a look of wonder. Ismail had the same expression when he read comic books. This connection to her son barely allowed her to see Sasha as a human being who was worthy of love and pity and protection.

Ismail was in his room. She hoped he was reading comics and not brooding. Knowing Ismail, though, he was probably at his door listening to what was going on in the kitchen. She hoped this was not the case. A tremor of panic and sadness came over her as she thought how her husband had always admired Ismail's inappropriate curiosity. He thought it would serve Ismail well: by refusing not to be shut out from action he could learn harsh lessons adults thought were too grown up for him. Her husband had never told this to Ismail, of course, though she wished he had.

The man finished reading the contract and shook his head in admiration. He straightened himself out of his stoop and stared at her. She wished he would leave. It was the worst day of her life and she wanted to be alone with her son. He didn't move, and with shock she realized she and Ismail must go, not him.

"Well," he said.

Her poise was leaving her. It had taken so much strength to stand up to this goblin during the negotiations. Eventually they settled on a complicated contract that allowed Sasha to sign a rental agreement that would take effect immediately with the guarantee of the sale after all the legal hoops had been jumped through (for this she made him pay more up front). He even had to go back to his lawyer twice and draw up new paperwork. After all that she could not ask for the mercy of one more night in their own apartment. But she could not bear the thought of being anywhere else either. Her sister's house would not work, not yet, so soon after what had happened that morning. The antiseptic Super 8 was so depressing she couldn't entertain the thought. She wished she had a friend she could call. If only for guidance. Though she knew many people, she wouldn't trust any of them to give her sound advice.

"Keys?" he asked.

"Surely . . ." Drita began, and then didn't know how to continue.

"I can take back check if you are not sure," Sasha said.

She reached down and unconsciously touched her purse, where the check was securely in her wallet. She planned on depositing it tomorrow on her way out of town but now thought it was perhaps better to do it this afternoon if she could get to the bank before it closed.

"No," she whispered.

Sasha smiled nicely. "You are scared because your husband killed himself and you are all alone. It is best if you do not stay here. Too much has gone on. You should give me keys. Find somewhere else to stay."

This was the first they had spoken of her husband since Sasha gave his condolences upon first arriving. She assumed he now mentioned her being alone in order to frighten her, but it had the opposite effect. It made her want to fight. Ever since she found out about her husband's death she felt the instinct to protect herself and her son. This reminder simply invigorated her. People here did not speak directly like this, and now it made her think of past run-ins with Albanian government officials. Back then their open intimidation usually worked—mostly because she knew if she didn't comply they would follow through with their threats. But now this man was using the same tactics to try and break her down quickly. He didn't want to give her time to think.

"Of course we need to file the paperwork," she said, hoping it made sense.

"What filing? You signed contract and I gave money. Simple transaction."

"No," she said. "I will talk to my lawyer tomorrow and he will file." By tomorrow she didn't care what happened. She would gladly hand him the keys. "You can do whatever you need down there tonight but we will stay in our apartment. Just until tomorrow."

Sasha frowned deeply and rocked his head back and forth. "I can work down there as much as I need?" he said.

She nodded.

"I do not care then. I was not going to stay tonight anyway."

She didn't want to ask for or receive his permission, and she was glad she didn't.

He left soon after and she could hear him downstairs moving chairs and tables, rattling kitchen equipment. The sound was comforting, almost as though the restaurant were operating normally.

Drita now turned her attention to her son, who was still in his room. She had not yet been able to explain to Ismail what had happened. She knew as soon as she saw the police tape across the door of the restaurant (and confirmed by the blood on the floor) what her husband had done. She also knew her son was in a precarious emotional state and that her silence could potentially damage him, but she still could not bring herself to speak when he finally asked her for an explanation. She wished she had driven straight to the police station for information, and then gently repeated it to her son, or that she could go and do it now, but the thought of putting her trust in any governing entity made her angry. She had been systematically manipulated by people in charge all her life, until yesterday when that inspector came in and unjustly shut them down, though they had done nothing to deserve it. No. The emotional scars inflicted upon her son were the horrible collateral damage brought about by her own inability to go to authorities. She recognized it, felt even worse (if that was possible), but still did nothing. It was time, though, to talk with him about what had happened. He was a smart kid and no doubt had figured it out, but she must explain to him how their life would be from that moment onward.

She called softly to Ismail to gauge if he was eavesdropping. He didn't respond so she went to his bedroom door and listened. She didn't hear anything so she knocked gently. Like his father, he tried not to show emotion in front of her, but she felt an overwhelming need to check on him, to keep him in sight. She opened the door.

His room was empty. She must have made a mistake. She went to check the rest of the apartment. The TV was not on and he had not walked past them in the kitchen. He could have gone out the back way, the alley—the way they had come inside in order to avoid going through the restaurant. She sat back down at the table and resisted the impulse to go downstairs and see if Ismail was in the restaurant. If she did not go down, she could hold out hope that he was there, still close. She went to the sink and drank a glass of water. She needed to sit for a minute—two at the most—and not think. Downstairs she heard something—a glass bowl, a plate?—break loudly against the floor. It was not her problem anymore but she instantly felt the loss of the object, as she always had when something in the restaurant broke. Something jettisoned that needed to be replaced.

≈

After leaving his office, Arthur stopped by Dave's Ace Hardware and picked up a can of Raid Ant & Roach Killer. He then parked behind Marty's, entered the building through the loading dock, and walked through the store unnoticed until he was in the produce section, close enough to spray the tomatoes with Raid. The stock boy who had tackled him was the first to notice and shouted at Arthur as he ran toward him, but Arthur only pointed the can at his face in response. Soon the produce manager and store manager appeared but were also kept at a distance. They could only stand by and watch as he finished off meticulously spraying each tomato.

"You need to get rid of these," Arthur said as he backed away from the group toward the loading dock.

"This isn't right," the store manager said.

Arthur agreed and nodded sympathetically until he was through the back doors, then he sprinted to his truck, which he had kept running.

The exhilaration he felt while driving away grew with the recognition that what he had done was inexcusably wrong and the fulfillment of a long-held fantasy. He'd always dreamt of forcing people to do what he knew was right.

It was getting late in the day so he focused on the restaurants near Millsville. He stopped asking. At each restaurant—Hot Stuff Pizza, the White Horse Inn, Hodorffs Bar and Grill, the Bobcat Supper Club—he showed his badge and ordered the manager around like a bank robber in a 1940s gangster film. They always complied. He would then ask to use their phone and, changing his voice as much as possible (making it sound midwestern by shoehorning in a "Oh yah" or "You betcha"), he called the city, county, and state police and reported that he was offered drugs at a hot dog cart out on Highway 9.

The Bobcat Supper Club was on the outskirts of town—the "nicest" restaurant in Millsville. It offered large pieces of meat, potatoes, frozen green beans or peas heated in the microwave, and plenty of white-bread rolls. Other than the prime rib and the 1970s charm, its main feature was that it overlooked the land to the south of Millsville, which was surprisingly hilly for this part of the country, thanks to a glacier that tore the flat land apart thousands of years ago. The restaurant got its name because it faced Bobcat Mound—the high point of north central Wisconsin and a picturesque reminder to Arthur that he had not taken advantage of the opportunities that surrounded him. Before he left the restaurant he stood beside his Cherokee and took in the view.

Ever since he resigned himself to moving here he had planned on morphing into an outdoor enthusiast. If he was the kind of guy who got off work and went immediately to his favorite trail and hiked vigorously until dinner, he figured he could shake off the nagging feeling that he wasn't doing anything worthwhile with his life. Instead, it took him months to buy hiking boots, more months to remember to bring his hiking boots to work, and then he got lost trying to find the trail. When he finally put the boots on and walked around for a while, he was so covered in ticks that he couldn't comprehend how it was worth all the hassle. But now, taking in this scene at the golden hour on what was probably his last day of work, he wished that he had pushed himself to become what he had wanted to be. If he had hiked even once a week, he would, right now, consider himself a better person. He told himself that if he made it through all this and kept his job, he would become a hiker. Then he lifted up each pant leg and checked for ticks.

That moment of reflection was enough to slow his momentum. He decided to take a more circuitous route to the remaining restaurants so he could drive by the pushcart and warn Anna about the police. After all, she had been nice enough to sleep with him, and she only abetted her father so she would be able to leave town faster. He could respect that. He didn't personally care what they sold—he was tired and wanted it all over with. Of course, if Sasha was at the cart, he would gladly keep driving.

On his way he was able to stop and remove the tomatoes from a Kwik Trip gas station that served salads and sandwiches, a small diner closing up after lunch that had heard the radio report and had already disposed of their tomatoes, and a roadside stand that sold fresh vegetables where he spent six dollars to buy all their tomatoes and tossed them in the back of his truck to throw away later. As he started to feel cautiously proud of his productivity, the highway traffic slowed to a crawl. Generally this meant there was a deer or semitruck-related accident, but now he knew better. And though he had orchestrated it, the fact it was happening caused his mouth to go dry and he briefly felt the overwhelming need to shit. When it came down to it, he wanted to compel the world to adhere to what he thought was right, but he didn't want to stick around to see the consequences.

A number of police cars up ahead had their lights on, but the rubberneckers slowed the traffic. When it was finally Arthur's turn he slowed down just in time to see Anna in handcuffs, being led to a police car. He tried to accelerate quickly away but this only made his truck whir loudly and stall as it caught between gears. Anna turned toward the noise, which allowed Arthur to witness her expression shift from frightened to furious before she spat viciously in his direction.

≈

Janet hung up on the reporter and picked the candidate forms off her desk, dangled them over the garbage can, and did not let go. She hadn't admitted anything but the reporter seemed to know quite a bit already. The reporter's chirpy Madison voice grated on Janet's nerves. She couldn't stand that city. So clean and full of Volvos. What kind of town brags about being an isthmus? Maybe instead of running for office it would be better to stay here with her house and dogs.

No. She would still run. She couldn't give up. Sure, in part she needed to win because Janet needed to win at everything. But that was how she won, not why she ran.

The first time Janet paid any real attention to politics was when the representative from her district was outed on the floor of Congress in the early nineties. At least she thought it had been her representative—with gerrymandering she never was sure. Her teammate had simply handed her a newspaper on the bus and pointed out the story, asking if that was where she was from. After that Steve Gunderson—a man Janet had never heard of before—became a legend. Janet had never voted in her life. She couldn't have named either Wisconsin senator. But then a fellow Republican accused Steve Gunderson of advocating for tolerance only because he was gay and Steve did not contradict him. Janet and her teammates joked that Steve Gunderson would be known as the Jackie Robinson of openly gay congressional Republicans, except there would never be a second one. With so much time on their hands that year, the team found many reasons to shoehorn Steve Gunderson's name into jokes. After a one-hit shutout, the first baseman gave the pitcher a mock interview in the locker room where she said, "This one's for Steve!"

Joking aside, Janet was shocked by Steve's admission. She had hardly ever heard of anyone coming out, certainly not anyone from where she grew up. It barely even happened on TV. It was as though a teacher ripped off his mask and revealed he was a space alien and then kept on with the lesson.

Steve Gunderson acknowledged who he was, continued his argument, and then ran for office again. And won! She had to say this for the people in her district: they were loyal. Or they really, really didn't like change.

The irony was that the debate in which he was outed—after which they voted in favor of a confusingly worded bill ostensibly designed to deny federal funding to schools for portraying gay people "in a positive light" but was ultimately red meat for the evangelical base—was one of many stepping stones that made it impossible for future Republicans to come out. Steve won that election after being outed and then retired. Janet hoped he ran only as a kind of "fuck you" to the asshole who outed him. She only wished that the door he had opened had not been firmly shut behind him. For gay Republicans now there was, who, Mary Cheney? Overall it seemed pretty bleak.

Her plan when she got into politics was to get elected. She could figure it out from there. Other than gay rights she was in step with the party. If nothing else, she couldn't see herself as a Democrat—least of all winning as one in the staunchly red Chase County. But instead of feeling more secure after winning a local election, she felt desperate to hold on to her position and increasingly cautious. Soon, electoral victories and a small amount of power became a substitute for any private ideals she once held. Now she wanted to run, and she wanted to win. If coming out or voting for her own interest diminished her chances, then she would not do it. That was simply what the world had become: she could do what she believed or she could win. Lately she had chosen to win. Luckily there had not yet been any moments of truth for her. Nobody had asked to rent out the town-square gazebo for a gay wedding. Nobody had been denied any service because of their sexuality. This allowed her to not directly confront who she had become. She would just have to hope nobody called her out on the congressional floor, should she get there.

She knew explaining this would have shut up that reporter, or at least changed the story. It might have even brought national attention. Maybe she could run for senator! But no. She was who she was. One negative story didn't ruin her. The exposure could end up benefitting her campaign. She could still spin it, though it made running on an anti-immigration platform appear more and more necessary.

She set her forms back on her desk and turned to her computer to look up statistics on immigrants in her district (if there were too many, she would start figuring out how to change the perimeters of her district) when she heard a thump against the wall. She brightened, thinking it was Katie playfully announcing her return by throwing a softball of her own against the wall. But this thump—which was soon followed by another and then another—was on the *outside* wall of her office, the one facing the street. As she stood to investigate, a tomato arced through her open window and landed directly on the glass case housing the softball that her teammates had signed after her last game.

She ran to the softball and lifted it delicately off the floor. It was ripped by the glass shards, and bits of tomato pulp stuck to the cover resembled open wounds. For the first time, the events of the last couple days struck home. She ran to the window. The two old people in view were wearing masks.

Had word gotten out about her withholding information about the tomatoes from the public? Were they rebelling? This probably was how an insurrection would start around here—a passive-aggressive act where the thrower doesn't even stick around to take credit.

She was starting to feel like she had the previous night, when she almost drowned. The thought of dying like that made her shiver. She imagined being found floating naked and bloated by some idiot fisherman. She picked up her phone and dialed.

"Burt?" she said.

"Speaking."

"There's a Packers game tonight, right?"

"For sure! Got the Thursday game this week against—"

"The curfew's lifted."

"That's good, you know, Janet. Because I took off tonight special just to—"

"You're going to Pokeys to watch, right?"

"Heck else would I go? Only place with DirecTV. Thursday game's not on network and regular cable don't have the—"

"Make sure to tell people, Burt. Tell everyone that they can go out and watch at Pokeys. Tell them it's safe to go out now, that everything's over. By the way, did you actually catch anyone out after curfew last night?"

"Nah. I mean, I seen some people but just told them to get on home and they complied. Oh yeah, and I saw that one fella works over there at the county building. The one in the paper today. Figured he was out on official business. Was walking out toward his work."

"Interesting," Janet said.

"Not really, just out walking."

Janet hung up.

She called the radio station, told them about the curfew being lifted, and asked if they would put in a plug for going to Pokeys tonight to watch the game.

"Figured it was lifted already," Brittany said. "Since it was the tomatoes and all."

Janet asked her how she knew that.

"That one fella came in and told me. Had a badge? Kind of beat-up looking guy. Gave his name as Officer Reilly. Said to announce over the radio about the tomatoes. Said you told him to tell us as much."

It was possible Janet had underestimated Arthur. But at least now she had a plan. She'd go to Pokeys Bar tonight. She would be with her people while they drank and watched the Packers. She wouldn't talk about politics. They wanted to feel comforted and to be reassured that life was back to normal. She would let them know she was with them, that she was one of them, that she had been as affected as everyone else. About this she would be honest, since she had indeed been exposed to the same risks. Janet's presence would show them that the worst was over. If she succeeded in assuring them they were safe, and the Packers won, and she bought them beer, then she was pretty sure they'd forgive anything.

≈

Ismail still had not actually been told what had happened to his father. Based on how his mother was acting and what that woman at the pushcart said, he essentially figured it out, but there was still some part of him that wanted to believe he might have understood it wrong. Each time he had asked what happened she had cleared her throat and said nothing.

Sneaking out of the apartment would devastate his mother, but he couldn't stay there after listening to her negotiate with that man. He couldn't pretend to be OK with her selling their restaurant and home. He didn't know anything else. Their best times were spent down there, working. That was the closest he had ever felt to his father. No matter how uncomfortable life with his father got—the endless silences, the constant criticism and needling—while they were working he was always smiling for customers or complaining about them to Ismail while they stacked dishes or cleaned tables at the end of the night. He couldn't imagine life without the restaurant any more than he could imagine life without his father. So before his mother could tell him the news he snuck off. If he was not there, they could not leave.

He walked along the same route he took to school. He drifted toward familiarity and routine, but somehow everything now seemed alien to him. Every house stood out as odd—he couldn't get over how a bunch of strangers lived in each one. So many trees lined the streets, and the fire hydrants in this town were yellow. He felt unsettled, as he recently had when he reread his favorite childhood book, *The Giving Tree*, and was shocked at how boring he suddenly found it. He also disagreed with the premise: he saw the tree as weak for giving itself away and the boy as selfish for taking it. The experience had been disappointing, and he realized that he didn't enjoy it anymore because it wasn't written for who he was now. Like how, walking down the street, he didn't consider if he was seeing the town differently because these were his first moments alone since the death of his father or because he was going to leave soon and was looking with a sentimental eye. If he did consider it, though, he would hardly think it mattered.

He planned on sneaking into school and going into the storage room next to the gym where the large tumbling mats were stored—the mats used to break high jumpers' falls and cushion the ground where the wrestlers landed. The room was filled with these cushions so you never had to touch the ground, and the farther inside you got the more hidden you were within the cliffs and folds of the torn, vinyl-covered mats. This room was not common knowledge—Ismail found it by accident one day when he skipped lunch to wander around. Ever since, he made sure not to go in too often for fear his favorite spot would turn into a popular place for kids to hide while they skipped class or into the default make-out room. If he could lounge around in this room for a few hours—or perhaps overnight—

maybe he could come to accept, while resisting, what seemed inevitable: that he needed to support his mother, or that his mother, really, was just trying to support him.

If only that inspector hadn't shut them down yesterday. It all started with that. Ismail couldn't get over the man's sneering face when he insulted his father. He was glad he stood up for his father as he did, though maybe that only embarrassed his father more. Maybe he thought Ismail was fighting his battles? For the first time, but not the last, Ismail wondered if he was responsible for what happened to his father.

The football team was still practicing, despite school being canceled. Ismail climbed up on the bleachers to watch but immediately felt an excruciating squeezing of his stomach. Blackness obscured the edges of his vision as his mind clouded with fear. He did his best to hide his panic and didn't want to clamber back down—he didn't want to be more conspicuous than he already was. Being up here was the opposite of going into the dark room with the mats. Here he was in the sunshine, watching kids more athletic and popular than him, at ease with their blondness and their toothy smiles. And here he sat on metal bleachers that dug into the backs of his legs, making him aware of the pain his body was capable of instead of sitting on mats in a conscious effort to forget himself.

Alongside the football field was a road that led away from the school, toward the subdivision where the inspector lived. Ismail had been at a friend's house once when he saw the inspector mowing his yard. Back then Ismail hadn't thought much of it—the inspector was just one of those people who orbited their lives inside the restaurant. Now, though, he considered the range of malevolence he could inflict upon the inspector. Pranks escalated to felonies: he could toilet-paper his trees, egg his garage, light a bag of shit on fire on his doorstep and run, break a window, slash his tires, set fire to his house, go inside and kill him in his sleep. The ease with which these thoughts intensified—the fact that he could just as easily think of hurting a man as egging his house—frightened Ismail. He looked around, startled, as though someone who had been close enough might have been able to hear his thoughts.

He detested the inspector even more for making him feel this way, and his attention became split between the comfort of the cushioned room and the road leading to the inspector's house. As nice as it sounded to be in the dark, hidden and comfortable, he couldn't help but imagine the look on the inspector's face if Ismail were to hurt him as badly as the inspector had hurt his father. Seeing that look could be enough to sustain Ismail through whatever came next. He mashed his legs back into the sharp bleachers and wondered if he was capable of causing such pain.

≈

Arthur didn't remember anything about the ride home. He saw Anna in handcuffs, she spat at him, and the next thing he knew he was driving by the Little League baseball field where he had been a volunteer umpire two summers ago. That Anna was caught wasn't his fault. Katie woke him up with the news about the drugs—not that Janet was the best about passing along information to the proper authorities. And yet he was overwhelmed with guilt. Someone he identified with finally came to town, they had fun, he wanted to get to know her, and he had her arrested.

The first people he saw when he got to town were wearing masks—two old people slowly crossing the bridge over the river, each carrying a small bag of groceries. Arthur gripped the wheel tight. They were afraid for their lives while walking to the store because of what he had said yesterday. He stopped his truck in the middle of the road.

"There's no reason to wear those," he called to them.

They shifted their eyes toward him uneasily and kept walking.

"Your masks, you can take them off. You never needed them."

The woman nodded at him politely (or Arthur assumed politely since he couldn't see her expression), and the man stopped and said, "Huh?" and pointed at his ears.

"The masks!" Arthur shouted over his jangling engine. "You can take off your masks! You won't get sick! I promise!"

The woman waved a placating hand at him, as though letting him know that nothing in life is worth getting so worked up about. The man scrunched up his eyes, confused. He looked over at his wife and said something, his wife's mask jostled gently as she murmured a reply, and the man shook his head, baffled, before walking on.

Arthur took a breath to shout more but let the air slowly escape from him. He felt like a tired father letting his children go off and play instead of insisting they learn a necessary lesson. The old couple seemed happy enough and would eventually know the truth. Or they wouldn't.

Before driving away, Arthur glanced at his back seat and noticed the tomatoes he had bought at the roadside stand. He came up with an idea that would, if nothing else, raise his spirits. The county courthouse was two blocks away, and Janet usually kept her window open. He couldn't imagine a better way of declaring war.

Another line he couldn't uncross. A direct assault on his superior—something Arthur had never considered before today. He parked and wondered again, while reaching into his back seat, what he wanted from all this. He still didn't know, but for perhaps the first time in his life the answer definitely wasn't that he wanted safety and security.

He parked near the memorial park and took out the bag with the six tomatoes. To his left he heard a deep and resonant cough echo from the gazebo. Eldred was there, sleeping on the floor, his cast dangling down off the top step. This time, seeing Eldred in that position didn't inspire Arthur to help him. He had made that mistake already. Now when Arthur saw the man—the "poor man," as many people referred to him—he wondered how Eldred had become who he was. Arthur had never asked anyone but assumed—based on the number of Vietnam War–related buttons and the POW-MIA cap Eldred always wore—that he was a Vietnam veteran. If so, either the war had changed him or he was living with a mental illness to begin with and the war made his condition beyond hope. Callously, Arthur hoped that the war was to blame. Though perhaps Eldred had simply been alone too much and became unhinged because he was slightly too incompetent to hold down a job. In more lucid times Arthur would not have compared himself to a person with debilitating mental problems, but he was currently a seemingly sane man holding a bag of tomatoes that he intended to throw at a government building. Could there really be many steps between this and sleeping in the gazebo?

With his eyes still on Eldred, Arthur shook his head confidently, as though he had been asked a question to which the answer should have obviously been no but was secretly yes. Would you sleep with your friend's wife? Would you shut down a man's business and take out your petty frustration on his son? Would you blame a man for causing a serious illness if you didn't think he was guilty? Would you see a dead body and not report it? Would you throw tomatoes at a government building? No. Of course not. He would shake his head if asked any of these questions because he believed all these acts to be wrong. After he shook his head, he walked over and threw six tomatoes at Janet's window. The last one made it all the way through and into her office. Then he ran away.

≈

People swathed in Packer paraphernalia were already drifting toward Pokeys Bar by the time Adam was finally able to close up the office. An unusually high number of customers had complained about delivery of the paper, which Adam attributed to tension and frustration over the illness. At no other time in his life was Adam as polite and solicitous as he was while dealing with complaining customers. He found that while responding to these complaints his Wisconsin accent—which he had tried so hard to lose his freshman year of college—came back in full force. He ended each interaction by saying, "So you going to Pokeys to watch the Packers tonight?" To which the complainant would answer with some form of "You betcha."

In principle, Adam respected that nearly all social activity around here was centered around beer and Wisconsin-based sports. It was the same wholesome, unpretentious fun of their fathers and grandfathers. Adam appreciated sports for their grounded, meaningless rules and their exposure of the corrupted nature of people supporting an enterprise that almost openly encouraged cheating and lying and hurting people for fun.

And yet Adam never went to Packer games at Pokeys Bar. He found it depressing in the same way he used to find visits to his grandparents' house depressing as a child, even though they lived on a lake and had a speedboat. Both activities made him confront his aversion to prescribed amusement with a finite end. All he could think about in these situations was the ride home. Or he considered why he wasn't having as much fun as the people around him. He did not enjoy amusement parks in much the same way.

But tonight he decided to go to Pokeys to get the unfiltered news of the town. Drunk people shouting their fears over droning announcers and yammering commercials would tell him what was really going on—not newspapers or radio or TV and certainly not the internet. So he would go not only to stay in the loop but also to indulge the firm tug of journalistic instinct telling him that something of greater importance would occur.

After locking up the building he checked his phone. Three new texts from Sasha but none from Katie. A year ago this would have been ideal. Now Sasha was distracting him from winning Katie back and convincing her to go back to work. Adam reached into his pocket to tap his copper coil and was momentarily dismayed upon remembering he had sunk it in the river.

His life seemed so close to being under control. All he needed now was the illness to go away, Arthur to be out of their lives, Sasha to leave his house, and Katie to go back to work. Basically, he wanted things to go back to how they were a year ago, before he messed everything up. He even thought, perhaps based on the quiet confidence Katie displayed that afternoon, that he would like to seal their renewed partnership with a vigorous bout of lovemaking, though now she might have closed that door to him. Losing Katie suddenly made her unbelievably desirable. Adam wanted her more and more with each unanswered text.

He knew he should ignore Sasha and head straight home. But the restaurant was only a block down the street—he might as well get it over with or Sasha would never leave him alone. Further delays might even cause Sasha to rat him out to Katie about Utah, and then Adam would have no chance to get her back. Plus, convincing Sasha to stay at the restaurant tonight would be the most effective peace offering possible if he hoped to reopen negotiations with Katie.

He'd have to hurry, though, if he hoped to have any chance to wrap up with Katie before the game began. He didn't want their fight to lose momentum by leaving to watch a stupid football game, but he did not want to miss the scene at Pokeys either. He also couldn't wait until after the game—if she had more time to think, she might realize she'd be better off without him.

He pushed open the door to the restaurant, but when his eyes adjusted to the darkness, he was startled to see Sasha sitting in a position oddly similar to Bogdani's body that same afternoon.

≈

Anna was viciously angry when she phoned her father from the police station. She said he was a dried-up stupid old man, he was an idiot for thinking it was a smart idea to move to this piece-of-shit town, it was his fault that her life was ruined, nobody liked him, it wasn't surprising that he had failed at everything he ever tried, and she had wasted her life trying to please him. She told him to come down to the police station and tell them everything was his fault.

Sasha responded, "It is OK. I have lawyer."

She hung up.

He slumped into a chair. His plan was finally falling into place, and suddenly he was worse off than he'd ever been in his life.

For as much as Sasha believed the world was a cold and corrupt place, he couldn't bear to hear bad news about people he cared about. This squeamishness was so intense that he never allowed his family to have pets—in fact, if a relative or close acquaintance even mentioned a sick or recently deceased dog, he would instantly change the subject. Nobody could remember him speaking his wife's name in the ten years since she died. But he couldn't run from his daughter being arrested.

And yet Sasha couldn't get up. He couldn't even call his lawyer (who was still, as far as Sasha was concerned, indebted to Sasha for having borne false witness against the inspector) to get the ball rolling on a defense. He could only imagine, after a few minutes of sitting, perhaps continuing to clean his restaurant.

Upstairs he heard the tentative steps of Drita Bogdani. The idea of her up there comforted him, but also reminded him that his daughter might never again keep him company, that he was hopelessly alone in a strange place. Again, instead of spurring him into action, this only rooted him more firmly into his chair. If he were a different person, he may have reflected on what he had done to deserve all of this. Instead, he decided to wait out the inertia until he could resume cleaning. The only thing Sasha was sure of was that it was better to work than not.

Before he could get up, however, Adam walked into the restaurant. The sight of his friend brought Sasha, infuriatingly, to tears. He had not cried in front of another person in over fifty years. (The practice had been put to a violent halt at an early age by his father, who slapped the tears off nine-year-old Sasha for weeping upon the news that he had to move in with his aunt when his parents could no longer support him.) But it was a relief to see Adam, especially after he had ignored Sasha all day. After being so openly derided by Drita Bogdani and then spoken to so cruelly by his daughter, he saw Adam's presence as a hopeful sign that somebody in the world wanted to be near him. He was willing to forgive Adam for losing all his money in exchange for one kind word. He would agree to never step foot in the Bender house again for five minutes of benign companionship. Unfortunately, Adam was as uncomfortable around a crying man as Sasha was crying around another man.

"My daughter," he said, resisting the urge to snuffle, allowing snot to run onto his upper lip.

"What about her?" Adam said, looking mostly at the floor.

"She has been arrested."

"For what?" Adam asked, snapping to attention.

Sasha looked at him helplessly. He could only bring himself to say, "The pushcart."

Adam sighed and said, "Let's go get her."

Sasha nodded but did not move.

"Where is she? The local precinct?" Adam asked.

"She did not say."

Sasha watched as Adam clenched his fists. He wanted to plead for patience, tell his friend that he needed him to understand that he wished he could do something himself but did not know where to begin. He was gratified when Adam took out his phone.

He didn't want to listen to Adam's conversation, which would make his daughter's arrest even more of a reality. Instead, he imagined what the restaurant could soon be. The Albanians had no sense of décor. Sasha would keep only the fake plants and perhaps add more. He would also put up pictures—many pictures, colorful paintings of European street scenes and landscapes and paintings of boats at sea. He would paint the walls a bright color, perhaps orange, and maybe he would sponge-paint them, for a modern look. Soon, when he made money, he would put in a fake marble counter (fake marble is, after all, just as good as real marble) and new, higher tables with stools. People like to spend time in a lively space.

If it brought to mind Europe (but without the liberalism) and seemed more hip, they would be willing to stay longer and spend more money. He would also put pictures in the window of the dishes he was to offer. The sight of them would make people hungry and compel them to come inside to eat.

He had this exact plan even before he had seen the place, and he had gone over every detail in his head each time he had been in the restaurant over the past three days. The idea of the decorated restaurant made him happy at his upcoming success and life in a house near a pond or a stream. So happy, even now, that he was finally willing to get up and continue cleaning. By the time he began to stir, however, Adam got off the phone.

"She's being held at the precinct here in town for the night," Adam said. "She'll probably be transferred to county in the morning."

Sasha slunk back into his chair.

"I have lawyer," Sasha said. "Vanderberg."

Adam looked annoyed. "He's an estate lawyer," he said. "You'll need a criminal attorney."

Sliding deeper in his chair, Sasha didn't even try to figure out the difference. A lawyer was a lawyer. "Vanderberg can help," he said. "He owes me."

"Fine," Adam said, throwing up his hands. "Call him."

Sasha nodded and did nothing. He understood the appeal of sinking into that chair forever, of not having to deal with the well-organized hassle of life. It was not lost on him that he was sitting in the same position Bogdani had been in that morning. He just could not convince himself to do anything else. He felt not envious—but he realized it had not exactly been weakness that drove Bogdani. More like succumbing to sleep even though there was work still to be done. But no matter how much you want to work, Sasha thought, sometimes you are too tired to stay awake.

It was that thought that got him to stand up and lead Adam outside to go to the police station.

≈

The Bender girls always had two sets of clothes with them. They left the house wearing one set, and they changed into the other when they were out of sight of their parents. Jenny, the leader, made them do this though she never completely explained it to Caitlyn, who was a year younger.

The clothes they changed into wouldn't have been unacceptable to their parents—especially their father, who was weird about dressing anyway—but Jenny still insisted. From what Caitlyn gathered, the need for the change was threefold: first, if something soiled the original set, they could change back and return home without comment from their mother; second, if they happened to stay out overnight, they had a better chance of sneaking in the next morning and not getting caught (they could say, for instance, that they had gone for a morning walk, which would be weird but technically possible); third, if they for some reason needed to look different—say, if the police were after them (which was not so rare for a teenager in this town full of bored cops)—they could quickly change their appearance.

Caitlyn knew Jenny was weird. But she was also smart and brave and very fun. Caitlyn took part in all kinds of adventures because her sister insisted she come along. (Caitlyn assumed this insistence was also calculated: if they were both in trouble, each would be slightly less culpable.) Like when these college guys Jenny met online came and picked them up and took them to Eau Claire and Jenny got so drunk or stoned or something that Caitlyn had to get her home all on her own, pulling Jenny along as Jenny repeated, "I can't believe you're my sister!" over and over. When they arrived only slightly after curfew (thanks to a nerdy and slightly creepy guy at the party who drove them all the way home in exchange for fourteen-year-old Caitlyn's phone number), Caitlyn had never felt such a sense of pride.

It was Jenny who struck up a conversation with the Russian woman who, for some reason, was staying at their house. Jenny was instinctively wary of her at first, and they seemed to eyeball and circle each other like boxers sizing each other up in the ring. Caitlyn could see the Russian woman was not to be trifled with, but she also knew Jenny would see this as a challenge.

Jenny pulled Caitlyn out of bed and into the Russian's room the second night they stayed. The woman was looking at her phone when they came in. Her eyes narrowed at the sight of them. Jenny tried to act casual, and said, "You're from New York, right?" The woman said, "That's right." Jenny then started talking about how she wanted to move there after high school, how her friend Kristi wouldn't shut up about how great it was. The woman's expression did not change. Caitlyn had never been so afraid of someone in her life. She had no idea why Jenny dragged her in here and hated that she was wearing the long purple nightgown her grandmother had gotten her for Christmas. Eventually, after a couple more failed attempts at conversation, Jenny asked, "So I'll bet you can get all kinds of shit in New York, right?" The woman asked, "Shit?" And Jenny said, "Like, drugs?" The woman finally widened her eyes while she suppressed a smile. She glanced first at Jenny, then at frightened Caitlyn, then back at Jenny. She seemed to be calculating something, and then shrugged and said, "What do you want?"

Their parents had no idea. They trusted the sisters completely. Most of this, Caitlyn assumed, was due to Jenny's calculations and careful consideration at all times. Jenny even insisted Caitlyn get on the honor roll so she stay above suspicion. Talking to the Russian like this was a risk, but Jenny must have known or seen or sensed something if she was taking it. In any event, Jenny was right.

So the next night when they each texted Katie and asked if they could eat dinner and watch the Packers and stay over at a friend's house, Katie texted back that it was fine and to keep her informed of their plans. Normally Katie would have hesitated to allow them to stay over on a school night, and skeptical because they texted for permission at roughly the same time. But tonight she was relieved to have fewer people in the house.

She had expected—indeed rather wanted—an emotional drubbing after she confessed her affair. That Adam had been too hurt to fight struck at something deep within her, a well of guilt and shame she didn't know existed. After he'd stormed out of the newspaper building, she continued to sit in his office for a few minutes, stunned. She pitied him.

The Russian man, thankfully, left immediately after eating her sandwich. She'd been unable to eat after the tomato incident so she did laundry to keep busy. Adam's texts started to arrive during the first wash. The texts were oddly pleading, at least for him. *Let's work this out, please?* And *We've built too much together to end this way, over a health inspector.* And *We owe it to Caitlyn and Jenny to at least talk like adults. They shouldn't see us like this, Kates. I know I'm to blame too.* The pity and humiliation she'd felt since he left the office seeped out of her a little more with each of his texts. Something was off. This wasn't the Adam she knew. Sure, he was hurt, but these were too calculated. Adam didn't say please, or sincerely use phrases like "We've built too much together," he never admitted fault, and he barely ever considered Caitlyn and Jenny except to goof around with them or bark at their mistakes. The man she fell in love with bottled his emotions—that she was the only person who could divine what he was feeling was much of the reason why they worked together in the first place. For all Adam's faults he was honest, not often passive aggressive, and his manipulations were on the surface. Those qualities allowed Katie to trust him, if nothing else. But now he wanted something from her that he wasn't able to ask straight out—what he wanted she didn't know, but if he was afraid to ask, she was sure it wasn't in her best interest. That was a breach she could not abide. For the first time she began to see how she could stop loving him.

She folded clothes in her bedroom—a large pinch of chew in her lip making her happily spinny—and imagined that she was packing a bag to leave. She went so far as to imagine being on the road in her Honda Accord, driving south out of town up and down the hills of the moraine one last time. The freedom she felt was even greater than in her fantasies of sneaking away to Arthur's, and she considered jerking off right there on the bed in the afternoon.

Back when Adam was gone on his motorcycle trip, her clothes-folding fantasies used to center on what it would be like if Arthur came to live in their house. This scenario, far from making her feel free, produced a fear closer to claustrophobia. Her problem, she realized, may not have been that she was with the wrong man but with anyone at all. Of course, she didn't know what to actually do with this knowledge since she was already so entangled. Now, the dream of leaving her family made her feel naked and unafraid—that is, like the person she wished she was. She saw suddenly, clearly, that her obsessive concern with the superficial comfort of others stemmed from her inability to admit her own discontent. It would be such a relief to not have to worry about anyone else anymore. Of course, the fantasy ignored the cruelty and callousness it would take to abandon Caitlyn and Jenny. Leaving them would be the kind of selfishness she had been disgusted by all day. She hadn't been through anything she could not endure; her life was simply imperfect. Four more years and her daughters were out of high school. Then she could do whatever she wanted.

She finished folding and went to the window with her half-empty bottle of Diet Coke that was gross with tobacco spit. Outside it was beginning to get dark. A neighbor named Jared Kudenhagen—who always walked his dog without a leash or poop bags—walked by wearing a green Packers sweatshirt tucked into his jeans, his dog sniffing the overgrown grass across from Katie's house.

The sweatshirt, besides looking ridiculous tucked in like that, reminded her about the Packer game tonight. Soon everyone will gather at Pokeys Bar. They will look at the screen long enough to be exulted or furious. They will drive drunkenly home listening to the postgame homer radio broadcast, nodding along with replays of touchdowns or maddening calls by the refs. They will get home and fuck in celebration or frustration—they will rut because their emotions are stirred and this is a way of sorting them out. During the game they will forget everything that had happened over the past couple days because watching the Packers is worth the risk of getting sick, a way to forget that people died. Packer games were a reason to live—during those three hours at least.

Katie knew this because she had been around these people her whole life. Her father and mother and brothers and entire extended family *were* these people. She had been one until she met Adam. That he wasn't one of them was the reason she fell for him in the first place—why she had overlooked his many faults and copper-and-colored-bead eccentricities. She felt more interesting and unique when she was around him. He was different, and he liked her even though she was the same as everyone else. But now, as she watched the dog and owner walk away, she thought how Adam wasn't so special. He was confident, and smart compared to most people around here, and probably depressed, which gave him a haunted, broody quality. But, objectively, she was able to navigate the world better than he was. She didn't claim to know everything the universe was capable of—she lived in a world of change and uncertainty and his world was fixed and definite. Her way was how things actually were, not how she wanted them to be.

She would go to the bar to watch the game. Whether this was to assert something new or to get in touch with who she used to be she didn't know. She was afraid of seeing Janet (who would no doubt use this as an opportunity to campaign), but facing her would also be an opportunity. She would go to the bar and watch the game with her people, see Millsville in its most pure state, and decide where she fit in, if she fit in. Who knew, maybe she would leave with or without Adam. Or maybe she would stay and run for Janet's county commissioner seat whether Janet ran for Congress or not. Maybe she would give her first speech with a big wad of chewing tobacco bulging out of her lip.

There was something in the air, maybe the expectation and nervousness of people wondering if the Packers would beat whomever they were playing—the Bears? the Lions? some animal. All the emotions of the past two days could come safely to a head, nestled in the comfort of a game with clearly defined rules, where the only people hurt were helmeted men on TV. Men nobody at the bar would ever meet.

≈

Watching Packer games, for Cal, was probably the way an insignificant member of the mission control team felt watching the Navy SEALs perform an extremely dangerous and vitally important assassination: he had no real control over what happened but the outcome was of grave importance. Also, his real life had to be put on hold for a few hours in order to concentrate. So while he felt guilty about leaving his sick son at home to go watch the game, Cal didn't see any way around it. Besides, even if Jake was well, he was too young to go to the bar.

Cal, a bar-goer, did not frequent Pokeys, but he went tonight because Pokeys was the only bar in town with DirecTV, which carried the game. He was a regular at the Red Lantern Tavern, only because he went there when he first turned twenty-one and so felt loyal to it. The bars around here were mostly the same—prices and selection identical, ambience consisting of promotional beer posters with NASCAR cars or football players and Wisconsin Badger or Green Bay Packer paraphernalia.

But he was glad Pokeys didn't happen to be *his* bar because, for as long as he could remember, it had been undergoing a halfhearted renovation that split it into two distinct sections. Half the room—the side with the bar—was outfitted with blond, highly polished wood that brightly reflected the harsh bar lights directly overhead. The other, unfinished half of the bar had the obligatory Big Buck Hunter video game and dartboard but little else. That side was dark and unpainted and had a sheet of drywall sagging against a wall, a stack of two-by-sixes in a corner, and a folding table with an empty Crock-Pot.

He was disappointed, upon arriving, to be relegated to this unfinished area with the other latecomers. As much as he didn't like the brightness of the actual bar, it was much preferable to this other, more depressing side where he had to stand to see the TVs. Normally he would have come at least an hour early to start on a pitcher and get a seat, but he'd stayed home listening to the pregame until Jake fell asleep. Now, with this poor vantage point and already aching feet, he felt he was being unfairly punished. He was aggrieved and determined to take the stool of someone who stood to go to the bathroom, not yielding it back no matter what, since he didn't deserve to be standing either.

Even stealing a seat didn't seem likely, however, in this big crowd, and they seemed drunker and rowdier than usual, probably because they had been cooped up for the past two days. Nobody was wearing a mask so, Cal assumed, word of the tomatoes must have spread. Or maybe people were just done with worrying or were sick of being told what to do. Cal shut off his mind to the fears of the past few days too. The booth announcers were on the TV, signaling that kickoff was imminent.

He didn't see the ball kicked, however. The moment the cameras shifted to the field, the door cracked opened and Arthur Reilly poked his head in, looking surprised that anyone was there. Arthur blinked hard a couple times as though he had just stepped out of a cave. (Who, after all—besides someone in a cave—would not know that the Packers were on tonight?) Cal was thoroughly uninterested in why Arthur popped in. He only wanted to escape anything to do with work so he drifted yet deeper into the dark recesses of the lousy side of the bar. Grubbing spectators immediately occupied the vacated space. He ended up all the way back against the wall. He felt violated and inconsequential as he squinted toward the far-off screen.

≈

All afternoon and into the evening Arthur hunted for open restaurants. On his way home, exhausted, he saw cars outside the bar and remembered that sometimes Pokeys served food on weekends but that Arthur had not (in a rare show of pliability) required them to get a permit. Today, however, he was unbending and, football game or not, they would comply.

All hope for a simple interaction—the manager informing him that Cal had called and they had already thrown out their tomatoes—was lost when he saw Cal evaporate into the crowd like a cowardly ghost. Another complication was that he had probably—that day—pissed off quite a few people here. Indeed, a cursory scan revealed the stock boy who had tackled Arthur standing with his produce manager at the bar. They were staring at the screen and drinking beer from identical glasses. For a second Arthur was touched that they were able to put aside their nominal difference in status and chose to spend time together outside of work. It made him regret that his own presence so swiftly drove Cal away.

The place was filled with problematic people: the lawyer Vanderberg was sitting at a table clenching and releasing the hand with which he had punched Arthur; Adam and Sasha—the only people not engrossed by the game—were standing in the unfinished part of the bar; Sandra and Jill from his office were sitting at a corner booth craning their necks toward the TV; Kent Mueller was standing with some buddies and, from the fit of laughter that overtook them when Arthur looked their way, was possibly telling them about his and Arthur's ill-fated trip to the hospital with Eldred; Janet was sitting prominently at the bar, demonstratively professing her desire for a Packer victory.

He was picking his way along the wall behind the door—not hiding but not coming out into the open—when he excused himself past another familiar face: the man who had forced himself into Arthur's Cherokee a few hours before. His eyes were so glued to the screen that he didn't recognize Arthur even after Arthur tugged at his sleeve.

"It's me!" Arthur whispered.

Distracted recognition clouded the man's face.

"Oh yeah. Hey," he said and turned back to the TV.

"Why are you here?" Arthur whispered.

"Packers are on. Don't got DirecTV."

Lowering his voice, Arthur said, "They probably have your gun. Shouldn't you be out of sight?"

The man shrugged and said, "Packers are on."

Arthur shook his head and the man groaned loudly at something that happened in the game. Arthur wanted to explain to the man that he should feel bad. Partly because of this guy's irresponsibility and stupid fascination with guns, Bogdani was dead and his family was devastated. He shouldn't care what was going on in Green Bay. He should want to *do* something. Or perhaps the man's focus and determination revealed something important was happening simply from the communion of all these people. Everyone in the bar agreed on a uniform idea, a Packers win. Arthur was the one with only his own interest in mind (even if that interest was, ostensibly, wanting what was best for the whole town), and he was willing to impede all these people who were doing nothing of value but something of great significance. These people moved past troubles by finding something else to agree on, since agreeing and having fun were better than seeking difficult truths. This seemed like the wrong approach to life, and yet Arthur was the only outwardly miserable person in the room. He was sore and blood covered and tired and was probably going to lose his job. Everyone else was having the time of their lives.

At the bar he waited impatiently for the harried bartenders to fill their pitchers and give back change that was pocketed wholly by the customer with no thought of a tip. A woman nudged him. Arthur didn't respond.

"Hey!" the woman persisted.

Arthur didn't recognize her so he nodded and shifted focus back to the bartender.

"You the guy from the paper this morning?"

Arthur focused harder on the bartenders and contemplated walking behind the bar to better flag them down.

"What's going on?" asked a male voice behind Arthur.

"This the guy from the paper," the woman said. "The inspector. You going to close us down in the middle of the Packers?"

There was a chorus of laughter behind him. A McDonald's commercial was on the screen.

"I'd like to see him try!" said another voice, followed by more laughing.

Arthur had often been through this type of hostility while inspecting in New York. He felt the same sweat prick his palms, the need to control his breathing, the heat under his arms. He couldn't tell where the threat was more serious. More people were killed in New York, but it was easier to hide a body here. He kept staring at the bartenders.

The voices behind him quieted. The game was back on. Arthur was relieved until he saw that the bartenders had stopped working to watch as well. He'd have to call to them to get their attention. He closed his eyes, allowing himself a moment of pure misery.

"Excuse me," Arthur called out, just louder than the din.

"Leave them alone," someone said, nudging his shoulder. "Let them watch."

Arthur called again, louder.

The woman behind him shoved him hard saying, "Cut it out! Watch the friggin' game."

"Seriously!" Arthur yelled to the bartenders, "I just need a second!"

They seemed not to hear him.

"The fuck is this guy?" a new voice behind him said.

"Guy in the paper," the woman said. "Inspector who made everyone sick or whatever."

"Dude, watch the game. We got the ball."

"I understand that!" Arthur said, much louder than he intended, as he turned to face them. "The fucking game is on! I comprehend." To demonstrate his understanding he gestured toward the TV, just in time to see the Packers throw an interception.

The cursing and groaning frightened him. The camaraderie he had witnessed before had turned into a biker-gang togetherness. He considered joining in by pretending to care about this unfortunate turn of events for the Packers but only felt his body sag as he waited for whatever befell him.

There were calls of "There you fucking go, asshole!" and "Who the fuck is this guy?" and "Get him the fuck out of here!" and "Nice going, shithead!"

For once Arthur wanted the game to be on the screen, but instead there was a Bud Light commercial.

"Here's your chance, dude!" came a new, louder, more familiar voice behind him. "Come on, what was so goddamn important?"

A wider area around their little group was becoming quiet.

"No, tell us. Here you go, let everyone know. What was so goddamn important?"

Arthur recognized the voice as the produce manager's from Marty's.

"I just need to talk to the bartender." Arthur said, his voice cracking, "I need to—"

"Can't hear you!" someone out of sight shouted.

"Let's get him up so we can hear him better," the produce manager said, his confident voice dripping with irony.

Before Arthur could do anything but repeat "no no no no no no" the produce manager and stock boy grabbed him under the shoulders and hefted him up so he was sitting on the bar.

This briefly lifted everyone's spirits, as if a monkey had been put up there to dance for them. Arthur stopped struggling and scooted away from his tormentors.

He stood and everyone raised their beers and cheered up at him. Some laughed, some called on him to speak. Burt Butzler, out of uniform and looking particularly unlike a chief of police, blearily smiled up at him a couple yards down the bar. When Arthur said, "Burt, come on—help me out!" Burt shrugged and said, "Off duty." Arthur scanned the crowd, searching for a friend, and realized he had none left.

With no other options, his panic gave way to clarity. Fear could do him no favors now. They wouldn't beat him up while he was up there—maybe on his way out of the bar, but not openly like this. Anyway, he had little to lose. He'd already been beat up, his car was wrecked, he'd surely lost his job, all his secrets were exposed, the Bogdanis' misery would be forever on his conscience, and he was being openly ridiculed while soaked in spilled beer and blood. But at least, finally, he got what he had asked for all day: people to listen to him. He couldn't let the opportunity slip away.

"Fine," he called out. The crowd hushed slightly and he took a breath to speak, to tell them everything. "First thing—"

"Hey, shut up there, game's back on," someone sitting near him at the bar said.

Arthur looked back and saw that the blue team—the Lions, he believed—had the ball. So he calmly turned around, sat on the wet bar, watched the TV, and waited for a commercial.

≈

Sasha didn't think it was possible for him to be interested in an American football game, but then they threw the inspector on the bar. Until then, when he accidentally saw what was happening on the screen, he was only reminded of how overly complicated and physically bloated Americans were. Adam had tried to explain the rules to him—something about "downs"—but quickly gave up due to mutual disinterest. They had come straight to Pokeys from the police station after being told there was nothing they could do for Anna that night. Sasha went to the bar only for a distraction—at least until the inspector was forced to make a spectacle of himself. Then he keenly watched and waited for one of the many commercials, during which the inspector would speak.

Through three commercial breaks (and, from what Sasha could tell, several good turns for the team everyone was rooting for), the inspector explained much of what had happened since the sickness began. Hecklers interrupted his speeches and he had to keep recapping what he had already said so that people of increasing drunkenness could keep up. Plus, a woman in front—big, strong woman—kept correcting and undermining him. Sasha liked this woman.

"So, like I said," Arthur, still standing on the bar, had said during the second break, "as far as we know, the MFR had no more to do with this than any other restaurant or grocery store. I closed that down for reasons that had nothing to do with the illness."

"You think that's true," the woman in front had said. "But you don't know."

"No, it's true. A random bad shipment of tomatoes—ordinary, everyday tomatoes—got people sick. Janet blamed me and then the restaurant so it would look like she knew more than she did."

"Totally untrue," the woman said calmly and stood as tall as she could to address the crowd. "We had valid reasons to believe that the man—an immigrant who came here from what I'm pretty sure could be a Muslim country—could have caused the outbreak. He," she said, pointing at Arthur, "is the one who told me!"

"Janet, you and I both know—"

This was cut short by a cacophony of voices telling them to shut up. The game was back on.

"He's doing pretty well," Adam said while they waited for another commercial break. "Holding his own. Can't be easy up there."

"If he was smart, he would not be up on bar," Sasha said. "This is not way to handle this. You cannot try to tell the truth. The woman, she is right. She acts as though she does not know—that nobody can know for sure—but she hints that it is one way. Since people already think that way, they want to believe her. People trust when someone says that someone else is lying and they pretend that what they want the truth to be is what is actually true. The inspector should either tell them exactly what to think regardless of truth or else just lie."

They were quiet again as yet another commercial came on. Sasha began to warm up to the sport because of how ingeniously it tricked people into watching so many commercials. It made him consider creating a commercial for his new restaurant and airing it during football games. He could present the renovated space and assure people that the mess had been cleaned up—he could mention that his kitchen is now safe and that they had not been operating during the sickness. He could also introduce his expanded menu, which would include pizza and gyro and panini and, perhaps, even an upscale tea service, which could get people to spend more money.

The inspector stood up again, but before he could speak someone shouted, "What about you and those foreigners? Heard you got a ride with them this morning and they were selling drugs. You with them?"

Arthur cleared his throat and was interrupted several more times.

"What's that on your pants?"

"Why's your jaw swollen?"

"You really spray someone with Raid at Marty's?"

"You the creep with the Vanderberg girl? You know she's only a sophomore?"

"Vanderberg really hit you? That why your jaw's hurt?"

"Damn right I hit the son of a bitch!" Nils Vanderberg yelled, his swollen fist held high in the air. Everyone cheered and raised their glasses.

Sasha did not like that he was mentioned. He watched as, between interruptions, the inspector looked around the bar trying to identify his questioners. Finally his gaze fell on Sasha and they held eye contact. When there was time to speak he was only able to say, "Well, about that hot dog cart out on Highway 9 . . ." before the game came back on.

Hearing Arthur (finally, over the course of two commercial breaks) expose the truth about the Bykovs gratified Katie enough to justify having come to the bar. Until Arthur started speaking, she had politely declined free beers from men at a nearby table and followed the game with, at best, mild enthusiasm. She naturally wanted the Packers to win so people would be happy but had little stake in the outcome herself.

It was personally rewarding to her, however, when Arthur explained how the Bykovs sabotaged the poor Bogdanis' kitchen, had indeed sold drugs, and illegally sold food out of their pushcart during the height of the illness. They should not, he said, be trusted to operate the MFR. He also said that he, Arthur, regretted accepting a ride from them and took full responsibility for not doing more to stop them. During Arthur's speech Sasha looked so miserable that Katie nearly felt sorry for him. But at least now she'd get her house back.

Arthur spent most of the second quarter and halftime clearing the Bogdanis and implicating the Bykovs as best he could. He used the remainder of halftime to explain that he had nothing to do with that Vanderberg girl but someone else did, and if it didn't stop immediately, he would hang posters around town advertising who the culprit was.

Katie admired what Arthur was doing—it was brave to force people to listen to the truth. He was so much different at work. At home he was hesitant and awkward, always guessing what she wanted to hear. Who knew if she would have bothered waiting for Adam if he had spoken up like this with her? Even the one night she and Arthur spent together when they did nothing special but only cooked and watched TV and slept in the same bed, he didn't once say something like, "This is nice. We should do it more often." He only occasionally stared at her helplessly, as if he knew the words but forgot the language to say them in. If this Arthur—the one standing on the bar, the one who very well might get beat up upon his exit—told her what he wanted from her, what he would do to keep her, then maybe they could be together. This Arthur she could get on board with. Though this Arthur, she also realized, reminded her much more of Adam.

Her stomach lurched as it dawned on her that someone might shout something about her up to Arthur. Having her indiscretions broadcast publicly was her greatest fear and she suddenly felt trapped in the middle of this beery-breathed mass. She wanted to claw her way out but thought that would somehow make her look suspicious. Plus, even if she ran, the words could still be said. She still turned around wildly, searching for an escape.

A few yards behind her she saw Cal Luedtke, whom Arthur had spent so much of their time alone together complaining about. Now that guy definitely didn't care what anybody thought of him. Last year he got so drunk at the county government Christmas party he threw up on the cake—and then he drove home! And yet he keeps bumbling along, happy as a clam, friend to all. Look at him now, not a care in the world, half in the bag here at the bar when his son was sick with the mystery illness. Katie didn't like going to work when one of her daughters had a cold. Sure, people poked fun at him behind his back, but what did that matter to him? Why was it that Katie cared so deeply about what other people thought of her? It felt somehow irresponsible to not worry about being judged, as though she shouldn't trust herself to do the right thing. Maybe, she thought for the first time in her life, this time it would be somehow freeing to get exposed.

Her phone rang. It was Caitlyn.

"Mom?" her daughter said with a shaky voice.

"I can't really hear you," Katie said, picking her way toward the exit.

"Mom, you need to come here now."

Katie stiffened in panic and stopped, blocking people's view. She said, "Are you safe?" but the shouts around her drowned out the reply.

Outside, after having stepped on toes and shoving one man completely off his stool, she finally heard her daughter's voice in between sobs. The phrases Katie most clearly heard were "I'm so sorry" and "police station."

"Caitlyn, honey?" she said and, not waiting for the sobbing to subside, added, "We're on our way."

Katie hung up and froze for a few seconds, torn between going inside to get Adam and rushing to her car. While she was standing there, motionless, she saw a lone figure across the street, looking lost. The figure walked under a street lamp, and Katie saw it was Drita Bogdani. She seemed exhausted—the guilt and fear and despair evident on her face even from where Katie stood. The desire to help this poor woman passed quickly through Katie, and she turned around to go inside and get her husband.

≈

Janet didn't like the direction the night had taken. These town-wide events—high school football games, the Heritage Days Festival, the county fair—were always difficult. Not that she struggled to make a good impression—quite the opposite—but the mental toll it took to smile and be charming in exactly the right way exhausted her. She preferred the confines of her office, where she could carefully craft her decisions and control which people she had to deal with. These big gatherings were free-for-alls of sociality that left her shaky and depressed. She had never enjoyed being in large groups but luckily had mastered the art of performing in them.

Her old plan had been to set herself apart—her softball prowess taught her that people liked her best when she excelled and performed for their amusement. But she could rope only so many cattle before people saw her as a cowboy. She needed them to trust her and agree with her, or at least trust that they probably would agree with her if they bothered to check what she was doing. So she worked hard at becoming a leader during social occasions. People needed as much guidance while having fun as they did while living their regular lives.

Until Arthur got up on that bar, everything had been perfect. The Packers were winning and Pokeys had given her a discount on pitchers. People didn't seem to notice her recent missteps, and they weren't overly distressed that the man she had wrongly blamed killed himself. The few times she swung the conversation toward these disagreeable subjects, people appeared confused about the facts, which was ideal. There was a fair chance people weren't expressing their concerns to her and instead were talking behind her back. But this only meant that it wasn't important enough to yell at her about, so they'd forget about it after a few days of grousing. According to the hospital, a few sick people were straggling in, but the illness had all but run its course. Nobody else was likely to die. Also in her favor—as Adam had informed her earlier—the widow of the immigrant was leaving town. Apparently another immigrant had bought her out, so there was no reminder left of Janet's mistake. She supported this immigrant-for-immigrant exchange, since it left a local representative for her anti-immigration platform.

But now that Arthur was up on the bar forcing people to deal with reality, everybody was drinking more, since they had entertainment during commercials as well. So far, Janet had managed to divert and confuse his message, but tomorrow, as hangovers lifted, people would think back to what that pansy New Yorker said and wonder if any of it was true.

Perhaps she could push him off the bar. People would probably cheer and raise their glasses to her if she did. It would be so satisfying to see him topple over, maybe fall on a keg and smash his teeth or break his neck. So many problems would go away. But the push might also legitimize the inspector—it could be akin to Janet admitting guilt. Though she considered herself a maverick, she avoided taking risks whenever possible. Even the calf she had chased down and hog-tied had been hobbled beforehand so it was easier to tackle.

Instead of shoving him, she argued with him about the topics that involved her and stayed quiet during the ones that didn't. When not arguing, she tried to look completely disinterested by rolling her eyes or staring blankly at the bar. She couldn't allow him any credibility at all.

Luckily, this disinterested posture gave her a clear view of Arthur's feet up on the bar. When the way to discredit him came to her, she couldn't help but smile. She had to wait to strike, which meant watching a long stretch of an increasingly boring game in the third quarter (the Packers were up 24–7) until a new set of commercials came on. Just as the crowd quieted down and Arthur opened his mouth to deny spraying any *person* with Raid at Marty's that afternoon, Janet interrupted him.

"Just one second!" she yelled, bringing Arthur and everyone else to silence.

"What?" Arthur finally said, hesitantly.

Janet cleared her throat and spoke calmly as she asked, pointing at his shoes, "Are those Rockports?"

≈

It felt so good—so right—to stand up on that bar and so honestly say everything he wanted to say. Then Janet pointed out his shoes and it was as though she had shoved him off the bar and cracked his skull on a keg. It threw him off so completely that he couldn't even pretend to deny it.

People were quick to bring others up to speed. At first Burt refused to fill in the gaps in the radio report—saying he couldn't talk about an ongoing investigation—but after enough cajoling, a drunken Burt finally admitted that there had been footprints on the floor of the restaurant.

Arthur felt trapped. Since gaining composure on the bar he had, from his high vantage point, kept prison-guard control over the crowd. Now standing up here only exposed him and made him vulnerable. When people yelled for him to show them his shoes, he shook his head petulantly but couldn't think of any reason not to if he indeed wasn't guilty.

The produce manager finally grabbed for Arthur's foot, and Arthur instinctively kicked his hand away—huge mistake. Before he could jump behind the bar and maybe keep them at bay by spraying them with the soda hose, his legs were grabbed.

He toppled hard onto the bar. The fall redoubled the pain in his ribs and face, and he offered little resistance as they worked to wrench off his shoes. He even allowed himself a few seconds to appreciate the cool, wet surface during an awkward moment while they discussed how to untie Arthur's tight double knot. Eventually someone yelled, "Yep! Ten-and-a-half!" Time seemed to briefly stop after the announcement while people digested this revelation. Arthur feared that they might drag him out of the bar and beat him senseless, just because they couldn't think of anything better to do.

Eventually Burt was persuaded to take Arthur to the station. Burt put up a fight—arguing that he took the night off special to watch the game, had indeed asked for it off "months ago! Months ago!"—but nobody cared. So he stood Arthur up roughly and shoved him out past the dirty looks of large men who jabbed their flanneled shoulders into him.

Being locked in the back of a police car with a drunk, angry Burt Butzler at the wheel seemed like punishment enough, but Arthur was taken in for questioning anyway. Once in the station Burt abandoned him to the confused officer at the front desk. He handed her Arthur's shoes and said, "Keep him here. I'm going back."

Ten minutes earlier, Arthur had felt euphoric, but the feeling had vanished completely after the frightening, stop-sign-running ride with Burt.

And when he assumed his day couldn't get worse, he saw Katie and Adam huddled in the waiting room where he was deposited. A deep depression descended upon him, and he briefly considered admitting he killed Bogdani so he would have to confront only the relatively simple problem of specific prosecution rather than vague guilt.

It was a long time before it dawned on him how strange it was that nobody was speaking. And though he welcomed the silence, something must have been seriously wrong if Katie wasn't yammering in a failed effort to make everyone else feel at ease.

"Why are you here?" Arthur asked.

Adam looked up at him, annoyed. Too much had passed among the three of them to talk normally now. This was his last opportunity to assert himself, to make the effort to become a part of Katie's life or else bow out of both their lives completely. Seeing them together in their pain, it was obvious there was no room for him. This, at the moment, was too great a loss to comprehend. He lowered his eyes and waited. He had to leave them alone.

Soon their daughters came out, accompanied by the officer at the front desk who was still, Arthur hoped, in possession of his shoes. The daughters looked scruffy and tired, makeup down their faces. The younger girl—Caitlyn—stayed against the wall, ashamed, but the older—Jenny—approached her parents boldly. Nothing in the room moved for a minute, then Katie screamed, "Heroin! My daughters were caught with freaking heroin!"

Caitlyn burst out crying and pressed her face against the wall, and Jenny said, "Mom—" but Katie held up a silencing hand.

Arthur was shocked. The two neighbor girls—whom he had first met when they were in middle school and still looked to him like small children—had taken, to Arthur's knowledge, the hardest drug there was to take. He reassessed them both and, though they were the same kids, they now had an experience that he himself lacked. He admired them and wondered why *he* had never tried heroin. He wished he knew how it felt. Since two small-town girls had done it, was he perhaps the only square who hadn't snorted (or smoked or injected?) it? He had done a little cocaine and some hallucinogens in college, but everyone did that. For confirmation of the bizarreness in all this, he looked at Adam—not at their father but at his friend—and found Adam already staring at him. Arthur made the facial expression equivalent of "*Jesus!*" and Adam responded with the smallest hint of a grin and a slight, modest cock of his head. Arthur suspected Adam was in some strange way proud of his daughters.

This was Arthur's last intimate moment with a member of the Bender family. There was no future with Katie; he could no longer be Adam's friend. He didn't cause their daughters to do heroin—they were probably being bored, stupid, impulsive teenagers—but he needed to get on with his own life, stop glomming on to theirs. The relief he felt at this was nearly palpable. He relaxed in his hard plastic chair, turned away from the Benders, and let them be. He had never been as big a part of their lives as they were to his; this realization was embarrassing and later would make Arthur very lonely. For now, he stared at a poster that featured a large set of handcuffs set against a dark background and was thankful that Burt, in his haste, had not handcuffed him, and Arthur was free to move his arms as he pleased.

≈

The Packers were winning, Cal was sure of that. But he wasn't able to follow the game. Ever since Arthur had mentioned Kristi during halftime—just before they beat him up and took him to the station—Cal could only steadily drink beer and try to hold himself together. For the first time in his life, he wished the Packers were losing, so he would have an excuse to look so miserable. But they weren't, so he staggered to the bathroom and splashed water on his face.

"Better pace yourself there, buddy," a man at the urinal said while Cal was staring at his wet face in the mirror. "Only the third quarter."

Cal glanced at the man and clenched his fists. It was Kent Mueller, Cal's HVAC guy. Kent had been a couple years below him in school and rode the bench on the football team.

"Yeah," Kent went on, unprompted, "you know, yesterday I was with the fella standing up there on the bar. Went all the way to Danville with him because he thought Eldred was sick when he was just sleeping one off. Nice enough guy, I suppose. A little standoffish. From New York and all. I was actually there when he first took a look at that cart where that Russian girl was arrested."

Cal shifted focus back to his reflection and wondered how long Kent was going to pee.

"You hear it about him and that Vanderberg girl?" Kent continued. "None of my business but I don't believe it myself. Guy like that with a stick up his ass—no offense, I know you work with him up there at the county—doesn't seem the type to take advantage of a young girl. Seems like a Boy Scout, if you ask me."

Cal bit his lip and could hear Kent zipping up.

"I know a guy does something like that to my daughter I'll do more than punch him. You're lucky you have a boy. Speaking of, how in hell is he? Heard he got what's going around. He going to play this week? Could sure use him. West Oran is right up there with us in conference."

Cal couldn't bring himself to respond and walked out of the bathroom. That Kristi was forced from him was for the best. If she had broken up with him, he might have reacted badly, and if it kept on, they could very well be caught. But Cal had assumed they'd at least end it in person, which would have led to tearful farewell lovemaking. This would have significantly softened the blow.

Worse still was the knowledge that he had a hand in this. If he hadn't called Bogdani and said what he said, perhaps Bogdani would still be alive and none of this would have happened. Arthur might not have come into the office earlier and pressed Cal to break it off, and he almost certainly wouldn't have talked about Kristi while up on the bar. The town seemed to go a little crazy ever since the news of the suicide. If Bogdani were alive, Cal could continue his affair, and even if she eventually broke it off or if they were caught, he would forever have additional memories of her. Before Kristi there weren't many variations to the rhythms of Cal's life. A particularly good meal or many-pointed buck or watching his son pancake-block an opponent into the dirt was as much elation as he could hope for, but all these produced were short-lived surface emotions. In Kristi he had dug himself a little well from which he could draw sustenance. Now Arthur had filled in and sealed that well forever.

He took out his phone and typed *We need 2 talk. Meet me at my work after midnight if u can get away*. His fingers shook and he did not check his phone again in case there wasn't a reply.

It frightened him that watching the Packers with all his friends wasn't enough to make him happy. If this wasn't enough anymore, what would be? Cal had never known the pain of heartbreak, and to learn at this relatively late age how much it hurt was overwhelming. Opening himself up to such heights of joy had also exposed himself to such depths of pain.

At what he considered his low point—when even a sixty-four-yard Packers touchdown couldn't rouse him from his despair—his thoughts, for some reason, went to Bogdani. But of course they didn't linger.

He would do only the bare minimum. Tonight he would get as drunk as possible and figure out a way to get away from his house so he could go break up with Kristi. It would be the hardest thing he had ever done—but only because he had done so little.

Kristi's father was sitting at a table between Cal and the TV, and each time he glanced in the lawyer's direction Cal couldn't help but recall a distinct sexual memory of the man's daughter. Kent's words about Cal being lucky that he had a son echoed back, and he recognized they were true: if his son had an affair with an older woman, Cal would perhaps be openly proud. But Nils Vanderberg was protecting his daughter—he didn't want to lose her. Cal, having recently come so close to losing his own son, felt for the first time the wrongness of what he had done.

Loud cheers snapped Cal out of his thoughts. He clapped without emotion but was able to keep himself from returning to the whirlpool that was threatening to take him under. He forced himself to smile, clap harder. He clapped so hard his hands hurt. Then he went up to the bar and ordered another beer.

≈

Sasha gathered his and his daughter's belongings from the Benders' house and drove his truck, with pushcart attached, to his new restaurant.

It had all gone wrong so quickly. It was impossible to open now after the way people at the bar glared when the inspector implicated him. He did not consider whether he deserved any of this. *Deserved* had nothing to do with it. Sasha did not believe in *deserved*. He had orchestrated everything perfectly, and because of one uptight man (at the station his daughter told him—or, rather, shouted at him—that the inspector had gotten her arrested) it was all taken away. Nobody gained from Sasha's downfall.

Now there was no restaurant. Now there was one more person in the jail. Now Sasha had to leave so there was one less productive person in their shitty nothing town.

He felt immense loss as soon as he entered the dining room. There was no regret since it was basically chance that had made him fail. No thought to what he should have done differently—if he shouldn't have paid that man to tear apart the Bogdanis' kitchen, if he shouldn't have allowed his daughter to sell drugs. It was bad luck that his arrival had coincided with a strange illness that randomly hit the town. Just bad luck.

He had mopped up the floor earlier in the day so it gleamed when he turned on the light. The tables and chairs were still arranged in a circle around the spot where Bogdani had been sitting. It reminded Sasha of a dance floor. Perhaps, he thought, he could have rented the place out on weekends for parties and wedding receptions, that this would be how it would look after a particularly rowdy and profitable night. He had to stop thinking of ideas for how to make the most of this place.

The remaining members of a family who hated him were upstairs. He would soon go up and ask the woman to buy back the restaurant. He would even be willing to sell it at a lower price. He needed money to help his daughter. Adam had been right—Vanderberg could not help except to refer him to a proper lawyer and estimate, with jaw-dropping calm, how much it would cost to give Anna a proper defense. Sasha did not hesitate when he said he would do everything possible for his daughter.

Though it was late, he took an extra moment in what was still his restaurant. He arranged the chairs and tables to make it resemble a place where people would eat. He walked through the kitchen that he had already made strides in restoring. He stood behind the counter and touched his fingers lightly on the buttons of the cash register that one day should have held the money to make him happy for the rest of his life. He wasn't asking for too much. He had worked so hard his whole life and had persevered through much harsher trials than attempting to live a modest life in a below-average town. He moved his family away from a country where happiness was such a distant dream, took any job necessary to earn the money to buy a stake in the restaurant in Brooklyn, raised a daughter, moved on with his life after burying his wife. Oddly, despite the havoc he was willing to create, all he wanted was peace—that was why he came to this country in the first place and why it was such a loss that he currently had nowhere to go. He would have to keep working, first to free his daughter and then to get back on his feet. Every morning he would get up and decide what he needed to do to keep himself moving forward, and he would begin by going upstairs and asking Drita Bogdani to take pity on him by buying back her restaurant. He sighed at such a miserable task ahead of him, then began to make his way upstairs.

≈

Ismail had nearly fallen asleep waiting for Arthur to come home. He had been in the woods behind Arthur's house since nightfall, sitting on his bike and waiting. By the time Arthur arrived Ismail was in a half-sleep state, dreaming that the area around him was full of animals that allowed him to pet and cuddle them. The headlights of the police car that dropped Arthur off stirred Ismail; the slamming of the car door woke him completely. His heart raced when he couldn't figure out where he was. Then he was afraid at being all alone in such an alien environment. He was also quite cold.

He didn't know why he was so intent on spying on the inspector. He didn't expect to gain anything from it. Any fantasies he had of hurting him had disappeared—Ismail lacked the courage and stupidity it took for a kid to harm an adult. He needed to see him. It was a place to focus his pain. Besides, Ismail liked spying. Watching someone while not moving a muscle or causing a sound was calming.

Ismail walked his bike forward until he got a clear view into the inspector's house. His breath came out in tight gasps. He had never looked so directly inside a house before, though he often desired to. Any time he was out walking at night his eyes were glued to lighted windows, to see what was happening inside, how it was different from his own life. Either the inspector's house didn't have blinds or curtains or he didn't bother to draw them. Ismail got off his bike and tracked the man's movements from window to window.

The inspector was barely inside the door when he took off his pants and left them right there on the floor. This fascinated and frightened Ismail. He thought maybe the man knew he was watching and was doing something gross to deliberately make Ismail uncomfortable. Ismail then went to the back of the house to keep the inspector in sight. Eventually the inspector flipped open his computer. Ismail nearly pressed his nose to the window to see the screen. The inspector was on Facebook. The banality of the next twenty minutes would have caused a less diligent person to give up, but whether it was boring didn't cross Ismail's mind. He watched this inspector, whom he had loathed so intensely for the past two days, act like a normal lonely person. Ismail had an impulse to go into the house so the inspector would have someone to talk to. In all of Ismail's spying efforts he had never seen someone so alone—the houses he looked into usually had families inside. Individuals, if he saw them on their own, seemed to be trying to get some time to themselves.

The inspector abruptly closed the computer and went to the kitchen, prepared and ate a peanut-butter-and-banana sandwich, drank milk directly from the carton, and took off his shirt. Now he was standing in the kitchen in his tighty-whities. The poor inspector. Ismail couldn't help but feel sorry for this balding, flabby man whom nobody cared enough about to make him keep his pants on or prepare dinner with or force him to drink from a glass or ask him about his day. No wonder he was such a stickler in his work. He had so little else. But this shifted Ismail's thoughts back to his father and a cry nearly escaped him. If this man humiliated his father and shut down the restaurant because he had nothing else in his life—if he had simply taken out his boredom on his father—it was almost worse than doing it for some kind of gain. At least if he had gotten something out of it—amusement or profit or whatever—there would have been a reason. The randomness was more hurtful because it needn't have happened. The desire to hurt the man again came over Ismail, and he watched him hawkishly, waiting to take some kind of advantage.

The inspector retreated into the bowels of his home, and Ismail, after circling the house completely to get a better view, assumed he was in the bathroom. Ismail went back to his bike to wait and after a few minutes began to get sleepy.

He jumped when the front door banged shut. By the time he located the nearly naked inspector he was almost out of sight. He was running down the street with a towel billowing behind him.

Ismail mounted his bike and pushed off, down the street past the Benders' house where a man's silhouette was visible in a lit upstairs window, from which he heard muffled yelling. It felt good to be in motion. To be trailing someone was, just then, preferable to waiting. If nothing else, it warmed him. He pedaled hard to get the inspector in sight—he had already turned two corners by the time Ismail reached the street. Ismail then slowed down, kept a couple blocks behind. The inspector, having turned onto Maple Street, stayed running in a straight line.

Despite the smallness of the town, Ismail didn't venture in this direction much. He took it in as if for the first time. The old-fashioned streetlamps downtown—where he lived—flooded the air with an odd glow, but the road in this direction, which passed by mostly residential neighborhoods, had normal lights that lit the street directly below. Coasting down a hill, Ismail saw each pool of light as a dot on a map that he had to follow to reach a treasure.

As he neared the courthouse, Ismail noticed a single lighted window on the third floor. The window was open and a person was leaning out. Ismail quickly stifled the impulse to stop and stare up, to see what a person in the courthouse would be doing at this hour. It must be something important. Certainly it was of more consequence than anything the inspector could be doing, since the inspector was such an insignificant man. But Ismail kept on, assuming that whatever he was up to had more to do with Ismail than anything going on in the impressive courthouse building. Ismail also held out hope that he could still perhaps harm the inspector in some way.

At the end of the residential portion of Maple Street, right before the intersection that marked the beginning of the business section of town, which included the Pizza Hut, car dealership, and, further up, the Super 8 motel and then the radio station, Ismail saw the Russian man who had bought their restaurant. He stood next to his truck in the middle of the road, both hands over his face, and looked up at the sky. Propped up behind the truck, like a scale with far too much weight on one side, was a hot dog cart that had come unhitched from the truck. The scene was so odd that Ismail, without thinking, stopped. The man faced Ismail angrily, ready to confront yet another enemy. When he saw it was Ismail his features softened.

"Your mother . . ." he began.

"Go to fucking hell you stupid Russian fucker!" Ismail interrupted, and then he got on his bike and pedaled hard, as though the man was in hot pursuit.

For the first time that day, Ismail could say that he felt almost happy. It lasted maybe ten seconds but while racing away from one repulsive man and toward another, something seemed right. This courage was new to him, the fearlessness a rush, like when he would sometimes close his eyes and take his hands off his bike handles while riding down a hill. He was proud to have said that to the Russian, and as he rode on thought of even worse insults he could have said.

In his rush away from the Russian, Ismail lost track of the inspector. He rode past the Subway until signs informed him that Maple Street was turning into Highway 9. Here the sidewalk ended and beyond the shoulder of the road was a dark expanse of barren field and, ahead, farmland. A semitruck sped down the highway and made his bike wobble. As the first signs of defeat began to creep in, Ismail thought he glimpsed movement down the road that led to the industrial park. He crossed the highway and followed.

The industrial park, then the county garage—areas that should have been bustling—were zombie-scary to Ismail. Such stillness in areas that were meant for movement was unnatural. Ismail felt exposed, as if anything that wanted to could come out and hurt him and nobody would ever know. That the road soon turned to gravel did not lessen his fears. With his heart in his mouth, Ismail abandoned his bike and dove into the ditch alongside the road when a truck turned swiftly out of a parking lot about a quarter mile ahead. The truck tore past him and Ismail stayed huddled for a minute to make sure he was OK and alone. He decided he would go as far as the parking lot, and if the inspector wasn't there, he'd turn back.

A second-floor light was on. Normally he would have been unwilling to enter this place without permission, but now he was afraid, tired, and cold. He wanted this to be over with so he could go home. He took a deep breath, leaned his bike against the wall of the building, and went inside.

≈

Arthur stood naked in front of the filing cabinet reading the report he drunkenly had written the night before. His towel, which he had hastily wrapped around himself as he dashed out of his house, was in a heap at his feet. The report barely made sense. It was riddled with typos and errors, and what should have consisted strictly of facts and numbers was basically a screed that explained how Arthur was to blame for Bogdani's death, even if he hadn't pulled the trigger. Would it really be so bad to shred it, as long as he wrote up another, more properly formatted one the next day? He hadn't thought this would be a difficult decision, yet he could not bring himself to move. Someone could have seen him running; he needed to shred the report and then burn the shreds. But he couldn't shake the fact that it wasn't his to destroy. It was his sloppy confession. He had spent all day trying to tell people the truth and get others to tell the truth and now he was about to burn this report because it told a truth that he didn't like. A truth that could ruin and expose him. If he did this, he would be no better than anyone else.

The police had seemed interested in finding reasons to let Arthur off the hook. Arthur assumed this was because they had been so quick to deem the death a suicide and then left the crime scene unattended and open to alteration. Burt wanted to keep himself out of harm's way—an investigation could only reveal their incompetence. Arthur was not even asked to give a statement. He was told to not leave town in case he was needed for further questioning. They had no answer when Arthur asked, "Where would I go?"

He closed the drawer to the filing cabinet. Whether he burned it or not, he had to do something; he would go crazy if it was filed away for anyone to stumble upon. He didn't even know to whom he could turn himself in, how to pay for what he had done. Janet? The police? Give it to Adam and let him publish it? Maybe post it up on telephone poles and let the town judge him? Every recourse seemed useless. He reminded himself that all he had to do was shred and burn and everything would go back to normal.

When he looked up, Ismail was standing in the doorway. Arthur jumped and screamed, the report slipped out of his hands. He caught it midair and used it to cover himself. The boy's presence made Arthur aware of his situation: he was freezing cold; he was naked; he was in his office when he shouldn't be, about to shred something that wasn't his to destroy; and he was about to cover up something that he should not keep secret. He had a hand in Bogdani's death. He was perhaps a significant factor in driving the man to kill himself. If he shredded this report, he would still have to live with what he had done. He had to stop acting as though he was less wrong than everyone else.

The towel was stiff with cold when he gathered it around himself. The boy had still not moved. Arthur glanced one more time at the paper in his hand and, after a brief hesitation, reached it out toward Ismail.

"Here," he said.

Ismail didn't move.

"Take this," Arthur said. "It's about your dad." His teeth began chattering and he added, "I'm sorry."

Slowly the boy reached over and took the report but didn't look at it, choosing to keep his eyes on Arthur. They stood like that for what felt to Arthur like a long time.

"I need to find some clothes," Arthur said. "I'm freezing."

He went to the break room, to a closet that held some old inspectors' jackets. He took the warmest and least patched one and put it on. It smelled like mildew. In a warped full-length mirror leaning against the wall, Arthur caught a glimpse of himself wearing only this jacket and a towel. He looked like a pornographic movie actor on break. The sight was painfully creepy and he looked away. He desperately hoped the kid would not be in the office when he came out.

But there he was, standing in the same spot near the doorway. Arthur had no idea what he was thinking. Ismail looked blank.

"I need to find some pants," Arthur said.

He once again wished he was a healthier, more together person who worked out regularly and kept sweatpants or at least gym shorts in his desk. And though he knew there was nothing of the sort in there, he still searched every drawer. Then he searched Cal's desk (where he found a surprising number of Little Debbie Swiss Rolls and Hostess Donettes but no pants). By the time he moved on to the accountants' desks, Ismail was looking through Sandra's.

Seeing Ismail like this reminded Arthur of the previous times he had inspected the Bogdanis' restaurant, back when it got perfect scores. This quiet kid Arthur had always had a certain respect for. Now, seeing him helping so attentively after all Arthur had done to him, Arthur thought of him specifically—the pain he had already endured and was about to have to face was unimaginable. Arthur wondered why this boy was here right now. He had been too surprised to consider it fully before, but seeing the kid rooting around inside desks gave Arthur a moment to think. He must have followed Arthur during his insane sprint through town. But why? Had he intended to hurt Arthur until he saw how pathetic Arthur really was, standing naked in his cold, lousy office? Or did Ismail lose his nerve? Considering these options made Arthur freshly abased. He saw how nothing he could do would undo the hurt he had caused.

"I don't think there's anything here," Arthur said after they searched all the desks.

Ismail stared blankly at him as though awaiting instructions.

"Let's check the other offices," Arthur said.

They moved on to the next office down the hall, the Department of Public Works. Arthur had been inside only once before, when the goose crashed through the window a couple weeks ago. The window had not yet been replaced. Instead, a sheet of plastic was duct-taped in its place. It flapped lazily with a breeze that made Arthur shiver.

Ismail went straight for the nearest desk and started rummaging. Arthur watched him search. The kid obviously enjoyed having permission to snoop, so Arthur slowed down, hoping Ismail would find something first. A regular act of adult indulgence, though Arthur hoped it somehow meant more than that. He then had to remind himself that such a petty kindness did not help anything. The harm he had already inflicted was irreversible. And yet Arthur could see himself fruitlessly attempting to atone for what he had done for the rest of his life. Or, more likely, he would feel bad for a while and eventually move on.

A few minutes later he saw a small arm shoot up into the air.

"Got it!" Ismail yelled.

Arthur laughed and went up to him. He took the purple cotton sweatpants and tried to hide his dismay after seeing that they were a women's medium. He took a couple of steps away, pulled them on under his towel, and took the towel away. The pants looked painted on and a giggle escaped Ismail.

"Thanks," Arthur said, hoping it sounded both appreciative and joking.

He took a set of keys off a hook in the Public Works office and borrowed a truck they kept in the parking lot, loading Ismail's bike in the back. Of all his infractions, Arthur could hope to be fired only for the unauthorized use of this vehicle. At least he could easily explain it away as an honest mistake during future job interviews.

Neither of them spoke on the short ride to the restaurant. Ismail held the report on his lap like a schoolbook he hardly cared about. He had actually misplaced it in the office, and he and Arthur made another short search through the desks to track it down before they left. Arthur wanted to explain everything to Ismail as they drove, tell him what was in the report. But what would it have done other than make Arthur feel better? It was better to live with the shame, let it fester and overtake him. Maybe then it could change him, make him better.

If Arthur had said anything during the drive, he would have talked about how they weren't so different. Both didn't want or really choose to be in Millsville, and both would probably be leaving soon. Arthur tried to think of advice or condolences, but when he glanced over at this boy who looked like a middle-aged man, he thought there was nothing he could tell him that he wouldn't figure out on his own soon enough.

The dining area of the restaurant was surprisingly clean. The tables were arranged as though they would be filled with customers in a few hours. By instinct Arthur began to walk back to the kitchen to inspect but changed course when Ismail made his way toward the stairs to their apartment. Less than two days earlier Ismail had sat at the top of these stairs and watched Arthur and his father.

Upstairs in the apartment, Drita ran to her son and clutched him hard to her, squeezing the boy's face against her shoulder. She pushed him away and shook him, as though angrily making sure he was real, and then she pulled him in again.

Arthur felt superfluous and exposed, especially when he remembered how he was dressed. The green and purple of his wardrobe appeared even more clownish in the bright overhead light of the kitchen. He shuffled toward the stairs and then stopped and cleared his throat. He spoke before he could talk himself out of it.

"You can call the police if you want to," he said.

She still didn't seem to recognize his presence.

"The report," he said. "Your son has it. You can get me arrested or at least fired." He paused and thought, *Arrested for what?* "You can do whatever you want. It's all there. I'll admit to anything. I can stay here while you do it."

Again she didn't move. Soon Ismail squirmed, trying to escape her, but she kept him close.

Arthur decided to wait it out. Being uncomfortable was the least of his problems. If he left now, he couldn't take not knowing what would happen.

Minutes passed and eventually Ismail got free from his mother, though she managed to hold him by the shoulders. She looked up at Arthur, not paying him any real attention.

"We don't care about you," she said quietly, and shifted her focus back on her son.

"But the report," Arthur said. "I was the one who did all this to your husband. I blamed him. I saw him. I should have done something."

She took the paper from her son's hands and dismissively threw it toward Arthur. It fluttered and landed on the floor between them.

"We don't," she said, staring up at him, "care about you. Get out and leave us alone."

Ismail freed himself completely from his mother but they were still together. Arthur envied them, though he wouldn't have traded places with them.

Arthur nodded and made his way out of the kitchen, down the stairs, and onto the street. Nobody was around. The only cars in sight were the Public Works truck; his own Cherokee had been parked down the street since he went to Pokeys. He decided to walk home.

He was in the clear, he supposed, though he didn't feel any better. The town was free from the threat of disease. He was done with Katie and Adam. On the run to his office he had passed Sasha's loaded truck and pushcart and assumed he was on his way out of town. Janet, he saw by the light in her courthouse office, was probably deciding whether to still run for office as well as possibly filling out his termination forms. He thought about going up there, talking to her like two old hands, maybe even laughing about what had transpired over the past couple days. He didn't hate her any more than he ever had. He didn't hate anyone right now.

He passed the gazebo and didn't see Eldred sleeping there. It was probably too cold. How Arthur had ended up here seemed as random as how any star landed in any distant, insignificant galaxy that nobody in the universe gave a shit about. He laughed. The people here liked their insignificance. They treasured it and wore it as a badge of honor. Arthur had always bristled at this characteristic: feeling superior to people who wanted to feel superior. Now, after all that had happened, Arthur only wanted to return to his old, inconsequential status. He wanted to simply live his life.

As he entered his subdivision he gazed up at Katie's bedroom window just in time to see the light go out. He turned away, toward his own house, where every light was still on. As he made his way past the Benders' he saw the lights of his house through the trees and was glad he lived here, at least for now, in this bright, comfortable house. Of all the houses in town, his, at the moment, was sure to be the brightest.

≈

Drita woke in a chair next to her son. It was dark, though his room faced the alley and never got all that much light. She hoped it was morning. Reaching out, she touched the blankets covering Ismail's body. He grunted, annoyed. Last night he had tried to get her to leave his room, but she made it clear it was not his choice. She had stayed up as long as she could, both to make sure Ismail did not escape again and to delay waking up this morning for as long as possible. She did not know what she would do with a whole day in front of her.

Stiff from sleeping in that straight-backed wooden chair all night, she limped down the stairs to the big kitchen to make coffee. She would have preferred to avoid the restaurant for one more day but did not want to wake her son. The Russian man had cleaned the dining area the day before, though, so she could at least be thankful for that. The chairs and tables were set up nearly the same as they always were. Outside, the sun was up but no cars were on the road. She assumed it was early yet. A full day ahead.

The kitchen was still a mess. The thought of all the work she had to do made her lightheaded, though maybe that was because she hadn't eaten since breakfast the day before. But it could be a fitting distraction to have a kitchen to clean on a day like this. If only that was all she had to do. If only she didn't also need to file insurance reports, cancel food orders for the next few days, hire a cook, figure out a way to regain people's trust. Plan a funeral. All this while managing to not break down in front of Ismail. Right now making coffee was a monumental task. She wondered if buying back the restaurant had been the right choice. Though she had made a nice profit from the desperate Russian, and she was glad that she did not need to wake Ismail and tell him they had to leave town forever, the idea of performing the same mundane tasks each day as though nothing had happened seemed impossible. Like right now: how was she supposed to remember how to make coffee?

If she had died and her husband survived, he would surely have had no difficulty making coffee the next morning. The first time she heard the English word "jerk" she had laughed and pointed at him and said, "My jerk!" And he was a jerk. Her jerk. He didn't apologize for it. Being a jerk was part of what made him strong. The men she had known all her life in Albania were not precisely sensitive. But he used to occasionally be vulnerable with her. When she was pregnant and he had passed up the opportunity to buy the restaurant with her sister's husband, she had held his head while he apologized for being afraid of taking the chance. But she liked that he was who he was. He did not change when he came here. This might be the reason why he was dead now, because he did not become who people wanted him to be. They did not know him. They did not know how he fit into their world and did not want to figure out where he came from. OK, she thought, perhaps I will have to change in the ways he did not. If she was to survive, she might have to become the person people wanted her to be. Her sister's husband, after all, attended all the high school football matches and worked hard to soften his accent. And look at how he thrives. It certainly was not a show of strength. It was simply survival.

The first step was to find the coffee. It would be where it always was, in the cupboard above the microwave. This came to her as she became aware of knocking noises. She turned and saw an exasperated man banging on the door with his knee while holding three boxes stacked in his hands. Of course, the deliveries. She unlocked the door and the man thrust the boxes at her.

"Been knocking," he said.

She took the boxes and allowed the door to close.

So many pastries. What would she do with all these pastries now? The answer was that she and Ismail would eat some of them and let the rest go to waste. She managed to get coffee and water in the pot. Seldom before had she felt such a sense of accomplishment. She decided she deserved a break and sat at a table in the back of the dining area. As the first whiff of brewed coffee reached her, there was a knock at the back door. She sighed deeply and got up. There were so many things to do this morning. For a moment, before she pushed open the swinging kitchen door, she thought perhaps Ismail had managed to escape again and was locked out, trying to get back in, and if she didn't arrive quickly enough, he would be gone! She ran through the kitchen and flung open the back door.

Outside stood the homeless man. They locked eyes for a minute.

"He always gave me a day-old and a coffee," the man said, looking over her left shoulder while he spoke.

It took her some time to realize that "he" was her husband, a "day-old" was a day-old donut, and coffee was what was currently brewing in the pot. She nodded. Another minute went by and it dawned on her that the only way to get him to leave was to give him these things. She needed him to leave because she did not want her son to come down and see this man here.

She sloshed some coffee in a to-go cup and grabbed one of the pastry boxes. She handed him the cup and opened the box to him.

He looked at the rows of donuts, his eyes scanning the box left to right as though he was reading. A worried look came over his face.

"He put one in a bag," he said.

"Here, have the whole box," she said, closing it.

His eyes widened and he looked at her, pleading.

She bit her lip in frustration and went and grabbed a paper bag and a square of wax paper. She took a donut at random and placed it in the bag and thrust it out to him.

With the slightest nod he took the bag and walked off down the alley.

By that time the smell of coffee filled the air. She poured herself a cup and sat in the dining area facing the front window. A car went by. Then another. It was, what? Friday? The world seemed to be waking up and going on its way. She did not know how she would do this every morning from now on. It did not seem possible that it would get easier. She tried to remember something from her past that would give her strength. But her memory seemed wiped clean. There was only now. Moving forward without a past felt like a nightmare. Like she was stuck in her body, forced to live out her life for no good reason at all.

She heard another knock, or a thud. She closed her eyes and thought, "What now?" From upstairs she heard, "Mom? Are you here?"

Of course. Of course.

Acknowledgments

I would like to thank Dennis Lloyd, Jackie Teoh, Adam Mehring, Diana Cook, and the entire staff at the University of Wisconsin Press for all their support.

I could not have written this without my incredible advisors and teachers at MFA@FLA. Thanks to Jill Ciment, for so much, including telling me to toss out the original first fifty pages; David Leavitt, for his sage advice and friendship; Michael Hofmann, for the title, advice, and lending a wonderful apartment to finish it in; and Padgett Powell, for being Padgett Powell.

Thank you to all my friends who took the time to read early drafts: Steven Hyden, Glen Lindquist, RL Goldberg, Sebastian Boensch, Heather Peterson, Richard Leson, Brian Malatesta, Patrick May, and especially Kennan Ferguson, who also suggested I send my manuscript to UW Press.

I'm immensely grateful to my parents. They have been unbelievably supportive during the writing of this book and over the course of my life. Any humor in these pages can be directly credited to my brothers, Andy and Joe. And my niece Bernadette and nephew Harry have provided some much needed breaths of fresh air.

Many thanks to Mimi Ibraimi from the Park City Family Restaurant in Janesville for sharing her stories, as well as Linda Smith for getting me in touch. Thanks also to Barbara Holla for her insight on Albanian culture.

Thanks to the NYC Parks Department for giving me a job as an inspector all those years ago, and to my fellow inspectors Joel Metlen and Jeremy Holmes. Thanks to Mike and Bella Gorfinkel, Mark Mitchell,

Chand and the Dalston Red Cross Refugee Men's Group, Judith Mitchell, Liam Callanan, Valerie Laken, Jocelyn Szczepaniak-Gillece, and my cohort at MFA@FLA.

Of course thanks Dan, the best dog ever, who was around when I started this but not when I finished.

Most of all, to my best friend, Elena Gorfinkel. The smartest, most caring partner and first reader a person could ask for. She challenges me in ways I could have never imagined and has made me a far better person than I ever thought I'd be. Without her this book certainly would have never happened, but more importantly I would be a miserable wretch.